LYN R. BARTLETT

A BOY
from
HAHNDORF

The Long Journey Home

outskirts
press

Outskirts Press, Inc.
http://www.outskirtspress.com

Paperback ISBN: 978-1-9772-1037-1
Hardback ISBN: 978-1-9772-1039-5

Cover Photo © 2019 www.gettyimages.com. All rights reserved - used with permission.

Outskirts Press and the "OP" logo are trademarks belonging to Outskirts Press, Inc.

PRINTED IN THE UNITED STATES OF AMERICA

Dedicated to

Cindy, my one and only Claire

TABLE OF CONTENTS

Chapter One: The Epiphany   1

Chapter Two: The Formative Years   16

Chapter Three: Change of Course   35

Chapter Four: A Year on the Farm   47

Chapter Five: Wider Vistas   52

Chapter Six: Teaching and Marriage   64

Chapter Seven: An International Tour and Divorce   87

Chapter Eight: The Swing and Sway of the World   104

Chapter Nine: The American Experience   126

Chapter Ten: The Easter Nationals   158

Chapter Eleven: Break up—Then Graduation   196

Chapter Twelve: A Road Trip to Remember   214

Chapter Thirteen: New Life, New Work   252

Chapter Fourteen: Back to Work   276

Chapter Fifteen: A Dream Come True   294

Chapter Sixteen: Coming Together   317

Chapter Seventeen: The Rest of the Story   347

Epilogue   370

Author's Notes   378

MAP OF AUSTRALIA

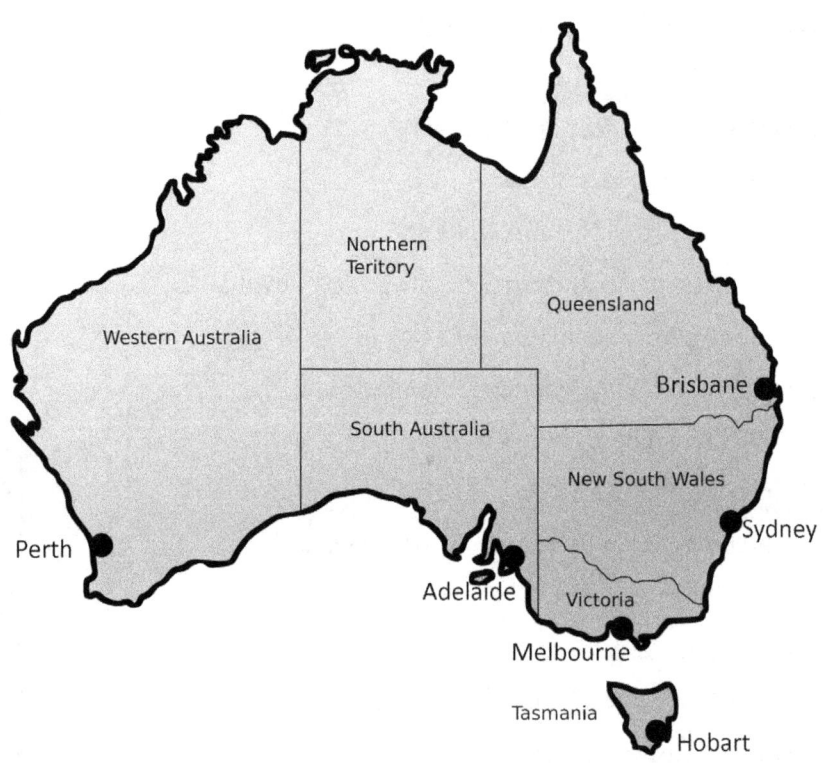

Partial Map of South Australia

Mount Lofty
Ranges

Adelaide

● Hahndorf

● Mount Barker

Gulf of St. Vincent

Adelaide Hills

Victor
Harbor

Kangaroo Island

CHAPTER ONE

THE EPIPHANY

"We are the dreamers of our dreams."
—Roald Dahl

Mark Schubert turned his face toward home. He had put Australia behind him once, but now it was calling him home. His talent had taken him many places, and finally to Annapolis and the United States Naval Academy. His academic quest had him pursuing a doctoral degree in music education at Johns Hopkins University in Baltimore. Music was his profession and he was world class. He played euphonium, and more recently, bass trombone. Not long ago, he had taken up conducting, but it was as guest adjudicator for the Easter National Band Council of Australia championships that was bringing him home. It was also his mother's birthday, and he needed to speak to her.

Six months ago, he was foot loose and fancy free. Sometimes he was glad of this and sometimes he was lonely, but increasingly he felt alone. Now, Christina was in his life. She had little idea of Mark's deeper concerns. She thought he was merely going home for the Easter Nationals and his mother's 70th birthday. Had they met earlier, Christina would have most likely accompanied him. So much had happened, and so fast, since their first date at Maria's Ristorante at the city dock in historic Annapolis. That's the way it is when you are older. Besides, he would be back in Maryland in three weeks, and they could take it from there. Even so, this didn't make it easier to say goodbye to her at the airport.

Mark sat back in his seat and readied himself for take-off. He pushed his head into the head rest and breathed deeply. He had repeated these same movements hundreds of times over the years, or so it seemed. He enjoyed plane travel. Always, he was impatient for the actual departure from the gate. There was a cathartic sense of relief and release in anticipating the thrust of the engines and the initial lift-off from the tarmac below. It meant closure to that which was left behind: what was done was done, and that which was left undone he had to let go for now. Usually, neither people nor circumstances would bother him for the duration of the flight. This time, it was different.

The flight from Washington-Dulles to Los Angeles was almost four hours. That gave him just under two hours to connect with his flight to Sydney. Mark had never liked the tension of not making this connection. He had been delayed before and waiting another twenty-four hours for the next flight across the Pacific was never his idea of time well spent. Still, today all was on schedule. This was good because he had more pressing thoughts on his mind. Mark knew he was leaving behind a woman of substance, or so she seemed, after a feverish six-interrupted months of dates and so many phone calls. Christina had forcibly occupied his loneliness and, as he looked down on the stately farm land of Loudon County, he felt as though he was betraying her. He had not been truthful with her. He had not taken her into his confidence. "What am I to do? Is it right to fall in love at the ripe old age of forty with this blasted disease?" he thought, as the Boeing 747 continued to climb.

He felt selfish and even a degree of self-pity. He had known about his medical issue for just over a week and, rightly or wrongly, he had decided not to tell Christina about it until he returned. This didn't feel honest, but he told himself it was best for Christina just now. His long-practiced ability to leave his worries on *terra firma* wasn't going to work on this flight. At least he recognized his emotional state and saw the long journey as a welcome time for reflection. Adjudicating at the Easter Nationals and celebrating his mother's birthday in Hahndorf had become nearly incidental to the fact that he also needed space to deal with his feelings. It was not really absence or a pause from Christina that he needed as much as the compulsion to revisit the beloved places of his early days before life was snuffed out. "Stop this nonsense," he said out loud, "You're being overly dramatic. You're not going to die."

He knew he was acting contrary to his Lutheran background and to most of his personal upbringing. This was not a time to wax and wane; rather, this was his moment to exhibit steadfast moral fortitude. Wasn't he Mark Schubert, the brass virtuoso of two continents? So, he had succumbed to the inevitable frailty of humanity. This was his opportunity to confront the male health scourge of modernity with grace and dignity. Instead, he wanted to escape to his childhood haunts of Hahndorf. He could all but feel the impulse to *run* to the pine trees that bordered the family farm, just as he had as a child and a teenager. Here, betwixt and between his German ancestors, he would find adequate courage to devise a plan for dealing with his medical problem and Christina.

United Airlines Flight 196 leveled off at 32,000 feet as it headed west into the setting sun. It was a beautiful early spring in the Washington, D.C. region, and Mark could also anticipate pleasurable weather in his home state of South Australia. It was autumn in the southern hemisphere and Adelaide, the state capital, had some of its best weather in the months of March and April. The days were warm and balmy, bookended by cool mornings and evenings. It was the season when people debated daily whether to shed their summer attire and don the new season's styles and extra layers. Mark smiled as he remembered the wool industry advertisements promoting *Pure Australian Wool.* The people who walked the streets of Adelaide instantaneously looked more affluent and professional in their autumn styles. He wondered if these same people had become more relaxed in lifestyle since his last visit. After all, Australians liked to think that they were more casual than most other nations. He shuddered a moment as he remembered the acceptance of shorts and long hose for business men during the summer months of the '70s. Mark had always been more formal than the norm.

"Sir, are you ready for your dinner? Would you like the chicken or lasagna?"

The flight attendant interrupted Mark's meanderings and made him suddenly aware of the bustle of activity in the aircraft as the in-flight meal was served. He took a moment or two to respond, such was the depth of his ruminations. "I'll … I'll have the lasagna. Can I also have a coffee with cream, please?"

He liked to control his food intake when on an international journey of such magnitude. He spoke to the uninitiated of crossing east coast to west coast, and then the Pacific, as a journey of eleven thousand miles, or six movies and five meals. To fully indulge in each of those meals while constantly passive was a sure recipe for a longer recovery from the inevitable effects of jet lag. To eat now meant the chance to walk vigorously in the LAX corridors before his departure from the U.S. mainland. Mark ate deliberately, appreciative that he had a window seat with no-one immediately next to him. He had only flown first class once before and business class three times. He didn't mind economy when he had an empty seat next to him. Would he be so fortunate on the Pacific crossing?

"Another coffee, sir."

Mark sipped his coffee slowly. He marveled at how much he had enjoyed his meal and the coffee, too, was good. His German roots had instilled in him the enjoyment of, and appreciation for, good food, wine, and tea and coffee. He was raised on *Deutsche Kuchen* and his love of Hahndorf stews, soups, sausage (never *bratwurst)*, schnitzels, rollmops, and especially breads and pastries, had spoiled him for ever after. Feelings of homesickness typically meant a longing for his mother's cooking; especially Black Forest cake, made with cherries. The Berliner doughnuts, with no holes, had caused many a light-hearted banter with his naval buddies in the Annapolis Dunkin' Donuts shop. He finished his coffee, pushed his tray into the upright position and reclined his seat. In three hours, he would land in Los Angeles.

"What about this life of mine?" he mused. He knew himself to be a foundational person. He had to start at the beginning whenever he pondered serious matters. Some would call it 'mulling things over.' Whatever the term, Mark knew he had a lot to sort through. He was nearly forty-one and he felt his life to be at a watershed. To him, the outcomes of this journey could affect the rest of his life—however long that may be. This included Christina as well. The sheer thought of her made him warm inside. He knew she was more than an attractive female friend with whom he was beginning to share his inner self. His stoic disposition, under control for so long, was inclining towards passion and, dare he say it, love. Was this the woman he could spend the rest of his life with? He felt twenty-one, not forty-one.

Mark's mother, Betty, the storyteller of the family, had given him a deep appreciation for his earliest years. Descending from one of the original German families in Hahndorf, Betty was a splendid product of the oral tradition. It was widely known that the people of Hahndorf, perhaps because of their unique station in an otherwise British country, sought to preserve the memories and perceptions of family and township with more vigor than other communities in the Adelaide Hills. The frequent car journeys from Hahndorf to Adelaide, while only eighteen miles and forty minutes, were moments when mother (and, at times, father) told the four children stories of family history. Some children resonate with the art and practice of narration, and Mark was such a child.

"I remember, Mark, when you looked back through the rainy car windows at the drum and fife bands in Victoria Square and said, 'I want to be a band boy when I'm big enough.' Your Dad looked at me and said, 'We'll see!'"

Obviously, Mark couldn't remember his childhood epiphany exactly, but over the years, his mother's recollections had become his own. His admiration for the drum and fife corps on that dreary Saturday was the early awakening of his future career path. Little did he realize (as do any of us), the magnitude of the task ahead. More than thirty-five years later, Mark could look over a career that had preoccupied his life far too long. He had embraced a vocation that was brass music: the banding world of Australia and New Zealand. His innate talent as a boy became an obsession to reach the pinnacle of brass band performance at an earlier age than others. His drive to achieve and excel dominated his need to establish balance and constraint. He did much more than toil as a teenager. Prodded by Mr. Paech, his first and most influential music teacher, Mark strove relentlessly as if he was afraid that his success and achievements could evaporate at any time. High school was a means to a greater end for Mark. Progressing through various music levels was standard fare in moving on to university and the music conservatory, both of which were mere words lacking real comprehension until Mark was to experience them personally at nineteen.

From a young age, Mark was the favored son of Hahndorf and his talent was acclaimed and recognized. Expectations were heaped upon him before he was a teenager. He chose to be a performance musician, a choice that had brought him immense satisfaction and self-assurance, but it had cost him dearly, too. After university, he tossed his hat into the ring of music education and the world of brass competition. At first it was within the safe confines of teaching music within a church-related secondary school. Yet, he was always hounded by the competitive worlds of state, national, and international championships.

Divorce led him to the Royal Australian Naval Band in Melbourne and then to the United States Naval Academy. He became a sought-after performer and teacher of music. All this while he was in pursuit of personal and professional excellence. He had succumbed to insidious allurements and severe pitfalls in his quest to be the best.

For several years now, Mark, despite all the acclaim, had felt an increasingly strange emptiness. He wanted to matter, for his life to have meaning, and a sense of purpose. The bright lights, the glitz and dazzle, didn't cut it anymore, if they ever did. He wanted more. It was not that he had come to the end of his career. To be sure, he was scaling back playing his euphonium and trombone for conducting and his best years were still ahead in this endeavor. Even so, right now he was facing a time of personal evaluation. It wasn't just his health issue, but Christina and the whole spectrum of what he wanted from life in the days and years ahead. Mark was confronting a major realignment of his very person. There was no question that he was facing surgery in as little as three months. Would he undergo surgery in Maryland, and thereby pitch his future in America, turn his back on the Royal Australian Navy, and settle down with Christina? Or would he return to Australia after graduating from Johns Hopkins, face surgery in Adelaide and continue his career in the Royal Australian Navy? This journey home would determine answers to these questions. Beyond doubt, Mark knew that his decisions over the next several months would dramatically affect the rest of his life, where he lived, with whom, and how. He was beginning to feel intimidated by it all. "Oh, dear God," he thought, "how did my dreams and idealism become so convoluted?"

The cabin crew had cleared the remains of dinner, and the movie announcement suggested headsets or sleep to most of the passengers. Mark rarely watched in-flight movies. Flying gave him the opportunity to transcend earthly matters. Why waste the time away from people and work by watching a movie under less than ideal conditions when the movie screen of the mind was rampant with all types of adventures, thrilling possibilities, and new discoveries? Thus, Mark settled back for some serious contemplation. If sleep came to him instead, it would be welcome. He remembered the second 'Eureka' moment that stimulated his desire to be a brass player. "It's amazing," he marveled, "but since I was eight years old, I have known I would play brass and teach music."

It was at the Hahndorf Public School Fete in the autumn of 1960 when Mark realized his attraction to brass bands. He had worn his Hopalong Cassidy outfit and jingled the five shillings his grandfather had slipped him in his pocket. He won a costume prize but didn't remember much about the fete itself. He did remember the assembling of the brass band under the huge Radiata pine trees in the school yard. He was mesmerized by the musicians and their instruments. The band members arrived in twos and threes, chatting nonchalantly and laughing as they took their seats, unpacking their instruments, and making ready for their playout. Mark recalled that nothing else around him seemed to matter. Even at eight years of age, he was captivated by the group dynamics and the effortless organization that was occurring before him. He witnessed the obvious camaraderie of bandsmen gathering for this annual civic event. On that Saturday afternoon, Mark knew in his young heart that he was going to become a bandsman. He also knew that he wanted to play the cornet, and to be like Gordon Kramm, first chair of the Hahndorf Town Band. At this moment, he was one step closer to his earlier illumination.

Mark emerged momentarily from his thoughts as if he was taking a television break for a commercial. He looked about him and was grateful once again to be alone in a row of three. "This happens once in a hundred flights, but I'll take it!" He knew his present frame of mind. It would last all the way to Los Angeles and then resume on the flight across the Pacific. By now Mark was familiar with his compelling need to visit and revisit the various stages of his life. It came from spending too much time alone. Closing his eyes, he indulged in the pathetic occupation of second guessing himself. Meeting Christina had made him realize that future contentment lay in confronting his past, both the ghosts and the glories of bygone days. He knew only too well that despite his confidence as a musician, he personally felt unsure of beginning a new relationship. He had been on his own now for over fourteen years, but his medical problem only made his uncertainty worse.

He remembered that three years after the school fete, he was given a trumpet for his eleventh birthday. Months before, Betty and Frank Schubert had been alerting Mark to the added demands of taking music lessons and the reality of becoming a band boy. He was one of four boys at St. Michael's Lutheran school, and another three from the public school, who were designated to join the Hahndorf Town Band. It wasn't expected of all boys, but the ever-watchful eyes of the town knew the right nudging to give a young boy for his best development. It had been the Hahndorf way for generations. Such communal shepherding of the town's youth had preserved the German traditions in the past and, hopefully, provided direction for the current generation now. In a town of some six hundred people, with another two hundred or so in the farming precincts, there were few secrets, and the chrysalis of youth was watched with a collective sense of unabashed stewardship. After all, there was no constabulary in Hahndorf; the closest police station was seven miles to the south-east at Mount Barker.

Music lessons followed two days after Mark's April birthday. The memories of nervousness about his first lesson remained vivid to this day. He had tried for two days to blow his trumpet. As yet he could not even make a proper sound. Worst of all, his efforts hurt his cheeks and lips. Would he ever be able to play like Gordon Kramm?

Alex, Carl and Lester joined with Mark and three other boys from the public school in beginning brass instrumental lessons. The week before their first practice session the boys talked of little else. Their bravado heightened the anxiety they each felt, and as four o' clock arrived their friendship turned more into timorous competition. Mr. Paech, the town's music teacher, immediately reduced the tension by offering the would-be-musicians cake and lemonade before their lesson.

Mark smiled now as he recalled the exhilaration of knowing that he could, at last, blow a clear, controlled sound. Soon afterwards he mastered the scale of C and the pitching of low C, middle C, and high G. He remembered the impatience he felt as he labored over the scales and a myriad of small exercises. He wanted to play *real* music and to be good enough to join the band. His father meant to be encouraging when he said, "Patience, Mark, Rome wasn't built in a day!"

For several months the seven boys remained in a state of friendly rivalry. Mr. Paech sat them in a row: seven boys sitting upright on austere chairs with music stands before them. They played scales and exercises in unison and each was given a tutor and weekly practice exercises. Mr. Paech, sternly watchful, expected to hear that daily practice had taken place—three times a week at the very minimum. After the ever-important scales, short pieces such as *Lead Kindly Light, Men of Harlech, Deck the Halls,* and *Scotland the Brave* came next. All were still intimately familiar to Mark, including the position on the page of his old brass primer. Some things, like the alphabet and tables, remain firmly embedded for all time.

By the end of June, the days were cold and short. It was winter time and Hahndorf looked drab during the many overcast days so typical in the Adelaide Hills. The main street, one mile in length and straight as an arrow, was lined with ash trees along the entire thoroughfare and gave welcome shade in the hot summer months and glorious color in the autumn. Without their foliage they added to the wintry bleakness of Australia's first German town. Most houses had an open fireplace in the living room and a wood-burning stove in the kitchen. Only the few stately homes had fireplaces in the bedrooms. All had supplies of wood in their back yards or somewhere on their acreage. A frequent topic of gossip by the women of Hahndorf spoke whispers of empathy for any housewife who had to cut her own firewood because of her husband's neglect or laziness.

As the eldest of four children, Mark was expected to help his father in maintaining the wood supply. Fortunately, he liked chopping wood and, several afternoons a week for about five months of the year, he would cut the hardwood eucalyptus blocks for fifteen to thirty minutes. Still in his school uniform but minus tie and blazer, he became adept at swinging the axe with precision and force. Some blocks had a twisted or knotted grain and they took extra effort to split. Mark knew how to sharpen the axe with the whetstone on Frank's workbench. Betty was always a little fearful of the serious injuries an axe could inflict. "It only takes a second," she would warn Mark. It must have worked because he was always conscious of being careful. Nonetheless, Mark had several near mishaps when the swing of the axe went awry, or wood chips flew wildly in the air. Once, a chip hit Ginger, the family's tomcat, and brought blood to the bewildered animal. After the wood was chopped, it had to be carried into the house and stacked against the wall in the playroom. Not all of Mark's friends had to cut wood, but he didn't mind.

The wood-cutting always came before supper, and so did trumpet practice, but only during the week days. As mother prepared the evening meal and the other children either watched television or labored at their homework, all quietly cheered their big brother during his thirty-minute practice. Just before the birth of their little sister, Mark and his brother Gary were relocated to a makeshift bedroom off the playroom. It was a narrow room where two single beds were placed along the outside wall with glass windows above waist height. There was a wardrobe along the inner wall and Frank's old radiogram from the early 1940s. Looking back, Mark marveled at how Gary and he survived the chill they faced nightly for many months each year. They would leave the warmth of the inner house and hurriedly undress, jump into bed, and curl up in a fetal position with the covers high over their ears. Even today, Mark still slept with the covers pulled up high and he suspected that Gary did too. Many a morning they awoke to ice on the inside of the window panes.

Mark kept his birthday present, his shiny silver Boosey and Hawkes trumpet, in the wardrobe. Every day he took it out of its case, assembled the music stand, warmed the instrument by blowing long, sustained notes, and then followed up with scales and the various chromatic scales. The initial reluctance to sit on his bed and practice soon gave way to the growing realization that he not only liked playing, he was improving. His last ten minutes of practice was always given over to learning some of the popular music he found among Frank's stacks of piano sheet music. *Smile* was an easy piece to learn and one he always liked to hear his father play on the piano. Usually Frank came in from the farm towards the end of Mark's practice and then the family would gather around the kitchen table, bow their heads for grace, and share the events of the day while they ate. On Friday evenings, the chatter could keep the meal going for two hours.

Life has a way of separating the lives of those who pursue a goal from those who do not. Mark didn't know what made him excel at the trumpet. He simply knew that he enjoyed playing his instrument whereas his other friends soon became bored and gave up. He even relished playing scales and routine exercises and accepted these as, in the words of Mr. Paech, "the building blocks to becoming a cornet virtuoso." Was he more talented than the other boys? It didn't feel like it, but he did realize that there must have been something in his genes that took him from Hahndorf and put him on premier stages around the world. He gave much of the credit to his parents; it felt right and appropriate to do so. Beyond question, he was raised in a home where both father and mother were secure, hardworking, and intent on encouraging their children to do better than themselves. But it took Mark a long time to understand the thinking of his parents. In fact, it wasn't until he graduated from the University of Adelaide, the Music Conservatory, and after he had accepted a teaching position at Luther College in Melbourne that he began to appreciate what his parents had done for their children.

Both Frank and Betty Schubert had been born and raised in Hahndorf. They were children of the Depression, but even more, the stigma of their German heritage had been thrust upon them by the impact of two world wars. Frank had inherited the family farm developed by his grandfather, Walter Schubert. Betty's family had been shopkeepers for generations. Both families were among the first German settlers to arrive in Australia.

They were religious immigrants, known as *Old Lutherans*, from Sileasia, one of the provinces of Prussia, where they had come under intense scrutiny and some persecution during the reign of Friedrich Wilhelm III. In 1817, he had decreed that the Lutheran and Reformed churches were to amalgamate and form one church under one government. A religious man and a monarch seeking to maximize efficiencies, Friedrich Wilhelm insisted that all congregations would adopt his new Order of Service. The Old Lutherans refused and clung to their traditional liturgy. As a stalwart group of dissenters, they eventually concluded that religious immunity was improbable for generations—in fact, it did not last beyond 1840. In the meantime, pastors, businessmen, shopkeepers and farmers were made examples of, and were incarcerated because of their defiance to the king. The fervent aspirations of these *Old Lutherans* for individual freedom and religious tolerance reached such proportions that immigration seemed the only responsible solution in providing for the future prosperity and well-being of their families.

Mark was well-versed in these stories of oppression for the sake of faith. It was all so long ago, he, and most of his generation, did not fully comprehend the religious struggle of his ancestors. What he did sense, and had taken into his very being, was a tremendous pride and respect for what his Sileasian forebears had endured.

The *Old Lutherans* found a convincing leader in the person of Pastor August Ludwig Christian Kavel who introduced the outlandish idea of sailing to a new life in the recently founded British colony of South Australia. The thought of journeying more than half way around the world to make a fresh start was, at first, daunting. Then, it became a romantic refutation to conditions in Prussia. On August 21, 1838, departing from Altona (Hamburg) on the right bank of the Elbe river, 197 anxious and naive Sileasian immigrants commenced the arduous journey of 129 days aboard the *Zebra* and arrived at Holdfast Bay on December 29, 1838. Due to low water, they did not land at Port Adelaide until January 2, 1839. Four days of waiting to go ashore after more than four months at sea was disheartening for those on board. Nonetheless, the wait was revealing as to the spiritual nature of these immigrants. Each evening as the hot sun set across the Gulf of St. Vincent, the 39 families gathered on deck and worshipped, largely in song. The British colonists onshore gathered to witness the harmony and devotion of these new German arrivals. It was a similar report at each destination on the long voyage; on the barges along the River Elbe, at Hamburg and later Liverpool. Music was the saving grace of these families. Mark felt the connection from his earliest days.

Two months later, accompanied by Captain Hahn of the *Zebra*, these German settlers trekked into the foothills of the Mount Lofty Ranges and over the other side to settle in an attractive valley with several water courses. Here, they gave thanks to God for their deliverance and safe arrival at their new home. The landscape round about was undulating with good areas of fertile soil and trees that were large and imposing. From respect and deep gratitude, these settlers named their *village,* "Hahndorf," after Captain Hahn. Mark always thought it even more curious because "hahn" is German for *rooster* and "dorf" is for *village,* and he was raised on a farm with poultry.

———⚬⚬⚬———

Mark shifted in his seat, pushed up the window shade and peered down at the American landscape beneath. He smiled as he thought about seeing his "rooster village" in less than one day's time. He was glad he was going home. Closing the window shade, he resumed his deliberations.

———⚬⚬⚬———

Hahndorf soon established itself and prospered as a rural village. Later, it consolidated with permanent buildings to become one of the many idyllic towns comprising the Adelaide Hills. As a community, it maintained certain celebrations and traditions. Besides the Hahndorf Public School fete, there was another major town event that further cemented Mark's boyish dream of becoming a "band boy." In November 1959, St. Michael's Lutheran church, his family's church, celebrated its centenary. Situated between the public school and Mark's Lutheran School, St. Michael's was the older of the two Lutheran churches in Hahndorf and was Evangelical in its outlook. The other church was St. Paul's which adhered to the mission-focus of the Missouri Synod. In 1846 a rift developed in the *Old Lutheran* congregation over doctrinal differences, and while the differences were more organizational than theological, these aroused animosities among town members and families that lingered to the present. Mark had been raised in a heavy religious atmosphere at home, at school, and within the entire town community. He had long recognized his natural propensity towards spirituality, and this factored in his formative years and early career. Now, older and wiser, Mark could look back and laugh at the wiles of organized religion. The tensions between individual spirituality and sectarianism still bothered him but, more significantly, he now despaired at religious aspirants who failed to act as caring and engaging people. So many religious leaders sought power under the guise of religiosity. They irritated Mark and he regarded them as twice as difficult as their secular counterparts.

CHAPTER TWO

THE FORMATIVE YEARS

"What doesn't kill me, makes me stronger."
—Friedrich Nietzsche

Family and friends, and, indeed, the town of Hahndorf, recognized Mark's musical talent even before he completed primary school. Mr. Paech knew how to motivate young musicians in and out of the musical arena. Every so often, he was fortunate to nurture a boy who had both the talent and the determination to excel as a brass player. Gordon Kramm had been one such boy twenty years earlier. While he played for special occasions at school, church, and town events, he also competed in the South Australian Band competitions, winning the Under-18 Cornet Championship. Later, he aspired to the National Open Cornet Championships, but times were hard during World War II and Gordon was expected to work in his father's grocery business. Then he married and became content to play first chair for the Hahndorf Town Band. Mr. Paech, though disappointed, understood. It was rare, particularly in rural areas, when a young man could catch a vision to rise above the safe confines of his prescribed community. After all, to join another brass band required an eighteen-mile journey through the Adelaide Hills to the capital city of Adelaide and this was considered a special trip not frequently ventured by many of the townspeople in those years.

Fifteen months after his eleventh birthday, Mark was invited by the Band Committee to join the Hahndorf Town Band. The letter of invitation was signed by Mr. Cleggett who was the band master and secretary of the band committee. Betty cooked a special meal that evening and the family celebrated Mark's long-anticipated invitation.

Seated around the large dining table, the Schubert family was pleased that Mark's hours of practice had now been rewarded. Frank's blessing on the meal extended to a blessing on Mark and on each of the other three children, although the youngest child's wriggling in her high chair caused suppressed giggles in the middle of blessing the food.

The next Thursday evening, Mark and Frank went to band practice for the first time. Frank had decided that the best way to support Mark, and later Gary, as young band boys was to join the band himself. There was a need for a bass trombone player and Frank still played the piano a little. He knew how to read the bass clef, and the bass trombone music in the Brass Band tradition was written in this clef. Mark's nervousness was diminished because he did not have to walk into the band practice hall alone on his first night. Both Schuberts were applauded as new members and Mr. Cleggett welcomed them before calling the band to order. The evening's practice began with *Lead Kindly Light* and continued with fifteen minutes of hymn playing to warm the instruments and develop tone and harmony within the band.

Mark played very few notes at first on his band cornet. He felt bewildered by the cacophony of thirty-four other instruments around him. It seemed that every eye was looking at him and he kept his head down, only looking at the music when he came to play. Everything was confusing to him and all he wanted to do was slip out the door and go home. He was the lowest chair in the brass band pecking order, he knew it, and accordingly felt small. The one pleasant memory of that first band practice was the melodious sound of the euphonium. It did not sound as brash as the cornet, and even the trombone sounded rasping alongside this new sound. Once, as Mark was fixated on a euphonium cadenza, Ray Sadler looked over at him and winked. A seed was sown.

In December of 1962, eleven Grade Seven students completed their primary education years. Mark played *Vigoro* at the Speech Night dressed in his band uniform and looking as gangly as any twelve-year old would in a suit designed for a grown man. One phase of life was concluding, and a new chapter was about to begin. First came the Christmas season, and then the summer holidays.

Mark's formative years had been under the tutelage of church education at Saint Michael's Lutheran School. Established in 1839, the very year Hahndorf was settled, the church school was a commitment by this Lutheran community to the biblical injunction "to train up a child in the way he should go in the days of his youth." Now, 125 years later, the Lutherans of Hahndorf still valued the daily lessons in the Bible as the main source of strength and well-being for an individual, a family, and a community. Sunday School attendance of all boys and girls was expected by the townspeople. Even Wolf Heise, the town drunkard and the most prayed-for individual in Hahndorf, would ask Mark and his mates, as he staggered past them at times, if they went to Sunday School. Deciding to enroll children at the public school or the church school was entirely the choice of the parents. Regardless, certain families felt a loyalty to "keep the church school open" by paying tuition rather than accepting the state-funded education of the public school only a hundred yards away. Historically, the farming families were noticeably more supportive of the church school than families involved in business who, in the past century, recognized the importance of learning English in both written and spoken forms and, as a result, many families turned to public education for their children's better integration into Australian life as a British colony.

There is little doubt that parental support of Saint Michaels would have been more unequivocal but for the intervention of the state years earlier. Hahndorf was not only the first German settlement in all of Australia, it was also the most symbolic of German traditions and the Teutonic way of life. As the rise of Germany posed a threat to the British Empire in the late nineteenth century, so did suspicions build toward the strong German presence in the Adelaide Hills, including the Barossa Valley. After all, the state of South Australia was of more than ninety percent British stock. Though small in number, Hahndorf's residents of German descent were a distinct aberration when contrasted with the rest of Australia. As World War I continued, increasing hostility was expressed towards the quiet and somewhat secluded German villages. By 1917 the residents were enduring a vitriolic campaign by the Adelaide press and state leaders who spoke against the *Kaiser towns* and their "disloyal" inhabitants. Ill feeling was exacerbated by the South Australian Premier, Crawford Vaughan, and in 1917, the Lutheran Day School was closed. It was not re-opened until 1946. *Hahndorf,* as the town's name, was changed to *Ambleside,* and not changed back until 1935.

In the post-war decades, Mark's father was known throughout the community as a respected contradiction. His farm was one of the more prosperous in the district. He was conservative in his Lutheranism and the maintenance of German traditions and values for the community were important to him. He believed that the future well-being of Hahndorf, and its Lutheran diaspora, was enhanced by understanding and respecting the past. The God of Martin Luther was Frank's God and *sola fide*—salvation by faith—was his by-line.

After the Centenary, Frank recognized that changes were coming to his family, his town, and his state. It was not possible to retain Hahndorf as a quiet enclave removed from the mainstream of South Australian life. Neither would this be possible for the other German communities, particularly those in the Barossa Valley. Adjustments were on the horizon and modes of mobility were among the greatest visible change agents. For townspeople, the bicycle was still a popular means of transportation. Children rode their bicycles everywhere with the only real caution imposed by parents that "you must be careful when riding down the main street!" Cars were increasingly purchased by farmers and townspeople, but it was not unusual for women to be dependent on their husbands to drive them whenever they wanted to leave the town limits. Some of Mark's school friends had been to the capital city of Adelaide, less than an hour away, only once or twice in their lives. Frank was acutely aware of the increase in traffic passing through Hahndorf. As an integral part of the Adelaide-Melbourne highway, the main street of Hahndorf was the main thoroughfare for cars, trucks, and transports, the eighteen-wheelers, that thundered through the town, especially during the night hours. Now, over fifteen years since the end of World War II, Mr. Wittwer still had his 1948

Chevrolet, Mr. Molen, his 1926 Chevy with a canvas roof. The Holden sedan was the most popular car, but English cars were still dominant— Austin, Morris, Vanguard, Vauxhall, and Land Rover. Some of the more affluent families owned Jaguar, Rover, Humber Snipe, Ford, Pontiac, Chevrolet, and Dodge. Farmers favored the Holden utility and small trucks like Bedford and Austin were preferred by local merchants and daily freight haulers. Frank spoke of his inner concerns about pending change to his family around the meal table. He was instructive in his words and encouraging in his questions as he sought to build awareness within his children. Mark came to see the world through his father's eyes.

Frank Schubert loved to read and often lamented that he did not pursue his first love, theology. He had the most extensive library in Hahndorf and enjoyed loaning his books to his pastor, the teachers, and other reading townsfolk. At this very moment *en route* to Los Angeles, Mark reflected on how much he resembled his father, including his determination and occasional stubbornness. Sometimes, assuming the same attributes of a parent occurs through more than just genetics. When it was clear that Mark was serious about his music, Frank invited Mark to use his study for daily music practice. Frank's study was also his refuge when life hurled its difficult barbs in his direction. This room, located in the old homestead of Mark's great-grandparents, was only a hundred or so paces away from the larger home the family occupied now. Revealing the old German architecture, the dwelling was too dear for the family to demolish. It came in handy as accommodation for visitors from time to time and one room was maintained as Frank's study and retreat. This room was the old main bedroom, with a large open fireplace and Frank's study desk facing the large window overlooking the sloping garden and beyond to the western border of the farm. To the left of the window was an imposing old walnut tree, which kept the family in walnuts, and in early spring a carpet of golden daffodils covered the ground right down to the little stream before the land climbed again to reach the trees. Mark migrated to the study for his daily practice and left his music stand set up a few paces from the large window. This became *his* cherished haven too.

Mount Barker was the commercial center for the eastern region of the Adelaide Hills and home to the district's hospital, police station, and high school. In February 1963, Mark enrolled for his secondary school education. Each day he would walk or ride his bicycle just under one mile down Balhannah Road to Hahndorf's main street, where he and another ten to fifteen students caught the school bus to Mount Barker High School. For the first time, he wore a school uniform consisting of grey trousers, grey dress shirt, a green and yellow striped tie, a grey sweater with yellow and green piping on a v-collar and sleeve cuffs, a green blazer with yellow piping and the school's insignia on the blazer pocket. Black lace-up shoes and grey socks were mandatory. Shorts were permitted in the summer months, but most self-respecting high school boys did not wish to appear juvenile and immature by wearing shorts and long knee-length socks. Wearing such a prescribed dress code presented two possible responses from Mark and his fellow first-year students. He could disregard his uniform and act as if he was wearing an ordinary shirt and jeans. Or he could behave as though his uniform was a precursor to the tailored suit of a professional adult male. Already familiar with his band uniform, Mark subconsciously opted for the second response. He wore his uniform with care and, later, with a degree of pride. He didn't like a tie at half-mast, and he avoided dirt and mud on his pants and shoes. He even learned to kick a football from end to end during play times and while waiting for the bus after school without acquiring much grime on his shoes.

High school took some adjustment. On the first day, all the Hahndorf first-year students took a series of tests along with another one hundred and fifty fresh and raw students from Mount Barker, Nairne, Wistow, Macclesfield, Echunga, Verdun, Mylor, Bridgewater, Aldgate, Stirling, and even Crafers. Once these aptitude tests were graded, the students were "streamed" into their home rooms; 1A, 1B, 1C, 1D, 1E, and 1F. Thus, began the separation of students according to innate ability. It alerted unsuspecting students, and sometimes oblivious parents, to the forthcoming generation's socio-economic divide. Secondary education was compulsory until fifteen years of age, but fewer than thirty per cent of those who commenced high school completed the final year. The American term of graduating with a high school diploma was foreign to Australians. Most students ended their formal schooling at the Intermediate Certificate or Leaving Certificate levels. Students in 1A studied Latin and were better predictably at English, mathematics, and general science. These students were expected to complete the Leaving and Leaving Honors certificates. Then, it was on to university and the various professions available to those with scholastic ability plus the determination, perseverance, and support base to make the arduous undertaking possible. With only one university in South Australia, the narrow rite of passage to the professions was usually reserved to the state's elite and professional families, and those few from the lower echelons who aimed high enough to make it happen. Country high schools were not known to produce an abundance of university students and most of these students left school at fifteen and took a job on the family farm or business or took up a trade. Unfortunately, for many just taking a job, the prevailing imperative was to be free from high school and all traces of required learning, teachers, and examinations as soon as possible.

Not only did Mark have to contend with regular homework and weekly tests, he also had music theory lessons and daily practice. While learning Latin declensions was arduous, cornet practice was enjoyable. Collectively, Mark's early high school years required a high degree of discipline and effort. In terms of hours in the day, Mark was *busy* for one so young. Each Tuesday, after the school bus returned the high school students to the main street of Hahndorf alongside Cleggett's shop, Mark pedaled his bicycle the half mile down the main street to Mr. Paech's house for his weekly lesson. This became his routine for four years, except when it rained, and then his mother or father would meet him at the bus stop and drive him to his lesson. Understandably, there was relief all round when Mark turned sixteen and could drive himself. Gradually, Mark advanced through his brass lessons. He learned music theory at the same time as he learned to play his cornet with the proper *embouchure* and techniques. Right posture was necessary for correct breathing and a precise sound. Mr. Paech worked with exactitude in teaching Mark, because he foresaw the potential of this young player and he understood his own part in shaping a musical talent he had not had the responsibility to nurture before. He knew he would have to surrender Mark to a more qualified teacher in a few years. He anticipated that Mark would be admitted to the Adelaide Conservatory of Music when he was eighteen or nineteen and he knew that Frank and Betty Schubert wanted their first-born to reach his God-given potential.

To this end, in the same February that Mark began high school, he was also enrolled in Grade Four of the Australian Music Examination Board's (AMEB) Theory of Music Musicianship and Brass Instruments (Trumpet) courses. Mark was to study both music theory and music performance with examinations for both in November. Mr. Paech challenged Mark when his enrollment was finalized. "Mark, you are skipping three grades as you begin your AMEB studies. If you work hard you can have your first 'degree' by the time you are 17!"

Mr. Paech was referring to the Associate in Music, Australia (AMusA) diploma. The importance of his teacher's words didn't fully resonate with Mark until he had successfully completed his Grade Four Music performance examinations and recognized that his trumpet performance results were spoken of as being "exemplary." Only then did Mark's thirteen-year-old mind begin to comprehend that he was working towards a significant goal.

In October 1965, Mark was entered in the Under 18 Brass Championships of the South Australian Band Association. Mr. Cleggett, the Band committee, and Mr. Paech spoke with Frank and Betty first, and then with Mark, stating that it was time for him to experience real competition with his peers and to taste the rigors of performing before professional adjudicators. With Mark's AMEB examinations completed in November, he immediately began working towards the South Australian Band Championships in the Centennial

Hall for the following March, with the National Band Council of Australia championships a few weeks later over the Easter weekend in April. Mark turned sixteen that same month. One event was really a rehearsal for the other, and Mark knew the importance of the Easter Nationals. For an adolescent, Mark had a lot going on in his life. He didn't have much free time and, knowing little difference, he didn't hanker after the "nonsense stuff" as Mr. Paech blithely labeled television, comics, meeting down at Cleggett's lollie shop, and other idle pursuits.

Alex, Carl, and Lester remained good friends of Mark's, but they were school friends and not close mates like they had been in primary school. In fact, some of Mark's friends became involved with a homosexual in an episode that concerned most of Hahndorf for several months. It was at this time when Mark's parents spoke to him about matters of sexuality. He also learned about masturbation and the bodily changes that were impacting his physical and emotional adolescent body. Shaving was now a new experience as was the embarrassing and visible onslaught of acne. Frank knew Mark had to get through the stage of puberty and needed to be kept as positive and as occupied as possible. Fortunately for Frank and Betty, Mark was a "home body" who didn't seek to be always with his friends after school and on the weekends. And, the other three children seemed to be following the same pattern.

When Mark wasn't reading, doing homework, and practicing the cornet, there were always chores to do on the farm. Frank was known as the "tidy farmer" in Hahndorf circles. It was a complimentary term and very much reflected Frank's character which tangibly carried over into the appearance, and success, of his 130-acre property. It was a highly compact farm and required an organized and agriculturally astute manager to prevent possible dysfunction resulting from the heavy animal count or seasonal climatic shortfalls. Fortunately, plentiful water was available. Frank had two permanent laborers and would hire seasonal workers as needed. The farm consisted of a Friesian dairy herd of 40 to 50 cows and some 300 Romney Marsh sheep. He also grew potatoes each year. An orchard of apples and pears had been planted years before by Frank's grandfather and, although much reduced from its original size, this provided good fruit for eating and for pies, preserves, and cold storage. Frank maintained 15 acres of Lucerne and cut this for green feed for his 2,000 or so laying hens and hay as winter fodder for his various livestock. He sold about half of his Lucerne bales. Frank's poultry was both free-range and shedded. Fifty per cent of the Schubert's egg money from the South Australian Egg Board was donated to the St. Michael's Lutheran school. As well, they sold cracked eggs to many of the townspeople and this cash money was given to the children to separate, count and bundle each Sunday morning before going to Sunday School. Once every quarter the children took the accumulated cash and placed it on the Thanksgiving table at the front of the church. Frank and Betty called the egg money their mission project. Mark never forgot the example of his parents' philanthropy, even in its small doses.

He had helped his father and one of the farm workers with the evening milking since he was six or seven. Now, almost sixteen years of age, Mark could handle the milking on his own if need be. It was the way of things for generations in this German farming community. Frank Schubert was expected to farm and thus, in his teenage years, he subjugated his innate desires to pursue the scholarly life. He was determined never to apply such familial pressure on Mark and Gary, although Gary was showing early signs that farming was to be the life for him.

The band championships came quickly, and Mark had his first experience of competitive pressure. He came first in the state competition and, emboldened, made ready for the Easter Nationals in Melbourne. Sadly, his experience was not positive and stung him deeply. Even some twenty-five years later, he wished he could erase some of the memories and some of the hurt.

The car journey to Melbourne was a happening all in itself. As a family, the Schuberts had only taken day trips to various places in South Australia. Frank had promised one day of fun for all before the championships began. Even on an overcast day, the Schubert family found a special magic at Luna Park in St. Kilda. From the moment they entered through the mouth of the huge clown, they were mesmerized by the fantasy world atmosphere of the carnival. Mark recalled feeling very much a naive country boy entering a form of amusement somewhat frowned upon by his pastor. As the first order of business, Frank directed the family into the walk-around inspection. Everyone expected this anyway. Whether at a new fruit and vegetable market, or a department store, or visiting a park, Frank liked to know the layout of the place under visitation by the family. Mark, Gary, and their sisters had their intended rides in mind by the end of the circumference walk. The roller coaster rides were pride of place—the Big Dipper and the Scenic Railway. The siblings stared in nervous anticipation at the thrills that lay ahead. Gary giggled as he dismissed the Tunnel of Love ride. With the family organized, the fun began and Mark's overwhelming competition ordeal on the next day was pushed to the background for a few hours.

Five hours later, the Schubert family re-entered the ordinary world after having indulged in a level of fun none had experienced before. Side Show Alley at the annual Royal Adelaide Agricultural Show was the closest comparison to Luna Park. Mark considered one as temporary while the other was permanent: Imagine being able to frequent Luna Park whenever you liked! How lucky were Melbournians and Sydney-siders to have a standing Luna Park. Mark found himself wishing for bigger, more expansive worlds to experience. That evening the family was glad to reach their caravan park. Not only were they tired from Luna Park, but the size, slowness, and intensity of Melbourne's peak hour traffic was exhausting. Adelaide and the Adelaide Hills were nothing compared to this!

Rain was falling gently when Mark awoke at daybreak. He knew it was impossible to return to sleep, so he quietly slipped out of his stretcher bed in the annex and decided to go for a walk. Before he left, Frank opened the caravan door and he stepped into the annex. "Feel like a walk?" he asked. Together, reaching for umbrellas, they strode out into a wet, yet significant, day in Mark's life. Frank knew some of the inner turmoil his son was experiencing.

"What if I mess up, Dad? What if I make a mistake and can't correct myself to go on?"

"Mark, I know you are feeling anxious just now, but you can do this. You've been preparing for months for this competition. Mr. Paech has prepped you as best he knows how. He wouldn't set you up for something you couldn't do. He trained Gordon, remember," said Frank. He glanced at his son.

"I know all that, Dad. It's just . . . what if I don't win?" Mark asked.

"You know my answer to that, Mark. You can't do any more than your best. Your mother and I are proud of you and we want you to win. We think you deserve to win. But there is no guarantee. Right now, you need to focus on your state of mind. Think of it this way: imagine all of the other players standing in their underwear and you are the only one in full uniform!" said Frank.

"Dad, that's a horrible thought."

"Maybe, but if it helps calm you when you come out on stage, then so be it!"

By the time they returned to their caravan, the rest of the family was awake, and the Schubert temporary abode was alive with the energy of a young family in close quarters. Treks to the shower block and breakfast on the run occupied everyone, including Mark. His nervousness and anxiety were replaced by his habitual role as helping the family make ready for the day.

By 8:00 a.m., Frank gathered his brood in a circle in the annex and prayed for God's blessing on the family for the day ahead and especially for Mark, "our wonderful son" who was "facing his most important competition so far in his young life."

Mark looked splendid in his black surge band uniform with the green stripes on the trousers. The green epaulets accented his ever-broadening shoulders. He had shaved, and his skin was clear except for one small pimple on his neck just above the collar line.

Betty hugged him, "You look so handsome," she said proudly.

"Okay, let's do this," said Frank as the family jumped into the Ford Galaxie. Mark would always remember that drive to Melbourne

Town Hall as a surreal experience. He looked out onto a city preparing for the new day and felt he was in a dream as they drove
along the crowded Whitehorse Road, crossed the Yarra River, past the
imposing Houses of Parliament, into Burke Street, and finally into
the Southern Cross Hotel parking garage. Amidst this incongruous
imagery, a flurry of sights, sounds and senseless speculation reeled
through his mind while his brother and sisters were chortling away.
In the windows of passing cars he saw other youthful passengers in
their band uniforms, and he wondered if his competitors were as
nervous as he was.

The walk to the Town Hall down Little Burke Street took ten minutes. Betty dearly wanted to linger at the George's display windows, but
she knew that while this may have been the right place, it certainly was
the wrong time. Sensing her interest, Frank squeezed her hand and said
quietly: "On the way back, you can look as long as you like."

Mark carried his cornet case and Gary carried the sheet music, even
though the notes had all been committed to memory six months ago.
In Queensbury Street the imposing arches and columns of the Town
Hall heralded the 1966 National Band Council of Australia championships. Beautiful flower carts and luminous banners added to the cer-
emonious nature of the four-day event. The Schubert family entered
the spacious lobby of the Town Hall and was greeted by Mr. Paech
who had traveled by train on *The Overland* to Melbourne and arrived
Thursday morning. Recognizing the importance of dedicated family time, Mr. Paech arranged to meet them an hour before the Under
18 Solo Championships commenced. He knew Mark was emotionally well-attended by Betty and Frank. Personally, there was not much
more he could do for Mark anyway.

"Good morning, Schuberts. What a great day for a little competition! You look good, Mark. In fifteen minutes, you will need to meet
at the top of the stairs over to the right. You will see the sign for the
Under 18 Soloists to assemble. You're number three on the list. It's
not a bad place to be. In fact, it is very good. Two will have finished
before you and then there will be five after you. It's a great placement.

We're fortunate." Mr. Paech stepped back and indicated that the family should find their seats in the upstairs front section of the main auditorium.

Mark was noticing the increasing swirl of band members around him of all stripes and colors. Fixated on the task ahead, he deliberated for a moment.

"Mum, Dad, I need to go to the bathroom and then I think I'll go to the waiting room and mix with the other players."

Mr. Paech interjected quickly: "Just remember, Mark, the other players are your competition and you shouldn't expect them to be all that friendly. Let me go with you and I'll leave you at the waiting room. Having a few nerves now is a good thing. This is what we have worked for and you're going to be fine. I will say no more; you know what to do, but most importantly, do your best."

Walking into the assembly room, Mark found five other anxious teenagers, including one girl, readying themselves for the competition ahead. A band association volunteer approached Mark: "What is your name, young man?"

"Schubert, sir, Mark Schubert from the Hahndorf Town Band."

"Good, Mr. Schubert, you are number three in the order of players. Come and sit over here. We are still waiting on the players from Willoughby and Hawthorn City. They need to be here in the next ten minutes. I will leave you for a few minutes; please, all stay in this room."

As the band monitor left the room, Mark took his cornet out of its case. He connected the mouthpiece and ran his fingers over the valves. Looking down at his sheet music, he was wondering if he should break the silence, when the Kew City young man said:

"Hey, Schubert, this is a bit out of your league, isn't it?"

"What ... what did you say?" Mark asked hesitantly.

"Well, for starters, you're a Crow-Eater. You're too young to be in this competition I don't think you've got it! Why don't you go back to Hannnd-dorf—where all the dorks are from!"

Mark looked around the room, bewildered. Two other players

looked at each other and sniggered. He knew the players by names only from the Under 18 Solo Championship list. He wondered if he had heard correctly what had just been said.

"Why did you say that? I haven't done anything to you!"

The band monitor walked into the room, accompanied by the Willoughby and Hawthorn City players. Both were taller and older-looking than Mark and exuded self-confidence. With the competition now only minutes away, and sensing anxiety in the room, Frank Jackson of Hawthorn gave his rallying cry:

"Hello all. Hey, we're going into a competition, not a funeral procession. Take it easy, we're all going to do OK."

"Yeah, all except the dork from Hannnd-dorf!"

"Now, hang on, Mr. Green," said the band monitor. "That's uncalled for. Apologize to Mr. Schubert and get ready to go on stage. The bell has just sounded, and the adjudicators are now waiting. Please do the right thing."

"Sorry, Schubert. You'll make Hannnd-dorf proud yet."

"Good, Mr. Green, now get on stage and best of luck to all of you."

Mark could not believe what had just occurred. He didn't want to look around the room, even though all the players were now pre-occupied with their own thoughts. He felt shaken by the unprovoked antagonism of James Green, the Kew City cornet player. His eyes watered and he wondered if he could clear them in time. He had been raised by the Golden Rule "to do unto others as you would have them do to you." For him that was not some idle platitude, rather it was a code of conduct burned into his very person. He wanted to leave. He longed for the familiar surroundings of Hahndorf where people were supportive.

Mark had been nurtured by a family, indeed, an entire community, where a genuine sense of self-esteem was neither overly competitive nor comparative. In fact, the German residents of Hahndorf had learned over the one hundred plus years of their settlement in a heavily British country that they must project a sense of humility and fairness and justice to all. As minorities, particularly through the bellicose half-century of both the Kaiser and Adolf Hitler, Hahndorf residents avoided arrogance, boastfulness, and the over-estimation of one's abilities. Lutheranism promoted a healthy self-esteem whereby one was neither at war with self nor with others.

Mark knew he needed to relax. He needed to dismiss the outburst as the action of an immature person who lacked self-assurance. It was time to focus. While Mark was the youngest of the Under 18 players in the competition, he had a good chance of placing first, perhaps second, and certainly no less than third. The next hour would tell the tale and Mark wanted to return to Hahndorf with the Under 18 Solo Championship trophy in his possession. The tinkling of the bell alerted the players that the solo section was about to begin and the second day of the 1966 Easter National championships was under way.

First on stage was James Green. He positioned himself and paused while the announcer welcomed the audience, competitors and adjudicators to Friday's proceedings. The bell sounded the readiness of the adjudicators and Greene placed his lips to his mouthpiece. He played with confidence and ease. The shrill of the cornet and the clarity of sound and tone filled the Town Hall and announced to all within hearing that musical talent was on display.

"Boy, Green can play," said Jackson of Hawthorn City, "It's a pity he's such a show off."

"Yeah, but it sure makes it hard for the rest of us," replied McIntrye of Willougby as he clutched his euphonium a little tighter.

Five minutes later, Green walked off the stage obviously pleased with his performance and basking in the manifest approval of the five hundred strong audience of family members, bandsmen, and other brass band enthusiasts.

"OK, beat that, the rest of you!" Green snapped at the other soloists as he walked by. There was as much provocation in his voice as arrogance, but he also closed his eyes with relief as he placed his instrument back in its case.

Next on stage was McIntrye. Mark listened intently as the mellifluous euphonium played the same competition music, yet the silvery, dulcet sound made the piece sound new and different. When it came to the *Andante* section, Mark felt a wave of emotion come over him as he experienced the sweetness and softness of the euphonium's tone. He knew he was next, and he felt inadequate for the exercise ahead. Why did Green single him out and put him down? Why did Green have to be first and then to have played so perfectly? Was this boy from Hannnd-dorf really ready to play in a national championship? Mark felt his hands becoming clammy and he felt dryness in his mouth; even in his youthful inexperience, Mark knew that both sensations were not good just prior to a competition.

"Mr. Schubert, you're next. Please make ready to walk onto the stage. Do you want a music stand for your music?"

"No ... no music stand, I'll be alright," replied Mark as he dealt with the myriad of thoughts rushing through his mind. Most of all, he tried to "see" Mr. Paech and "hear" his words, "... *this is what we have worked for ... you'll be fine.*"

"Worked for what? And how can I be fine after being called a dork?" questioned Mark to himself. He knew he was in trouble. "Steady down, dork. Please, Jesus, give me calmness. Help me through this piece."

"Ladies and gentlemen, boys and girls, our third player in the Under 18 Solo Championships is Mark Schubert of the Hahndorf Town Band. Mark is playing cornet and has been with his hometown band since he was twelve years of age. Turning sixteen years in a few days, Mark is the youngest player in the Under 18 Solo category this year," said the announcer.

With this introduction, Mark took a sip of water and lifted the cornet to his lips. He knew his family was in the balcony straight ahead, but he didn't have time to look for them. As the piano played the prelude to his piece, Mark steadied himself and felt ready to give the music his best. His first notes were clear and on pitch. He had played this same piece of music several hundred times and he had played it in many moods. Mr. Paech had deliberately positioned Mark over the years to play certain important pieces of music at the very times when he did not wish to do so. Mr. Paech called it *conditioning* for the time Mark may need to have "all his wits about him." Mark was now at section C and he knew all was well thus far. He was coming up to his cadenza and this was his first moment to demonstrate his tone and control, particularly on the high notes. From his favorite triplet segment, he landed on middle C for the pause. Taking a breath, he tongued down to low C and began the chromatic semi-breve run with a trill on high B flat and paused. As he took another breath, the word *dork* flashed into his mind and he instantly mis-pitched his next note which would lead him to his last run of semi-breves and his final pause before section D, *Largo*. He recovered as quickly as he flubbed the note, but he knew the damage was done.

Largo, with its slow, somber, and subdued tempo, was Mr. Paech's secret weapon in Mark Schubert for this competition piece. This was Mark's moment to exhibit his maturity of tone and instrument control. The thirty-four bars were played accurately, and the notes were clear and precise, but the *Largo* didn't sing. It had none of the Schubert passion and empathy that had brought tears to Mr. Paech's eyes so many times over the past ten months.

The final section was the *Presto*. Mark was glad to arrive at the conclusion and attacked it with a flurry of fingers and staccato tonguing as if he was on automatic pilot. The notes fairly flew from his cornet as he tripled-tongued his way to the final crescendo and arrived at his last pause which he held as the piano completed the accompaniment. He took a deep breath, lowered his instrument, bowed courteously, and then exited the stage as quickly as possible. Mark knew he had played poorly, and he felt like running to the pine trees and bawling his eyes out.

Mark came fourth, but it felt like last. He saw himself as a usurper, a mere child trying to cope in a class way beyond his reach. As of this moment, he rejected any prospects of future performance championships. And, to be honest, Mark was re-thinking continuing with his cornet and playing in the band. The hurt was not worth the hours of practice and memorization of music. There was always football and the season was just getting underway.

The ten-hour car journey back to Hahndorf on the Western

Highway was quieter than usual for the Schubert family. Frank and Betty talked together and pointed out sights of interest along the way. Mark watched the scenery go by, but the ticking of the hours turned him sullen and resentful. He was giving up on music. He was tired, and sleep brought him some physical rest, but not emotional repose. Meanwhile, Gary and his two sisters intuitively understood that this was not a time to fight, act flippantly, or complain about being cramped in the car.

As the United flight continued its way to Los Angeles, Mark finally succumbed to sleep. Even thirty minutes of fitful rest at this stage would be good reinforcement for the thirteen hours across the Pacific to Sydney.

CHAPTER THREE

CHANGE OF
COURSE

"I took the one less travelled by,
And that has made all the difference."
—Robert Frost

"Ladies and gentlemen, as we approach Los Angeles International Airport, we ask that you prepare for landing. Your seats need to be returned to their upright position. We will be landing in 15 minutes."

Mark was awakened from his stupor and complied by taking out his ear phones and bringing his seat to its upright position. He felt rested, although a little tense as this was only one quarter of his journey home. He had slept a little and his foundational mindset had, once again, revisited earlier times and accepted the inevitable; there was no way to change the past, but the present was the doorway to the future. Mark needed his future to be better than his present. He had not thought of Christina once over the last few hours, but he wanted her to be part of his better days ahead. At least, he thought he did.

The aircraft landed, and Mark made his way to the Tom Brady Terminal where Qantas departed for Sydney at 11:40 pm. He had ample time to wander around the growing number of shops at LAX. Mark remembered when there were very few shopping opportunities in airports and now there seemed almost too many fixated on enticing passengers to shop up to the moment of boarding. Mark always bought Sees Candy for his mother and this meant *Nuts & Chews* for her. Also, he needed to eat as he rarely ate food served in transit. Finally, Mark found a seat far enough away from the milling crowd of rambunctious passengers, the majority of whom were rowdy Australians anxious to return home to the "best country on earth." They had been to

Disneyland, Universal Studios, the Queen Mary, tramped the streets of Hollywood and Rodeo Drive, explored the mountains and desert country behind Los Angeles, and the beaches on the Pacific Ocean, "which were disappointing compared to Australian beaches!" It was a similar scenario to every flight departing LAX for Sydney, or Melbourne; Australians going home to their *Lucky Country*.

Mark, too, felt a little like them but he was embarrassed at their vocal arrogance which knew no reserve around the LAX staff tasked with boarding passengers on QF12 for its flight across the Pacific. Calmly, toting only hand luggage, Mark boarded and was fortunate once more with a spare seat next to his aisle seat. Was this an omen for a positive time in Australia at the Easter Nationals, and with family and friends in Hahndorf? He hoped so, and he found himself quietly saying a prayer for a safe flight and seeking God's blessing upon all that was ahead, even Christina.

The Boeing 747 climbed into the darkness of the night sky. Weather reports foretold of an uneventful flight and good autumn weather in Sydney. After the evening food service was over, Mark settled back to resume his reflections. *Where was he? Yes, he was just sixteen a few days after his first experience of national championships.*

There was no question—Mark considered himself a failure and, for now, pursuing a career in music had dropped to the bottom of his list of priorities. Perhaps, he reasoned, Mr. Paech had given him unrealistic expectations. Maybe Hahndorf had made too much of its favorite son. Possibly Mark himself had developed an ego and thought he was too good to lose. Whatever the case, Mark felt hurt and humiliated by his experience at the Easter Nationals. Clearly, the months of preparation did not match the outcome. After many visits to the pine trees, Mark decided to abandon his cornet for now. After all, it was the onset of winter and football dominated the thoughts of most teenage boys in the Adelaide Hills.

Mr. Paech was more than annoyed at Mark's decision to stop

playing his cornet. In fact, he called him a "selfish young fool." In further defiance, Mark left the Hahndorf Town Band as well. Mr. Paech appealed to Mark's parents and asked them to exert pressure on Mark, but they refused to do so. Instead, they advocated a hiatus of three to six months. They had no idea if this would turn Mark around. Undue provocation was not their style.

Mark was a good football player. Center half-back was his position. The Hahndorf Colts had the challenge before them of reclaiming the Hills Championship from the last two years. Practice was on Thursday nights and Mark felt liberated to think that he now only had one routine practice on his weekly agenda; no more cornet and band practice for him. Saturday afternoons, week after week during the winter months, the Colts advanced on the Hills football ladder. The team coalesced into an enviable force and Mark proved to be a valuable addition. He was a solid barrier to the forward advance of every rival team. He was an aggressive player, fast, with a towering leap, and he built an impressive mark ratio. It felt good to be part of a team which worked together, to have a coach that cheered you on no matter what, and townsfolk who gave wholehearted support, even if Mark was no longer their cherished musician. By the end of the season, Mark was part of the winning team. It had been a wonderful five months. Mark was physically more fit than ever, and his state of mind had recovered. Thoughts of the Easter Nationals no longer haunted him, made him physically ill or kept him awake at night.

In early Spring Mr. Paech deliberately encountered Mark as he stepped off the high school bus one Thursday afternoon. "Mark, can we talk?"

The initial moment was awkward as Mark recalled the incident as clear as a bell. There was nowhere to go for a confidential talk in the main street of Hahndorf. There was no coffee shop, no library, no public seating, and so they walked across the road to the old Academy where Mark left his bicycle each school day. Mark wondered what was coming.

Mr. Paech got directly to the point: "Mark, I can't let your talent go to waste. Please listen: I know you were hurt by the Easter Nationals, but you have had a few months to get over it. Won't you please pick up your cornet again, and let's start with some more lessons. I promise you that you can become an A-grade champion."

"Mr. Paech, I must be honest when I say that I have felt like a quitter many times. After the Easter Nationals, I never wanted to play my cornet again. But now that football season is over, I'm not sure what to do with my time. I guess I'm saying that I miss playing," said Mark.

Mr. Paech saw his opening and he pounced: "You have lived a disciplined life for years. Music practice was what gave you meaning and the challenge of becoming a champion was what we both worked at so hard for so long. Many boys your age can only dream of opportunities that are within your reach. Let's try to get it back, slowly at first, until you become sure."

"Mr. Paech, I have to get home to do my chores. Dad will be wondering where I am. Let me talk to Mum and Dad and I promise I will think seriously about it," responded Mark.

As Mark rode his bicycle home, he felt alright, even a little grateful that Mr. Paech had approached him. That night, after dinner, Mark spoke with Frank and Betty. All his jumbled thoughts and feelings that had been bottled up during the winter months came tumbling out. Ever the honest person, Frank told Mark that Mr. Paech had asked permission to speak to him about starting music studies again. The conclusion of this outburst, which Frank and Betty had listened to without interruption, was that Mark wondered if he should not restart his music dreams again.

Frank glanced at Betty and then said quietly: "Mark, we've been praying for this moment. We knew you needed time. We think God is leading here. Even so, it is your decision. Don't rush into it. Sleep on it and pray about it too!"

Mark did pray before he went to sleep. Belief in a personal and interventionist God was the Old Lutheran way. It is what brought Mark's descendants to Australia in the first place. Frank often said it took a strong belief in a personal God to undertake that voyage into the unknown in 1838. Mark was raised in a 'take it to the Lord in prayer' family and community. He determined to make a considered decision, knowing that it was time to grow up and to focus on becoming a champion.

The Leaving Certificate examinations were looming and after the Royal Adelaide Show in September it was a full onslaught in preparing for the state finals in mid-November to early December. Always a good student, Mark melded his farm chores, family life and school into this tight three-month schedule. He did not include cornet practice, but it was on his mind. One Saturday afternoon when he and Gary were under the pine trees, Gary asked, "Are you going back to your music, Mark?"

"Yeah, I think I am," replied Mark, "But, it is going to be different this time."

The festivities of the Christmas season came and went, and the Schubert family embarked on a new year in the usual holiday fashion with many visits to Brighton Beach. Mark was in his Matriculation year, the final year of high school for students who had university in their sights. It was February when Mark announced to the family, and later to Mr. Paech, that he was going back to music, but he was changing instruments. He was going to play the euphonium. The family was surprised but supportive. Mr. Paech, on the other hand, was upset.

"Mark, where did this come from? Do you know what you're doing? The cornet, the trumpet," he spluttered, "this is the king of brass. This is *your* instrument! My dear boy, do you know what you're saying? The euphonium is a beautiful instrument and melodious, to be sure. It is the leader of the bass end of the brass band, but it hardly has parts in a concert band or an orchestra. Mark my word: you are going to limit yourself! I recommend you seriously rethink this. I want to make a champion of you and to point you in the right direction for a super career that best fits your talents. The euphonium will certainly make *my* job more difficult!"

———∞———

Mark smiled and shook his head slightly in his seat half way across the Pacific, remembering how he 'handled' Mr. Paech in his seventeenth year: "Mr. Paech, I have spent a lot of time thinking about this. I am going to play the euphonium and you can *still* make me a champion."

———∞———

A week later, Mr. Cleggett dropped off a euphonium for Mark at the Schubert home. He was glad that Mark was returning to the Band. On reflection, Mark remembered his final year of high school as being a watershed year. The euphonium was his major challenge, but he knew he had to focus on his academic work as well. Added to this was his AMEB Grade 7 theory and practical examinations. He was now a year behind schedule in completing his AMusA diploma. Ultimately, he wanted to go to the University of Adelaide and the Music Conservatory to study both music and history—European History, with a focus on the Sixteenth Century and the German Reformation. As a child, Mark was often found on the floor of his father's study engrossed in books on medieval times, Luther and the wars of religion.

Mark's final year of high school revolved around the core elements of family, school, farm, community and music. He sensed he was maturing and more in command of his own person. His decision to switch from cornet to euphonium was evidence of this. He retained his trumpet-birthday present, but the band cornet was now replaced with a band euphonium. Sitting next to Ray Sadler as second *eupho* player was a big deal for Mark. He was growing up, no longer that little kid who sat in the lowest chair as third cornet.

Neither Mark nor the Hahndorf Town Band participated in this year's Easter National championships. These were convened in Launceston and the Bass Strait separating the Australian mainland from Tasmania added to the cost and complexity of attending unless participation was sought by Mark or the Band. Mr. Paech was adamant: "Now that you are playing euphonium, we have a lot of work to do, my boy. No *Nationals* for you this year!" It was true; Mark did have a lot of work in making the transition. All the same, Mr. Paech had his eye on next year's Easter Nationals in Sydney. Mark would still be under 18, although only by five days.

Now as a euphonium player, Mark liked the way it felt to hold his new instrument. "You have to wrap your arms around a euphonium; it's my new girlfriend," Mark recalled saying for a week or so, until he dropped it as too corny. The first order of business was to form the correct embouchure, the shaping of the lips to the mouthpiece. The mouth piece from cornet to euphonium was significantly larger and Mark looked back to the formative moment when Mr. Paech touted his old mantra: A (Air) + E (Embouchure) = T (Tone). While this equation also applied to all wind instruments, it was especially so for brass instruments. It was the correct embouchure which produced the tonal quality and only with brass instruments did the vibrating force of the lips add to the production of good tone. Mr. Paech had already taught Mark the old trick of looking in a mirror in the early days of forming a proper embouchure. For over twenty years Mark had used this method repeatedly with his students. It worked for him, and it worked for them.

The approach of winter gave Mark time to re-engage with his music and adjust to his new instrument. The shorter days and cooler weather encouraged the people of Hahndorf into the warmth and security of their homes at an earlier hour. His weekly lessons with Mr. Paech were becoming more meaningful as his teacher was accepting Mark's decision. Especially was this so as Mr. Paech was recognizing that Mark and his euphonium were beginning to flourish. This was looking to be a perfect union. The other component in Mr. Paech's equation was *air*. Mark recalled having an abundance of this and he always attributed this to living in the country where the atmosphere was clean and natural. Equally important was Mark's physical fitness; *as fit as a mallee bull* was the colloquial phrase in Mark's recollections. Collaboratively, the Paech formula was working and it was only a matter of months before Mark was demonstrating the euphonium's distinctive tone, its wide range and the variety of its character and agility. Mark especially enjoyed the extremes of the instrument's span; its high notes with the sound of the sweetest song bird and the low, commanding notes which equated the euphonium to the double Bb bass instrument, even if only faintly.

Life has the tendency to interject trials and hardship into a family's equilibrium. The Schubert's were entering the winter season as a contented household. Farming activities had slowed as excess livestock had been sold, the spring crops were dormant until the incalescence of the spring sunshine, the orchard was drab and bare, all poultry were now in their sheds, the cattle and sheep became friendly with the daily allotment of lucerne hay, the pond was full and overflowing, the firewood supply was stacked, and Betty's wood stove was now the sole source of cooking in the kitchen. The electric stove became inert during these cold months. The wood stove's other advantage was the cozy warmth and the distinct aroma of eucalyptus. Nothing could be more Australian than this, reflected Mark—how many times had he come into the kitchen to warm himself by the wood stove.

Then, in July, Frank became ill. At first, he complained of back pain and upper abdomen soreness along with bloating. Two weeks later this was followed by erratic bouts of fever which took him to bed early. By the end of the month, Betty noticed a slight yellowing of the skin and told Frank that he was "jaundiced," and he must see the doctor. The prognosis was the need for gallbladder surgery. The winter calm now turned to panic as it became clear that Frank was going to hospital for an operation. The younger children did not want "Daddy to die." Betty and Grandma called the family together and, with Frank sitting in his chair, they talked over what was ahead and prayed for Frank's speedy recovery. Mark, always Betty's right-hand man, assumed added responsibilities and kept the fear level of his siblings at bay by reassuring them that Dad would be back to normal by the time of the Royal Adelaide Show.

By the first week of September, Frank was not completely healed, but he was walking, and he did make the effort to take the family to the Show for most of the day. He endured the discomfort by sitting frequently. It had been an intense five weeks and Mark remembered how good it was to see the family laugh and enjoy Show food in all its greasy and over-sweet flavors. Naturally, Frank had to forego most of it. When they arrived at the Car Pavilion, Frank was keen to see the General Motors Holden display. There, in front of them, was a beautiful new pillarless four-door Blue and White Chevrolet Caprice. The idea of a new car came to Frank during his convalescence. He was spending more time with the daily paper and he saw the promotions for the new cars on display at the Show. Frank was aware that the children were growing, and more room was needed to take Grandma with the family too. Admittedly, the Ford Galaxie was not ten years old, but family comfort was important, and Frank considered it a necessary expenditure. Besides, the excitement of a new car would be good for morale after what he had put everybody through.

Frank's psychology worked. It was a good spring which followed as Frank regained his full health and strength. Always the systematic farmer, he embarked on two new ventures and challenged his two workmen to take these projects as their own. He would pay for all expenses and even send them to Victoria to learn from current successful operations. Each would take the lead in his small business and the other would work alongside. Both men would continue their regular work on the farm, but this would enable them to don the entrepreneurial spirit where they could share in the profits and thus be more than just wage-earners. The first idea was a potted plant operation and the second was raising turkeys for the Christmas market. Both young men jumped at the idea and within two weeks were working with Frank to bring both projects to life.

Mark remembered how Frank made it a practice to include the family in the operations of the farm. This aided in the maturity and a degree of awareness in the children from an early age. They skipped much of the silliness and aberrant behavior so common of the teenage years. Indeed, Mark and Gary, as the older siblings, were developing a business sense vicariously.

The last three months of high school were less than tranquil for Mark. His father's surgery dislodged his balance somewhat because Frank had always been there no matter what came his way. His father's illness meant that Mark now thought of himself as the head of the family. How could he do this with everything else he had to accomplish between September and his final high school examinations? Little wonder that Mark doubled his efforts in all his endeavors. He rose earlier and went into his father's study to review, memorize and practice past examination papers. When the family began to stir after 6 am, he played his euphonium. Endlessly, he played the scales: the diatonic, the chromatic, major, minor, progressive exercises, double and triple tonguing, and cadenzas. He was also committing his test piece for the upcoming Easter Nationals to memory. Frank insisted that Mark be excused from many of his farm chores, so Gary was given more of these to do. It was the farming way. Nevertheless, Mark knew what it was to schedule every half hour segment from morning to night. December was in sight and he had to accomplish his goals.

One irrepressible moment of reflection flashed into Mark's deliberations as a welcome juxtaposition to the grueling task of revisiting the past with typical Schubert accuracy. As a prefect at Mount Barker high school in his senior year, one of Mark's duties was the supervising of first-year students giving ten minutes of their time once a week every term to the *Tidy Yard* program—in essence, to pick up papers and other trash around the school grounds. A cute, precocious thirteen-year-old named Claire had a crush on Mark and made no bones about it. Knowing he was leaving high school in a month or two, she would come up to Mark at lunch time with a friend and ask Mark if he could "supervise" her in picking up papers. There was always light-hearted banter in these exchanges with Mark insisting that she was "adorable, but way too young." Even after all these years Mark remembered Claire's comment, tossed off with a smile on the last day of school: "I may be too young for you now, but every year I am getting older!" Mark had to admit these innocent encounters were flattering, but he dare not lose focus on reaching his dreams. He was a Hahndorf boy by birth and upbringing, but he would have to leave the Adelaide Hills to realize his ambitions. Yet, here he was, at 35,000 feet, coming home and wondering what he had really accomplished by leaving.

Mark's spring-time regimen saw him through until Speech Night, or graduation in his adopted American context. His state examination results were not as stellar as he wanted, but he earned three A's and two B's, and this gave him entry into the University of Adelaide and the Music Conservatorium.

Attention now turned towards harvesting in the Hahndorf farming community as it did for the entire Adelaide Hills. The Schuberts only had a small acreage under crops and the haymaking left the paddocks with their stubble. It was early summer and each week the landscape turned more of the shades of yellowish-brown. Gone were the greens of spring and by May the countryside would ache to lose its ecru sallowness and to experience the soft, refreshing autumn rains.

With the heat of summer came the season of Christmas and the frenzy of parties, primary school end-of-year festivities and the Lutheran church Nativity celebrations. The Hahndorf Town Band featured in many of these and Mark was now wearing a new band uniform. The Schubert family was involved in most of these events and after the Christmas Eve service, Christmas Day usually meant a complete day at home with family, food and presents. Often, the day was hot, and before air conditioning this meant that the family had the Christmas mid-day meal in shorts and sleeveless dresses. Nevertheless, tradition was maintained, and the meal was turkey and roast vegetables followed by hot English pudding with silver coins cooked inside. The delectable dessert was covered with brandy sauce, and ice cream if desired. It was always an untroubled day and there were squeals of joy as the family opened gifts, many of which had come from their Christmas lists. Mark gave Frank a book he had mentioned several times, *The Theology of Martin Luther,* by Paul Althaus. It did not take Frank long to read part of a sentence that thrilled him: "… it is through the gospel, through Christ, that 'we learn to look straight into the face of God.'" The author was quoting Martin Luther, and Frank said that he wanted each of his children to understand the beauty of the Gospel because it would keep them all close to God throughout their lives. Looking back over more than twenty-five years, Mark knew he had drifted from this, but the wish of his father never left him.

CHAPTER FOUR

A YEAR ON THE FARM

"I gained it so, by climbing slow."
—Emily Dickinson

Christmas and New Year's always seemed like a continuous vacation. Indeed, for most Australians this was the season of annual holidays and could mean that a return to work was not until the third or fourth weeks of January.

Almost as momentous a decision as changing from cornet to euphonium, Mark deferred going to university for one year. He had discussed this possibility with his parents back in September, but their recommendation was to wait for his examination results, his acceptance into university, and his state of mind after the New Year. A year on the farm would be his *catch-up* interval. He had lost momentum after his Easter Nationals saga and he did want to complete his AMusA diploma with minimal disruptions and give full attention to the National championships coming up in Sydney this Easter. Moreover, Mark knew that he was young to be attending university, and a year where he could coddle himself in an uncluttered life, even for twelve months, would be good for him in the long term. Ever since Mark was thirteen, Mr. Paech had kept him so focused on his music that he had missed many of the mundane aspects of his teenage years. Frank and Betty had an emotional investment in Mark's decision as well. They fully appreciated that Mark's future lay in the world of music and not agriculture. It was likely that Gary would be the son who stayed on the farm. However, Frank and Betty had two daughters too. On the horizon, they must confront the complex matter of succession and estate planning. They were the fourth generation on the Schubert farm and now they were staring at the fifth generation. There were three foremost objectives they sought to meet: to maintain a viable farm business for the next generation, to treat all their children fairly, and to provide for their own retirement. As a family, the Schubert's embodied the rural cultural outlook on farming as a way of life. For Mark to have this "year on the farm" was important to them. They knew that all too soon he would be far away from all things close at hand and agricultural.

Mark's first full day on the farm began at 8:00 am on Monday in mid-January. He was sporting an enviable suntan as evidence of many days at the beach with the family over the last three weeks. He wore shorts, a sleeveless shirt, and new elastic-side boots. He had enjoyed his Christmas and New Year's and now he was joining the ranks of the workforce. Each day he would toil by the sweat of his brow, and more than five days a week, as this was farm life and not your *nine to five* office job. Even twenty-five years later, and high above the Pacific, Mark distinctly remembered thinking on this first day on the job that from now on he was the maker who shaped the road that lay before him. If farming was not his lot in life, then he had to be intentional how he contrived what lay ahead. He was optimistic, although a little hesitant, but overall, his dreams were ambitious.

On the other hand, Frank was suddenly ambivalent about Mark's "year on the farm" as the family was beginning to call his hiatus between high school and university. What if the interruption in the discipline and habit of music and academics caused a complete re-evaluation of Mark's desire to become a music teacher or a professional musician? It would be understandable if Mark was to take the road less strenuous and join the family farm enterprise instead. After all, he could still pursue his music in the Hahndorf Town Band, although he had really outgrown a C grade band long ago. He would have a lot less pressure on his shoulders and one day the farm could be shared by the Schubert brothers. Frank decided to keep these apprehensions to himself and determined to act as a coach and a guide toward the intended outcome.

With Mark on board for an entire year, Frank could proceed with his egg cooling room extension. Over the last three years, Frank had expanded his poultry operation because the price of eggs was worth his extra effort and he could also sell the two-year-old laying hens on a regular rotation basis. Even the manure, which was highly sought after by the Italian and Greek market gardeners from the Adelaide plains, brought a nice profit. By trebling the size of the existing cool room, Frank could grow his egg production even more as the market continued to expand.

Summer turned to autumn, and Mark prepared for the Easter Nationals. He resolved to do all in his power to win the Under 18 Solo championship. Since early February, he had played up to five hours a day. Working at home allowed him to practice at mid-day as well, and even after seven years of playing Mark never thought of the heavy practice routine as drudgery. Mr. Paech came to the farm twice a week during the lunch hour. Everything was done to facilitate Mark's endeavors.

It was decided that Frank, Mr. Paech, and Mark would fly to Sydney for the Easter Nationals. There was no other way to do it. Betty and Grandma, Gary and the girls, would stay and keep the home fires burning. The Ansett Airlines flight from Adelaide to Sydney was a first for all three men and was exciting by itself. Once in Sydney, it was a taxi ride to the hotel and then two days for further practice, with a little time for sightseeing. Naturally, Sydney Harbor was the big attraction and the ferry ride to Manly introduced Mark to a new vista not found in Adelaide or Melbourne. It was a stunning day and the bright blue sky on the choppy water made for a convenient pause in the presence of mounting competition tension. Mark had never seen such urban beauty woven into the very fabric of nature at every turn. The many houses built on the rock formations that extended down to the water's edge, the numerous tidy alcoves of beaches and parklands, the distant landmarks of Lady Macquarie's Chair, Fort Denison, the Taronga Park Zoo perched high above the harbor; all were new geographical experiences for these South Australians. The one familiar element was the Norfolk Island pines at Manly reminding these visitors of their own seaside resort of Glenelg. An ice cream cone and a walk along this strip of the Pacific Ocean rounded off a good day. Mark was in bed by 9:00 pm in readiness for his contest performance on the morrow.

It is interesting how two years of maturing can change the dynamics of a band competition. Mark awoke feeling some tension, but not apprehension or a feeling of inadequacy. Today, he had a job to do: He must play music he had rehearsed hundreds of times. He was ready. The intrepid trio from Hahndorf arrived at the town hall, Mark registered, and, after final best wishes, he left his father and Mr. Paech and disappeared into the waiting room. By noon, the Under 18 Solo championships were over, with Mark placing second. He felt good about that. The next day they flew home.

Even though Mark continued to work on the farm, his major preoccupation was his music. His parents understood and so did his siblings and Mr. Paech. Competition work was over until next Easter, yet Mark still played the euphonium for two hours every day and worked on his AMusA examination repertoire. His practical examination in November required him to play for 30 to 40 minutes, a rather foreboding prospect, but by the end of winter he was feeling more comfortable with his performance selections. His daily routine had Mark playing each piece of music a total of four times plus his usual exercises. To the family, it was as if he had evicted his father from his study. Mark occupied the old wood paneled room early in the morning and then each evening. The family had adjusted to the more mellow sound of the euphonium over the more piercing sound of the cornet. He was becoming more familiar with his instrument as well. While the euphonium was easily overwhelmed by the cornets and trombones, it had the sound that all other brass players admired and envied. It was the leader of the lower brass section, and yet it was also the principal tenor voice of the brass band. Its role resembled that of a cello in a symphony orchestra. When asked what instrument he was playing, Mark knew people would never forget the name *euphonium* when they heard its sound and range. He was delighted he had made the switch; now he had to make his career and his reputation as a euphonium player. In November, Mark passed both his practical and theory examinations. He was now an Associate in Music, Australia (AMusA).

In July, Mark was invited to join the Kensington & Norwood City

Brass Band as its solo euphonium player. It was an honor, something Mark had wanted for a few months. As Mr. Paech had indicated, Mark knew that the Hahndorf Town Band could not develop him further as a promising solo player. Nonetheless, the transition was not without its difficulties. Weekly practice was on Thursday evenings in Norwood, a suburb of Adelaide fifty minutes from Hahndorf and longer during the winter months when rain and fog made the journey hazardous.

Like most farm teenagers, Mark had been driving a tractor since he was eleven years old. He obtained his official driver's license at sixteen, and though he was a good driver, Frank and Betty were concerned about him driving weekly to the city in the big family car at night. With Mark going to university in a few months, they decided it was time to give him an early Christmas present—a car of his own. Besides, half of Mark's weekly wage had been withheld as part payment for a car at year's end. Mark and Frank had already decided on a new 1600 pale blue Volkswagen Beetle. It was economical—a young person's car—although not high on the safety register. It was an exciting day when the family went down to Adelaide and bought the new car from Light Motors in Light Square. When they lifted the bonnet, Gary said, "Just enough room for the euphonium!" Of course, the engine was in the rear in a Beetle.

Within a few months at Kensington & Norwood, Mark vaulted ahead with his playing. He was young and inexperienced to be playing solo euphonium for one of South Australia's two premier brass bands; the other was the Tanunda Town Band. Mark did not take the confidence entrusted to him lightly. He felt the challenge and his appreciation of musical performance in an excellent band spurred him to give his best. With his weekly trek to the city for band rehearsal came the beginning of Mark's break with Hahndorf. It was gradual, of course, but Mark was leaving the safe and secure cocoon that had been his nurturing home since his birth. He was to face many more transitions in the years ahead, but none were as difficult as leaving the farm and his home town.

CHAPTER FIVE

WIDER VISTAS

"There is one subject-matter for education,
And that is Life in all its manifestations."
—A. N. Whitehead

In rural communities, higher education and a career path were not valued the same as they were in the suburbs and cities. Clearly, in the '50s and '60s many rural young adults did not reach the point where it was meaningful to speak of them ever reaching their full potential during their work lives. It was an unknown concept to most, and what you do not know, you cannot miss. While still adolescent, they left high school and went to work, and there they remained for forty years. Too often it was more important to find a job rather than a job of choice. The fortunate ones went to work on family farms and family businesses. Young women hoped to marry early, and young men girded themselves for a pay envelope at the end of each week. For many men work became loathsome drudgery and was allayed by *mateship* and the local pub where six o'clock until closing became the haunt for too many. Raising children and the life of a housewife was the lot of most women. Few women sought work after marriage, and weekly shopping trips to the local town, or a monthly gathering at the Women's Country Association, along with church, were the main social outlets. Television was not standard in homes until the early 1960s. It would be wrong to call it a drab life; rather, it was their life and they were living it as best they knew.

Hahndorf was no different to other country towns in that it emphasized work over a profession. Owing to its unique German heritage and its collective shepherding of its sons and daughters, it was the hope of the community that the next generation would endure better than the last. There was a general understanding that those who stayed in Hahndorf and toiled for parents and community were the ones who prospered in later years. It was implied that leaving the community was tantamount to flirting with the devil and there were numerous sorry souls confirming the economic folly of abandoning one's roots.

For those fortunate to hail from farms, the first expectation was to ensure that this tradition continued. The farms of Hahndorf were etched in the German ancestral psyche and it was betrayal to abandon the sacred trust of maintaining these for the greater good of ancestry and the community. Yet, adjustments were coming and many of the old ways were giving way to the use of machinery, with tractors making the greatest impact. New post-war homes were built on smaller lots, thereby dismantling the original *Hufendorfen,* or farmlet-village, design. Many of Mark's contemporaries had already commenced farming and were now content within a mostly twenty-mile radius of the post office. Where sons were in abundance and funds insufficient to expand the farm or stretch an existing business, the final alternative was to leave the community. This is where the apprenticeship system came to the rescue.

By the '60s, South Australia was experiencing steady growth and expansion and there was a shortage of skilled trades people. The metal and engineering trades, the automotive trades, the electrical and fledgling electronic trades, the building and construction trades and food trades—all provided occupational pathways for Australia's youth. Why, even Hahndorf's only barber would be retiring soon. There was no ladies' hairdressing salon in town and yet more women were seeking weekly and monthly appointments in Mount Barker, Stirling, and even Adelaide. One of Mark's best friends was in his second-year apprenticeship as a butcher. In such ways, the apprenticeship system provided support to Hahndorf as an emerging community integrated and interlaced with nearby towns and the capital city itself. Notwithstanding, for a few more years it remained a sleepy hamlet, a bedroom community of Adelaide on the other side of the Adelaide Hills.

Mark was released from any obligations to remain close to his heritage. To be sure, as a chosen son, most of the town recognized that his future lay beyond its main street and the undulating countryside of the District Council of Mount Barker. His career path would first take him to Adelaide, then to Melbourne or Sydney, and finally, should fortune be kind, to the world. This was the talk of the community and if Mark felt any pressure at all, it was to leave Hahndorf with confidence and to step boldly into the future.

It was a process to be sure, and in March Mark commenced his tertiary studies at the University of Adelaide. He selected a combined degree, Bachelor of Arts/Bachelor of Music, a four-year degree program which enabled Mark to include his emerging interest in Sixteenth Century Reformation Germany.

His lecture schedule had him driving to the University of Adelaide and the Elder Conservatorium of Music three days a week. On Thursdays Mark remained in the library until it was time to go to band rehearsal in Norwood. It made for a long day, but Mark soon fell into a routine as best a university student can. He still worked at intervals on the farm, as Frank advocated a work-study regimen being crucial for a well-rounded individual.

The Easter Nationals were approaching right on the back of settling into university, and this year they were held in Maryborough, Victoria. This was the competition in which Mark strove to become the Australian Open Solo champion. This time the calendar worked against Mark as his nineteenth birthday occurred several days before the competitions. Even so, he was still young to be challenging Australia's finest brass band soloists. But, challenge them he did, and he surfaced from the grueling match as the nation's youngest brass band solo champion of all time. Interviewed on television and numerous radio stations, with his photo in national, state and local newspapers, Mark was experiencing acclaim for the first time. On campus and in class, Mark was met with more "Good one, Mate" accolades than he was with mocking and scoffing, but there were some who derided his euphonium playing as antiquated. Mark remained largely impervious to the acclamation. Inwardly, he sensed that something in his demeanor had changed by his new title. Yet, his family and German roots had conditioned him to react with restraint in all matters. The one crack in his make-up was the sudden attention from girls. He did not anticipate this, and found it bewildering.

"Let's face it," tuned in the older, wiser Mark from his Qantas flight, "not only was I warned against girls, I was instructed to leave them alone as they only bring trouble!" Of course, Mark was remembering the most influential voice in his life, Walter Paech—his music teacher, his stern disciplinarian, his mentor and the one who had dominated Mark's life from before he was a teenager. Paech operated under the guise that he was making Mark a champion, but the truth, Mark realized much later in life, was that it was Mr. Paech who needed the personal satisfaction that *he* had made Mark a champion. In fact, he had latched onto Mark from the moment he saw the first glimmer of an extraordinary music performer. Mr. Paech had schemed to live vicariously through Mark and his achievements, and to do this he had to dominate and control his protégé. "It was wrong of the silly old coot," Mark voiced aloud followed by, "Excuse me, I'm just remembering something not pleasant," as he reassured the woman across the aisle that he was alright.

University years were the times when young men and women looked to each other in the quest for future life partners. Serious relationships were forming all the time on a campus the size of the University of Adelaide. However, this postwar generation was dismantling the traditional mores. For many Baby Boomers, it was a time of countercultural and social revolution. It was the era of feminism where more changes were occurring for women than for men. Confusion of roles and clarity of acceptable behavior were often jumbled and even inverted. Marriage was becoming an increasingly fragile institution and more couples were living together first. Women were the customary guardians of morality and they were expected to act accordingly. Ideally, a young lady would meet her future husband in a Pollyanna courtship, and this would lead them to the alter, and to live happily ever after. When all expectations were shattered by the stampeding forces of change, it was towns like Hahndorf where the impact was most profoundly felt. Why? Even at the Spring Strawberry Festival during the early '60s, dancing did not begin until the Lutheran pastor politely excused himself and went home. It was no longer the romantic violin but the barbaric saxophone and the thump of the bass guitar that dominated the dance scene.

For a decade or so, Saturday night dances were scheduled on a fortnightly basis among the local towns. When it was Hahndorf's dance night, there were sometimes a hundred cars or more parked on either side of the main street from the Pioneer Gardens to the chemist shop at the junction of main street and Pine Avenue. All too often the talk of the town on Monday was rife with rumors of this girl or that girl who had spent too much time in the back seat of a car and not enough on the dance floor. In this changing milieu, Betty had every reason to be deliberate in her prayers that her eldest son would find the *right* girl.

Mark took all this in stride, as did most of his generation. Generally, Australians knew they were living in the *Lucky Country* and problems were few, even though the Vietnam conflict had left a festering scar, the threat of encroaching communism was still of political concern, and Japan was buying too much of Australia and, in return, infiltrating the country with small, high-revving cars with radios as standard fare. More funding was being injected into education. Primary and secondary schools were increasingly offering more programs in music. High school brass bands were being formed in schools where teachers possessed the vision, talent and drive. These were most successful in communities already possessing a current brass band, or the history of one. Some of the elite private schools had impressive youth bands which would rival the community bands in competition work at least up to B grade. All this bode well for Mark's career path upon graduation.

In the meantime, Mark was pre-occupied with completing his studies at university and the *Con*. In his final year two new interests came on his radar screen and took hold of him in serious fashion. He found that his coursework in conducting was opening a whole new vista that he had earlier sworn he would never succumb to any time in the future. He was such a staunch instrumentalist; he vowed he would never take up the baton. Yet, here he was at the ripe old age of twenty-one, thoroughly enjoying his course in "Analytical Studies for Conductors." Next, his "Advanced Conducting Project" saw him conducting choirs and orchestras even in St. Peter's Cathedral on King William Road. He became a friend of the Master of the Choristers and forever developed an affection for English choral music, particularly the superb choral compositions of John Rutter of recent times.

His studies in Brass Pedagogy provided Mark with a far greater understanding of the dynamics of brass instruments and how to teach, develop and motivate brass players from beginners to those who sought to excel and become professional solo performers. He came to appreciate music as metaphor, to listen and to recognize the significance of developing the concept of sound. The same playing techniques so forcibly instilled in him by Mr. Paech now took on new meaning, as the physiology of posture, breathing, embouchure and articulation were re-examined by numerous musicians specializing in various brass instruments. It seemed that Mark was mildly obsessed with finding that quality of tone in his personal playing which would forever distinguish him from fellow euphonium players. How to make his euphonium "sing" was the way he asked tonal questions over and over.

There were some afternoons when Mark just did not wish his class sessions to end. So, often, he would linger and chat casually with these professionals. From them he learned so much that many a day he would drive his Beetle home through the Hills fully engaged in reflection on his newly-acquired knowledge. While his university milieu stimulated so much personal growth, nonetheless there were times when self-doubt cast its shadow over all his progress. He would feel deep discouragement and question if he had the strength and perseverance to bridge the gap from rank amateur to a truly professional musician. At these moments, he would push his Beetle through the twists and turns of the

Adelaide Hills to *get to the pines* more quickly. Stretching out on the familiar pine needles, gazing through the branches into the sky and reviewing the lessons of the day, Mark knew he would find consolation, and a tranquility in nature that brought him rest, and, at times, even peaceful repose. He was not, by temperament, prone to diffidence and timidity. He did know that he was a loner and such moments were best handled by himself in the comfort of his pine trees.

While Mark was advancing in knowledge and skills with his formal studies, he still saw himself as a promising young novice in his involvement in the Australian and New Zealand banding worlds. He had yet to prove himself with staying power. Three years after joining the Kensington & Norwood brass band, his playing had lifted the morale of the band and its status in the national band league. At twenty-one, he was still a developing performer, though he had now won the National Open Championship title twice. He amazed himself in that he had a relaxed and somewhat cavalier attitude to competition work overall. Mark saw it more as pitting himself against himself in the endeavor to become a more skilled and accomplished euphonium performer. He was his own hardest taskmaster. Unquestionably, this was the direct opposite reaction to the aggressive stance advocated by Mr. Paech after Mark's original humiliating ordeal during his first competition experience. It still produced a raw affect.

The other unexpected interest for Mark at university was his dual academic focus in Early Modern European history. The History department had an American visiting professor who was a specialist in John Calvin, Geneva and the French Reformation. He was a gentle professor who lacked the stereotypical brashness most Australians heaped on many Americans. This scholar introduced Mark to the compelling importance, even now, of the significance of the European Reformation. Mark took to this field of study like a duck to water. It was his father's favorite avocational academic interest and Mark had some familiarity with the subject matter through family discussions and numerous books in his father's study. Mark developed an affinity for Luther and post-Lutheran Germany. He linked this with his own family heritage and admired the courage and bravery of the Old Lutherans in embarking on their voyage to Australia and in flourishing as they had done for over 100 years.

Throughout his undergraduate studies, Mark continued to adhere to his Lutheran faith. Few of his university friends even bothered with religion and neither did many of his older fellow Kensington & Norwood bandsmen. Nevertheless, for Mark, a religious commitment was ingrained. He was the product of a happy family and a cohesive community with clear origins in the Lutheran church and the Protestant Reformation. As a young adult, Mark had made his choice and he had decided it was important for him to follow Jesus Christ as his personal Savior. Within Australia of the 1970s, this placed him in a minority as more and more people were turning their backs on organized religion and even the practice of a personal Christian belief system. Curiously, Census statistics revealed that more than three-quarters of Australians still believed in God, or at least the supernatural, but it was abundantly evident that church attendance was in steep decline. The University of Adelaide had various religious associations on campus and Mark was a member of two: the Lutheran Association and the Evangelical Fellowship group.

In addition, just a mile away in North Adelaide was Emmanuel College, the Lutheran Seminary and training college for future Lutheran primary and secondary school teachers and ministers. In conjunction with his university studies, Mark attended lectures here and was subjected to a philosophy of Christian education for the first time and its practice in Lutheran Education—the largest Protestant Education system in the world. Its focus was on combating the secular forces of individualism and a *laissez faire* attitude of letting things take their own course, without the interfering notion of a personal God. The emphasis on rank individualism was a bane to a Christian who believed in a "thus saith the Lord" and recognized that there was right and wrong in life and it was the mark of a Christian to know the difference. Such a belief system impinged on how a young adult conducted his daily affairs and planned his future. (Now, high above the Pacific Ocean, Mark acknowledged increasing shades of grey where his world had been once black and white.) By way of contrast, too many of Mark's friends and acquaintances were deliberately choosing uninhibited indulgence in the erratic use of drugs and alcohol and sex. So often Mark retreated to his car, grateful for the personal value system that had been instilled within him by family and community. He was not a prude, but neither was he someone who was loose with word or conduct. It made him appear reserved and even aloof in some company, but no one ever challenged Mark or openly mocked him. He was often the peer to turn to in times of need and personal distress.

In October, during Mark's final months at university, the Kensington & Norwood band travelled to Ballarat for a regional competition weekend. Mark's family went along too as Frank and Betty understood fully that soon, perhaps next year, Mark would be living away from home. Already he was looking at possible music teaching positions in the various Eastern states. The capital city of Melbourne was high on Mark's list of desirable locations and all he really needed was a suitable job offer. He did not know that this was just around the corner.

The important memory of this visit to Ballarat was Mark's first meeting with Roslyn. The Saturday night concert was a relaxed occasion where two brass bands performed to an audience of family members, local brass enthusiasts and other guests who found themselves in the town hall that evening. The Kensington & Norwood band occupied the stage for the first half of the concert. Mark was the soloist for the contemporary lyrical piece, *Be My Love*. The Master of Ceremonies linked the music to "the good-looking, eligible euphonium player, Mark Schubert," with the quip that Mark will be signing autographs in the vestibule during the break. Band members laughed at this and Mark tried to look unaffected. The solo went very well. It was silvery music made popular in the '50s by Mario Lanza, the Italian opera vocalist. The acoustics of the hall were favorable to the honeyed, soothing voice of the euphonium and Mark felt the transmission of his sound soar to pleasurable heights.

At half-time a photographer was taking promotional photos of Mark with his euphonium at the Queen Victoria statue across the road from the town hall. Frank and Betty where there too, taking some family photos. As Mark entered the vestibule, he was approached by two young women who asked if Mark would sign their programs. In between smiles, giggling, and furtive glances Mark recognized that one of these young ladies was extra special. Roslyn Schneider was her name. She worked in Melbourne and came from a farm in Horsham. The ringing of the bell warned that the second half of the concert was about to begin. That night Mark went to sleep in his hotel room with intermittent thoughts of Roslyn on his mind. On Sunday, he and his family drove home to Hahndorf. Three weeks later, Mark completed his undergraduate degree and looked forward to officially graduating in May of 1972.

Rejecting work as a secondary teacher for the State of South Australia, Mark accepted a position as music teacher at Luther College in Croydon, an eastern suburb of Melbourne. Naturally, Frank and Betty were pleased with Mark's decision on several fronts. The first was selfish they readily admitted; Melbourne was only a full day's drive from the farm. The second reason was also very personal: their eldest son had chosen to work as a Christian teacher. He could have focused fully on music performance and advancing his career, but his decision was a strong validation for all their years of spiritual nurture and prayer.

With the decision to move to Melbourne came the end of Mark's nearly five-year association with the Kensington & Norwood brass band. At the Christmas party, the bandmaster gave an emotional farewell speech.

"Mark came to us as a youthful, idealistic lad from Hahndorf. It has been a good fit for both of us. We have given him opportunity in which to grow as an excellent champion soloist. He has given us dedication and commitment as a player on the rise. He has now completed his tertiary studies and won two national solo championships. It is appropriate that he goes to Melbourne to begin a new phase in his already impressive life. Our loss is their gain. Damn, they get too many of our top musicians and sportsmen!"

"Seriously, Mark, we wish you every success and are going to miss your humble but intense presence in our midst. I have come to cherish you as a son. And, you remain the only euphonium champion I know who doesn't swear like a trooper!"

Mark arrived home late, but Frank, Betty and Gary were still up. For the next hour, they talked about all the changes that were ahead for the family. Afterwards, before they drifted off to sleep, Gary posed two questions: "Are you scared about all the changes that are going to happen to you next year?"

Mark thought a few seconds and replied: "Scared! Yes, I could be if I let it happen. But you, Mum and Dad and the rest of the family are only a day away. It's not like going to Britain or America. That's when I would be scared. Whatever happens it is good to know that I can always come home."

"What do you really, I mean really, want to be?" questioned Gary again.

"It's late to be getting philosophical, isn't it, little brother?" responded Mark. "I do know what you are asking because I'm asking it too. I guess I want to be the best euphonium player I can be, and I want to play in some of the best brass bands in the world."

"All I want is to be a farmer," interjected Gary.

"You keep thinking that way. I think you were born to be a farmer," said Mark intentionally seeking to reinforce his brother's goal.

"Mark, what if you become the best and you want more?" asked Gary slurring his words as sleep was upon him.

"Hmm, what if I want more? Sounds selfish and somewhat futile. Whatever happens it is good to know that I can always come home to Hahndorf and the farm," replied Mark as he heard Gary turning on his side.

As the eldest child, Mark understood he had been the trail blazer. Gary had looked on as Mark began his musical journey and had seen the successes and the struggles. Mark wondered if he may have been the culprit causing Gary to give up on learning a musical instrument. Did he see the challenges Mark confronted and decide against pursuing music? If so, then Mark could feel guilty of robbing his brother of the innate joys of music because of his own relentless drive to be the best. He decided against asking the question at this time. With that, both went to sleep aware of each other and the commitment that was theirs as brothers.

For now, Mark and his family looked forward to Christmas and New Year's together. Mark did not need to be at Luther College until late January. Despite the busy weeks before Christmas, the Schubert family felt that the pressure of the last four years was lessened for a little while. Next in line was Gary, who had just completed high school and wanted to immediately begin his work on the farm. He had said for months that his transition from school to work was going to be "much easier than Mark's. I am not going to cost you so much!" However, Frank had persuaded Gary to enroll in Roseworthy Agricultural College as a residential student. His diploma course was two years and his full-time work on the farm would be delayed while he learned greater insight into agribusiness—a new term for most farmers. Gary would be home most weekends as Roseworthy was in the Gawler-Barossa region. All too soon, the Schubert family would be torn asunder. Within two months both sons would be leaving the family and while it was disquieting to Frank and Betty, they were proud of their sons. They were grateful it was not war that had taken their boys or some other calamity. Their young men were beginning to make their own way in the world. This was as it should be.

CHAPTER SIX

TEACHING AND
MARRIAGE

"The easiest relationship is with ten thousand people.
The hardest is with one."
—Joan Baez

There were many unforeseen experiences awaiting Mark on arriving in Melbourne. He had persuaded his parents that it would be best if he contended with these on his own. Luther College helped him locate a flat, introduced him to the school's bank, and new colleagues gave him pertinent information daily about the Croydon, Lilydale, and Ringwood suburbs. One of his first pursuits in his new city was to attend band practice at the Kew City Band in mid-January. With the Easter Nationals looming on the horizon, all Australian competition bands commenced their rehearsal schedules while summer holidays were still in progress. Banding was a major commitment and the "brass band widow" syndrome was more than a mere expression. At least this year the competitions were held at Ballarat, less than two hours west of Melbourne.

Kew City Band considered Mark a significant coup. Attracting a young solo euphonium player only enhanced their own national standing, especially when their current soloist was looking to retire within the year. On the first night of practice, Mark arrived late. Negotiating Melbourne traffic was very different to little Adelaide. Feeling flustered he entered the band hall as the bandmaster was castigating his players for giving less than a full effort in preparation for the Easter Nationals. The next minute, applause broke out and Mark was given a raucous welcome. He sat down on the inside chair next to the euphonium soloist. Then, both the soloist and the bandmaster ushered Mark to the outside chair and said, "This is your seat and we look forward to you staying for many years." Mark blushed and looked awkward, but the soloist took his arm and motioned that it was what he wanted. With the tap of the baton, the band began their tonal warm up with fifteen minutes of hymn playing. In like manner, so began the most fruitful span of Mark's development as a young professional musician and aspiring performer.

The first few weeks at Luther College were indelibly etched in Mark's consciousness. These were not the most rewarding, the most memorable or the most difficult times of his life. Rather, it is best to describe them as an enormous awakening to the reality of existing in the real world. Until now he had always lived under the shelter of his parents, of the family farm, of the Lutheran church and, most of all, under the collective sense of all that was Hahndorf. Suddenly, it was as though his every waking moment was dominated by the needs of someone other than himself. Rambunctious students, new teaching colleagues, expectant administrators and concerned parents; all fine and wonderful people, but they all wanted something from Mark from morning to night. Then, there was the constant class preparation the night before and always consuming large tracts of every weekend. Mark had never known such legitimate tugs on his emotional and physical strength before. He found it nigh to impossible to steal thirty minutes for his euphonium practice, let alone his usual morning and evening regimen of up to two hours of essential practice. If he wanted to retain his championship standing, practice was an imperative, not just a choice. The physical circumstances were even worse, he could not play a brass instrument (even muted) in his flat. This left him the church on campus or his music studios and both were not readily available until after hours. Amidst personal and professional frustrations, Mark recognized that he had no option but to begin his work day at 5:00 am. This way he could be at the church or studios by 6:00 am leaving the best part of two hours before Luther College came to life for the day. In time, Mark was permitted to schedule an additional thirty minutes after the school day (including meetings) for his instrumental practice. Afterwards, he would exercise, eat, grade papers and prepare for the next day. Rarely did he get to bed before 10:30 pm and when he did, he fell asleep within seconds. By March, with the Easter National championships approaching, Mark questioned whether he wanted to make high school teaching his career path. It was just so demanding and exhausting. There had to be something better, and easier.

Most Sundays Mark was in church and, increasingly, involved in teaching the Sunday School class to teenagers. Many of these were his students during the week. Mark liked the challenge of teaching from the Bible. He considered the Gospel to be the best "good news" that any person could ever hope to hear and understand. He believed in the great controversy between God and Satan and that, just as there was a beginning when sin, or separation from God, entered this world, there will be an ending when Jesus will come again and restore peace and harmony to this world through the eradication of sin and Satan. Using the motifs of a battle between good and evil, Mark's presentations both in class and at Sunday School drew the attention of pastors and parents. They saw the impact he had on youth. Some began to ponder offering Mark a position in youth ministry and to encourage him to expand his presentation skills and his range of topics. With churches combating the ever more sophisticated assaults of secularism, discovering a young teacher and musician who could communicate and inspire an audience towards Christian ideals was increasingly rare, and needed to be nurtured.

Mark was flattered by their confidence in him and wondered if maybe this was a convenient way for him to escape from the rigors of teaching. He thought about these new opportunities and he prayed about them too. In the meantime, immediacy eclipsed his meanderings about his career path. It was only a couple of weeks away from Easter and he had an Open Solo Championship to win.

On one of those sunny autumn Sundays before Easter, and after church as many of the worshippers were milling around, a female voice called out, "Hey, Mark, remember me?"

Mark turned, and there was Roslyn Schneider from Horsham.

"Well, hello there. I wondered if we would ever see each other again?"

They spoke for some time, and when Mark asked what Roslyn was doing for lunch she replied, "Nothing that I can't alter as quick as a flash!" He liked her spontaneity. They walked to Mark's Beetle and drove into Croydon to a sandwich shop and became more and more transfixed with each other throughout the afternoon. It was the beginning of their whirlwind relationship.

Roslyn was a nurse in Box Hill. She was two years Mark's junior and made it clear that she wanted to marry but not have children. Mark's reaction was mild. He said that he had just not thought about it much. Mark told Roslyn that he wanted to take his music as far as he could, even if it meant relocating overseas to Britain or America. Roslyn assured him that she relished an adventure and it was all good so long as he made plenty of money with his music. It was after 4:00 pm when they left the café. Roslyn had agreed to take the early evening shift for a fellow nurse. They said goodbye and Mark said he would call her later that week. "A good afternoon!" Mark said to himself. Within the hour, he was in his music studio ready for some solid practice and rehearsing his competition piece several times without accompaniment.

Mark won his third solo championship and immediately decided to tackle the New Zealand Championship next year as well. Now, into the winter months, Mark was settled into a manageable routine. He was much more relaxed and his preparation time for his classes and the ever-present grading were now under control. The fledgling student brass group was developing nicely and he out-sourced string and woodwind part-time teaching needs. He was happy, or as close to mature happiness as he had ever known. Roslyn was heavily involved in his every day and they called morning and evening and spent as much time together on the weekends as possible. His music practice was habitually scheduled in the early hours of each day. It was the only aspect of his daily regimen which did not change as Roslyn assuredly became his *piece de resistance.*

With the spring came the Royal Melbourne Show. Like its counterpart in Adelaide, it was a magical experience for Mark to go several times during the ten days of its duration. Years later in the United States, Mark never saw a county fair on such a grand scale as found in the various states of Australia. This was the first time that Mark had gone to a show with a girlfriend, and this girl was hanging onto Mark for dear life. Rarely is the Show not an enjoyable time. They went on dusk and stayed until the fireworks. They ate way too much junk food, but isn't that what such festivities are all about? One thing new to Mark was the adamant stance Roslyn took as to what she would look at and what she would not, despite Mark's desire to do otherwise. Roslyn did not want to look at the livestock pavilions. She did not care for wood chopping. She became bored with events in the main arena after fifteen minutes and pouted with her sad lament, "Please let's go, I'm bored." Although, she did spend an inordinate amount of time in the embroidery, cooking sections and looking at various displays in the exhibition halls. Mark saw nothing wrong here, and was, in fact, impressed that Roslyn knew what she liked and did not. He considered that he obviously came from a family that essentially liked the same things in life, and on rare occasions when they did not, they were all curious enough to expand their horizons with patience. Not Roslyn, for her life was clearly delineated, and always in her favor.

In September Mark's fledgling student band performed for the first time at the Luther College Church. It was a significant moment. The local newspaper ran a comprehensive story with photos. The school board and administration had made a calculated investment in funding a brass band in addition to the regular music program. This first successful performance brought accolades to Mark.

Group music was receiving a lot of support throughout all education departments in Australia and the same was occurring in New Zealand as well. Current pedagogy was fostering sustainable group involvement in K-12 curricula in all disciplines. The aim was to stimulate group involvement in the young as a precursor to more group emphasis in the workplace. Individualism was considered detrimental to the development of a healthy productive society. To learn to work and think in groups while an adolescent was to suggest that group emphasis would follow through every phase in the life cycle. Such a progressive philosophy would enhance democratic principles for all Australians and quell the age-dominant belief in rank individualism.

In October Mark was asked to participate in an Australian Broadcasting Commission (ABC) television program exploring the current state of the brass band movement within the nation. Even though he was one of many musicians and music educators asked to contribute, he was targeted as the aspiring brass band champion soloist and music educator. Mark protested his inexperience and relative youthfulness. The ABC program managers retorted, "Mark, that is the very point! We want someone who is young, accomplished and able to inspire. We want to appeal to a wide audience and to *sell* brass bands. We want to argue that communities, families and schools are better off when music is promoted in groups and not just as an individual enterprise. There is a tradition of brass bands in Australia, especially in the rural parts. Most of that has now disappeared. Today, it is three or four young guys getting together in the garage and forming a rock band which will most likely fizzle in a year or two. We hope to create an awareness that brass bands are part of the *public* good, as are choirs and other expressions of musical groups, but we want to delimit and focus on brass bands. We need you, and we suggest that it will help your career as well. Can we count on you?"

What could Mark say? Of course, he would be part of this documentary program. Roslyn was elated when she heard that Mark was "becoming a TV star."

"It will be so good for all my girlfriends to see you on TV and to know that you are mine!"

"Mine" sounded both corny and confusing to Mark. Yet, their relationship was nearly nine months old and Roslyn was talking of marriage and "their home" more frequently. Mark asked Roslyn if she would go home with him for Christmas, and while she demurred at first, a week later said that she only had a week over Christmas. Her nursing schedule was fixed three months in advance and there was no changing it at this stage. Mark explored various scenarios where he could fulfill some time in both Horsham and Hahndorf. Roslyn would not shift. She did not mind if Mark only spent a day or so in Horsham and then went onto Hahndorf, but her schedule was so tight that it was not worth making a quick trip to Mark's family; it would not be enjoyable. Again, Mark accepted her decision. He told his family that he would be coming home alone the day before Christmas and would stay until New Year's Day.

Closing Exercises for Luther College ended Mark's first year of work. The student band, now expanded to two dozen players, played for the final speech night. Mark was pleased with the band's progress and was quietly thinking of entering the band into a Junior Band competition next year outside of the Easter Nationals calendar.

Roslyn and Mark drove to Horsham three days before Christmas, and then early on December 24, Mark drove on to Hahndorf via Bordertown, Keith, Tailem Bend, across the Murray River and then into the Adelaide Hills. As soon as he came to the familiar undulating terrain, he began to feel the excitement of home. It was a visceral aura of well-being that came over him. This was home territory. It was where he belonged; where he first understood well-being and happiness. It was the land of his forebears. It was where he could let down his guard and relax completely at any time and still find acceptance. He slowed down, as he turned into Balhannah Road, put the Beetle into third gear, and dawdled for the last mile to the family farm. Everything looked so familiar and agreeable. The entire family came out to greet him as he pulled alongside the garage. He was home.

After an hour of small talk, Frank said that he wanted to check on the water to the poultry. Gary walked out to check the irrigation time clocks and said to Mark with a certain glee in his voice, "Only one more year and I will be a professional agriculturalist!" Mark envied Gary's sense of humor and his carefree spirit. He knew that by contrast he was more intense, driven and fragile. However, for the next week he was home and he determined to embrace family and Christmas with minimal toleration for anything else. Betty hugged Mark once more and said that she and the girls were going to scuttle off and attend to the evening meal. This suited Mark and he replied that he would just look around.

He found himself heading straight to the pine trees. He walked into the low branches and was locked into their confines. This was his sanctuary of many years; he dropped to his knees, scooped the pine needles into the shape of a bed, and rolled over onto his back. He peered through the branches to the sky beyond and breathed deeply. He felt fully unencumbered for the first time all year.

Roslyn! This time last year she was not in Mark's life and now she was dominating it. Why would she not make the effort to come and meet his family, and see where he grew up? Did she really love him? Did she know what genuine love was? Did Mark? Were they both ready for marriage; possibly later next year? Mark asked himself, "Am I up for all this?"

As he questioned himself, he realized how tired he was. He had been driving for over four hours, but he was home now, and in his favorite spot in all the world. He drifted off as the smell of pine and the gentle sound of the summer breeze through the branches added to his lethargy.

He awoke suddenly as Gary appeared between the branches.

"Sorry, Mark, didn't mean to startle you. Mum says that dinner will be ready in fifteen minutes. You know I come here too when I am home from Roseworthy. You showed me there is good karma here in the pines."

They both walked back to the house and, when inside the kitchen, Mark went over to his Mum and hugged her and declared: "This looks so good, Mum. And to think that I have not done one thing in preparing this meal. Do you know how much I have missed your cooking?"

Mark marveled at how rowdy it was eating around the Schubert table. Several times he just gazed at the scene before him. Frank saw the pensive look on his face and asked, "Is everything alright, Mark?"

"Sure is, Dad. I'm just glad to be home."

It was Christmas Eve and a warm pleasant evening. The forecast for

Christmas Day was good; it would be comfortably hot. This was one of the distinct advantages of living in the Adelaide Hills as the temperature was often ten degrees cooler than on the flat Adelaide plains.

The washing up was done, and the dishes were put away when Betty said to Mark, "Are we going to hear you play your euphonium?"

Mark smiled and replied, "Well, I need to play as I haven't in four days, but I didn't want to appear anxious on my first night with you. Truthfully, I can't wait to go into Dad's study and play. I have missed it so much. Plus, I am playing at church tomorrow and so want to go over the carol medley several times."

Betty, Frank and the girls had some more gifts to wrap and Gary wanted to watch a Christmas program on television. So, with that, Mark went to his car and brought in both his presents and his euphonium. He placed his gifts under the tree, walked over to the old home, and opening the door to his father's study began an hour's music that was savored by the whole family. Such a close-knit family having nurtured and listened to Mark's brass playing for thirteen years, couldn't help but miss it when it suddenly stopped, and he moved away to Melbourne. They all knew his routine: first came the long, sustained playing, then scales and exercises, and tonight, on Christmas Eve, rather than some competition piece, Mark played Christmas Carols and ended, as always, with the hymn *Abide with Me*.

On Christmas morning, they all went to St. Michael's for the Christmas service. Mark played for special music and afterwards was engulfed with extended family and many friends, both older and younger, who felt that they each had some part in Mark's musical development. Then it was home for the Christmas repast with the entire house smelling of roast turkey and vegetables. The table was a joy to behold, with the family's finest china and crystal goblets. There were nuts and dried fruits in silver trays and chocolates in crystal bowls. It was all so familiar. Frank prayed before carving the turkey and thanked God for blessing and protecting his family for the past year. Next, came the cracking of bon-bons, and the silly paper caps which appeared on everyone's heads.

It was a memorable festive few days and the family had gone beyond expectations in arranging and coordinating visits here and there and activities that were high on Mark's list of favorites. They went to Loebethal to see the Christmas lights, to Adelaide, to Glenelg where they had fish 'n chips on the beach. They went to Victor Harbor and had a double-coned ice cream in keeping with past visits to the coastal town. They had a barbeque at home with cousins, aunts and uncles, along with some of Mark's closest friends. Every day was full of conviviality and good tidings.

Even over Christmas, farm chores still had to be attended to daily. This gave Frank and Mark opportunity to talk by themselves. Roslyn was the prime topic of conversation several times. Mark's main naïve question was this: "How can I be sure she is the right girl for me?"

Frank was guarded, but finally said: "Mark, I suppose finding a life's partner is personal and different for each of us. With your mother, I struck gold and we have been very fortunate. We love each other and have been blessed with four wonderful children. And very important, we still live in the community of our birth where family heritage runs deep."

"One thing I know to be true. You don't just marry a girl; you marry her family and her background."

"You have to trust your instincts and continue to ask for guidance. You will know when it is right. You must believe this."

On New Year's Eve, Mark was called to the phone by Gary, "I think it's Roslyn, and she seems upset." Mark took the phone. Roslyn was distraught and told him that she needed him to return to Croydon immediately. The long and the short of her call was that she was now back at work and was missing him and wanted him. He said that he had planned to leave early in the morning, but she insisted that he leave now and be in Croydon before she went to work at 7:00 am. Mark told her that meant he would be driving all night, and he could do this if necessary. She replied that "surely, you have spent enough time with family by now" and that she needed him. Mark responded that it would make more sense for him to start out in the morning and be with her after she finished work in the late afternoon. He could sense that this did not please her, but she calmed down when he told her that he missed her and that the family were sending presents for her.

As he got off the phone, he made light of the call by saying that she just was missing him. But later that night Frank said quietly to Mark, "One more comment, Mark. Make sure you marry a happy person and one who will bring you joy and peace. Establishing a good marriage takes time, but it is doubly hard if you do not begin with the best ingredients of love and respect for each other. Above all, you need to be true to who you are at all times."

The next morning, after a hearty breakfast, Mark said goodbye and turned the Beetle toward Melbourne. He knew it was his last visit home as a single man. He consoled himself that change was part of living and he had to recognize this fact in all areas of life. He was among the fortunate few who was raised in an intact, caring family, on a modest yet successful farm, in a small stable community, and in a democratic country with its best days ahead. Yes, it was fortuitous to be an Australian, although he always thought the term *lucky* was a brash and flippant way of describing Australia. Beyond doubt, he was now really leaving home. He knew that Roslyn had a wedding in her sights for the year ahead. He had to put family in second place and "cleave" to Roslyn as his soon-to-be wife. It was the way life worked. He *did* love her. That was the answer to one question, but did he *know* her? This was the question that was pressing on him as he headed east towards the Victorian border. His thinking dwelled on *what it is to know someone* for most of the return journey. As the outskirts of Melbourne came into view Mark ended his ruminations with another question: Do you ever truly know the girl you fall in love with? The potential truth of the question unnerved him.

It was 4:05 pm when the Beetle pulled into Roslyn's drive way. She came bounding out and hugged him tightly. Through tears she declared how much she loved him and missed him, and Mark got lost in the emotion of the reunion. The opening of presents revealed more about Roslyn. She reacted with delight to those gifts which pleased her but asked, "Why would anyone buy this for me" when she didn't like another one. Mark was careful but did defend the purchaser by saying, "Probably because they don't know you but would like to have met you this Christmas." But Roslyn was in a happy mood and merely said, "Mark, don't be hard on me." That was it. They went to their favorite café that evening and then Mark went home to his flat to make ready for his second year in the workforce.

The flight was becoming arduous and Mark came to his senses feeling the discomfort of a flight that never seemed to end. He went to the bathroom and stood long enough to stretch and regain a little composure. He requested a coffee and then settled back into his seat. He was feeling somewhat impatient with the flight and his cogitations. He was recalling too much, and he wanted to be finished before he landed in Sydney, and certainly before Adelaide. Of course, he admitted to himself, he was now entering the part of his earlier life that he wished he could erase. It was full of twists and turns where he had acted on impulse and undue pressure from Roslyn. In short, he was not himself for several years and he had allowed himself to be manipulated until something just snapped within him. Fortunately, survival skills took hold, and he had lashed out and fled. Slowly, over many years, and largely in the evening hours when he was alone, Mark came to realize that while acclamation will come and go through life, holding onto integrity is forever. He could hear his father now, "As a son of God, and my son, be true to who you are, always." With this recollection, Mark teared up and looked out the window only to see darkness and the blinking of the aircraft's light. Again, he was grateful for the spare seat next to him. He felt like an emotional mess. Nevertheless, he was going home to pick up some of the pieces and to reconnect with family. His ultimate quest was for peace of mind.

The year he married was a tumultuous one in so many ways. The

ABC program, *Brass Bands Alive and Well in Australia,* was aired in early March and received positive comments across the national spectrum. It brought renewed focus on Mark as a musician and music educator. The Lutheran Church wrote extensively about Mark as a Lutheran professional and public figure heralding the Christian ethic before the secular world. He could not honor all the church-related speaking appointments that came to him. The education world sought to use him as an advocate for music education, and the arts in general. Radio and television requested interviews and panel discussions where he would speak words of motivation to youth caught in a lifestyle of despair and disillusionment. Roslyn wallowed in all the attention this brought to *her* Mark.

Rapidly, Mark was appreciating that there were really two levels of work for the average person. There was essential work directly related to the salary a person received from one's employer. This was his teaching assignment at Luther College. And then there was the extra-curricular work which pushed his cognitive capabilities, created value for him in the marketplace, and improved his skill levels to an extraordinary degree. Mark needed his primary work position to eat and survive, but, increasingly, it was his professional activities beyond teaching that came to consume him more and more.

For a fourth time he won the Australian Open Soloist championship at the Easter Nationals, and followed it up by winning the New Zealand championship as well. Thus, Mark became the first person to win both the Australian and New Zealand Open Solo championships in the same year.

Mark shifted uncomfortably in his Qantas seat. He was about to reflect on the most agonizing phase of his life. He knew he had to go there, but he also knew that he would like to bypass a decade. Oh, for a magic wand to obliterate this segment. Yet, almost fifteen years later, he recognized that what's broken can be mended, and what hurts can be healed. Somewhat consoled by his own counsel, he began the review of his marital years.

With competitions behind them, Mark and Roslyn moved forward in their relationship to betrothal. On June 25, they officially announced their engagement. Quietly, Mark worried about the price of the ring and was grateful for the fact that Frank and Betty had arranged that each of their children would receive an annual stipend from the farm once they turned 21. While it was not a huge sum, and was payable on his April birthday, Mark had banked this each year. Now in its fourth year, it more than paid for the engagement ring. Mark did not tell Roslyn about this source of extra income. Even at this stage, the warning signals were there. To be sure, there was so much that each did not know about the other; despite dating for fifteen months.

Roslyn wanted the wedding as soon as possible and October 6 became the date. "A spring wedding would be perfect," she exclaimed. She did not want her wedding in 'sleepy' Horsham. Mark and Roslyn surveyed Lutheran churches in Melbourne and decided upon the Good Shepherd Lutheran Church in Ringwood. It would be wrong to say that Mark was precluded from all the wedding decisions, but he was clearly not in the driver's seat. This was Roslyn's domain and she forged ahead to arrange "her" wedding as she had dreamed from her early teens.

Mark's parents were quietly alarmed. Had they not come to Melbourne for a long weekend after the engagement was announced, they possibly would not have met Roslyn prior to the wedding, and as it was Gary and the girls only met Roslyn at the wedding. Mark apologized to his parents for the unilateral developments of the whole relationship. "It is what I want," protested Mark, "even though Roslyn is always three or four steps ahead of me." Quietly, Betty said to Frank, "He was so in charge of his own life and so wonderful as our son all his growing years, I worry that this girl will be his undoing." Frank agreed but said that Mark was his own man now.

In his inner self, Mark knew that he was in trouble. He tried to talk with Roslyn and, one night in early September, she exploded and yelled, "Mark, if you are having doubts and want to delay our wedding, then it's off for good. There will be no wedding. Is that what you want?" It wasn't what Mark wanted, but he told Roslyn that he wished they'd had more time to become best friends without the need to fight, yell and be at war with each other so much. He said marriage was for an awfully long time when happiness was in scarce supply.

Roslyn placated him and on Saturday, October 6, 1975, Mark and Roslyn were wed. The day lived up to expectations and spring was truly in the air. It was a pretty wedding and went off like clock-work. After the reception as Mark and Roslyn came down to leave for their honeymoon, Gary shook Mark's hand and said, "She's not as pretty as I thought she would be." On that dubious comment, the married couple drove off for two weeks at the beachside resort of Port Macquarie on the Pacific coast in northern New South Wales. Mark left his euphonium in his flat, although he did take along his mouthpiece.

The honeymoon, Mark recalled, was more like a business trip with a few days of respite on the beach. Probably too much time was spent driving from Melbourne through Sydney and half way to Brisbane, and back again. They could have gone to Lakes Entrance, or to one of the many closer beach towns like Merimbula or Batemans Bay. Roslyn was not a road trip girl; that was not necessarily her fault as the Beetle was aging, small and hardly a cruising machine. Before they reached Sydney, Roslyn was suggesting that they should look at buying a larger car and she gave as her preference a Holden Monaro. She considered it would be a good plan to keep the Beetle and she could use it as her work car. Besides, she was thinking that she would change to night shift nursing as a means of earning more income for their new home. In these few words, Roslyn had declared the strategic plan of the newly-formed Schubert household. When Mark interrupted and spoke of their earlier discussions of him advancing his musical career, Roslyn said, "Yes, of course, and that too!"

The weather in Port was kind to them and they were both glad to finally arrive at the beachfront hotel. The week went by quickly as they unwound and connected as a honeymoon couple. Mark intentionally dismissed all the weeks of tension and hyperventilating as due to the pressures of the approaching wedding. At least, he hoped so.

Back in Melbourne, their last few days were spent moving Roslyn's goods to Mark's flat. On the last Friday before returning to work, they purchased the previous-year model two-door Holden Monaro GTS. After putting $2,000 down, they owed $3,000 on their new gold car with a black vinyl top. Roslyn agreed to make the car payments while Mark paid for the monthly rent and food. Mark had never owed big money before: he was absorbing yet another reality of life as an adult wage earner.

The remainder of the year hurried to a conclusion. The newly-weds were now looking at their Christmas to New Year's plans. The decision was made to spend Christmas in Horsham at the Schneiders and on December 27 to drive to Hahndorf to the Schubert farm and stay until early January. This journey was the first major drive in the Monaro. Both felt proud of their new car and enjoyed the extra comfort and room despite the higher fuel bill. Mark was a country boy at heart and liked nothing better than driving through a rural landscape and into the setting sun. Roslyn's family lived in the Wimmera district of Victoria. It was a very flat region with vast plains suited to wheat cropping and large holdings of sheep. After passing through Stawell and seeing the sign to Hall's Gap, Mark commented that one time they must go explore the Grampians. Roslyn said, "You will like it. We camped there many times as children."

After a quiet Christmas with the quiet family in Horsham, Mark and Roslyn drove on through Mallee country with its monotonous sweep of short trees interrupted by the towns of Dimboola, Nhill, and crossing into South Australia at Bordertown and journeying onto Keith. It was a landscape so different from the Adelaide Hills of Mark's upbringing and the Yarra Valley beyond Croydon and Lilydale where they now lived. Even so, he was curiously drawn to the Mallee topography, and he knew this terrain would continue until the rolling hill country returned after Murray Bridge. Mark felt heightened excitement after crossing the River Murray and Roslyn said, "I have never seen you so excited. They're only family!"

Mark replied, "Yes, but they are my family, and I love and miss them every day."

Roslyn came back, "Interesting. So, am I not good enough for you?"

With mild exasperation Mark responded, "Roslyn, for crying out loud, you are my wife and I love you. But that doesn't mean that I don't love family. Why do we always have this type of conversation? It is not a competition. Why aren't we growing closer together? You should know what I mean because you know me!"

Suddenly, Mark swerved as a kangaroo jumped out of the bush. It veered away immediately and was not even close to their car. Nonetheless, it did suspend their conversation and silence pervaded. Mark was glad of this.

The minute they drove into the farm, they were surrounded by family with all the glee, affection and happiness that was so familiar to Mark, but seemed invasive and threatening to Roslyn. Gary commented first on the Monaro and took Mark by the sleeve and led him over to his new HQ Holden Ute. This was his Christmas present. His smile said the rest. Betty hastened all to the dining room table where a late lunch was consumed with much talk and laughter.

The next five days were full of day trips showing Roslyn the favorite family haunts of Adelaide and its surroundings. She relaxed finally and gravitated to Mark's sisters most of all. On New Year's Eve, the entire family drove to Glenelg on a warm afternoon for fish 'n chips on the Reserve and then to the jetty and the beach to watch the setting of the sun across the Gulf of St. Vincent. Next came the side show lights and the frenetic action of the traveling carnival. This always attracted large crowds and the raucous sound of rock 'n roll and the side shows were fun to see from one end of sideshow alley to the other. There were rides too, and Frank bought everybody tickets for two rides each. By 10 pm, Frank called it a night. He had little tolerance for the behavior of drunken revelers. It had been a good day, and they could look forward to sleeping well and long as the new morning was New Year's Day.

At lunch, the last day for Mark and Roslyn in Hahndorf, Frank asked an innocent question: "Are you still planning to go to the U.K. or the U.S., Mark?"

The family knew what Frank was asking as this was part of Mark's long-term dream from his teens.

"Probably not," interjected Roslyn, "We will buy a home as soon as we can and get established in Melbourne."

The Schubert family with one accord stopped eating and stared at Mark who looked dumbfounded, if not stupefied. Suddenly aware of the disharmony she had created, Roslyn continued: "What? What's wrong? Mark can travel to the U.K. or America if he wants, but we are going to live in Melbourne, aren't we, Mark? Help me out here?"

"If the opportunity comes for me to advance my musical career by going to Britain or America, then I still want to do that. Australia will always be our home. We are young yet and in the music field, I need to carve out my niche before I am 40! You and I need to have an understanding here; I thought we agreed about this before we got married?"

"I didn't mean to cause trouble," said Frank. "Let's drop it now and enjoy your last day with us. You can talk about this on your way back to Melbourne tomorrow."

Unfortunately, the harmony of the day was broken. Roslyn went to the bedroom to be alone and to sleep. She blurted out to Mark as he left the room: "It is obvious that I am the bad guy here. They hate me!" Mark kissed her on the forehead and told her to get some rest.

The family had farm chores or personal matters to occupy them for the afternoon hours on this holiday. His family had witnessed too many faux pas not to be concerned that Mark was becoming entwined in an impossible impasse with his wife. Alone, Mark found himself drawn to the *pines*. It was a warm and beautiful afternoon. He scooped the pine needles into a fort and into a bed and lay down looking up through the branches. It seemed only yesterday that he was doing this and wondering what he would be doing in five years and then in ten years. How innocent he was then and how old and tarnished he felt now. Weariness overcame him, and he closed his eyes, conscious that seeking sanctuary among the pines was not real life, but given the circumstances, it was an escape he sorely needed just now.

Years later, Gary told Mark that Frank said, after more low points in the marriage, "Mark has hell to pay with that woman!" Over the next year, the family knew that there were only two things they could do—pray and wait.

The journey home was in almost complete silence. Roslyn feigned sleep most of the way. Mark was wrapped in his thoughts and for the first time found himself plotting on how he could extricate himself from this increasingly caustic marriage—all four months of it.

By February, Mark's third year of teaching had begun. His junior brass band was preparing for its first experience with state competition. Mark had personally decided not to enter any competitive events this year. He needed to concentrate on others and not on himself so much. At least, that was what his chastened conscience was telling him. He was in survival mode. His early morning practice continued and became his devotional time as well. After all, he was playing his euphonium in a church. It worked well. For further distraction, he had returned to serious reading of church history, especially the Reformation era. In fact, he met with the chair of History at the University of Melbourne and was permitted to enroll in a maximum of nine hours of Early Modern Europe coursework before he had to be approved as a degree candidate. This would give him ample time to complete the regular application process.

Providentially, Mark's better judgment reprimanded him and brought him back to earth. Church history must remain his avocation for now. His career path was already heavily invested in music performance and music education. He reminded himself of this fact and immediately settled down. A day later, he made a second appointment at the University of Melbourne and was accepted into the Conservatory of Music's Master of Music degree in composition and performance. Later, he vowed, graduate work in the Reformation would follow. For now, he had made the right decision.

When Mark informed Roslyn that he was thinking of starting his graduate degree, she said fine as she would be starting night duty in three weeks and he would need to have something to occupy his spare time at home. She concluded by announcing that in a year's time she would begin her Accountancy degree. She would nurse at night and study during the day. This would enable them to buy their home more quickly, and then she could work from home as a CPA, her final goal. With some hesitation, Mark asked about the possibility of children. Roslyn shot back in an adamant voice, "There will be none from me!"

How do couples reach such gridlock? They were still in their first year of marriage and it resembled a war zone. Civility toward each other was rare, each tended to their own needs for food, washing, ironing and social activities. Intimacy was gone and the marital bed, only shared two nights a week, became the loneliest place Mark knew. How does a staunch Christian fall to the level where his thoughts and behavior become un-Christian? Roslyn stopped going to church altogether and refused to pray with Mark or engage in regenerative talk. She had one focus: to purchase a home in the next two years. Capitalizing on the battle field metaphor, Mark felt like he was suffering from shell shock. His head was not working properly, either in thoughts or actions. He continued to play solo euphonium for Kew City, but this was no longer the privilege and challenge as when he first joined because he was further advanced as a solo player himself. He had enough resilience to perform his duties in the classroom and to conduct the school band. At the Junior Band Championships in Box Hill in late April, Mark blamed himself that the band came second in its performance. This intensified his malaise. He withdrew from interaction with teachers and administration, all the while projecting a busy and pleasant persona. He was fortunate in that there was currently a lull in his noncollegiate activities. Mark really did not have any close friends and he realized that he was retreating into his inner self. Still retaining some sense of humor, he wondered if he should consider joining a monastery. There was one in the mountains before Warburton.

By May, Mark and Roslyn were living like ships passing in the nights as one came home to the flat while the other left for night duty. In the mornings Mark was at Luther College for his euphonium practice before Roslyn arrived home. On the weekends, when they did share some time and space together, they were both preoccupied with their studies. There were snippets of time when they enjoyed each other's company, but it never lasted. Something always snuffed out the good times and left weeks of animosity and vitriol. Mark was becoming no better than Roslyn and they both recognized that they were in a cycle of intractable conflict, increasing defensive behavior, growing contempt for the other, and a breakdown of trust between each other.

One evening of the last week of the school term as Mark arrived home, Roslyn accused him of prying through her personal records, bank statements and other documents. Mark protested his innocence, but Roslyn responded with contempt and as she stormed out the door, she flung over her shoulder that she wanted a divorce. With that she got in the Beetle and steamed off down the road to night duty. Mark stood in the doorway, shaking and beside himself. This had to stop. He could not live this way anymore. He slept little that night.

The administration, teachers and staff all knew of Mark's perfunctory early morning practice in the church or his studio. The next morning, the principal appeared in the church as Mark was practicing and asked if they could talk. They both sat in the front pew and the principal began: "Mark, some of us know that you have been under enormous emotional pressure for some time. I have been concerned for months. I do not want to intrude into your personal life, but I do want you to hear me out."

Mark looked at the principal. "We have noticed that Roslyn has stopped coming to church and that you are suddenly alone in attending many school and church functions. Along with many of your fellow teachers and staff, I have noticed that you look preoccupied and burdened. Your work is still exemplary, and you are one of the most valued teachers at Luther, but I know something is wrong."

"Back in February, the ABC wrote to me asking if you could be granted a leave of absence from Luther for two months to work with them on a music education program they had scheduled. It would require you to go to America and the UK with the team. I replied and stated that you could not be released from your duties at Luther. But last week I had a phone call from the project manager asking if even at this late stage you might still be able to join the team."

"Mark, I have been seriously worried about you all year and with this late request, I took the liberty of speaking to the chairman of the Board and asked if we could release you for next term on compassionate grounds. You need a break from us and perhaps your marriage, and we wondered if this project may act as a vital restorative moment for you personally and professionally. What do you think?"

Mark had his head down, and when he looked up at the principal, he was fighting tears and the compulsion to break down completely. He replied: "Sir, I don't know how I have gotten into this situation. I have worked so hard and I have been so careful in planning my career path as a means of furthering my musical talents and serving God at the same time. I just can't believe that my marriage is in such bad shape and there seems to be little I can do to make it better."

By this time the principal was holding back emotion as he said: "Mark, it takes two to tango. It is not just you in this marriage. Roslyn is part of it too. If she's not working for the success of your joint relationship, perhaps there is little that you can do to save it."

"The Board chair and I think that taking next term off for you to tackle this project with the ABC will provide some space for Roslyn and you. Perhaps 'absence may make the heart grow fonder' and the two of you will be able to re-kindle the romance that you seem to have lost at this point."

"Will you at least think about taking on this project? You will retain your salary and benefits during your term off. So, you don't need to worry about that. You will need to work with the deputy in finding a substitute conductor for the band while you are gone. The good news is that the term ends this Friday and we have two weeks to work on your replacement. We will cover your other classes."

"One point of pressure on you is that you will need to give the ABC manager you answer on Monday before 5 pm."

The principal stated that the Board chair was waiting in the pastor's study and that he would like the three of them to have prayer together. He left Mark for a few minutes. Mark was overcome with the care and concern of the principal and even more so for the obvious opportunity that had been given to him and, yes, even to Roslyn. It may be that *space*, as the principal put it, would be beneficial for them both in the hope of salvaging their marriage.

Mark ensured that he arrived home earlier that night and told Roslyn what had transpired with the principal and the offer from the ABC. She flared immediately, accusing him of leaving her in the lurch as he went off to see the world. She said that she didn't care if he never came back. Was there nothing that would soften her? What had made her this angry? Mark did not sleep well that night; it was a mixture of worry about Roslyn, and a lot of excitement about joining the ABC team and the eight weeks overseas.

Officially, Mark became part of the ABC project after his phone conversation on Monday. He knew many of the members already and over the next month he was fully versed in the project and working extensively on its success. In late autumn, Mark tried to say a kind farewell to Roslyn, but it was impossible. In despair, he wrote her an imploring letter and left it on the kitchen table. He locked the flat and stepped into the taxi bound for Tullamarine Airport. He prayed that God would be with them both, and if their marriage was to dissolve that God would be with them as it unraveled. With that he left Melbourne and Australia for his first major foray into the world of international music.

CHAPTER SEVEN

AN
INTERNATIONAL
TOUR AND
DIVORCE

"The world is a book
And those who do not travel read only one page."
—Augustine

It wasn't only the ABC investment in this music education tour. Federal, state, tertiary Schools of Education, curriculum specialists, the Arts Council and music interests throughout the nation were all seeking a better understanding of how Australia could fund group music education in K-12 public, private education, and the wider community. Already the initiative was late in converging. Academic research and studies had shown beyond doubt that Australia (and New Zealand) was languishing in the provision of artistic development for its youth. Australia had a distinguished global reputation through its military prowess from the Boer War to Vietnam. Its sporting achievements in the fields of cricket, tennis, swimming, the Olympics and more: all promoted the image of a country capable of winning on the international stage against nations with quadruple or greater the population base. However, in the arts, and especially music, Australia was in its embryonic stage. Certainly, there were individuals who became "tall poppies" in music, painting, literature, poetry and the like, but for too many children joining a choir, playing the piano or other musical instruments, was not the Australian way, unless socioeconomic pressures stated otherwise. "It is sissy" was heard too often among adolescents when invited to participate in group musical endeavors.

Mark was one of four selected musical personalities to speak to these issues and to suggest, on camera, various initiatives whereby Australian music education could enhance its appeal in the minds and experience of the current K-12 generation. Mark was the youngest of the quartet, but deliberately so as he had the look and charm of a passionate music teacher who just happened to be a performer in a traditional group genre: the brass band. It was the long-established, time-honored, conventional musical assemblages that were now under attack. Brass bands, choirs and the ethnic chorale were the main expressions of regional communal pride and festivity throughout Australia before the postwar era. Mark's German roots fostered both bands and choirs as did the Cornish mining communities on the York Peninsula, and this was just South Australia. The Welsh *Eisteddfod* had pockets of interest throughout Australia in its competitive festivals of poetry, singing, dancing, acting and musicianship for school children. A century later, these manifestations of local aesthetic utterance, so important to the small, isolated community before the Second World War, were now falling behind the ongoing support of local sporting activities. Besides, the preferred music of the '60s was loud, raucous acoustical rock 'n roll bands, often of little talent or lasting value. With the decline of community artistic opportunities, children and youth were left with the growing acceptance of television as the passive provider of ideas and notions of beauty, style, imagination, creativity, art and music. This was typically outside of the local community and rarely hands-on. The result was a deficit in stimulating the gentle arts throughout society.

In many ways, the full agenda of the ABC music tour was overly ambitious. Not only would an hour-long television program be produced. Additionally, the program managers and the myriad of educators involved in the genesis of this tour envisioned workshops, discussion groups, research projects, and the final, essential challenge for the public to rally and promote group musical activities at the national, state and local levels. As the four future luminaries boarded their Qantas

747, they joked that they felt no pressure as the project began, no, *no pressure at all,* and they all held up their hands with fingers crossed. For Mark, this would provide necessary research data for his current graduate degree.

Emerging from San Francisco's International Airport into the warm night air was an unforgettable moment for Mark. The energy, frustration, noise and pandemonium of hundreds of cars, hotel shuttles and taxis confronted the four tour members, and their film crew, simultaneously. This was their introduction to the big league; the United States of America. And, it did not stop for the next three weeks as they made their way from California to New York, from Michigan to Florida, from K-12 school systems to state research universities, from elite private universities to liberal arts colleges where music programs were paramount. Each day brought new appointments, subject-matter experts to meet for stimulating conversation and unique ideas and concepts, laughter, sharing, and the consumption of an abundance of food and, at the end of the day, the comfort of a hotel room far superior to any found in Australia. The team members were overwhelmed by the degrees of size, professionalism, diversity and cutting-edge richness of the American music sector. As they flew into one state or city to visit one conservatory or college with a pre-eminent music program, they had to fly over so many more. It dawned on them, slowly at first, then like a deluge, that they were hearing comparable stories to those at home that all was not well within music education in America.

Dilapidated Carnegie Hall was a prime example of lost glory in renowned concert halls. The '60s and '70s was the era of Woodstock, the Newport Folk Festival and the violent Altamont Speedway Free Festival. These were spectacular outdoor concerts made possible by the latest in audio equipment which blasted sound and beat barely resembling music much of the time. Alternatively, there were the lavish Las Vegas and Atlantic City gambling casinos featuring big show business stars like Liberace, Chairman of the Board Frank Sinatra and the King of Rock 'n Roll, Elvis Presley. Patronage of traditional forms of musical performance suffered in these years. It was a time of listening to music on the radio or while driving rather than attending conventional concert halls. This brought about a state of bewilderment for music educators and established providers of classical and traditional live musical performance. Absence of vision, scarcity of funding, curtailment of program growth, a dearth of marketing and promotion: all, and more, of these organizational components were lacking in the furtherance of music education at all levels of American society. The United States, for all its musical talent, its dominance in almost every classification of music, its vast music education opportunities—for all this, its music educators ached to be able to do more.

Most evenings, the entire team would gather for dinner in the hotel and discuss the progress, and at times, regress, of their project. Already, they had gathered a wealth of information and they felt good about its potential outcome. Mark did find some time to focus on brass education and brass and concert bands. Public education was one arena where music education was alive and well, not so much in formal music classroom learning, but in the pragmatic approach of learning to play an instrument in a group setting. Many American children and teenagers gained valuable experience playing in bands, orchestras or singing in choirs or ensembles. This was part of their formal education and was most successfully developed in high school. Band, or its equivalent, was a legitimate part of the secondary curriculum, as was physical education. Mark could readily see this was a contributor to the building of self-esteem so evident within American youth.

He met with many brass specialists who suggested that he consider coming to America to advance his career in this larger context. They were genuine and assured Mark that they would lend him the support he needed to make the change. It was flattering, but Mark had personal matters to deal with first. He wrote several letters each week to Roslyn, but he heard nothing in reply. He called their flat when he knew she would be home. Roslyn did answer once and was noncommittal at first, then she broke down crying, and accused him of "leaving her in the lurch to cope all by herself." It made him feel terrible and selfish. He slept little for two nights and was not fully attentive in his meetings, so he called Roslyn again. This time she was confrontational and told him to stop calling her so often and disrupting her work pattern. Strangely, he needed this and felt calmer and ready for work once again.

The final month was given to visiting music education programs first in France, and then in Germany, Italy, Norway, and Britain. The beauty, architecture, history, and culture of these countries astounded Mark. Any of these aspects could easily have distracted the team members from their purpose in gathering data on music education. The team also felt the sheer physical toll on their bodies of having been on the road for over a month. They discussed this and agreed that they had to provide at least one day a week as a personal day. They also reviewed and reduced some of the data gathering assignments. They decided there were four core questions about music education which they would ask in each country: *What was the state of formal K-12 and tertiary music education? What were the plans for enhancing formal music education programs in the immediate future? How was non-formal music education dispensed to children, adolescents and adults? What were some of the barriers to expanding both formal and non-formal music education in each country?*

With new parameters before them, the ABC team began their investigations. The French concert and opera halls were magnificent edifices and the plentiful choral music was excellent no matter where the team visited in Paris, Limoges, Lorraine, Aisne or Marseille. Public music education in K-12 was highly centralized, systematic and diversified. In the private sector, Catholic education dominated and, as in the public schools, emphasis was given to vocal training and listening to music. Music came under artistic education and lacked the political and economic clout of the traditional subjects like language, history, mathematics and the sciences. Even so, the various partnerships with music academies and conservatories kept avenues open for all students who were intent on pursuing music as a career.

In Italy, the home of opera, there were few trained music teachers at the primary or secondary levels. Music was not sought after by many students and their parents, and this meant that musical studies were usually taken outside of formal schooling. In one interview a power-ful comment was made: "Italian conservatories focus on developing professional musicians and make little effort to train music teachers."

The disappointing element in visiting Germany was that both East and West were still divided by the Berlin Wall. With Berlin and Leipzig, and the Luther towns of Efurt and Wittenberg in the Eastern bloc, Mark was not able to make his desired Reformation pilgrimage. He could have obtained permission, but it did not suit all members of the team and the project took priority. With summer in full bloom, superb film footage was collected of parks and gardens in Munich, Frankfurt and Hamburg. Twice they came across Oompah Bands in the parks. On a warm evening this *Volkstumliche Musik* with its polka flavor and the clarinet mixed with the brass instruments made for a very pleas-ant half hour while enjoying an ice cream cone. The pinnacle of the four days in Germany was attending a Wagner opera at the Richard Wagner Festival Theater in Bayreuth. Not dissimilar to other European countries, music education was compulsory in primary, *Gymnasium* and *Gesamtschule*, although students did not typically learn to play an instrument at school. Band, choir or orchestra were offered as extracur-ricular activities. Classroom music consisted of singing and listening to music.

In exploring how music education operated within the educational system of Norway, the team was intrigued to discover that they were really looking at Scandinavian music education, and what happened in Norway was also standard in Denmark and Sweden. All education was very centralized and there was little contact with the local levels of schools or communities. Scandinavian teachers were highly trained as subject-matter-experts and in pedagogical skills, but local initiatives in curriculum development were not encouraged. While about eighty percent of students had instrumental and vocal training, all of this hap-pened outside of regular school hours and its impact was short-lived.

It was fortuitous that Britain was the last country on the schedule, for it was here that the learning and comprehension of music education in the select countries came together. Perhaps it was simply that Mark and his colleagues did not have to worry about understanding their hosts speaking a foreign language. Even in America, nuances were not always picked up and some misunderstandings occurred. Whatever the reason, the team spent productive time meeting with politicians, educational superintendents, administrators and actual classroom music teachers at both the primary and secondary levels. It was fascinating to interact with committed professionals who were struggling with the same issues of access, funding, curriculum and student needs in music education and the arts in general. The ABC team began to see very clearly that while each country had its issues and overall philosophy of music education, all countries were struggling to understand how they could do more and do it better.

One discussion highlighted the conundrum where it was one thing to declare that British schools teach music and yet another to believe that learning about the social and cultural context of music is the same as playing an instrument. Indeed, most news articles conflated music education with learning an instrument. Mark liked the analogy, "Being a young high school student playing a cornet or the piano isn't the same as studying and thinking about music!" After listening to superlative Welsh choral music in Cardiff, the group came away from a meeting with the understanding that with music tuition being so expensive, it was very important to expose children to practical music, especially those in the lower-income brackets.

Then in London, at a conference on formal music education, a plenary speaker emphasized that "we now know that children tend to be more self-assured and happier from engaging in practical music." At the same time, absence breeds apathy, which in turn breeds mockery. Academic, or formal music, is seen by many students and parents as a soft option. The corollary to this truism is that educators also know that students learn practically nothing about the actual functioning of music by sitting in mute surrender before it. In support of children gaining hands on experience with music, the speaker said, "The sounds produced may be clumsy and crude, they may lack form and finesse, but the sounds are theirs!"

"The sounds are theirs" was hardly a desirable way for the ABC team to end its fact-finding tour overseas, yet it worked and profoundly so. They had gathered more than enough data in the form of video footage, interviews, and ideas and concepts. They had investigated music education programs, canvassed professional musicians, questioned government officials, brainstormed with educational specialists, and talked to hundreds of students in small and large groups. Collectively, the four weary interviewers were inspired by what they had seen, learned and experienced. They had marveled at some of the best music programs and music educators available. They had beheld majestic concert and opera halls of a by-gone period and thrilled at the dedication and commitment of young musicians performing classical and contemporary music. They digested talks, lectures, debates and conference presentations, all dedicated to the present and future of music education. They had also encountered the frustration, the despair, the promise and the vision of music as an aesthetic medium necessary for the profound emotional development of people in all countries and from all walks of life. The upcoming challenge to the team was to translate this information into various television, radio and print media, and thereby provide a springboard for the further development of music education in Australia.

On the last long weekend before returning to Melbourne, everyone in the group pursued his own interests. Mark had arranged for several meetings with premier brass bands in the Midlands around Manchester. He was excited about these few days and a little nervous. For most brass band aficionados, the Midlands of England was sacred grail territory. It was here in the late eighteenth century that industrial factories encouraged the growth of music, and brass bands emerged as the one strain of working-class music that grew and then flourished. Mark had read on the history of the bands and followed their competitions for years. He knew many of the players by name from magazines and contestant results and thought of them as competitors from afar. He enjoyed meeting various members and attending a concert by the world-famous Black Dyke Mills Band. Then, he travelled by train to

Grimethorpe in South Yorkshire and met with several members of the Grimethorpe Colliery Band. He was alarmed by the small town and its depressed surroundings. Band members spoke of the high unemployment rate and of crime and drug abuse in the community. The band continued to be of social and emotional importance for the region, but not all was well within the community. Mark returned to London glad of his few days in the Midlands and grateful for his homeland to which he was returning on the morrow.

The flight to Sydney via Singapore was long. Most of the twenty-four hours found Mark mulling over his future with Roslyn. Her one constant was unpredictability and he knew better than to anticipate his homecoming. Even so, he could imagine her preparing to unleash numerous stratagems. It had been eight weeks since Mark had left Australia, and during that time they had spoken on the phone several times and she had replied to his letters twice. The last time she had accused him of writing about sights and happenings that she had neither knowledge of herself nor could understand. Why didn't he write more about them and how soon they could buy a home? Mark's answer to himself was simple: why would I want to buy a home for us when I am doubtful there will be an "us!" Then he muttered to himself as he posted the last letter, "This isn't rocket science, Roslyn!"

There was a two-hour layover in Sydney, so Mark called their flat and left a message. He offered to take a taxi to Croydon if she could not make it to meet him at Tullamarine. She wasn't at the airport and the one team member he had confided in several times while on tour said, "The best to you, Mark. Just remember that to stay married and be unhappy is an awfully long time. We will talk in a week's time." He grabbed Mark by the collar and whispered, "Now, you hang in there, man, and don't let the bloody woman get you down."

Easy to say, but hard to do. The taxi pulled into the curb and Mark stepped out into drizzle and darkness. It was August in the southern hemisphere and Mark was missing the warmth of summer in Europe. He fumbled through his brief case, found his key, and opened the door to his home. The house was still and dark. He walked into the kitchen to find an envelope on the table addressed to him. He opened it quickly and scanned the first page: Roslyn had left him. He hurried into the bedroom and then to the study. Her personal effects were gone. He came back to the letter and read the second and third pages. Roslyn had moved in with her mother who had left her husband because he was having an affair. Mark could expect to be served divorce papers within the week. There was no telephone number and no contact information at all. Mark sat down and looked around the room. "She's left me, and that is it? No further explanation!" He was incredulous. He stood up, filled the kettle with water and made himself a cup of Earl Grey tea, only to find the milk sour. It was too late, and he was too tired to bother going out for more milk. There was nothing else to do but take a shower, unpack his case, put his second case of materials in his study, and go to bed. As he listened to the gentle rain on the roof, he felt a measure of comfort, but he longed for the pines on the family farm where he could think. Looking up in the darkness, he imagined he was looking through to a blue sky on a warm spring day in Hahndorf, and he recalled the words of Jesus, "Peace I leave with you; my peace I give you. I do not give to you as the world gives. Do not let your heart be troubled and do not be afraid." He felt numb, quiet in mood and spirit, but he knew he would deal with it. He closed his eyes and drifted into sleep.

The next three weeks were given over to organizing and sorting through the video footage the team had brought back from their fast-paced tour. A much larger ABC team would now focus on putting the documentary together. An entire production cohort would dissect the materials and determine how media could best utilize the myriad of discussion points. Mark could relax for now. Soon enough, he would be called upon for additional documentary interviews and, later promotional interviews on television and radio.

Alone once again in his flat, Mark prepared his classes for the new term commencing in early September. He informed his principal about the divorce proceedings and was assured of his support by all at Luther College. Emotionally, he felt empty. His accumulated annoyance and frustration after a difficult marriage, of almost one year, had quickly dissipated. He recognized his inability to cope with dysfunction in a relationship. He knew that he was naïve about relationships, probably because he came from a happy and secure family and he saw no reason why he and his wife should not be able to arrive at a genuine state of harmony. Sensing his need and confusion his pastor and his principal spent time helping him understand the realities of relationships when compatibility is missing.

When Mark called his family to break the news, Frank was sympathetic. He was keen to tell his son that sometimes couples who supposedly begin in the same direction, decide to take separate roads—and they never converge again. "Mark," he said, "the emptiness will go in time and soon you'll feel invigorated to tackle life as a new person without the hindrances of this last year." Then, he added, "Do you want Mum and me to come over for a few days?" Mark's eyes welled up with tears, but he murmured, "No, I need to get through this new term. I'll be home for Christmas."

The next three years saw Mark consolidate his reputation as a music educator, a brass band conductor, and a performer. He completed his master's degree and felt good about it. But a new role had subtly attached itself to Mark; increasingly, he was regarded as a motivator of young people. Youth clubs and church groups were eager to have this clean cut, clear speaking, and believable late-20s professional at their presentations and conferences. He advocated right living, right thinking, right behavior and promoted the notion that *we are always what we are becoming*. But it was getting to be too much. After a time, the high idealism he was promoting became a heavy burden for him. He deliberately scaled back these speaking appointments because he did not want to be the role model of goodness and moral rectitude. He would rather be their quiet advocate than their lectern-stomping salesman. Church leaders wanted more from him, but he declined. They applied pressure and he withdrew from all church travelling appointments. His present work was at Luther College and his chosen career was in music. Future speaking appointments would build on his growing acclaim as a music educator. Mark reasoned that he could still be the harbinger for ethical decency in this context.

Mark knew he was grounded in his faith and his family roots. He saw the fragility of popularity and acclaim. When tempted by the wiles of fame, Mark could recall his pastor's words: "Beware of public acclaim! You can be cock of the walk one minute and a feather duster the next!" That was enough for Mark. Besides, he was now divorced, and he secretly carried this as a painful stigma. He felt a deep sadness that he could not save his marriage. He thought of his parents: he had never seen them angry at each other or in any way out of love. They were his perfect standard. He wanted to love and be loved in his marriage. From the outside, it may have appeared as though Mark was the model young adult, but inside he was struggling to hide the blemish he wore on his conscience. Even so, Mark would say to himself, "Well, Mate, you may feel this is a blot against you, but it will keep you from becoming an insufferable pain in the neck!" With that Mark handled his celebrity status as a means of helping others experience some hope in a world which is often cruel and heartless. Sometimes he felt more counsellor than motivational speaker.

Media prominence brings with it the potential ugly side of being among the beautiful people. In the prime of life, and with a message of hope and aspiration, Mark was an easy target for the Australian media. Their approach was to report the ordinary, exaggerate the slightest slip, and sensationalize any word or deed that would guarantee headlines. He could rarely go to a football game without appearing in a magazine a week later. Shopping along Bourke Street made him a target for the *paparazzi*. Even photos of Mark arriving at church were popular. He took this in his stride, but he lived a cautious life. It was only a matter of time before something deleterious shook his public image.

That moment came two years later, after Mark had won the Easter Nationals Open Solo Championship for the fifth time following a hiatus of three years from contests. On the way back from Canberra, Mark and two other members of the Kew City band were coming into Lilydale when another car ran a red light and hit them on the passenger's side. Mark was shaken but uninjured because he was in the back seat. Both the driver and front passenger sustained injuries. The ambulance took the injured to the Box Hill Hospital and the police drove Mark to his flat, where he picked up his car and drove to the hospital to be with his fellow bandsmen.

His two friends were still in the Emergency Room and he was asked to remain in the waiting room. Within minutes, an ambulance pulled into its bay and its medical team wheeled in a large man on a gurney into the busy ER. Several photographers and journalists descended on the scene. An agitated woman followed, shouting at the nurses and ambulance crew, "If he hadn't cheated on me, I wouldn't have hit him so hard. He abused me for years. Did you hear me? My husband abused me for years! All he thought of was himself and his political career."

The ER nurse who had come over to calm the wife glanced up briefly and saw Mark. It was Roslyn. Their eyes locked and awkwardly Mark waved to her. He saw her mouth tighten and then she said to the wife, "It's alright. I know how you feel. I was abused too. See that man over there? He's the creep who abused me. He is a famous musician. That's Mark Schubert. Everyone loves him. What they don't know is that he neglected me to become a big shot."

Mark turned away, his face burning, but not before the crowd of photographers and journalists closed in on him with questions. He shook his head and said, "No!" and walked hurriedly out of the hospital.

The next day, the newspaper carried the story—replete with photos—of the politician's head injuries, sustained by his jealous wife attacking him with his own golf club. This had been a growing story for some months, as the politician had been associated in an affair with the wife of a prominent land developer. Also mentioned was Mark, seen in the same ER, whose ex-wife was calming the distraught woman with words of sympathy as she, too, claimed to be a victim of spousal abuse. Two photos showed Mark turning away and walking out of the hospital. The caption raised the question of Mark's credibility, and while incorrect, wrong, and mean-spirited, it hurt, as Mark recoiled in anger at Roslyn's words.

Luther College did not budge in their support of Mark, neither did its constituency nor the Lutheran Church. Mark spoke with his principal and they both agreed that it could have been worse. Some negative press was bound to occur sometime. Meanwhile, there did not seem to be any backlash about Mark's public standing. A few months later, his first book, *"Music in Your Life,"* was released. Targeted at the best seller market, the book extolled the benefits of including music as a positive influence in people's lives. It contained stories of young and old, rich and poor, rural and city, sacred and profane, all suggesting that music enhances the value and quality of life. Mark wrote from his heart when he eulogized the enjoyment of music, in some shape or form, as one of life's greatest gifts.

The book sold well. Its theme resonated with the intended audience, and Mark was kept busy with interviews on television, radio, and innumerable appearances in major retail department stories around the nation. These signings, where he sat at a table and people lined up for his signature and a few words, were exhausting events. He was literally on the road every Thursday to Sunday for two months. Along with wider acclaim, he was making a substantial supplemental income, and as his bank account grew, he began making investments. He did not want to purchase a home of his own. Something inside told him it was not yet the right time.

The Royal Melbourne Show came around again in September, and naturally, this country lad attended several times. These days he did not have to assuage anyone as to where he went and what he saw on the showground. Gary came over to Melbourne and the two brothers were like peas in a pod each time they went to the Show. The added enjoyment for both was taking the rail link from Croydon to the City and then the Flemington Racecourse line to the showground. They felt like kids again. They took in the full ambience of the show grounds, consumed too much junk food, and devoured facts and figures on all manner of agricultural and mechanized products and machinery. Gary spoke about the farm and family, catching Mark up on details missed in telephone conversations and letters from Frank and Betty. Thinking in comparative terms, Gary regarded the livestock of Victoria to be superior to that of the Adelaide Show. It stands to reason, he said, larger farming population, greater fertility and more water. It speaks for itself. They saved Sideshow Alley for last to enjoy the unique atmosphere of flashing night lights and the razzle dazzle of the loud music.

Suddenly, and out of nowhere, two inebriated young women caught hold of Mark and said, "Hello, Mark Schubert! Can we get a photo with you? You're our favorite musician!"

Gary was brushed aside, and Mark was in the middle of these two rambunctious girls as cameras flashed. Then, one of the girls held Mark's head and kissed him on the mouth while the camera flashed again. A few seconds later the girls disappeared into the crowd and people round about hardly knew what just transpired.

"Are you Okay, Mark? What was that all about?" questioned Gary.

"I think it is called notoriety. It is the dark side of what I do. Let's go home," Mark replied, and they made their way to the rail station and back to Croydon.

Two days later the kissing photo appeared in the newspaper along with the caption *Who's having fun at the Show?* This was the final straw. Mark decided to end his full-time teaching position at Luther College. He had had enough embarrassment and of walking on a tightwire. In a fit of self-righteous indignation, Mark was at the end of his tether and needed to make a change in his life. He knew he was overreacting, but somehow it didn't matter. He was his own master and slave to none. This was not who he was, or who he wanted to be. He was driven by his ethos of excellence, but sadly, he never felt good enough in all his endeavors. His instructional role was an example. Teaching in the classroom was never easy for Mark. He worked at it but always experienced a certain dissonance with the awarding of final grades. Too often it seemed the struggling students were more deserving of the higher grades than those who breezed through their studies. Nevertheless, he had tried his best. His school band had progressed very well and had earned respect and standing within the school, church, local community, and banding world. He had expanded his horizons outside of the education field and had become an acknowledged national figure in music education, a motivational speaker of youth, and a desirable discussant personality on television and radio. Even so, he had reached a self-imposed plateau. It was time for a change.

He wrote his letter of resignation and submitted it to his principal, Mr. Bacchus. In the interview that followed Mr. Bacchus was sympathetic with Mark's personal dilemma.

"Mark, I am going to accept your resignation," he said, "but with reluctance. I think you are making the right decision for yourself and the College. You have given so much to Luther and this school is richer for your dedicated service—and especially for the marvelous band we have today."

He paused, and then went on. "You've been through a lot in the last six years. You came to us as a fresh, young university graduate. Sure, you had won some brass competitions and that gave you greater perspective than most. But, frankly, Mark, you were otherwise a naïve, honest young farmer about to enter the tough world of a professional city."

He looked at Mark and smiled. "I'm two decades ahead of you in years, but, long ago, I came from the Mount Gambier area. My first visit to Adelaide, the capital city, was at twelve years of age, and then not again until I went to Teacher's College. Life in the country is much different to life in a complicated city. I understand you and I admire how well you have come through all this. Especially as a Christian, trying to interact with the secular world like you are now doing, it's not easy. Some may be hell bent in trying to catch you out; to tarnish that polished image of the young Christian professional. I'm not sure they are, but it is conceivable that there may be some truth to this."

"I do want to say something to you now, Mark," he said, "and I hope you will understand and think on it. As your administrator, I have never worked so closely with someone who has such potential for a successful and prosperous career in the public eye. Your music performance record, your commitment to music and arts education and your growing media profile—all this, and you are just coming up on thirty years old! It is amazing, Mark. To be sure, you have had a tough marriage, but that is now behind you. So, you married wrong; it happens. Now, leaving Luther College, and stepping boldly into the new unknown, please jettison all the baggage of these years as you go forward."

He looked Mark in the eye and said, "Stop being so hard on yourself and let go of this perfection bent. You're not perfect and neither am I." He shook his head and laughed, "And this side of Heaven, we never will be! Try and relax more. Try to enjoy working with people as a guide rather than as their taskmaster. It may take a little longer, but it will be much more pleasant, and even fun."

"Enough preaching from me!" he said. "Let's work together to make sure the next few weeks of this school year are memorable for you. I want you to leave Luther College on a high. You are dearly loved here, and we are going to miss you. Do you know what you will do next year?"

Mark got to his feet. "Thank you for your sage words and your patience and generosity," he said. "You have been the mentor I have desperately needed. I don't know how I would have gotten through the marriage breakup if it wasn't for your nurture. I will always treasure my years at Luther. The band has been my first big project and I will cherish the memories." He shook Mr. Bacchus' hand: "You will still see me from time to time as I am going to continue instrumental teaching with some of the students."

He paused and took a deep breath. "Next year, Mr. Bacchus, I am going to join the Royal Australian Navy Band."

CHAPTER EIGHT

THE SWING AND SWAY OF THE WORLD

"Life is a dance between heaven and earth,
The ebb and flow of life."
—Maurice Spees

Mark was accepted into the Royal Australian Navy Band in January of 1979. This was not a recent and impulsive idea. Ever since the ABC documentary tour, Mark had pondered a major change in furthering his career path. Especially in the United States, he sensed his narrowness in his loyalty to brass bands. As a teenager, he stubbornly pledged his fealty to this genre. Even as obsolescence threatened long-established community brass bands, Mark vowed not to let them disappear on his watch. The first real crack in his stance came in the second year at Luther College when he encountered some reluctance by female students and their parents. Woodwinds were preferable for girls. This irritated Mark initially, but slowly he embraced the wider diversification of the musical experience for high school students if they played in a concert band. It was years before he would admit that the sound was more variegated. His conversion came about almost entirely from listening to, and observing, the Australian Defence Force bands in concert and on parade.

Another confirmation from the tour caused Mark to forcibly recognize that he must master a second instrument. While he had played some trombone over the years, chiefly the bass trombone, this was still a brass instrument. For several months, the thought percolated in his mind, and his decision to tackle the sacrifice and devotion required to learn a new instrument came concurrently with his pronouncement that he was joining the Navy band. While exploring details on enlisting, Mark became pleasantly aware that Navy music was enlarging its styles of music, and jazz was inching its way into military music as a new offering in the larger cities. He would learn to play woodwinds and specialize on the tenor saxophone. Immediately, Mark felt right about his choice. It was like stepping out of the shadows and into the light. Now he could be loyal to his euphonium and classic brass band music and, also, be in step with contemporary trends. Similarly, he was enhancing his performance opportunities and strengthening his instructional skills for woodwind students. Why hadn't he done the same logical reasoning in some of his more important decisions of recent times? Enough, he thought, what was done was now behind him!

Mark joined the Royal Australian Navy Band as a Qualified Entry Sailor with a degree. His instrument category was euphonium. After his satisfactory musical audition, the Director of Music's office welcomed him as a considerable asset for Navy Music. This was followed by eleven weeks of basic training at the Navy's Recruit Training School at HMAS *Cerberus* in Western Port Bay, south-east of Melbourne. His most challenging feat during training was the Naval Swimming Test where, among other tasks, he had to tread water for fifteen minutes wearing overalls. Mark spent weeks preparing for this test.

On the last Friday of basic training a welcome finale was the Graduation Parade with all the pomp and fanfare of a military event. Mark marched in step with his fellow graduands. It was the first time in his banding life that he had marched *listening* to a brass band and not playing himself. The entire Schubert family attended the graduation exercise and celebrated with Mark as he began this new chapter in his life. At dinner that evening, Betty whispered in Mark's ear, "It's good to have the old Mark back again!" He smiled and said, "It's good to be back!" After a long meal with much conversation and laughter, Frank gave Mark a tenor saxophone as his graduation gift from the whole family.

"Mark, this is a wonderfully maintained 1965 Selmer VI saxophone, just like John Coltrane played. It was hard to find but I was given good help by a jazz friend in Adelaide. I know it will bring you hours of enjoyment."

Frank had acquired a taste for smooth jazz as a young man listening to the ABC radio jazz program hosted by Kym Bonython. After thirty-eight years, this program ended in 1975. Always somewhat *avant-garde* in his aesthetic interests, Frank exposed his children to all forms of music and was quietly proud of Mark's second instrument choice. He saw this as Mark having a vital "second string to his bow" as he forged deeper into his chosen vocation. Gary followed his father and gave Mark a collection of some of the best long-playing jazz saxophonist records.

"Now as you learn to play the saxophone, you can listen to the best: Charlie Parker, John Getz, Sonny Rollins and, of course, 'Trane, Dad's favorite," said Gary as he gave his gift to his big brother.

Ever the father, Frank said, "You will study and learn from these great jazz men, Mark, and you will discover that there is a lot of spirituality in their quest to harness the mystery and emotion of jazz. Just know that some of these greats also had sad encounters with drugs and depression. I don't want that for you. Keep close to our Luther's personal God as you reach out and uncover the wonders of jazz. May it always lift you up and never put you down."

Once again, Mark recognized his good fortune in having such a healthy and well-balanced family. He felt blessed, like a little kid at Christmas time surveying his whole family after unwrapping his gifts. Tomorrow, he would be back to an adult again. He almost regretted the thought. It was a luxury to be from such a family.

Mark was posted to the Melbourne-based Navy band. There were six bands throughout Australia. The Sydney and Melbourne bands were staffed with full-time musicians and stationed at HMAS *Kuttabul* in Potts Point, Sydney and HMAS *Cerberus* where Mark completed his initial training. The other bands were Reserve bands and were positioned at Brisbane, Adelaide, Hobart and Perth.

On a Monday, three weeks later, Mark was a Navy musician reporting for work. Gone were the numerous and, at times, conflicting roles and responsibilities he had assumed each week at Luther College. No more teaching, no more college band rehearsals and tutoring, no extra-curricular school duties, no rushing to Kew City band practice, no church youth groups and no one at home to worry about. Suddenly, shared life commitments vanished, and Mark was, of necessity, fixated on his own self. This was his job. Naval musicians performed at ceremonial and training parades, provided musical entertainment in the public interest and at official naval and government functions. This became his new mission; delightfully clear and concise and rigidly followed. His daily schedule was provided for him and the weeks became months as the Navy way became a very acceptable career path.

Over time, Mark had begun to recognize a degree of dualism growing within his personality. His thinking, his preferences in food, sports and entertainment, even his predilection for mornings over evenings— all spoke to his new singleness and, therefore, a penchant to choose, if he liked, one kind or category over another. He only had himself to please or to disappoint. He was captain and crew of his ship, and he liked it this way. He relished old Western movies where there was a clear division between good and evil, and where good usually triumphed. He was observant enough to appreciate that this black 'n white mindset, taken to extreme, would breed traits that were not always pleasing in a social context.

Notwithstanding, Mark knowingly shaped his lifestyle in a decidedly dualistic manner. When he was "at work" he was his normal, pleasant self, and when he was "off duty" he was usually alone and either walking along the many foreshores and trails on the base, or practicing his instruments, reading, studying, watching TV, or listening to music. Occasionally, he ventured out to eat or to a movie, but mostly he was content to be alone. He would joke sometimes about returning to his monastery and as he closed the door to his apartment, he always felt glad. This was his time and he could busy himself with the many self-imposed assignments he had placed on his monkish agenda. Underlying all this was the guilty conviction that after his failed marriage, now was his time to repair the breech and to heal himself through music with the Navy as his catalyst.

A new Navy musician recruit did more than 'play' music. There were other duties as well. Few joined the Navy Band with Mark's acclaim as a brass teacher and performer, and even more significantly, his national recognition as an emerging music educator of merit. It was of interest to the media that he had joined the Navy, and *The Women's Weekly* devoted two pages to Mark in his uniform graduating from basic training. HMAS *Cerberus* considered this a public relations coup for the entire Navy. Consequently, Mark was assigned to the base Public Relations Office. He protested his inexperience, even while he savored the opportunity to learn how to work with the civilian media networks. He saw this as a stroke of luck to be training under professionals in an arena which had such a sway on his future career plans—to be forewarned is to be forearmed. So far, he had been fortunate in his media exposure despite the few awkward photographic moments. Here was his chance to understand communications in a broader sense.

His other assignment was to tutor the lower brass players. He was a team leader, at least this is how he spoke of his role. For Mark, this was not work, but pure professional pleasure. Personally, he continued to play his euphonium one hour a day outside of rehearsal scheduling. His tenor saxophone was his current chore. He was being tutored, but he was impatient and pushed his learning curve as much as he could. He knew this was not the best way to achieve professional efficiency, but he was on a fast track to play smooth jazz. In the evening solitude of his apartment, Mark would play repeatedly the LP jazz records Gary gave him. Little by little he came to echo, or was it *mimic*, the style of the Master, John Coltrane. As relentless as Coltrane was in his pursuit of music excellence so was Mark to imitate his newly-acquired idol in style, mood, and sound. Again, his tendency toward dualism was evident. As a euphonium player, he could pound out the commanding, driving sound of the lower brass in a traditional march piece and then bring tears to eyes as he reached the melodic heights of a ballad or

Schubert's *Serenade*. Now, he was moving full force into this alluring, unbridled and emerging world of jazz.

In the '70s, Australian jazz was still developing and was most readily found first in Sydney, and then Melbourne. Jazz was widely known and followed, but rarely with local competent and successful jazz musicians. As Mark delved further into the scope of Australian jazz, he became aware of its underground and cultish appeal. He had become good friends with a fellow Navy musician at *Cerberus*, a percussionist. Together, they ventured to Melbourne, when not on duty, and to the club scene where *cool* jazz and *free* jazz held reign. Mark didn't care much for the smoke, but he endured it to soak up the music and the performance techniques on display. One group was extraordinary and worthy of emulation. Mark and Mike became friends with these serious jazz players who were boldly stepping out, hoping there was a future for them financially in jazz in the city of Melbourne.

Three months later the Music Director of the Royal Australian Navy Band in Sydney approved the proposal and request from the Music Director of *HMAS Cerberus* for the formation of the first Navy jazz quartet at the Western Port base. The Navy had had big bands and stage bands before, but not a small jazz quartet. At first, the four musicians were allocated five hours each week for initial practice, and if the base Music Director approved of their progress and quality, then the quartet could look forward to increased recognition and privileges. Conscious of breaking new ground, the quartet melded together saxophone, piano, bass and drums. As relatively young sailor musicians, all were eager to make their mark as they devoted hours of personal time to understanding the basic rudiments of jazz and to forge a style which suited them and would appeal to future Navy audiences. It was not long before they arrived on a format loosely classified as smooth jazz. The challenge facing each of these traditionally trained musicians was to become proficient with improvisation and at ease with polyrhythms.

A month later, the quartet was questioning their sanity in thinking that, as professional musicians, they could make a relatively easy transition to becoming accomplished smooth jazz performers. This was going to take effort, dedication and commitment. To be comfortable and adept with improvisation was one challenge, and then to play in harmony as a quartet in relaxed tempos and lighter tones was another. Even the term "harmony" was inaccurate as discord and dissonance are often deliberate ploys in achieving the polished and velvety sounds of smooth jazz. One commentator spoke of playing in "pastel colors" compared to red-hot, fiery colors.

Slowly, the quartet assembled its repertoire. It was tediously built one number at a time. A month later they announced their first performance, purposely held at HMS *Cerberus* before a home audience. Promoted as a bold initiative by the Navy to launch into the jazz field, the free concert attracted most of the musicians on the base as well as new recruits and local people of Western Port. Nervousness is not a trait usually exhibited by skilled and seasoned artists, but the members of the quartet were all apprehensive, none more so than Mark. He knew his instrument was the one most prominent, and thereby, the most vulnerable to gaffes in sound, style or flow.

Ninety minutes later their initial gig was over. Their performance was interspersed with speeches by several base officers, including the Musical Director, on how the Navy was breaking new ground in a new category of music. This was a forerunner of even more styles of music to emerge gradually in all branches of the Australian Defence Force. One of the officers spoke of this innovation occurring at a similar moment to Australia's own awareness of a greater sophistication in its musical capabilities and offerings. No longer does the nation need to feel left behind in its musical diversifications, he said. The quartet was hailed for its first recital and they felt as though their heavy practice sessions over the last three months were worthwhile. Mark was a realist and knew that he had more work ahead if he was to truly become a smooth saxophonist. Even so, they had come a long way, and continued effort would enable them to tackle compositions of much more exacting complexities. They all slept well that night except Mark.

He was becoming a worry wart, and he knew it. His concern was the double life he was creating for himself as an established euphonium doyen and now the budding saxophonist jazz marvel. Could he keep this all together? This was the question that bothered him. It was dualism again. Already the push into the jazz arena, largely at his behest, was disrupting his monastic preference. Rather than retreating into his shell after official duties, Mark was frequenting the Melbourne jazz scene weekly, spending large swaths of time with his quartet colleagues and becoming outlandishly social. This was not part of his game plan six months ago. The final irony was the fact that he was relatively impressed with his new self. He was laughing more, enjoying the company of others, drinking a little and jogging with buddies instead of solitary walks along the beaches skipping rocks across the water. Most likely it had something to do with the finalization of his divorce from Roslyn. At last it was settled. She got a fraction of the money she sought, but it was now over. Mark could see why his hop, skip and jump, his bounce, was returning.

With six bands throughout Australia, Mark was principally seen as a lower brass player, and he soon was assigned on a regular basis to brief stints with the Reserve Navy Bands in all states other than New South Wales. At least once each year, Mark or the entire HMS *Cerberus* Navy Band would travel overseas to Malaysia, Japan, Hong Kong and once to Britain for various Navy tour functions. A new experience was the occasional ship board tour. Living at sea was an adjustment as was rehearsal on deck of a frigate as it sailed to its next port. Mark's public relations duties doubled his importance to the Navy on these missions. He was involved in the tour details as well as the media coverage, and he frequently interviewed military, political and local dignitaries in an official capacity. With his resonant voice, his amiable demeanor and the ability to engage people, he was a natural and he was soon recognized by the Navy as more than a professional musician.

After three years, Mark re-enlisted, and in his fourth year he applied for an officer's commission. He was given encouragement to do so as his proclivity towards leadership was evident. To become a junior naval officer, he had to complete the New Officer's Course at HMAS *Creswell* at Jervis Bay, some three hours south of Sydney. It was a five-month residential course focused on what it means to be a naval officer. Mark continued to be sanguine about Navy life. It promoted self-government and nurtured self-mastery. He had always subscribed to the core values of honor, honesty, courage, integrity and loyalty. He extolled the primary responsibility of an officer; the welfare of his sailors. What was there *not* to like in becoming more entrenched in the Navy as a career path? The one downside to this training course was the severance from his musical routine, and especially the jazz quartet. There was an intermittent music presence at HMS *Creswell*. Mark took his two instruments to his single-person cabin, but he could not practice there. It was so small. Showers and toilets were communal, with the emphasis on promoting *mateship*. Mark had to seek out practice space and his practice time was reduced to two half-hour sessions each day. He was astute enough to realize that his jazz sojourn had just taken a severe interruption.

The New Officer's Course was intense, fast-paced and diverse. The administration, leadership, personal development and communications segments were standard fare for Mark, and he readily absorbed the content knowledge and its application to Navy and Australian Defence Force practice. Less familiar were components in systems management, equity and diversity awareness, and Royal Australian Naval History. On the other hand, Mark excelled at history and saw it as his avocation. Part of the assessment for this course was a military history essay with the Naval Historical Society Prize awarded to the best essay. Mark set his sights on winning this prize. His topic detailed the formation of the Band of the Victorian Naval Brigade just prior to the twentieth century. This band was deployed to China as part of the naval contingent that assisted in the quelling of the Boxer uprising. The essay concluded by describing the band as the Commonwealth Naval Force band, which was present at the arrival of the U.S. Navy's *Great White Fleet* into Port Phillip Bay in 1908.

Mark graduated with the rank of Midshipman, and once again, his parents were in attendance, as was Gary and his fiancée, Helen. Mark did not win the essay prize, but it did receive an honorable mention, and it was published. That was enough for him. With his commission came word that in six months Mark was being transferred to HMAS *Kuttabul* at Potts Point, Sydney. He was to join the Sydney Navy Band as instrumentalist and assistant conductor. Similarly, he was given an administrative position in media within the public relations office. These were clearly advancements and Mark was pleased. Yet, it was the death knell for the jazz quartet. When he spoke with his music director at HMS *Cerberus,* he was told that the intention was for him to form a similar jazz ensemble in Sydney. The three other members were being dispersed to other bands, too. The Navy did not have adequate funding to grow new musical groups and was looking to its internal talent to evolve, and then it would provide support through release time and exponential budgeting on a year-by-year basis.

Living in Sydney was a formidable change. There was nothing slow or relaxed about Australia's largest city. Especially was this so around the Sydney Harbor Bridge. Potts Point was less frantic, but still bustling. By comparison, Western Port was the boondocks. Mark knew this new location would take considerable adjustment on his part. Sydney Harbor was unbelievably beautiful and expansive, a modern city partially cloistered into segments by nature. There was an excitement in the city's countenance and a clear mindfulness of its national premier status, even if this bordered on arrogance. Mark was determined to embrace the titillation that was Sydney. As a country boy to his core, he quietly hoped that he would be able to find tranquility here as well. The compulsion to *escape to the pines* remained a coping mechanism for his continued contentment. His years in the Navy had brought him a certain fulfillment through belonging to an organization and a cadre of colleagues, many of whom were now simply "mates" at a time when much of society was overtly abandoning many of the mores of earlier times. Mark's main lament was the loss of dignity, etiquette and decorum among the nation's youth. Television's influence appeared to supersede that of parents, church and the time-honored traditions of society. Always the educator, Mark was adamantly opposed to passivity and idleness evident in so many children and teenagers. Mark retained his belief in God and the traditions of the Lutheran Church, but his attendance on Sundays dissipated. His deep involvement with church youth had ceased after leaving Luther College. He bemoaned this; yet did nothing to correct it.

As a Navy musician, his routine and obligations remained much the same. The Sydney Navy Band had a demanding performance schedule, both nationally and internationally. Mark joined the jazz band and soon branched off with the formation of a new quartet of piano, saxophone, bass and drums. The vibrancy of the Sydney jazz scene had Mark associating with Galapagos Duck, the Don Burrows Quartet and others. He frequented the El Rocco Club, the Basement, the Manly Jazz Festival, and the jazz component of the Sydney Festival. With the advent of the 1980s, the jazz scene in Sydney slowed. Jazz had lost its main champion in the energetic promoter, Horst Liepolt. As the glamor and razzle-dazzle dimmed, this opened the door for Mark's jazz quartet and the jazz combinations of the other branches of the Australian Defence Force. They were not found in the club scene (unless individual Navy musicians were playing in other jazz combos, as many were when off-duty), but rather at public holiday events and regularly scheduled performances at the Opera House and other key sites around Sydney. One of the highlights of these years was the three recordings made by the Sydney Navy Jazz Quartet. Playing saxophone and jazz music had given Mark an added dimension to his musical prowess. Gaining more confidence in improvisation and jazz techniques each year, Mark broadened his human sensitivity as well. He felt more alive and more in search of his best self. Still known foremost as a euphonium player, Mark continued to delight in the sound of his beloved instrument and played both instruments several hours each day unless Navy schedules prevented this.

A few months into his HMS *Kuttabul* posting, Mark attended a lower brass workshop in Brisbane for all branches of military bands throughout the nation. These work assignments were his preferred musical gatherings. While a soloist performer, sometimes a conductor and always a music educator, Mark derived pleasure in the interaction and learning when fellow musicians came together. There was a unique camaraderie when lower brass *ragamuffins* assembled. Some said it had to do with the degree of "huff and puff" required to blow lower brass instruments. There were few women in lower brass, and as a result there was a level of crudeness that had to be either tolerated or ignored. Nevertheless, Mark liked such occasions. On his return to Potts Point, he opened an invitation to Gary and Helen's wedding.

St. Michael's Lutheran Church in Hahndorf was the venue and Mark was glad to take a few days to attend the spring wedding and to spend some time with family. Mark respected his brother for waiting to marry the right girl, Helen, who had become his best friend for several years before he proposed. Now almost thirty, Gary had assumed leadership of most areas of the family farm. Frank was now in his mid-sixties and was not well much of the time. The doctor had not diagnosed anything specific, but Frank had an aging back not helped by the hauling of bags of potatoes and bales of hay in his younger days. There was a loss of energy and a general fatigue within Frank. He retreated to his study and his books and music as Gary became the lead farmer. Mark was delighted to be groomsman for his younger brother and basked in the happiness of the wedding and the time with his parents afterwards.

With Gary on his honeymoon and Mark's two sisters now married and with babies, it was just Mark and his parents for two days before he flew back to Sydney. It was a memorable time for the three of them and each meal took several hours as they just sat back after eating and talked about anything and everything.

Betty was serving Mark his third cup of tea on his last breakfast at home when she leaned over and asked: "Now Mark Franklin, what's going to happen to you? Why are we not hearing of any special girls in your life?"

Mark looked at his father who winked back and said, "Interesting questions, don't you think?"

Mark looked sheepish and squirmed about in his chair. He thought for a moment or two and replied: "It's not that I am not interested, and it is not that I don't look from time to time. I guess I am wary of making a mistake again. Perhaps I am afraid of girls, or of getting too close to a girl and developing intimacy. At times, I feel too selfish and too involved in my work."

"Since joining the Navy Band, the jazz side has taken so much time and I have obsessed over becoming a good jazz player. It's quite a switch, you know, from euphonium and *Colonel Bogey* to playing smooth jazz. I guess I have been married to my music and haven't had much time for anything else. I must admit that I am starting to feel weary from it all. I feel constantly on guard when I am at these jazz clubs. I love the music but not necessarily the atmosphere," explained Mark as he concluded his defense on no active social life.

Frank nodded in assent, "I hear you, Mark. I don't think a jazz club is the best place to find a girlfriend. It will happen when it happens. Your Mother and I just don't like to think of you living your life alone. We pray for you daily and that you will find that special girl who will light up your life."

Later that day Mark flew back to Sydney, and as he arrived in his residential street, he could say that it was beginning to feel like home. It was a second-level apartment with a car-port garage and best of all, it was only ten minutes from his work. It was now city living for Mark. He did not mind it, although he reasoned, it would not be forever. One day Mark anticipated a home on a few acres, with someone by his side. For now, it was all a nebulous yearning in a cubbyhole of his consciousness.

Mark's public relations work in the Navy continued to provide him with good skills outside of his music, and important professional contacts should he ever depart Navy life. Fortuitously, he could see parallel applications between his musical world and his public relations work for the Navy. Mark's focus was government and community relations with an emphasis in event coordination. He had developed a certain confidence in dealing with the media and senior Naval officers in the interplay of communications. In Sydney, the two large ceremonial events were Anzac Day and Remembrance Day commemorations. His work, continued from Melbourne, was the planned and sustained effort to establish and maintain goodwill and mutual understanding between the Royal Australian Navy and the Australian community. Most of his work was local, but the implications were pertinent nation-wide and internationally, too. With Mark's previous television and radio exposure, the Navy (and the Australian Defence Force in general) began using Mark as a junior-ranked spokesperson.

Two years along, the Navy hired a civilian to head Mark's division. Periodically, the Navy would engage a communications specialist with a certain set of skills to supplement its full-time public affairs capability. The overall task of protecting the good name and reputation of the Navy was paramount and crisis and issue management skills needed to be sharpened at regular intervals.

The person chosen for this role was to have a negative impact on Mark. Alison Terkel came from the Australian Broadcasting Commission and, thus, had a semi-government and private corporate relations background. She was loud, jocular, self-opinionated and insecure. At her first chaired meeting with Mark's division she waxed garrulously for a full hour on her personal gifts and talents, and her accomplishments in the public relations field. As she spoke, Ms. Terkel would close her eyes for extended periods, all the time talking on the topic at hand. Mark and the other ten people around the conference table picked up on these and other idiosyncrasies and furtively glanced at each other at moments when the eyes were closed. What did all this mean? Who hired this person? They listened for a sense of direction from her; there was none. They asked at the end of the discourse what length of time did she see in her adjustment to Navy public relations. "Only a few weeks" was her reply as she understood she was a change agent on how the Navy did public relations. The final question was how Ms. Terkel planned to develop her team. She replied that she would have one-on-one meetings with all in the department and hold a staff meeting every two weeks. With that she brought the meeting to a close. Her final statement was that she expected full loyalty to her and the direction in which she would be taking the department. In stunned disbelief, the eleven

Navy professionals went back to their desks. Had they seriously just witnessed what had occurred?

The old axiom proved true: first impressions are often lasting impressions. Ms. Terkel failed in her ability to coerce a willing team under her leadership. Frequent changes to job descriptions and the inability to provide a consistent course of direction resulted in each department member continuing to do as they had done before her arrival. Change appeared on paper only, never more than the semblance of change. This led to silos of operation with all endeavoring to do their best and, above all, to survive. Morale plummeted, and a once cohesive team now splintered regarding the quality of work. Talk was rampant among the team of seeking new employment within the Navy and even without. Mark coped for two years, but Ms. Terkel increasingly intruded into his event coordination, and became overly critical of his style and technique in his television and radio segments. She required more reporting, but never followed through afterwards.

She resented Mark's half-time status. She found it particularly annoying when he was called away on music assignments at short notice, sometimes for two weeks or more. As a result, Mark found himself actively pursuing as many music assignments as possible. And then a plum opportunity arose for Mark to travel to the U. S. Naval Academy in Annapolis, outside of Washington, D.C., for a music conference and a lower brass workshop. Mark could not respond quickly enough. There was little Ms. Terkel could do to stop this, and it was with irritation that she signed his leave papers granting him an additional two weeks of vacation attached to the end of his music workshop obligation.

It was spring when Mark arrived at Dulles International Airport in Northern Virginia. This was his second visit to the United States and to be positioned in the nation's capital was exciting for Mark. He was somewhat overwhelmed by the extent and majesty of the Federal buildings around the Mall. He found a pride and ownership that Americans exhibited towards their country's history and accomplishments. The blending of architecture and nature was appreciated when Mark understood why there were no skyscrapers within the precincts of the Capitol. The cherry blossoms were spectacular, and Mark felt a longing to walk leisurely under the canopy of gentle pink and white cherry petals with the girl of his dreams. Instead, he watched so many others do what he could only imagine. His solitude was made more difficult given the fact that it was his birthday week too. The crowds of people were constant. He took every tour he could and soaked himself in Americana on the Mall. Even then, he knew he had only seen a fraction of what would take years of steady focus for the serious student of the Smithsonian.

When he arrived at the Maryland state capital of Annapolis, he came face-to-face with an immediate and unexpected revelation. Before him was a living piece of colonial America: quaint, historic buildings on narrow, cobble-stoned streets all the way to the waterfront. Three hundred-year-old buildings now played host to shops, restaurants, pubs and the like. The Maryland State House is the oldest state capitol in continuous legislative use, dating back to 1772. He was awed as he reveled in sights that he had reserved in his mind for Europe. Yet, here was captured early America as he had seen in so many exhibits on the Mall days before. It was real, alive and enduring, a constant stream of traffic with capitalism hard at work. He enjoyed a seafood lunch and tasted salt water taffy for the first time.

When Mark entered the grounds of the Naval Academy, he was visibly moved by its size, dignity and power. He found himself muttering quietly, "Oh, poor little *Cerberus*!" This was to be his home for two weeks. The conference had military band personnel from numerous countries, including Britain, Canada, Japan, France, several Scandinavian nations, New Zealand, Egypt, Malaysia, and Brazil. One of the pressing topics was the role and funding of military bands in an age of declining audiences and national pride.

Mark was fascinated in learning that the United States had eleven "premier ensembles," as well as more than one hundred smaller, active-duty and reserve bands. All military bands in the United States were composed of regularly enlisted or commissioned military personnel. This was a departure from British, Canadian, Australian and other military bands where personnel formed *voluntary* bands, or bands composed of unpaid civilian musicians who dressed in military uniforms when performing.

It was clear that all countries faced the dilemma of lessening interest and support from the public in military banding. Britain had the advantage of historical tradition and pageantry, whereas the United States had the distinct advantage overall of funding, size and quantity of its military bands. The conference concluded, recognizing that there was no substitute for quality in military music and the draw on national pride. Get these factors in correct sequence and public support and admiration is guaranteed. Mark and the other Australian and New Zealand military musicians in attendance were tremendously encouraged and even inspired in their association with so many fellow military musicians.

Over the duration of the conference and then during his two weeks of vacation, Mark explored casually at first, then with deliberation, opportunities of him finding exchange, sponsorship or scholarship programs for doctoral studies at an American university known for its graduate programs in music. It did not take long for Mark to sift through the many suggestions and to zero in on the potential of returning to D.C/Maryland on an exchange basis as a euphonium soloist at the Naval Academy and a doctoral student at the Peabody Conservatorium of Music at Johns Hopkins University in Baltimore. As Mark travelled to New Norfolk, Williamsburg, Gettysburg and other military and historical sights, he was also able to meet with several key people at both the Naval Academy and the Peabody Conservatory to gain further insights into how he should proceed. He determined to make this become a reality. It was now or never to pursue that elusive doctorate.

When he returned to Potts Point, he was immediately assigned to work on a report of the conference for all branches of the Australian Defence Force bands. He and others were assigned to travel to each capital city and conduct workshops on enhancing the value of all the Defence Force bands at civic and public events, as well as tactical strategies and methods of garnering wider public support. This took another three weeks and when Mark returned to his public relations desk, he had been absent for seven weeks. Ms. Terkel was not pleased. She greeted Mark with sarcasm; "It's good to have the Wandering Minstrel back from his travels. I wonder how long before you are off again gallivanting around the globe?"

Taken aback, but not one to meet ridicule with more ridicule, Mark dismissed her nastiness and walked on by to his office with a curt comment, "It is good to be back, and to see you too, Ms. Terkel!"

The interpersonal assault by Alison Terkel continued to affect most who worked in and around the public relations office. There were several people who were nick-named *Terkel's darlings*. These, like Terkel herself, were not enlisted, career Navy; they came from government and industry and, by and large, were mild mannered people. Indeed, they fit the stereotype of personalities that could be manipulated and swayed by a scurrilous leader. It was apparent to many that she had a disdain for military types. In her mind, the role of the Australian Defence Force was to fight and win wars. This was its sole function and this opinion quelled any need for additional qualification. In the less structured world of public relations, where planned and persuasive communication was necessary to influence significant publics, Terkel believed this was her domain, her strength, her professional expertise, and not that of the military. Such was her hubris. She genuinely believed that her arrival at HMAS *Kuttabul* was the occasion for the Navy to engage in, and embrace, palpable public relations practice. Otherwise, with "them in charge all you will continue to get is crude propaganda."

For the old team, this was like a bad dream. How did this woman pass interview protocol and, after two years, why was Navy administration not picking up on the bad vibes which were so obvious to those working under such duress every day? While Mark and his colleagues continued with their routine production of Navy public relations, the general tenor of the office suffered, and innovative productivity atrophied. Mark was fortunate in his part-time capacity. His prime vocation was his musical calling and he recognized this fact more than ever under the Terkel regime. He had become the face of Navy news, events and promotion. It was this aspect that Terkel wanted to control. It was a power maneuver and she wanted to be the frontispiece, the ornamental façade of Navy public relations. Despite her lumbering appearance, she had the aplomb and effrontery to believe that this was her suite, her executive privilege and her irresistible destiny at this point in her career.

Mark had reached his limit. He had no further capacity to endure a toxic work environment. By this he meant the public relations position, and not his music. All in all, it was time to pursue his academic ambitions and to begin a new chapter in his life. The next four months of investigating, researching, calculating, estimating, analysis, applying and, finally, clearance and approval saw Mark ready to embark on his doctoral studies at the Peabody Conservatory of Johns Hopkins University and a musician exchange appointment at the United States Naval Academy in Annapolis. Mark had two months before he left for America and during this time, he took vacation and went back to the farm at Hahndorf. Perhaps this was providential because Frank Schubert suffered a heart attack only three weeks after Mark arrived home.

Now bedridden, Frank knew his time was short as did the entire family. Daily, Mark sat by his father's bedside and talked to him when he had strength and watched over him when he slept and rested. It was an anxious time for the household, although they knew that Frank, while only sixty-seven, was ready to meet his Maker. Frank was especially keen to learn from Mark what he planned for his personal life in the years ahead. His prolonged single status had become a mild obsession for both Betty and Frank. They had quietly prayed for a long time that Mark would meet a new sweetheart; this time around a best friend and someone who would love him and nurture him as he would her. Mark knew their inner desires for him and felt burdened by the stress this had brought them over the years. One afternoon, Frank asked Mark to "fetch Betty as I want to talk to you, my son."

Mark knew what was to follow. The three of them sat and talked for over an hour. Frank opened his heart and said: "Mark, you have always been such a wonderful son for us. We have cherished you from the moment you were born. You are our first born. You were blessed with extraordinary talent and have made a name for yourself despite a poor marriage. Now, you are preparing to leave us again and this time to leave Australia and go to the other side of the world. I know it is the right thing for you to do, but you will be so far away from us. It is a huge blessing to your mother and me that our other children are close by, but you will be so far away."

At this moment, Frank broke down and cried and Betty did the same. Mark held their hands and felt the intense emotion of the occasion. More than this, he felt awful; here he was nigh on abandoning his parents to satisfy his own selfish cravings while his father lay dying. Then, Frank continued: "Mark, we don't want you to live your life alone. We want you to find a sweetheart."

"I know you do, Dad, but it is something I can't make happen just like that!"

"I am sorry," said Frank, "It is my medicine making me this way and I know that I don't have long. I just want you to know how much your Mother and I want you to be happy and content."

"Dad, I am not unhappy. I know that it may seem that being on my own makes me incomplete. But I know what it was like to be with someone and be totally miserable. I will be fine. I promise you on this. I have wanted to earn my doctorate for a long time, and I am now going to do this. Let me focus on this for a few years and then I can perhaps look deliberately for my dream girl. I will come back to Australia, I promise. Don't worry about me. God will look after me. I am more worried about you, to be truthful."

The conversation ended there as Frank gasped for breath and Betty motioned to Mark that she would calm Frank down alone. Mark clasped his Father's arm and leaned over and kissed him on the cheek. "Thank you for being the best Father a 'fella could ever wish for!'"

Mark left their bedroom and headed for the pines. The neat tidy cubby holes that Mark and Gary formed years ago were no longer possible as the branches closer to ground level had all disappeared and the lowest branches were now too high for Mark to reach. So, he sat down and leaned up against one of the trunks, sighed deeply and closed his eyes to listen to the wind moving through the trees. He tried to think of nothing of any consequence, but this tactic failed. What was hammering at his conscience was the reality that he was not close to God anymore. He still believed fervently, although he had let go gradually of that daily walk instilled in him from childhood. So often the pastor of St. Michael's eulogized from the pulpit "talk daily to Christ and you will never pay for advice from a professional counselor." It was the Old Lutheran way, and Frank and Betty had sought faithfully to infuse this Christian assurance into the ethos of each of their children. Mark had lived it for so long and it had saved him from many a pitfall over the years. It was his inner voice, but he had paid less and less attention to it and let it slide into the recesses of his mind. He knew when this occurred: it was when he had obsessively pursued his desire to master smooth jazz and the tenor saxophone. Those umpteen rushed trips from HMS *Cerberus* to Melbourne seeking out the jazz scene in the smoky night clubs may have produced a pseudo-jazz virtuoso, but it came at a cost. Mark, in fact, surrendered much of who he was as a person. He became caught up in the manic infatuation of an art form and it dominated his personality for a time. He could see it now. He was living for himself, and this was not his early intention. If life is a gift from God, then it is best lived by being useful to others. Mark determined to refocus.

Frank died a week later and the whole Hahndorf community came to the funeral. Betty was stalwart and dignified in her grief. The four Schubert siblings were there to support their mother and each other. They lingered at the graveside while the community withdrew to the church hall for the wake. Gary suggested that they sing one of their favorite hymns before they left the cemetery. *Praise to the Lord, the Almighty* was one of the great Lutheran Pietistic hymns, and it had been sung in their home innumerable times, and in the two Lutheran churches of Hahndorf. As the grieving family came to the last words of the third stanza, they held each other tight: *"Ponder anew what the Almighty can do if with His love He befriend thee."*

Mark remained on the farm for one more month. The family finances were healthy as Betty and Gary had shared in the stewardship of the Schubert farm and its investments with Frank for years. Betty was a strong and beautiful Christian woman with many years ahead of her. Mark knew he could now leave confident that Gary and his sisters would care for their mother. On his last evening at the farm, he went into his father's study and played hymns on his euphonium for about an hour. The next day, as he walked across the tarmac to board the plane at the Adelaide West Beach airport, Mark felt again the pangs of selfishness in leaving his family to further his own career path. Nonetheless, he knew his family was proud of him and wanted him to continue the course that was charted for him thirty years earlier. This thought both humbled and comforted him as the plane soared into the skies above Adelaide.

CHAPTER NINE

THE AMERICAN EXPERIENCE

*"Many people will walk in and out of your life,
But only true friends leave footprints in your heart."*
—Eleanor Roosevelt

It occurred to Mark, as his flight landed at Dulles International Airport in Northern Virginia, that he had been travelling for almost thirty hours with very little sleep. He was too alert to do any more than doze after leaving Los Angeles. Nonetheless, as he gathered his luggage and musical instruments from the luggage carousel, weariness threatened to overcome him. Added to this, he needed a shower, a shave, and was certainly not in the mood for rousing his charming self as he met his hosts who were taking him to the United States Naval Academy. Yet, appreciating that their kindness was distinctly for his benefit, he reached inside his exhausted frame and, as he emerged through the electronic doors to the gathered public, his endearing nature took over. Glenn and Clive were Naval cadets who worked in Transportation as the work component of their naval course. They had been waiting for two hours and Mark soon learned how far they had travelled to meet him in the heat of summer.

It was Thursday evening in mid-July and Washington, DC was a flurry of activity everywhere Mark looked. Traffic was flowing in ways it only does in the United States. Mark commented on the orderliness and functionality he saw as the van continued to approach the Mall. He was getting the scenic drive to the Academy. He asked Glenn and Clive question after question as they left DC for Maryland and headed eastbound toward Annapolis on US-50. It was almost dark when the van entered the gates of the Naval Academy. Mark was checked in and taken to his guest quarters where he collapsed on the bed so thankful to have finally arrived at his new location. He mustered the energy for a shower and then got into bed and was asleep within minutes.

The next day began Mark's *American Experience.* Over a five-year sojourn, he would complete his PhD at Johns Hopkins University and mature into the *military* musician he had contemplated years earlier. He used the term *military* because he would have to say professional *novice* otherwise. Mark knew what he meant, although it sounded like a contradiction of terms. Prior to joining the Royal Australian Navy Band in Melbourne, Mark was a high school music teacher who had risen from the fading columns of Australian rural brass bands. There was no question that he had excelled to become a national euphonium champion and went on to be the first university graduate in his family. His years with the Hahndorf Town Band, Kensington & Norwood, Kew City were thoroughly enjoyable and they each helped to fashion and shape Mark as he became a *military musician.* This may not have happened had he stayed married to Roslyn. Maybe more to the point, he played an instrument that was out of step with modern times. A trumpet or trombone would have connected Mark to contemporary music, but he intentionally chose the euphonium. Certainly, he could play some trombone, but his leap toward the saxophone and his frenetic enthrallment with jazz while at HMS *Cerberus* meant that he never did transcend the trombone as an instrument. Thus, Mark saw himself as a traditional musician and a highly competent clinician of the euphonium, but not a truly professional specialist, especially as he began to compare himself with the barrage of euphonium players he was now meeting.

Here was the difference. Mark's world expanded exponentially from his first day at the Naval Academy and, a few days later, at the Peabody Conservatory. Back home, each progressive step forward with his music was considered and manageable. In his new setting, it truly was a *barrage,* an encounter of size and force with the best, so many of them jostling for position and recognition, yet with a civility which made them peers in a joint quest for excellence in music. Such individuals invariably had master's degrees, and increasingly doctorates, in euphonium or their specialty instrument. He was fascinated by the perspicacity of Americans and their endless drive to take matters to the very boundaries of what is possible. He found that euphonium players in some regions were beginning to enter the jazz arena and even that of experimental music. He would have dismissed this advance only a few years ago. Perhaps this was why he was a traditional military musician.

It was all very humbling for Mark to be among the best of musicians and music programs anywhere in the world. The good news was that Mark was placed by the Naval Academy so that he could taste as much of the American banding realm as possible. His exchange assignment was deliberately flexible. He was assigned to the Naval Band cohort and the Marching Band. However, within that arrangement were conducting duties and a relief player position which would have Mark assigned on short notice to play in other United States Navy or military bands, usually on the East Coast. He could hardly believe his luck with such a posting. Over his five years, he would travel much farther than the Atlantic coast; sometimes he was assigned to ship duty and sometimes to San Diego and Seattle. From the Navy perspective, Mark was a stable, single male who had few personal obligations. He rarely said No! Hence, his assignment was mutually beneficial.

Mark's rich and rewarding mission continued at Johns Hopkins University and the Peabody Conservatory. In his exploratory visit to the University the previous year, Mark was pleased to discover that he could earn both a Master of Music degree in conducting and euphonium and then continue to a Doctor of Philosophy from a joint program with the Graduate School and the Conservatory. He had a scholarship for his doctoral program, but he had to self-fund his master's degree. He did not mind and argued that he had only himself to please, and besides he was drawing both his salary from the Royal Australian Navy and an annual gratuity coming from the family farm enterprise. When combined, Mark knew he had the finances to tackle both degrees.

The far more significant question was, did he have the time? He had five years: ordinarily a full-time graduate student would be struggling to complete both a master's and a doctorate degree in this time frame. Mark's standard response to his skeptics became "I must put the pedal to the metal; I *will* finish in five years. " One major advantage was that some credit was awarded to his master's degree from his Melbourne University Master of Music degree completed five years earlier. He had persevered to finish this degree in the middle of his divorce, teaching and working on his media projects. Now, his agonized exertion was realized. Ultimately, it was the very concession which permitted Mark to complete both degrees in his allotted time span.

For his doctorate, he was granted permission to embark on a multi-disciplinary degree program. Mark would combine history, education and music to research a comparative study on the influence of community bands on music education in Australia and selected states of Virginia, Maryland and Delaware. This became his dissertation topic and enabled Mark to delve into communal aspects as to why community bands were established in the nineteenth century and how new competing factors led to the demise of so many of these same bands in both countries after World War II. A parallel focus was the development of music education at the state levels of K-12 education in Australia and the three East Coast states. For years Mark had pondered and lived around the edges of these themes. At last, he had the opportunity to become somewhat of a resident expert on these besetting questions. He convinced himself that his research outcomes would be good for Australian education and the Australian Defence Force as he became a reinvigorated champion for community music programs throughout the nation at a time when both funding and programs were diminishing.

Mark was a natural student and it was easy to retrieve and reestablish his monastic tendencies. He was renting a two-bedroom apartment in Eastport and, from his desk, he could look across the water to Old Town Annapolis and the Naval Academy. In his eyes, it must have been one of the prettiest urban vistas a person could ever wish for. Nevertheless, he understood that he would have limited moments to leisurely indulge in the panorama from his desk. He was going to be busy and had to keep his wits about him with time management and lifestyle efficiency like he had never known before. He had bought a current model Buick Regal two-door and this two-tone gray beauty would be his reliable transportation for five years. Mark would put one hundred and fifty thousand miles on the odometer, and most of this was tripping from Annapolis to Baltimore to Washington, DC.

Each day began in devotional time with his God. Part of maximizing his full strength was to include his spiritual side and he knew that he owed it to his father to be faithful in this endeavor. Indeed, he had brought with him several of Frank's books, beginning with Leslie Weatherhead's *The Transforming Friendship: A Book about Jesus and Ourselves*. It was a very old book written when Frank was a child, but Mark cherished it, as he had grown up with its many stories. Frank had also cautioned Mark to only read the early works of Weatherhead, saying, "He goes off the rails in his later years!"

By six o'clock, Mark was out on the streets of Eastport for his morning exercise and on the road to either the Naval Academy or Hopkins within the hour. He established his routine and slavishly maintained long days every day, except for Sunday. When he was not away with his musical obligations, Mark was in church and soon he was teaching Bible classes to Lutheran teenagers. The weeks turned into months and the glorious colors of fall gave way to the cold and snow flurries and the dead of winter. Mark had never known such cold and curbed his jogging, which had diminished to a hop-skip-and-jump exercise over snow and ice, for personal safety as much as the piercing chill of the wind from across the Chesapeake. At first, he found the snow exhilarating and walked whenever he could, even when the snow was falling hard and driven by the wind into his face. Driving in snow was a learning experience and he soon came to appreciate that the winter months had to be endured, but there was always the promise of spring. As March came nigh, there was anticipation in the air as the days became brighter, birds were heard again and, one day, Mark saw buds on the trees. His birthday fell on the first week of April and this was the expectant epoch in the calendar year when the cherry blossoms burst upon the Tidal Basin in the nation's capital. Cherry blossom trees were everywhere in Maryland too, and Annapolis was alive with the colors and sounds of spring. Mark had never viscerally participated in a change of seasons as he did in his first spring in Maryland. The sheer joy and intoxicating madness of it all did, honestly, throw him off balance with his strict daily regimen. He knowingly spent more time outdoors and reveled in the daffodils, crocuses, tulips, rhododendrons and the long-lasting azaleas, which bloomed well into May. In his letters home to his mother and family, Mark extolled the beauties of the season and vigorously apologized for his photos which "didn't even come close in showing the color and magnificence of the season."

With the end of April and the beginning of May came the plethora of graduations which continued across the education spectrum for two months or more. Again, Mark witnessed the American spirit at work as sons and daughters, men and women, of all ages celebrated their academic prowess by wearing their academic regalia on their proud day. Parties followed, and Mark was astounded to see walls of graduation cards bought from Hallmark stores and supermarkets. Australia with its small population and less established traditions and practices could not hope to compete, but Mark did think his own country would gain from an injection of American-type pride and patriotism.

The observance of ANZAC Day was a definite link to Australian national pride. ANZAC Day dawn services were convened in Washington, DC, near the Lincoln Memorial and at the Korean War Memorial. The Australian Embassy invited Mark to attend and he arrived before the dawn service began. It was always a commemorative service in memory of those Australian and New Zealand troops who had paid the ultimate sacrifice in the First World War, and every war thereafter. On the lighter side, it was enjoyable to reconnect with living, breathing Australians and New Zealanders, and to hear their accents and irreverent shenanigans. Each year, Mark was always glad he had rallied his tired body so early to attend this *in remembrance* gathering. At his first appearance, he was startled by the sight of a Mall he did not know; one shrouded in early morning mist and emptiness. As he walked past the eerie statuary shapes of Korean War G.I. soldiers in their wet weather gear, he looked forward to heading back to Annapolis to his favorite diner for a greasy breakfast and a long cup of coffee.

After his meal, Mark returned to his studies. The semester was rapidly drawing to a close and he had papers to complete. Because he was slow with word processing, Mark had found a good typist, and this meant that he had to complete his work ahead of most of his fellow class mates. When the semester ended, he was glad for a couple of weeks of respite before he began his full-load of summer coursework. The cycle continued, and he completed his Masters' degree in the fall semester, at the same time beginning his doctoral studies with a refresher course in German.

Three years later, Mark was feeling very comfortable with American life, his work at the Naval Academy, study at Hopkins and his Lutheran church. He was playing his euphonium four times a week over and above the rehearsal schedule for his two assigned ensembles. While the saxophone had taken a decidedly second place, it was not forgotten. Mark had consistently attended church and, in fact, had become a key person in youth ministries. In his second year in Annapolis, at one brain-storming session to derive new endeavors to keep the youth connected with church life, Mark suggested the formation of a small concert band, with the thought that a jazz group might evolve as the teenagers showed their talent and enthusiasm for music. The church was grateful for Mark's expertise and his willingness to "begin band" at St. Paul's. The one negative aspect was that he emphasized that in two years, or three at the most, he would be returning to Australia. Thus, forming this musical program was predicated on church leadership finding someone to continue as sponsor after Mark departed. When this was agreed to, Mark invested good energy and time in the first class of brass players. The first ten weeks of the initial class took Mark back almost thirty years to the days when he sat, with his mates, under Mr. Paech's tutelage. The sheer accomplishment of being able to blow a clear note was still vivid in Mark's memory. Several of his Naval Academy colleagues gave invaluable assistance and the brass section soon saw the inclusion of woodwind and percussion players too. Nine months later, the first venture into carol playing to raise funds for the church school, saw the fledgling concert band assemble on the streets of Annapolis for ten play-outs. It was cold, but the energy of these fifteen young musicians was arresting, and they received an encouraging reception from neighbors, friends and visitors alike. Collectively, the funds raised exceeded $2,000. The whole venture was lauded as a success by the church and the Annapolis community. In fact, many of the small businesses along Main Street openly praised the St. Paul's musicians for increasing their Christmas sales by adding to the festive spirit of the buying public. The band was overwhelmed by the generous supply of hot chocolate and cookies that came its way at each playout. The following Christmas season saw even more enthusiasm by the band, church members, community, and Annapolis business owners, and the amount of funds escalated to over $5,000. The group was featured on television and in several newspaper articles.

Mark was rightfully pleased with the band's success. He grew it to a concert band of forty young musicians and it had a positive influence on St. Paul's as a church. It was also a community band with several parents joining to play alongside their teens, and even the pastor dusted off his clarinet and played when time permitted. Some of the teenage players were not of St. Paul's, but found a place of meaning as they learned music through the rigor of practice and emulating a player better than themselves. Mark did not do all this alone. He had an active band committee, and these adult musicians and church members gave of their time, energy and means to ensure that the young band knew it had support, supervision and cheer leaders at practice, at church, on parade and at concerts throughout the year.

Mark used the St. Paul's band to gather data for his dissertation. It was the test instrument against his comparative data of selected Australian community bands and the American bands in three states. These were splendid and rich days for Mark, and they kept him breathlessly busy. His life revolved around the Naval Academy, Johns Hopkins and St. Paul's. He lived, ate, breathed and slept music in his work, his study and his avocation. He had no time for a personal life outside these all-consuming pursuits. Sometimes, usually at night in the sanctified moments before sleep, he would ponder before God exactly what was ahead in the way of a companion. Would he ever find the love of his life? At these moments, he envied his parents, his brother and sisters. They had realized the bliss of true togetherness in a life partner. Sleep always overtook him before he could feel reproach.

Fortunately, Mark's time in the United States was not entirely devoid of family. Betty came over for one Christmas and New Year's, and she savored the cold of the season as opposed to the heat of an Australian Christmas. She loved the caroling with the St. Paul's band and afterwards walking Main Street with its lights, the festive windows and the hustle and bustle of shoppers reveling in Christmas cheer. Her favorite adventure was driving into Washington, D.C., and around the Mall in the early evening, and seeing the magnificence of the monuments amidst the colored lights and decorations of Christmas. Mark's last year, while he was writing his dissertation, Gary and Helen brought Betty with them and during the month of June, they took a long road trip to New England, across into Michigan and then back to Maryland via Indiana, Ohio and Pennsylvania. It took them almost three weeks, and as Gary said, "We can be grateful for Grandpa and Dad in paying for this trip from our successful farm." Mark insisted, as a car load of farmers, on a visit to Lancaster and the Amish region of Pennsylvania. They rode the vintage steam train and then took a buggy ride along the roads of Amish farms as they listened intently to their guide impart a plethora of information that, in so many ways, paralleled their own beginnings as religious immigrants to Hahndorf. Mark made sure that they ate at a typical Pennsylvania-Dutch restaurant and understood what American *comfort food* was about. Betty commented as they emerged from the restaurant, "Not that much different from good ole' German cooking from Hahndorf; just so much of it. Can you believe the size of those helpings?" It was good for Mark to have his family with him for a while.

However, when they departed and returned to Australia, Mark felt their absence viscerally. He experienced acute homesickness, but more to the point, he had two unscheduled major Navy band events in San Francisco and then Seattle thrust upon him. Both required mastering new scores quickly. The family visit had put Mark behind in his dissertation writing, although he could compensate for this. What threw him way off schedule was the two West Coast events. He would lose an additional two weeks of critical dissertation focus. For several days, he languished and accomplished virtually nothing. He could feel the onslaught of panic and the foreboding, sinking sensation if he should not complete his dissertation on time. He knew that he had to be back in Australia by June of next year, just under twelve months.

He did not sleep well that night. He awoke early and walked the streets of Eastport, over the bridge and up to the Maryland Capitol building, as the first rays of daybreak streaked across the government buildings. Suddenly, he knew what he must do: he jogged to the Naval Academy, past the Chapel, in front of Bancroft Hall, and down along the water front to the intersection of the Severn River and Annapolis Harbor. Here, under a row of trees, was Mark's favorite place at the Academy for quiet reflection. It had none of the secrecy of the pines escape on the farm, but it was a tranquil place with the therapeutic advantage of the sound of rippling waves coming in from the Chesapeake Bay. Mark was alone, and he closed his eyes and implored God to bring him calm and resolve.

"Are you Okay, Schub?" asked a concerned voice.

Mark sat upright abruptly and then stood up, startled that another person would be in this section of the Academy's grounds so early.

"Schulzy, for crying out loud, what are you doing here so early? You frightened four years of life out of me!"

"Perhaps I should ask you the same thing. Are you alright, Mark? You look as though you are either asking God for help or battling with Him on some matter!"

John Schulz, senior pastor at St. Paul's, had been one of the early supporters of Mark founding a band at his church four years ago. He was married and his two children were enthusiastically involved with the band. He motioned to Mark to take a few paces and join him lean-ing on the railing overlooking the rock wall and Annapolis Harbor.

"You know, my friend, I did not sleep well last night. I had that pas-tor's inkling that someone close to me was in trouble and needed me. I awoke this morning and said to Shirley that I needed to go for a jog to clear my head. I don't normally go onto the Academy grounds until it is truly functioning, but here I am and so are you. What's wrong, man? Do you want to talk?"

Mark looked at John. He put an arm on his shoulder and said: "You are a good friend, perhaps my best friend in America. I couldn't sleep much last night either. I just wanted to escape and retreat to my childhood fort under the pine trees on our farm. It's where I went when life was too much, and I always emerged with any problem or burden pretty much solved. I think it is where I learned to talk to God. But all that is back home and there is no cluster of pine trees in Annapolis. Yet, this is the spot that has taken its place. I often rest here on that bench half way through my run. Many times, I just close my eyes and thank God for His watch care over me. Sometimes I take my burdens to God right here in the early mornings. Just now, John, I am … I'm feeling overwhelmed by all the work ahead of me. These last two Navy jaunts have tipped me over the edge, and I feel I'm losing control and will run out of time before I finish my dissertation."

Pastor Schulz gestured to the bench: "Let's talk for a while, you, me and God. How did all this happen? Why do you feel you won't complete your thesis on time?"

Mark took a deep breath, looked at Schulzy with a wry smile and began. "This may be more than you bargained for, old buddy, but I am going to buy us coffee and donuts when we're through."

"Sounds like a good deal to me." replied John, "I'm here for you no matter what!"

"And, it is good to know that, John," said Mark, "I can't imagine what it would have been like if I had tried to tackle both the Naval Academy exchange and my doctoral work at Hopkins without St. Paul's in my life."

"I think ever since I was a ten-year old child, I was aware of my tendency to take on too much in everything I did. I felt the need to help Dad on the farm, to help Mum with the other kids or the cooking or house work. Then, when I started music, it was one more chore that I added to my daily and weekly list. I don't remember ever worrying about this or losing sleep, but I do recall Mum and Dad saying to each other that they wished I was not so intense about life. All I knew was that I was busy most of the time and I needed to be organized and to be able to work quickly and efficiently."

Mark went on, recounting his teen years, early work years at Luther College and his progression in the brass band world. His marriage was difficult for him to discuss, even though he had talked to John many times about snippets of married life with Roslyn. He spoke confidently of his decision to join the Navy band and of his success in music, competitions and the broadening experience of his public relations roles in Melbourne and Sydney. He glossed over his altercations with Alison Terkel and how this determined him to pursue his current posting at the Naval Academy and his doctoral program at Johns Hopkins. Lastly, he described how much his "ministry" at St. Paul's had meant to him personally and professionally.

"My father was a great one for giving back to God. He taught us kids that setting aside cracked egg money for St. Michael's was a privilege for us. We could spend it on ourselves and 'silly things,' as Dad called candy and trivial items, but week by week 'the pennies add up' and they can do 'mighty things when given over to God.'"

"Working with you, John, at St. Paul's has been like this. It has been a privilege and working in youth ministry has been my opportunity to give back to my church and its kids."

"I think it is just that I feel I have hit a brick wall and I must get beyond this. I know that I have been pushing it for over four years now and that I am tired *from* my constant routine with the Naval Academy and Hopkins, but I'm not tired *of* either assignment. I love what I do, and, if honesty is what you want to hear, I am angry at myself for getting into this bind over the last two weeks. Yep, I am angry at myself!"

With that, Mark made some apologetic comment about prattling on for too long and then sat quietly as he let out a huge sigh. John, too, sat for a moment and then he took Mark's arm and said, "Let's pray to our awesome Father in Heaven."

After prayer, John asked, "Can I ask you a very personal question?"

Mark replied with a grin on his face, "After all I have just told you, what else is there you need to know about me?"

"Mark, why are you not showing any interest in girls? I have known you for four years now and not once have I heard or seen you show any inclination in dating, or even being with a woman about your own age and stage in life?"

"Well, that is coming right to the point, isn't it? Is Shirley asking this too?"

"All your good friends are! We see one of the most decent men we know, and we all are baffled by the fact that you have everything to give to a relationship, except that you don't seem to know how to engage."

"Engage?" queried Mark. "That seems rather mechanical, don't you think? No, that's not fair of me. I know what you are asking, and I probably don't have an answer for you or me. I know that I have forced myself to be focused on my career and it has worked for years. I kid myself that I have been too busy with work to *engage*, as you say. To be truthful, I am afraid of beginning a relationship with another woman. Roslyn traumatized me and destroyed my idealistic view of dating and marriage. It's my problem and I have avoided the whole scene. Is it that obvious?"

John knew it was time to end this conversation, but he spoke reassuringly, "Put it this way, Mark, we think too much of you and believe you are a good-looking guy going to waste by your fixated devotion to your work and your degree. You deserve to know and to share real love and happiness. We believe the right girl is out there for you, but you must want to look. Now, let's go for that coffee and donut."

While Mark was appreciative of all his friends in the U.S. and in Australia, he was very grateful for a friend like John Schulz. John had given him a wake-up call and reminded him that he was not an island unto himself. Intuitively he knew this, but he was trying to cope through to the end as he had always done since his first band competition in Melbourne. Realistically, he was fully aware that in his most arduous times, when he was so intent on *battling it through* himself, he still had a cadre of supporters assisting on the sidelines. All the same, he rarely turned to them for support or strength. Many a time Mark would mutter under his breath, "Schubert, you are such a dope!" Strangely, such self-abnegation always made him feel better.

A week later, Mark had wrenched himself from his pitiful state. He was still in a predicament with his timeline to finish his dissertation, but his anxiety had gone. John helped immensely and so did constant prayers to God for calm and a sense of a way forward. Through a *eureka* moment one evening, Mark came upon a provision that he knew about but had not consciously thought of invoking until now. As an Australian in his nation's workforce, he was entitled to Long Service Leave after continuous, full-time work with the same employer for a decade. Mark had served in the Royal Australian Navy now for over eleven years. Technically, he was eligible, and upon application and approval, he could gain himself another three months to focus on completing his doctoral dissertation at Johns Hopkins University.

Mark applied for, and was granted, *long service leave*. This gave him the breathing room he needed—in fact, more than he needed. He worked with the Naval Academy and the Royal Australian Navy to reconfigure his original contract so that it would end on September 30 rather than December 31 of the present year. However, Mark agreed to be available for last-minute instrumentalist or conducting assignments over Thanksgiving and Christmas to New Year's. He considered this was the least he could do for the Naval Academy Band after his supervisors had made every effort to ensure he had a rich and varied sojourn while in Annapolis.

He determined to give of his best to the Naval Academy over the remainder of his agreement. Come September 30, Mark would continue to live in his apartment in Eastport for seven months with no required commitment to the Naval Academy Band. His full focus would be his dissertation. The St. Paul's band would be a pleasant distraction from the intensity of his doctoral writing. The sheer contemplation of this release gave Mark such elation he decided to take himself out to dinner that Tuesday evening.

It was a balmy evening in early fall as Mark walked across the Spa Creek bridge to the Main Street Circle to Marie's, an Italian restaurant looking onto Ego Alley where all the yachts of distinction moored while in Annapolis. He had been to Marie's a few times and had always enjoyed the food and the company of his friends. This time he was alone, but in good spirits; a weight had been lifted from his shoulders. He picked up the menu as the waitress approached.

"On your own tonight, Sir?" asked the attractive black-haired woman. "I will be your waitress this evening. My name is Christina. Can I get you something to drink?"

"Well, thank you, Christina. Yes, I am alone, but celebrating some extra time I have been granted to complete a major assignment. I can give you my full order now. I would like a glass of water and one of white wine, and the *Salmon alla Griglia*."

Mark didn't go out to eat very often, and when he did, he liked it to be fine dining in an upscale restaurant. Italian was a favored cuisine and salmon was his mother's favorite seafood. He smiled as his memory flashed back to the many summer evenings when the family ate fish 'n chips on Brighton Beach. They always stayed to watch the sun dip below the horizon across the Gulf of St. Vincent. There was therapy in watching a day come to its conclusion. Even more so when Frank and Betty gathered their children close with beach towels around them as the evening cooled. Frank spoke in a pastoral tone as he directed the family's thoughts away from the setting sun and towards the providence of a loving God who watches over His children all the days of their lives. Returning to the present, Mark tasted his wine and nodded in agreement about the wine and his memories, "They were truly wonderful times!"

As he completed his salad, he reached into his inner coat pocket and pulled an envelope from it. He read the letter a second time and spoke to himself, "I wonder if this now becomes possible?"

The letter was from the National Band Council of Australia. They were asking Mark to be an adjudicator at the Easter Nationals this next year. His return airfare would be paid as would his accommodation and this all came with a stipend. Had the letter arrived even three weeks ago, Mark would have summarily dismissed it as a needless distraction from his looming obligations in Maryland. However, Mark now had his extra time, plus the opportunity to return home to see his family for a week or so as he fulfilled his role as an adjudicator at the annual Australian brass band championships convening in Adelaide. It all pieced together so well. He read the letter a third time and determined that he could spare ten days to make this happen. His aim was to complete his dissertation by mid-January, with his defense sometime in February. This would leave adequate time for corrections and alterations, although he hoped these would be minimal. Besides, the rejuvenation this would bring to his weary body could begin immediately after Thursday evening's telephone call with the president of the National Band Council of Australia. Mark was feeling optimistic as his meal arrived.

His food was delicious. He had noticed Christina moving from table to table and admitted to himself that she was a fine woman; friendly, caring and beautiful too. She found time to check on Mark every few minutes and they were both smiling at each other as he continued his meal. He ordered a coffee and then she persuaded him to have "the best tiramisu on the East Coast." And it surely was good: moist, the right amount of coffee-flavored custard and mascarpone cheese. It complemented his coffee and Christina added one more virtue about the dessert, "it is real cocoa, not chocolate!"

As Christina came to collect Mark's payment, she noticed the substantial tip and blushed as she thanked him. She walked away, paused, and then returned.

"Mark, do you mind if I call you by name? I saw it on your credit card. Why is a good-looking, single man with a foreign accent—I would say Australian—eating alone in Marie's on a Tuesday night?"

Christina had noticed that most customers had left the restaurant and she decided in that moment to discover more about this man who looked only a few years older than herself.

Mark smiled and replied: "This single Australian—not sure about the looks department—is a musician on an exchange agreement between the Royal Australian Navy and the U.S. Naval Academy. I am also trying to complete my doctorate at John Hopkins University."

Feeling emboldened, Mark asked: "So, why is an attractive and smart woman, probably just a few years younger than me, working as a waitress at Marie's? Is this your full-time work, or is it a part-time job?"

Christina nodded seriously: "Fair question. I got divorced fifteen months ago. I was married to a major jerk and now I am working my tail off trying to complete my MBA degree in Marketing at the University of Maryland at the Baltimore County campus. Before that I was a United Airlines stewardess on the European hops, usually Germany and Italy. My mother is Italian."

"I am divorced too," responded Mark. "I'm trying to figure out the rest of my life."

Christina smiled: "Perhaps we should do it together!"

Mark stared into her dark eyes, stood up, placed his folded napkin on the table and replied: "Well, maybe, but not tonight, I have to get back to my writing. Thank you for a wonderful meal and for being so pleasant. ... Are you working on Friday? Perhaps I could stop by and see you."

"I work until 4:00 pm this Friday," said Christina, "If you come by, then you can buy me dinner. Oh, I am sorry, I didn't mean to be so forward."

It was Mark's turn to smile, "I didn't take it that way; I will see you at 4:00 pm and bring your appetite."

As Mark left the restaurant and walked back to his apartment in Eastport, it was dusk, though there was enough light to enjoy the reflections of boats and masts on the still waters of Spa Creek. He thought about the entire evening: the pleasant meal and flirtatious exchanges with an intriguing waitress, the letter and the opportunity it gave Mark to see family, and reopen contacts in the Australian music, education and public relations arenas. He was beginning to see that he must make this trip home. He sighed with satisfaction: It had been a superb evening!

With the light at the end of a tunnel no longer a speeding train, Mark returned to his dissertation with renewed enthusiasm. His research was complete, his data had been gathered, and he had finished his introduction, literature review and methodology chapters. Now he had to organize and conclude the writing up of his research and his findings in the last two chapters of his study. He labored to clarify his assumptions and the limitations of his study. Clearly, there were several areas of research which would add to his current dissertation. It was not easy keeping his bibliography in order, and worst of all, he was reliant on a professional typist and the frequent meetings this involved.

By Friday, Mark had mapped out his new schedule, with the completion of his dissertation projected for mid-January. The Easter championships were at the end of March, and he would graduate in mid-May and be back in Australia permanently by early June. On paper, at least, it looked good.

Mark met Christina outside Marie's just after 4:00 pm. It was a cloudy afternoon, but soon they were in his car, driving to her apartment so Christina could freshen up for their outing. They both laughed when Christina asked Mark if he was taking her on a date. A date it was, and they were both happy for it to be so. Mark suggested seafood for dinner at a restaurant just on the Eastern Shore side of the Chesapeake Bay Bridge. Christina agreed. The drive took them thirty minutes. In the summer months, this could have taken over ninety minutes with the Ocean City beach weekend traffic. Mark was always in awe of crossing the Bay Bridge. Almost three miles long, it was one of the longest in the world. At the restaurant they found a table outdoors looking back at the bridge.

Dinner was long and slow, and while they enjoyed their food, it was superfluous to their conversation. For over two hours they shared their stories and laughed, but at times the conversation took a turn that drew on deeper emotions. At one point, Mark paused, and asked Christina if she would come to church with him one Sunday.

"Are you serious, Mark?" she asked.

"Yes, I am. I am a practicing Christian and it is an important part of my life."

"Wow, I guess that is Okay. I believe in God and was raised as a Methodist, but I thought most people our age had given up on going to church regularly a long time ago."

Mark thought carefully before he replied, "Well, I have not been the best example of a consistent Christian at times, but over the last half dozen years it has become my rock and stability. It is now as natural to seek to walk with God daily as it is to breathe. I know that can sound corny, but my life goes better this way."

Christina moved awkwardly in her seat, "Well, you have said it. I have become so accustomed to bumbling along on my own, I suppose I am a believer in making my own way in life as best I can and then one day you die."

Mark replied quickly, "But, isn't that sad? It's all up to you ... and then you die, either having had a good life or one of misery."

"I guess it is sad, if you think of it that way. You are telling me that no matter what happens in your life, you don't feel alone."

"That's right," said Mark, "I feel that God is with me every day. Sure, I still find time to get into too much trouble, but every morning and every night, I thank Him for being with me."

"You mean to tell me, that tonight after our date, you are going to thank God for being with you?"

"Yep, that's right. For being with us on our first date," Mark stated with a final resolve.

They sat together quietly, and just enjoying the feeling of being together. When they walked back to Mark's car and he opened the door for her, they embraced and kissed for the first time. Then, they kissed again and again. Both breathed deeply, and Christina kissed Mark again.

"Man alive," said Mark, "Is this what I have been missing all these years?"

"Believe me," whispered Christina, "There is this and much more waiting for you!"

Mark straightened. "I can see that, but let's not discover it all at once."

As they drove back to Christina's apartment she said, "Will I see you again, soon?"

Standing outside her apartment, Mark smiled and sighed. "I've got to work solidly this next week on my dissertation," he said. "Don't you have a term paper due soon too?"

"Let me give you my phone number," Christina said, as she rummaged in her purse for pen and paper. "And here is mine," replied Mark. "Good night," he whispered. He leaned in for a kiss as she looked up and smiled. As he drove back to Eastport, Mark was still shaking his head and smiling over his first date in almost fifteen years.

As the morning sun shook the shadows from the buildings and brought recognition to all things familiar, Mark was still analyzing the night before. He spent a longer time jogging the streets of his neighborhood and was so deep in thought that he narrowly missed a cyclist threatening to cut him off through sheer over-exuberance. He had to admit, he did enjoy the time with Christina. They had shared a lot of their lives with each other and the intimacy was amazing. No, it was pleasurable and arousing. "All well and good," sounded his logical voice, "but you have a dissertation to complete and you owe it to the Naval Academy to give them the best you have in the remaining few weeks of your exchange program. Then, my friend, in eight months you are back in Australia."

Mark was fully aware of the complexities Christina could bring to his newly-structured life. The possibilities of new-found companionship and further intimacy were alluring; even so, his overarching goal, yea mandate, was to conclude all his obligations in Maryland and to be back in either Sydney or Melbourne in early June. His new appointment from the Royal Australian Navy Bands would come in the next month or two since he was returning mid-year.

With that settled, Mark embarked on the busy, pre-holiday season with Navy band commitments, writing his dissertation and waiting for the telephone to ring. Christina took the lead in this budding relationship and would often call, seeking times and places when they could meet, eat together and further their friendship. Mark coaxed her to go with him to St. Paul's on Sundays and she did, admitting that "some decent religion" would do her no harm. She was surprised to witness Mark's involvement with the church programs and the endearment expressed by children, teenagers and older church members. It gave her pause to question if she wanted this level of religious commitment. She knew Mark had his answer, "This is more than a commitment, it is my chosen direction in life." For her, however, much of it was foreign and a stalemate for a *laissez faire* lifestyle she could neither defend nor explain.

Mark encouraged church attendance as he needed John's approval of Christina. Pastor Schulz was rather non-committal, but he did acknowledge her attractiveness. He said: "I know I encouraged you to look, but just remember in less than eight months you are returning to the Land of Oz. So, she doesn't have to be the one!"

In many respects, this was good advice for Mark and the next six weeks saw the couple dine once a week, often in Washington, DC on the Mall and the Smithsonian, or even at the University of Maryland while Christina did some research on her interminable paper due in early December. Mark, himself, had previous commitments for Thanksgiving as well as on Christmas Day. His continued single status made his offer to be available over major holidays a valued option by the Navy Band in filling the inevitable gaps of musician absences. On Thanksgiving he was aboard an aircraft carrier in Japan and by Christmas, he was in San Diego. Christina understood and went home to Philadelphia for both holidays.

A snow storm greeted Mark as he landed at Baltimore-Washington International Airport the day after New Year's. Gone was the balmy weather of San Diego and the salubrious sailing of the previous two days with a group of boisterous fellow sailors. The drive from the airport on I-97 was slow and treacherous. The Navy van inched along as commuters grimly squinted through the snow towards Annapolis. Mark took in the scene wistfully, knowing this was his last winter living in and around snow. He was going to miss the distinctly different four seasons he had come to appreciate. His farm roots endowed him with a deep sense of awe and gratitude for the visual delights each season brought. Winter caused Mark the most adjustment because, while Australia may have its snowfields, no capital city had snow that settled in the streets and created mayhem for regular living. He knew he was going to miss winter, fall and spring. Summer was not so different in either country.

Mark was glad when the van pulled up at his apartment, even though he could see there was some shoveling ahead of him. Once inside, he opened the mail which had accumulated over the past week. One letter was from the Music Department of the Royal Australian Navy and contained details of his new appointment. He was going to Melbourne as the newly-appointed director of public relations for the Royal Australian Navy Band and, secondly as an associate musical director for the Melbourne Navy band. Mark almost jumped out of his chair as he read the words from the Musical Director. He was asked to create a whole new interface in Navy bands and to be responsible for bringing Navy music to the Australian public. His assignment to the Melbourne Navy Band, a new position, would require a unique, visionary, strategic plan ensuring that all six Australian Navy Bands were reaching the public to the greatest possible extent. Though his job description was still in general terms at this stage, he was tasked with putting together greater structure and definition to his new appointment when he arrived in September. Mark went to bed that night a happy man, even if he still had his dissertation to complete.

The next two weeks saw Mark put the finishing touches to his 210-page dissertation. He intended to use it as the basis for a book within the year, but for now he was glad to have it finished. Next came the final approval from his major professor and his defense before his committee. This was an important milestone in his life, and he entered the small committee room for his defense somewhat apprehensively, but he was consoled by the remark of the sole Navy officer on his committee three weeks earlier: "Just remember, Mark, you know more about your dissertation than the committee, so be confident with this fact!"

An hour later, Mark was asked to be excused while the committee made their decision. When he was called back in, it was to the greeting of "Congratulations, Dr. Schubert!" Mark's most demanding and vexing goal thus far in his life had now been achieved. He had very little correction to do in the follow-up phase. He remembered hearing nightmare stories out there of considerable corrections and rewriting. He had a renewed appreciation for the careful revisions he had made along the way and for the close, collaborative association he had had with his advisor.

After a casual lunch with his committee, he walked to his car and sat for a few minutes. He thanked God for guiding and watching over him while in the United States. He was somewhat numb and unable to grasp the reality of having completed his doctoral degree as he started the car and drove back to Annapolis. That night Christina cooked him a meal and then gave him a gift in celebration of his successful defense. As they sipped their wine and cuddled on the couch, Mark suddenly sat up and said, "Christina, I have something to tell you. Remember, I told you before Christmas that I may be going home for the Easter National championships. Well, I now have the official word that I *am* going. I will be leaving in three weeks from tomorrow and will be gone for ten days."

"Mark, you have got to be kidding!" Christina exclaimed. "You were gone for Thanksgiving, Christmas, and now this? When you get back, I'll be cramming for semester exams, and then in June you'll be heading back to Australia for good! When do we get to know if we are going to make it as a couple? When? Just tell me when?"

With that, she stormed into the kitchen and began slamming around pots and pans. Christina's reaction was justified, and Mark knew it. He had been covertly using his work obligations as a means of gaining more time in trying to understand his own emotions and intentions toward her. He had no doubt that this was one of the reasons why he had suppressed all potential dating or romantic dalliances of any kind. He was not good at being a charmer, a smooth dude or an instant success with the ladies. It was why he so often came home and went into his father's study and played his euphonium after the flirtation on the school bus from Mount Barker to Hahndorf. It is why he never wanted to linger after church or to play tennis on Saturday afternoons on the Hahndorf Reserve courts in summer, or to loll around on the lawns at university between lectures, or to wander away from the group with a girl at the beach or the Royal Adelaide Show.

He had always been busy, preoccupied with chores, projects, family, music and life in general since childhood. Most of the time he was content to be alone. When he was not, he knew how to avoid confronting what was bothering him. Wherever he was, Mark would retreat within himself to his fantasy world, conjure up an image of the Schubert farm and of a community exactly like Hahndorf, always under the ultimate protection of his Lutheran God. These were the realities and images he could rely upon.

Now, as an adult approaching mid-life, Mark knew enough to recognize that he exhibited aspects of avoidance personality disorder. He felt a lack of confidence in forming intimate personal relationships. With Roslyn, she was in charge from the beginning and Mark could sense that the same was becoming apparent with Christina. What caused this stress and anxiety in forming a close bond with a female? Mark had never taken the time to analyze the cause of his reactions. He acknowledged there was a problem and recognized that it had something to do with his adoration for his immediate family unit. Perhaps he was afraid that no one else could aspire to the heights of the pedestal on which he placed his family. If this was true, then the problem was his. Nonetheless, at this very moment, he stood in Christina's kitchen and had to fix the Pandora's box he had created over the last few months.

He walked over to Christina and took her in his arms and held her as she resisted at first and then relaxed in his firm embrace. After several minutes, she said: "Sometimes I wish we had never met. I want a man who needs me and loves me. I am not sure you know how to do either."

Mark sighed deeply and then led them to the sofa and they both sat down. He began slowly and gently: "Christina, I am afraid to love again."

He took her hands in his and said, "Look, today, I passed my dissertation defense. I can hardly believe that it is all done. I am sure that I have been too preoccupied all this time. Let's see if we can't have a fun time over the next few weeks getting to know each other better. Can we just concentrate on being good friends? I can help you complete your paper. I will go to Australia and adjudicate in the Easter Nationals, see my mother and family and then come back to you. Then, we can really focus on our relationship."

Christina teared up as she peered into Mark's eyes. "Yes, yes we can. We owe it to ourselves not to rush whatever is ahead of us." Then she stood on tiptoe, kissed him, and walked him to the door.

Mark returned to his apartment with mixed emotions. He should have been experiencing tremendous relief—and he was, as it related to his academic life. He had finished his doctorate and was now Dr. Mark Schubert, pending the official conferral. It sounded good, but the Christina factor was on his mind. Did he like her enough to return to the United States and call it home for the rest of his days? This was an irksome question. He did not know what his answer would be in a year or two and it would take him that long, maybe even longer, to work through the complexities of returning permanently to Maryland or elsewhere on a Green Card. What he did know with increasing certainty was a deep desire to settle down and develop some semblance of stability and predictability in his life.

A week later, Mark had his annual physical at the Naval Academy. He expected it to be routine and was apprehensive when he received a phone call a few days later that he had to return for more tests. A few days after these additional tests, he was again called to the doctor's office. His doctor looked at him gravely and said: "Mark, I have been a physician for thirty years and the conversation you and I are going to have now never seems to get easier. I guess it is because I like people and I like helping them experience their optimum health and strength. I need to inform you that you have prostate cancer. I will work with you and we will get you through this. We need to schedule more tests to know more about the cancer and how to deal with it. As a fellow Navy man, I am sorry to give you this news."

Mark looked at his doctor in disbelief. He had heard the words, but they did not make sense. *He had what? Where did this come from? He did not have time for this nonsense? Cancer! That can kill you!* He leaned forward and stared at the floor without seeing it, collecting his thoughts. Suddenly, he sat upright and looked at his doctor.

"I can't believe this! How did it happen? I am going home to Australia for ten days in one week's time. I don't have time for this."

"Mark, it is going to take time for you to absorb what I have just told you. We must do more tests and I can arrange for these to be done in two days. Then, we will know more and can talk about what steps we will have to take together. I have already spoken to the urologist I want to work with us. We can give you a full report on Friday after the tests on Thursday. "

"Should I not go to Australia?" asked Mark in a calmer tone. "I am adjudicating at the Easter National championships in my home city, but I guess I can arrange something else if need be," he said resignedly.

Mark's doctor came around from behind his desk and put an arm around his shoulders, "I think it may be a good thing for you to go to Australia. It is only ten days. When you come back, we can arrange a schedule for you. I am sorry, but life is not always a silk road. The good news is that your life is not threatened."

"No, you are right there," replied Mark, "but my way of life will forever be changed. I can't believe that I have cancer." The enormity of what he had just been told was beginning to sink in.

"Yes, you have cancer, but we will deal with it!" said the doctor reassuringly. "Let me suggest a few things to help you cope with all this. Go somewhere now and be kind to yourself as you take in all that we have talked about this morning. Then, go tell your most intimate friends. I know you are a single man in a foreign country, and this will not be easy for you. This is the reason returning home to family in Australia will be good for you. You won't feel so alone."

"One more thing before you go, Mark. A big plus to all of this is that you and I are fellow Christians. We have God on our side as we tackle the big C!"

The two men shook hands and Mark walked out through the corridors and to his car. Rather than leaving the Naval Academy grounds, he walked on to his place of contemplation; the seat where Spa Creek intersected the Severn River. This was Mark's open-air refuge and he sat for over an hour. The myriad of emotions that rushed through his mind and body threatened to overwhelm him. He felt selfish, he was angry, he breathed heavily, he looked out into the Bay and asked, *"Why me at this stage of life?"* After a long time, Mark knew that he owed it to Schulzy to tell him about the medical prognosis. He drove to St. Paul's and met John in the nave of his church polishing the brass fittings. They talked, and John put his arm around Mark and prayed out loud for God's peace and comfort to descend upon his friend. They talked for a long time and Mark concluded that this was yet another obstacle in life to overcome with God by his side. John's last words were "Go to the Psalms, for there you'll find peace and strength," leaving Mark grateful for their friendship. On his way home, though, one thing he determined vehemently and that was not to tell Christina until after he returned from Australia.

That evening, Mark and Christina ate at the Chart House in Eastport with its wonderful view of Old Town Annapolis and the Naval Academy. It was situated right on Spa Creek and was part of Mark's jogging circuit he had used now for almost five years. So much had happened since coming to the Naval Academy and to Hopkins for his study program. He had matured in so many ways as a person, as a Christian, as a professional, and even as a traveler in the journey of life. The one arena where he needed a greater comfort level was in intimate relationships. It sounded so mechanical to think of it this way, and so Mark jolted himself out of his brooding and decided to enjoy his dinner with Christina, a truly attractive woman. Despite all he had learned today, he was, indeed, a fortunate man.

Thursday loomed as an eerie day for Mark. He knew that he was going to be prodded and invaded in parts of his anatomy that he considered his and his alone, by doctors and instruments. And it was as he imagined. At the end of the day, he just went home and sat in his small living room-cum-kitchen. He felt humiliated and wanted to return home to the farm and have no further medical treatments and let the damn cancer do what it may. He wanted to be alone and a bother to no one. Christina called and said that she was in the Mekeldon Library at College Park working on her paper with friends. He was glad to hear that and to know that she would not expect to meet with him that evening.

Mark intentionally chose his devotional reading on Friday morning to provide as much encouragement as possible before his revelatory meeting with his doctor and urologist. John had given him a book on the Psalms and suggested that Mark may find comfort as a single person from knowing more of the content and purpose of the Book of Psalms. As always, John proved to be correct for Psalms spoke so personally to its reader.

He read from Psalm 28:7 *"The lord is my strength and my shield; my heart trusts in him, and he helps me."* Mark read one more Psalm, but only partially, Psalm 40:3 *"He put a new song in my mouth ..."*. Mark *needed* a new song to help him cope with all that would transpire at his doctor's appointment.

His doctors were both caring and decent men and they took note of the fact that Mark was a single man of talent and accomplishment in the throes of returning to Australia permanently in a matter of months. Mark's PSA was elevated to 12 and the biopsy indicated that the cancer was in the fourth quadrant, but it had not spread beyond the prostate into the lymph nodes. Both doctors stated this was good news as it had not metastasized to other parts of the body. They recommended surgery as soon as possible—within three months.

To further assist Mark while in Australia, they gave him an envelope containing all pertinent test information about his cancer. They had even researched a recommended urologist in Adelaide and made initial contact with a Dr. Lawson. They asked Mark if this met with his approval. Immediately, Mark was appreciative and, together, they reviewed his travel schedule and agreed that the following Friday after arriving home would be ideal for the first appointment. Just like that, it was decided, and his doctors offered to make a firm appointment to take the pressure off Mark with all he had to do before his flight. They emphasized that delaying surgery would increase the risk of the cancer metastasizing. Between now and when Mark returned from his Easter trip home, there was nothing more to be done. Their advice was to go and have an enjoyable time with his music and family, and to come in for an appointment two days after he returned to Annapolis.

Mark was becoming accustomed to these significant meetings where the outcomes were dramatic and the results profound. Whether it was his farewell from the Navy Academy Band, his dissertation defense or now his prostate cancer report—all would affect life as it rolled out going forward.

He did, however, feel surprisingly calm and more resolute than he had thought might be the case. He would get beyond all this, but one thing was worth serious contemplation: he wanted to have the surgery done back home in Adelaide. He spent the afternoon digesting the details of what his doctors had explained and suggested to him, and tenaciously resolved that he would not divulge any of his medical issues to Christina for now. "That's right," he said to himself, "I have a medical issue." That evening he had a late supper at Marie's after Christina had completed her shift. She brought him a wonderful bowl of mushroom fettucine and they talked and savored each other knowing that come next Wednesday, Mark was off to Australia for ten days.

On Sunday, Christina accompanied Mark to St. Paul's, and they worshipped together. John and Shirley invited them home for lunch and they spent the afternoon in a real home with wholesome food, pleasant children and a husband and wife that Christina could see Mark adored and wished he could emulate in his own life. That evening, Mark and Christina walked along Main Street and around the Capitol grounds. They talked about her pending job for a marketing company in D.C. and how wonderful it would be for them both to graduate in May one week apart, enabling each to attend the other's graduation ceremony. Christina told Mark that she was moving to another apartment in two weeks and that she was going to share it with her sister who was starting a new job with the Maryland state government. In fact, Carol was arriving tomorrow, and they were going to look at the apartment one more time and then sign the rental agreement. Mark was pleased and suggested that all three go out for dinner on Tuesday night and that Carol come to the airport, since he was worried about Christina returning to Annapolis on her own. As Mark drove her back to her apartment, Christina leaned over and thanked him for being so caring. With her head on his shoulder, Mark parked in front of the apartment and they enjoyed a long, lingering kiss.

Mark spent Monday taking care of numerous small matters. He had several short meetings at the Naval Academy in the morning. He went shopping for several belated gifts for his family. He knew he would get his mother *See's Candy* at Los Angeles airport. He packed expeditiously knowing that he could wash his clothes at the farm. He requested his mail to be held for the duration of his trip and he wrote checks for some bills. He was ready to begin his journey across the Pacific. Nevertheless, his excitement level of anticipation seemed some-what anticlimactic because he was coming back to go home again in three months. And what about Christina? Mark buried the question for now. The next evening, he had a pleasurable dinner with Christina and her sister. Mark was picked up at mid-morning and taken to Dulles International Airport for the first leg of his homeward bound journey.

"Ladies and gentlemen, we are approaching Sydney International Airport and will be landing in fifteen minutes. Please make prepara-tion for landing. All seats must be returned to their upright position and you should ensure that you have your seat belts securely fastened."

The stewardess's announcement brought Mark quickly back into reality. He had been asleep, he did not know for how long, though looking at his watch it must have been over an hour.

"Sydney in fifteen minutes! Wow, Mum, I am almost home," Mark muttered to himself. He was nearly forty-one years old, but thinking of his Mum, made him feel like a teenager again. In just four hours he would be back in Hahndorf. It had been a long flight, but it was always an everlasting time from LAX to Australia. He felt his stubble-face and immediately longed for a shave and a shower. Perhaps he should have taken a day to rest and recuperate in Sydney. He had friends who would have gladly given him a bed for the night. Even so, he was mindful of his restricted timeframe. He had a lot to accomplish in eleven days before he caught the return flight back to Los Angeles. He knew that his mother and Gary, at least, would be at the Adelaide West Beach airport and after that he was less than an hour from the farm.

After clearing customs and immigration, Mark took the bus to the domestic terminal and went immediately to his gate and waited for the call to board his flight to Adelaide. He had time to call his mother from the pay phone.

"Hello, my Darlin', how are you? I'm in Sydney, waiting for the flight to Adelaide."

"Mark, is that you?" Betty Schubert asked excitedly. "I have been praying non-stop for your safe arrival. I can hardly wait to see you! Gary and I are coming to the airport. Helen is staying behind with the children."

"Can't wait to see you too, Mum," said Mark, "I have a lot to talk about and a lot to do in my few days at home. We must make every day count. I better go and wait for my flight to board. Love you, Mum."

Mark had a window seat and the aircraft was only half full. Such were most of the domestic flights scheduled mid-morning to mid-afternoon in Australia. The morning and evening flights were heavily booked, but otherwise flying was still pleasant and passengers were treated with courtesy and politeness by stewardesses who were not harassed and stressed beyond limit. Mark looked down on a brown landscape and knew that it would remain arid until his flight approached the timber and green patches of the Adelaide Hills. It was early autumn and there had been insufficient rain to turn the brown to green. Even so, the rains would come and by the end of May a lush green would take over the rolling hills, the valleys, and the farm land. Then would come the cold, damp, forlorn days of winter. Mark had a history with this portion of South Australia, and he knew how drenched and soggy the soil could become from June to early September. Suddenly, spring would arrive and with the daffodils and jonquils and the bright yellow of the wattle trees, livestock and people felt the beneficial warmth of the sun and better days ahead.

"Whoa, you are jumping ahead of yourself, old boy," muttered Mark to himself, "Sure, you will be back permanently in the winter, but you have a lot ahead of you before you see next spring."

Of course, Mark was thinking about his graduation from Johns Hopkins and tidying up his affairs in Maryland. Fortunately, he had done most of this already with the Naval Academy. Then, there was Christina. What future did they have together? It had been wonderful to feel close to someone again, but did she have a place alongside Mark for the rest of their lives? This was a much deeper question and the ramifications were still troubling him. For now, he would rather concentrate on meeting his mother, brother and other family members and friends. It had been over two years since he had been home.

The aircraft flew into the Adelaide airspace and over the seaside towns of Glenelg and Henley Beach, and out into the Gulf of St. Vincent and then turned, came back over the water, over the sand dunes and onto the tarmac at the Adelaide West Beach Airport. Although it was only a small airport the plane took a few minutes to pull up to the terminal building and Mark could already see his mother and Gary waiting for him. He was first out of the aircraft, and as he descended the stairway onto the tarmac, he could feel the cool, sea-salt air of the Adelaide beaches. He broke into a run as he approached the gate. Betty had her arms outstretched and Mark picked her up and twirled her around as he kissed her.

CHAPTER TEN

THE EASTER
NATIONALS

"And we know that in all things
God works for the good of those who love him."
—Paul, Romans 8:28

The drive home to the farm was full of talk and contentment as Mark let Gary and his mother channel the conversation. He was weary, although elated to be with family. As Gary chatted away about farm matters and Betty told of the baking she had done for Mark's arrival, he kept one eye on the passing sights of Adelaide. He knew the journey from the Old Toll Booth at Glen Osmond to Hahndorf by every twist and turn in the road. However, the twists and turns had their effect and Mark had to tell Gary and his mother that he would catch a few winks before arriving at the farm. He went into that half-conscious state where his mind wandered from his last medical session to Christina to the music repertoire of the Easter Nationals to his bed in his Eastport apartment. Suddenly, Gary said, "Mark, we are turning onto Balhannah Road now."

Mark awoke abruptly. There was the old Academy, St. Michael's church and *no* Monkey Nut tree. "Who cut down the Monkey Nut tree?" exclaimed Mark in alarm.

"It came down a year ago. The trunk was rotten from the inside. It was too bad, but we sure did enjoy those pine nuts, didn't we?" explained Gary.

"It had been around a long time. Your Dad and I would gather pine nuts with the other kids from St. Michael's too!" added Betty. "So sad things don't last forever."

Mark reached over the seat and placed his hand on his Mum's

shoulder for he knew she was missing Frank at that moment. She held his hand tight as Gary drove into the farm and up to the house just before the garage. Helen was outside waiting with the two children by her side.

After a shower and some freshening up, Mark went with Gary for a farm tour while Betty and Helen prepared the evening meal. Gary asked Mark to sit on the wheel guard of the tractor, so they could talk. They ventured down the main graveled lanes and Gary gave Mark his verbal report on the state of the Schubert farm since he had seen Mark last. Gary was equally as tidy a farmer as was his father. In fact, Gary had planted more trees, pines and deciduous, and had sections set aside for just mowed grass areas; "I just can't stand to see piles of logs or old drums. If they don't have a purpose, I get rid of them. They only make the farm look untidy." Mark slapped Gary on the shoulders gently and said, "At this rate, you are going to have a more fastidious farm than Dad!" Gary beamed. It was what he wanted to hear from his big brother.

Gary had been working on his lavender project for two years now and had six rows of lavender stretching for three hundred yards each, a large production shed for storing the harvested lavender with machinery to wash, dry and bag lavender sachets for the tourist markets in Hahndorf and other Hills' towns. Gary was ecstatic most of all about his oil extracting process just installed in February. As they walked into the shed, Gary was giving Mark his pitch on extracting lavender oil when they heard the dinner bell ring. Mark smiled and said, "Some things never change!"

"This will only take a few minutes longer. Mark, I really want you to see this. I know this is going to be a successful business. Did you know that there are 39 different species of lavender? They all belong to the genus "*lavandula*," and can be used to make distilled lavender essential oil. Just a little longer, Mark. *Lavandual Angustifolia* (or English lavender) is the best variety for making essential oils. It also has the sweetest scent. This is what we are growing!"

"You see, Mark," Gary was on a roll now, "We are going to produce the best essential oils on the market. We grow our lavender without the use of pesticides, and we will be able to legitimately use the Latin name, *Lavandual Angustifolia,* and promote our essential oils as 100% Therapeutic Grade."

With that, Gary said, "I wanted you to see this. It is my dream becoming a reality. The sachets of lavender are selling extremely well, but the lavender oil is going to do much better, I believe, even though it won't be ready for sale until early next summer. We better go for tea!"

"Gary, before we go in, I need to tell you something, and it's not good!" said Mark as he cleared his throat, realizing that the dreaded moment had arrived when he spoke with his family.

Gary look dumbfounded as Mark told him about his prostate cancer. Mark just kept going until he had told him everything.

"Are you boys coming in for tea now, or do we start without you?" asked Helen with very little demand in her actual question. She knew it was two brothers catching up and she had to give some leniency.

"Perhaps I should not tell them all tonight. Perhaps I should wait until tomorrow and tell Mum first," queried Mark who suddenly recognized that there was no painless way to tell the family that he had the dreaded cancer disease.

"No, Mark, you should do it tonight while we are all present. I can help you cope with the alarm this will cause. Mum will probably take it better than Helen. My kids will need help understanding it all."

The dining table looked splendid with the Schubert family's best every-day china and glasses, salad bowls, a cold turkey platter, bread and pitchers of juice adding to the color of an already vibrant spread. Gary had assumed the role as head of household in Mark's absence, and he called the family together for the blessing. As there was no hot food, Gary saw his opportunity and introduced the idea that Mark had something serious to tell the family, and that this would be followed by the blessing on the food and an appreciation to God for bringing Mark safely home. All eyes looked at Mark, especially Betty. Her motherly instinct rose to the fore immediately, and she cried out, "Mark, are you alright?" This was a good segue and Mark acted on it.

"I am Okay, Mum," reassured Mark, "and we can talk later about the details. We need to eat, and I need to get some sleep before much longer. It's … err, it's that I am going to need surgery when I come home in June. Less than a month ago, I had my routine physical and it turns out that I have prostate cancer."

With one accord, or so it seemed, the family gasped. "It can't be, Mark, you are too young!" "Oh, Mark, that is so wrong!" "How far along is it?" Then, Betty calmly spoke up and caught everyone's attention.

"Mark, we are here for you and, thank God, you will be back home in Australia for the surgery. Please just tell us what will be involved and then let us eat and be very thankful to God for his watch care over this family."

Mark felt a sense of calm because of Betty's reaction and he went on and told the family what was ahead of him and that he had an appointment with a good surgeon in Adelaide tomorrow afternoon. His final comment was that the cancer was contained within the prostate and he should be able to look forward to a long life beyond surgery.

With that Gary prayed a deep and moving prayer and the family reached for each other's hands as they felt the intensity of his supplication before God. He concluded, "And now, may the God of Luther and the God who brought our families to Australia all those years ago be with us all, and especially Mark, for we ask these things in the name of the Father, and the Son and the Holy Ghost, Amen."

"Gary," nudged Betty, "You forgot the blessing on the food."

Dutifully, Gary, with a grin on his face, asked the family to bow their heads again: "Sorry, dear Lord, but I ask that you bless this bountiful food before us. May it do us good. Also, we are thankful for Grandma and that she is having her birthday on Sunday. Amen."

This caused a chuckle or two, and before they all began to eat, Betty got up from the table and came to Mark and hugged him and kissed him, while the family gave assurances that he would make it through the surgery and be back to normal in no time! Mark wondered in his mind what "being back to normal would feel like." But, for now, he was home and with family, and that cold turkey certainly looked good.

The next morning Mark was awake at 3:30 am and could not go back to sleep. By 4:00 am he gave up, got up and quietly made his way out of the house and over to the old home and into Frank's study. The family maintained the old home just as they did the current home which was now really Gary and Helen's residence. Betty had given up the main bedroom and had taken one of the smaller bedrooms as her own. She could have gone over to the old homestead but felt closer to family by taking another bedroom. Mark knew his old euphonium was to the side of Frank's favorite leather chair. Mark sat in the chair for a few moments and sighed deeply as he thought of his father's prevailing influence on the entire family. More and more, Mark was remembering Frank as a good man who had many talents outside of farming and that, perhaps unknowing to both, these attributes, and dreams, were passed onto Mark. Clearly, Gary was the farmer, and Mark was the itinerant musician.

There was only one light on in the study, but Mark could see his father's books all neatly lined to within one inch of the edge of their respective shelf in the impressive book case that held almost two thousand books. Next, Mark looked over at the long-play records that Frank accumulated from the old 78 days to 33 rpm in recent years. Some of these recordings were collector's items, as Frank had some of the finest classical orchestras playing the works of the Classical Masters and then Jazz and Big Band recordings from Paul Whiteman through until *Galapagos Duck*, a Sydney-based jazz band Mark knew personally from a few years earlier.

After some time, Mark sensed that a certain sadness was coming over him and he reached over to his euphonium, took it out of its leather case, and began to loosen up the valves, stuck solidly from no use since Mark last played the instrument two years ago. He went to the cupboard by the window and took out the *Silvo* polish and rags, as well as the valve oil and Vaseline to place on the slides. He put a small tarpaulin on the floor rug and went to work returning his old euphonium back to working order again.

There was a knock on the door at around 5:45 am and in came Betty with a tray of hot Earl Grey tea and some Arnott's Granita and

Milk Arrowroot biscuits. Yes, these were biscuits and not cookies, Mark reminded himself once more, now that he was home. The tea and biscuits were delightful, but the next hour or so he spent talking to his mother was priceless. She had reconciled the prostate cancer surgery in her mind and was so grateful that Mark had made the effort to have the operation in Adelaide and not Maryland. She also told him how much she was looking forward to him only being a flight away or one night on the *Overland* by residing in Melbourne for his future work.

"Mum," said Mark, "Do you realize that I will have two full months to recuperate here on the farm after my surgery before I go to Melbourne."

"No," replied Betty with a smile on her face, "I had not thought that far ahead. That will be wonderful. I will be able to bring you tea and biscuits each morning."

"Thank you, Mum," chuckled Mark, "I will enjoy that, but be careful as I may want to take you to Melbourne with me."

"I would come," Betty said eagerly, "No, it would not be fair to you. You must live your own life. You still have to find that special girl I know God has for you somewhere."

With that comment, Mark told his mother about Christina and how they had been dating somewhat seriously for the last four months. As quickly as he told Betty, he retracted the dating part and said that he felt it wrong to let the relationship develop too far when he was due to return permanently to Australia. Betty's reaction was exactly Mark's in that it was wrong to thwart true love, or the possibility of it. Mark put his arms around his mother and said, "Mum, I love you for being you and I want true love too, but I want it to be right, and not like before. It was so awful with Roslyn."

"Fortunately, Mark, I don't think there are too many girls like Roslyn out there; at least, I hope not." Betty then looked at the rays of sunshine coming in through the windows and said that she must go back to the main house and help Helen with breakfast. Then she looked wryly at Mark and said, "Well, I don't have to, but I like to as it makes this old grandma feel useful."

Mark finished one more polish of the euphonium and checked the valves with his flurry of fingers on the three keys. All was working, and he would look forward to playing his old instrument later that evening. He could smell coffee and the thought of a home cooked breakfast was just too inviting. He headed for the kitchen.

After a farmer's breakfast of eggs and fried potatoes and so much family chatter, Mark went to take a shower and shave and prepared to go see the urologist in Adelaide whom the Naval Academy had recommended. Betty went with Mark. He was received very well at the doctor's rooms and Mark knew immediately that he could put his trust in Dr. Lawson as his specialist and surgeon. They were about the same age and his new-found doctor lamented that Mark had to deal with this men's dreaded curse so early in life. Mark's medical file had arrived a few days ago and Dr. Lawson had studied Mark's case ahead of this appointment. He told Mark that he needed him to come back next Monday for a series of tests to ensure that the cancer had not spread outside the prostate or elevated to an aggressive cancer. Whatever the case, Dr. Lawson cautioned Mark not to delay on surgery when he returned permanently to Australia in June.

"In fact, Mark, when we have the tests done next Monday, I am going to fast track the analysis and have the results for you by Wednesday of next week. Let's set an appointment for you at 10:30 am in the morning. We can go over the results together and I would like to schedule the date of surgery at that time for a few days after you return in June. If you must cancel, you can, but I suggest we deal with this sucker as soon as possible."

As Mark walked to the waiting room, Betty had her eyes closed and Mark knew she was praying. He introduced Dr. Lawson to Betty and the doctor said to them both, "From here on, please call me Paul."

They walked out into autumn sunshine and Betty squeezed Mark's hand and said, "I know everything is going to be alright. You are in God's hands." As Mark started the car, he looked at his mother and said, "Since I am with my favorite girl and this appointment went better than I expected, why don't we go down to Glenelg and I will buy you fish 'n chips for lunch." Betty smiled, and they continued down North Terrace to West Terrace and then onto the Anzac Highway and all the way to Glenelg, one of South Australian's best-loved suburban beaches. They walked along the foreshore to Mosley Square and to one of the family's preferred cafe's in the summer months. Mark ordered King George whiting and chips and two salads. When Mark returned to the dining table, Betty was looking at him with that girlish grin that he knew so well.

"Come on, what are you thinking?" asked Mark knowing that it was nothing bad or sad.

"I have just remembered that I have not called you Dr. Schubert until now. Dr. Schubert, my Dr. Schubert! It has a nice ring to it, don't you think?" questioned Betty.

"Is that what you are thinking? Well, it is not official until I graduate in May, and then we can say that my degree has been conferred?" Mark gave Betty the official line of academe on the matter and thought to himself, "Yep, I have accomplished what was a dream for so long. I am glad it is finished as I will be glad when my surgery is over!"

They enjoyed their lunch and then walked out to the end of the jetty and mingled with the many fishermen who were trying their luck. Walking back to the foreshore, Mark looked beyond to the outline of the Adelaide Hills. This was home, but he knew he would miss Maryland, and Annapolis especially. As his mother clung to his arm, he wondered how Christina was and what would be the outcome of their relationship. His mind refused to dwell on the question other than for a second; could he, indeed, call it a relationship? Betty tugged Mark's arm and said: "Mark, look at that little boy with his kite. I remember when your father and you would fly kites your grandfather made for you. We had so much fun watching it dart and dodge and you trying to keep it in the sky. We have slides of those beach days packed away in your dad's study. I must get them converted into prints and make all of you children an album to keep before I am gone."

"Don't plan on leaving too soon, Mum," Mark added adamantly, "I hope to spend a great deal of time with you in the years ahead here and in Melbourne when you will help me set up my new apartment. I must start calling it a flat now, mustn't I?"

They arrived back at the farm late in the afternoon, and Mark could feel the cool of the evening drawing upon the farm odors and giving off that mild damp, musty smell Mark knew so well. It had been a good day and, again, he was so glad to be with family. After tea, he excused himself and said he was going to play his euphonium. The next hour had him playing more hymns than classical or contemporary music, and he, along with his family in the main house, knew that dealing with cancer was a sobering thought even though the prognosis was entirely positive. As Mark continued to play, his mind raced with flashes of boyhood, of school days, of church festivals, of special occasions in Hahndorf's calendar, and of his musical beginnings. Tears came to his eyes as he played *Near to the Heart of God;* he so wanted to feel close to someone special. He did not think this was Christina.

Friday morning brought light rain and Gary was anxious for more. The end of summer saw even the Adelaide Hills thirsty for autumn rains. The farm dam was maintained by the faithful bore water pumped from the ground as needed. It was the pastures that had browned over the hot months of December to February. The lucerne patch was deceptively green in contrast to the scorched acres of grazing land for the cows and sheep. Gary's beloved lavender fields were kept watered by the mechanized water boom that rolled ever so slowly along the rows of scented purple. March was the time of year when nature waited patiently for the ferocious sun to wane, and this year it looked as though summer would linger and go out with a roar. Abruptly, one morning, the weather pattern would change, the temperature would drop, and mornings and evenings would become cooler each week until it was bracing to walk outside without a jacket. The sky would fill with clouds and light rains would fall and the dry grasses would soak up the moisture and turn various shades of patchy green. Come June all the paddocks would be vibrantly green again.

Standing on the front verandah, Mark was conscious of his tight daily schedule and he looked one more time at the farm vista before him and then turned and went back inside to make ready for the activities ahead. Today was the one open day for Mark, and Helen insisted that Gary take Betty and Mark to Victor Harbor for lunch and the afternoon. It was one of the favorite seaside locations for most South Australians; one hour from Adelaide, and Hahndorf too, if you went through Strathalbyn. On the way, they drove down the main street of Mount Barker and slowly passed the high school which had changed so much since Mark was a student there. Continuing through the undulating hill country, all three just talked casually about former recollections both in scenery and people from earlier days. As Strathalbyn came into view the farm land became flatter and gave way to vast expanses of wheat and sheep grazing properties. The trees were shorter and sparse, except for the ravines and water courses where pockets of tall eucalyptus escaped the greedy hands of earlier farmers. The grazing and cropping landscape continued until they came close to the ocean.

Suddenly, Mark cried out, "I see the ocean first!"

They laughed as this was the anticipation of the Schubert family when the children were small and always wanting to know when they would arrive at their destination. Frank would raise the question, "Who will see the ocean first?", and the whining of "how much longer?" was gone for the rest of the journey.

Back in those carefree days, it was the sight of the ocean that held Mark and Gary in suspense on their many visits to the Fleurieu Peninsula. Even now, as Mark gazed to the distant horizon, he commented: "You know, I always remembered thinking if only we could see forever, the Southern Ocean would eventually end up at Antarctica. I know many of my American buddies would give so much to be here with us today."

They drove through Goolwa and Port Elliot, and onto Victor Harbor.

"Hey Mark, remember how lucky we thought we were if we saw a steam train along this stretch of track? Dad took some great photos with the ocean in the background," recalled Gary, obviously feeling the excitement that Victor Harbor engendered in most people.

"Gary, please drive down the Esplanade and cross over the tracks so Mark can see if the tram is approaching. I always loved the draught horses when I was a little girl. Before tractors that was all we had to do the heavy farm work," reflected Betty.

"What say we go straight to the Hotel Victor for lunch? I am feeling hungry," directed Betty as she pointed out several changes along the foreshore, she did not want Mark to miss.

"Sounds good to me," answered Mark, "just so long as you both know that I must climb the Bluff before we head back home."

Lunch was wonderful. It was as if Mark could not get enough of sitting at a table and talking over food. He was so accustomed to eating alone, and too often on the fly. His second meal of King George whiting and chips was even better than the meal in Glenelg yesterday. Betty chimed in, "See, I told you the best fish 'n chips are to be found at Victor Harbor. Are we ready to walk over to Granite Island?"

Mark was glad for a walk. He had not exercised sufficiently since he landed in Adelaide. There was now a chairlift on the Island. Mark did not think it was a good fit but kept his opinion to himself. He took some photos, but the afternoon sun, while welcome through the clouds, obstructed him from taking clear photos looking back at the mainland. Never mind, it was time to climb the Bluff.

More correctly known as Rosetta Head, the Bluff was one of Victor Harbor's main tourist attractions for the active set offering a fabulous 360-degree view of the picturesque coastline to the west, and it was the highest point on the coast from which to gaze for miles out to sea. Mark was puffing more than he liked to admit after he climbed the 300 feet to the top. Gary assisted Betty and they climbed more slowly than Mark, ever the eager beaver. The view was superb, and the time of day awarded Mark some stellar photos. Looking back over the landscape of Victor's sprawling township and the two islands in the foreground made the physical effort by all three entirely worthwhile.

"Oh, Mark, I am so glad that Gary made me come to the top. Until we parked the car, I was sure that I would not even try and reach the peak. The views are magical, you know, even spiritual. Look at that sea and the rays of sunshine hitting the coastline. Oh, how glorious it all is!" Betty spoke in a reverent tone as she memorized each view.

They took their time descending, each one absorbed with staying on the trail as they edged by the people climbing upwards. They mulled over their private thoughts and said nothing out loud. When they were in the car and Gary started the engine, Betty reached over the seat and put her arms on the shoulders of her two sons.

"I have had such a wonderful day with my two boys. I will treasure this day in my memory," said Betty.

Gary suggested they pray, and he asked God to be with them as they drove home. He thanked God for the blessings of life and for giving them this special day together.

They arrived back at the farm at dark, Gary apologizing for being later than expected. Mark and Gary played with the children while the evening meal was prepared. Before retiring to bed, Gary asked Mark to go with him out to check on the new chickens that were hatched only a week earlier. They both wore their coats as the temperature was dropping. After all, it was nearly Easter.

All the people of *old* Hahndorf knew that Mark was coming home. It was, after all, still a German village in many respects. The opening of the South-Eastern Freeway may have taken away the heavy flow of interstate traffic which had pounded relentlessly through the long main street day and night for all of Mark's formative years, but it had only been replaced by the invasion of tourists who came to see this quaint, historic, whitewashed town resembling less and less its original self as each year passed. It was the townspeople and district farmers from earlier days who had watched Mark grow into a state, national brass champion, who cheered as he became a Lutheran music teacher, who proudly watched his television appearances and read his articles in the popular press, and who were supportive when he joined the Royal Australian Navy as a musician. These were the people who gasped at the breakup of his marriage and were a little apprehensive when the family told of his pending American sojourn. To all of them, Mark was not only a boy from Hahndorf, he was *their* boy and he was home, with much accomplished.

Saturday was the designated day to gather and celebrate two occasions: Mark's arrival home and Betty's birthday. It was a glorious day with blue skies and a coolness in the air unless you were out in direct sunshine. St. Michael's grounds became a picnic setting and the Hahndorf Town Band was the musical entertainment for the day's celebrations. The tall pines, the church and outer buildings, and the remains of the old cemetery provided a backdrop for the tables of food and drink and the seats arranged in two sections. The Schubert cars arrived together: Gary, Helen and the children, Mark and Betty and the two sisters, their husbands and children. As the program got underway before the food and fellowship, Pastor Bakken officially welcomed Mark home and gave birthday greetings to Betty. Mrs. Kuchel spoke to Betty, and all those assembled, as another person representing the original families who settled Hahndorf in March 1839. She spoke of the hardships the German women endured in raising families and making "homes" out of the bush environment. She remembered the years when she and Betty were growing up suffering the indignities thrust upon people of German ancestry during WWII, and their parents in WWI. She brought laughter as she told stories of Betty falling in love and dating Frank immediately after the War. She called Betty one of her dearest friends and wished her much happiness and long life, and then she gave a curt admonition to Mark to return to Australia as soon as possible, and to remain in his homeland. As the laughter and applause died down the bandmaster came to the podium to tell the story of the Hahndorf Town Band and how Mark became an aspiring member at the age of twelve. He spoke of Mark's determination and consistent effort to excel. "We can all be justly proud of our Mark and his accomplishments, especially since he remains today the same humble person he was when he first joined our band."

The bandmaster rallied the band and nodded to Mark in readiness to play. The Band was to play one special item before eating began. The bandmaster turned to the hungry onlookers and said: "We won't keep you from this wonderful spread of food much longer. We are asking Mark to assist us with this next piece of music. In fact, he is going to play the solo part of Ennio Morricone's emotionally haunting theme from the movie *The Mission*. I know many of us have seen this film in the last three months. Ladies and gentlemen, the band and Dr. Schubert playing *Gabriel's Oboe*."

Mark had been playing this solo part for several months. He had seen the movie in Annapolis with Pastor and Mrs. Schulz. Together, they considered it to be one of the most impassioned films they had seen in years. A euphonium is not an oboe and they were outdoors which typically meant that the mellow sound of Mark's instrument tended to get lost in the atmosphere. However, Mark gave a stirring rendition of the movie theme. As he lowered his euphonium, he looked at his mother to see that she had tears streaming down her face. It caused Mark to choke up with emotion and to stay bowed as he tried to regain his composure.

Pastor Bakken quickly asked the hundred, or so, people present to bow their heads for the blessing on the food and on the Schubert family. This was followed by several ladies from the Lutheran Women's Association issuing instructions about how to proceed with the food. Children under twelve years were to go to the tables with the blue checked tablecloths and the elderly to the tables with red tablecloths; drinks were over to the left and ice cream and cake would be served last. It didn't seem that anyone listened, yet within a minute or two all was going according to the instructions.

Mark was encircled immediately, and it remained that way for over two hours. He ate a little and had to request a drink of juice to help his dry throat from talking and laughing so much. He saw so many people from childhood days—some he had not seen in twenty years or more because their paths had not crossed when he returned to Hahndorf from Melbourne and America. He listened more than he talked. He heard stories about so many people, tales of woe and exaggeration, and recollections that brought peals of laughter with frequent hand-holding and embraces. He saw, too, the press of time encroaching on so many; farmers and townsmen, once robust and brusque, now bent and fragile, and women so alive and vital, now wrinkled and diminished. Yet, in all, there was joy at coming together as a community of faith and common heritage. At the end of the picnic, Mark could not count the number of times he had heard the lament, "We don't do this like we used to. Thank you for coming home!"

It was late afternoon by the time most had departed. Mark was finally able to sit down. He had been in conversation with Mrs. Paech for a long time. Her husband had died several months before and Mark had written to her at the time of his death. She was intent on imploring Mark to forgive her husband for driving him so hard as his music pupil. Mark protested that there was no need to apologize. In fact, his aggressive tutelage was probably what Mark needed to break through the barrier of mediocrity. Betty came to the rescue and helped Mrs. Paech to her feet and asked how she was faring. Mark hugged her and thanked her for all the biscuits and juice at the Paech home when he was having his music lessons. Mark walked over to Gary who had finished helping put the chairs back in the school storage shed across the road from St. Michael's.

"How are you holding up, mate?" Gary asked.

"Now that is said in true Aussie fashion, dear brother," replied Mark. "I'm Okay. In fact, it has been good. Gatherings like this give you a perspective. It makes me realize that we are all getting older. I envy you having found Helen and now you have a family."

"Well, Mark, I am grateful, but I will never be able to achieve what you have done," Gary replied.

"Oh, I see, so I have done more than you. Is that what you are feeling?" asked Mark. "Let me tell you what you have done. You have always loved the land and farming was what you were born to do. You have made more of a success of the Schubert farm than either Dad or Grandpa. You light up when you talk about the animals, the walnut trees you have planted, your lavender project and the money you are bringing in. I am proud of what you have done and more than a little envious of your family."

"I'm sorry, I guess I asked for that!" exclaimed Gary.

"You have nothing to apologize for," consoled Mark. "We all follow our dreams and our talents. I think Dad not achieving more of the academic side of his nature, and his interest in music and theology, drove me more than I knew. Mr. Paech also made his mark and to think that sometimes I almost hated him. You have stability. I long for it. I think I am also longing for the right girl too. It would help ground me."

"Gary, can we go home now? The kids are tired." asked Helen as she approached. "You two look as though you are in heavy conversation."

"Just talking about life, my darling, but it's all good," replied Gary.

Mark and Betty drove slowly back to the farm. Although tired, Betty had thoroughly enjoyed the party on the church grounds because it was so reminiscent of bygone church social gatherings. She said to Mark: "We used to socialize as a church and a town much more before television." Thus, ended a memorable day of community and fellowship at its best.

Mark was awake before the church bells pealed from the valley to the townspeople, the farms and beyond. He was pleased to hear them and to know that this practice was still going on. He had not asked about it because he had not thought about it recently. As various traditions were let go and news reached him in letters, or when family visited, or he was home, the usual response had to do with the march of progress. Mark rarely agreed with the changes reported to him. He was a traditionalist in most things, although he agreed wholeheartedly that cars, tractors and trucks were a great advance on the faithful horse.

After breakfast there was the usual rush associated with getting to church on time. Mark decided that he would stay close to his mother and was pleased that he was not besieged like yesterday. Pastor Bakken did welcome Mark along with other visitors and the sermon droned on as Mark fought drowsiness. Lunch was a welcome leg of lamb and roast vegetables, followed by apple pie. Then, the day was given over to rest and relaxation. Mark took the opportunity to sleep and to prepare for the medical tests ahead of him tomorrow.

The medical procedures were a repeat of what he had already

experienced with the Naval Academy doctors. He felt sorry for himself to have to suffer the indignity of all the pushing and probing twice. It seemed to take longer than in Annapolis and there were times he would close his eyes and try and imagine that he was somewhere else. It made Mark think of the pine trees. He had been home for almost a week and not once had he thought of them or the need to go to them. Right at this minute, he wished that he could enter in through the branches and be cut off from all people-contact. The medical tests ended finally, and Mark dressed and met with Paul Lawson in a small conference room, with Betty joining them.

Paul told them that the tests went well, but it was the results of these tests that will be discussed on Wednesday. Paul could see that Mark was tired and he said: "No going out for fish 'n chips for lunch today. We have taken blood and the biopsy means that you lost blood too. Go back to the farm and rest for the remainder of today and take it easy tomorrow as well. I will look forward to seeing you on Wednesday at 10:30 am," counseled Dr. Lawson. He shook their hands and they went out into cloudy skies and drove through the Hills to the farm.

Mark rested and so did Betty. She had been on an emotional high long before Mark arrived home. "Quiet time," as she called it, was not only for physical rest, but prayer and reflection on life and family, of days long ago and those just now, and maybe most of all, for the gift of life for herself, her deceased Frank and the children they brought into the world. Helen was glad for some respite too as she had been doing double duty in the kitchen even before Mark arrived.

Wednesday was test results day. Gary began early as he had to be with the Kaesler Brothers' engineers as they worked on the pump for the lavender paddock. He gave Mark the thumbs up sign as he and Betty drove through the farm to Adelaide. They were at the doctor's rooms with ten minutes to spare. Dr. Lawson did not keep them waiting long and told them all was well with the tests and that the results were not much different to the medical reports he received from the Naval Academy.

"Let's begin with the good news," said Paul, "The CT scan does not show any sign of metastasis. Therefore, we can be reasonably certain that the cancer has not spread to the lymph nodes or outside the prostate. The biopsy from which we removed about a dozen small pieces of tissue from several areas of the prostate suggests that your cancer is between Stage 1 and 2. The digital rectal examination did not reveal any abnormalities and you have said that you have not experienced any irregularities in urinating, even at night."

Paul continued to explain that there were far more good signs than bad. However, Mark still had prostate cancer with a PSI level of 12. If surgery did not occur within three months or so, this level could rise, and metastasis was a real possibility.

"So, why my son, doctor?" asked Betty, knowing full well that this was a repeat of the same question asked earlier.

"I don't know, Mrs. Schubert. Medical science can't answer the question adequately either as to why Mark has it and not his brother or his best friend. There is not a lot Mark could have done to avoid it either. I have given you all the printed information about prostate cancer and I think you need to read it again and again."

"I will say this. We know that the prostate produces the fluid that nourishes and transports sperm. The protein excreted by the prostate, prostate-specific antigen (PSA), helps semen retain its fluid state. An excess of this protein in the blood is one of the first signs of prostate cancer. Your PSA is at level 12, as I said before. Level 4 or less is considered normal. How does it all start? We know it usually starts in the glandular cells. This is known as *adenocarcinoma*. Tiny changes occur in the shape and size of the prostate gland cells, known as *prostate intraepithelial neoplasia*."

"I need to stop. I'm lecturing you and I don't mean to. It's all in the brochures. The important thing now is to remove the prostate and ensure that you are set for a long life ahead."

"As your Naval Academy urologist recommends, I think you should have radical prostatectomy surgery. We will remove the prostate and you are looking at a recovery time of up to three months. You are younger than most and so it may be less."

"I have two questions. When do you arrive back in Adelaide? When do you need to start full-time work with the Navy in Melbourne?"

Mark and Betty looked at each other and she reached for his hand. They had read all this information many times, but somehow it seemed more reassuring to hear it from Mark's new urologist and surgeon.

"Well, I graduate in the last week of May. I am returning to Maryland next Wednesday and will spend the rest of April and May tidying up personal matters. I have not booked my flight home yet, but I plan to be home around the end of the first week of June."

"I start my Navy job in Melbourne in the first week of September, or I will have to apply for more leave if I am not ready for work."

"No, no. I think that will work very nicely for us. What if we schedule surgery for the second Tuesday of June? This will give you about ten weeks for recovery. And, I expect that you will get there in less time," replied Paul.

Mark and Betty drove back to the farm with ample time to talk through various questions and concerns relating to all aspects of the next two months before the actual surgery. They were calm and introspective in the main. Mark had time for lunch and then had to return to Adelaide for the afternoon and evening in preparation for the onslaught of the Easter National Championships. He knew that the next three days were going to be grueling, yet he hoped, personally rewarding as well.

Bandsmen and women from all over Australia, and some from beyond, were descending on Adelaide. This annual event represented the culmination of a year of practice and rehearsal in musicianship and marching for individuals and bands all trying for the highest scores possible in the dozen or so categories of competition. Mark was the main adjudicator for the solo and band sections. He knew the musical scores and was ready to see how this all compared from his American experience over the last five years.

The dignitaries of the South Australian Band Association and the National Band Council of Australia (NBCA) hosted Mark for the entire weekend. Indeed, they feted over him completely. He was somewhat of a curiosity. Unknown to some as he had been absent from Australian banding for five years, he was a returning champion to most. Additionally, he was an Australian Navy musician returning from a work assignment at the United States Naval Academy and now with a newly minted PhD in music education from an Ivy League University. These were the essential facts about Mark from the NBCA program. What it all meant did not matter to most other than an appreciation that Mark represented the pinnacle of brass performance and excellence, and it would be interesting to see how he would *judge* players, bands and their music.

Later that evening, Mark drove home alone into the Adelaide Hills and to the farm. It was a clear moonlit night and he opened the car windows in order to feel the cool gulley air as he left Glen Osmond and approached the Devil's Elbow. "Out West," Mark mused to himself, "these would be called canyons!" As he approached the Eagle on the Hill Hotel, he pulled over at two places and took time to look down on the lights of Adelaide. "There are few cities in the world with a close-up view of city lights like this," he spoke to himself with a sense of awe as a returning son who had lived in the presence of American grandeur and bravado. At Bridgewater, he was on the eastern side of the Mount Lofty Ranges and as the landscape flattened out after descending Germantown Hill, the soft light of the harvest moon bathed the Hahndorf rural mural in a glow bespeaking peace and serenity. He felt annoyed at himself for uttering yet again for the "umpteenth" time, *he was glad to be home*!

He wore his Royal Australian Navy uniform to the first day of the Easter Nationals. By mid-morning, he was immersed in adjudicating the Junior Solo championships. If Mark had empathy for any category of competition music, it was for solo performers, especially the young. Etched on his memory was his first painful introduction to solo championships. His recollection of that day was linked to the weather: both were bleak and unpleasant.

There was a total of twelve junior soloists; five in grade A, four in grade B and three in grade C. The first soloist was apparently so nervous there was a dramatic and early wrong pitched note, followed by silence for about three seconds and then the player joined the piano again. The remainder of the performance was close to excellent. Mark was especially thrilled to listen to the last and difficult cadenza. The cornet landed on the pause and with gathering crescendo accelerated to a high F# on the final pause and onto the last segment for an exemplary conclusion. Mark was delighted, but he was also judge and he had to act on the pitch mishap and long pause in the introduction of the test piece. This was the part of adjudicating that Mark liked least. Here was a potential champion in the making and he had to grade this player down for a few seconds of composure issues rather than matters of talent or skill. He knew the turmoil of emotions being experienced by this young player. While waiting for the next soloist, he sipped on his Earl Grey tea and enjoyed some Arnott's biscuits as a distraction and a reminder that he must remain impartial, especially when human frailties were on display.

Nonetheless, it was as if the first soloist had calmed the nerves of the other junior players. There were no further dramatic mistakes. Next, was a euphonium player who struggled valiantly to find the full sound so necessary for this mellow instrument. The performance was technically correct but lacked emotion and tonal qualities. Mark pressed his lips together in mild disappointment because the plain solution was one of evolution, both as a musician and as a person. Mark hoped this young player would persevere.

A tenor horn soloist was the best of the morning. He listened to, and discerned, precise sensitivity throughout the performance. Breathing effectively, so often a downfall in young brass players, only added to the pleasure of this stellar recital. Mark wanted to immediately go to this soloist and share encouraging words to ensure that this musician continued with the brass band journey; tenor horn players were not easily available. However, he could not act on his raw impulse. He was, once again, the adjudicator.

As the final solo musician commenced to play, Mark reflected just how the number of Junior bands throughout all states in Australia had increased in his years of absence. However, most were not involved in competition work. He hoped that he might act as a catalyst in encouraging more of these fledgling junior players to enter regional, state and national solo competitions in the future. He knew, too, that music teachers, administrators and parents of both public and private education, held the key to greater involvement in competition and music excellence. There was little doubt in Mark's mind that when he left Luther College, he took with him a passion for growth and development within youth music whether it be brass, concert, orchestra or choral.

He was viscerally thrilled at the quality of music he was experiencing from these teenagers. Even the poorest performance was still acceptable music, and Mark could only applaud the dedication of the soloists, and their parents and teachers for the countless hours of practice and persistence. He did not find it difficult to evaluate these Junior players.

At the end of the Junior Soloist championships, he walked on stage and addressed the soloists and the audience. He only had time for brief comments, and he chose to emphasize the joy of learning to play a musical instrument as an "unencumbered teenager" before the burdens of adult life made it more difficult to commit time and energy to playing in a band. He praised the bravery of young soloists for standing before their peers and families and playing under competition conditions. Mark concluded by challenging parents, bands and K-12 education to seek to increase opportunities for more children and young people to have the experience of joining a band. "Remember," he said, "the person who learns to blow a cornet, will never blow a safe!" He announced the winner of the Junior Solo Championship for 1991, then second place and third. Cheers and clapping followed as did the lunch break.

In the company of his hosts, Mark ate little as he had consumed copious quantities of tea and biscuits brought faithfully to him every hour during the morning session. And, as a farm boy accustomed to early mornings, he knew of the dreaded mid-afternoon doldrums ahead when required to sit for lengthy periods of time. Nevertheless, he was more than busy listening to the chatter of his hosts as they unburdened themselves with their personal concerns and ambitions for the future of banding in Australia. They asked him few questions about his time in the United States, it was mostly advice to him as a musician of merit returning to his homeland. It dawned on Mark that this was a salutatory moment for him. He should recognize now that colleagues, friends and, perhaps, even family and other close intimates, were not really interested in all the amazing experiences he had in his work and study in America; it was mainly about what he could do for them now and tomorrow. Once he realized this human phenomenon happening before him, he could chuckle to himself and say, "No tall poppy syndrome for me, that's for sure!"

The afternoon was given over to the Junior Bands. This round of competition required Mark to be sheltered from a visible viewing of the bands. He did not care for this, and he found himself taking a deep breath almost in protest as he entered his cave should there be insufficient fresh air when it came time for his next breath. He smiled to himself and wished there was a better way to do his job as chief judge. He settled in his chair, arranged his papers in front of him and pushed the buzzer to signal the first Junior band of seven to begin its performance. Each Junior band was to play four pieces of music: the test piece, an own choice, a march, and a hymn. The first of three A grade junior musicians were underway. These were followed by the two B grade bands and, lastly, the two C grade bands.

The junior bands comported themselves according to their grade classifications. Mark understood, as did all adjudicators, that he was listening to the future of Australian banding. He was among a new breed of music educators who believed the best means to growing a strong banding culture was by setting and maintaining high standards.

One of the C grade bands performed way below the benchmark. Style, intonation, accuracy and adherence to the score were all missing. Yet, this band, and its conductor, was doing its best. Mark knew that his duty was to turn negative criticism into encouragement and to challenge this band to compete again next year. Resilience was best demonstrated by showing up again.

Not surprising to Mark was the overly ambitious selection of music in the Own Choice segment. Junior bands were no different to their adult counterparts in that their aim was to impress and to score maximum points at a competition. The freedom to select their own music often became a trap as they frequently chose music not entirely suited to the true capacity of their band.

Another cup of tea arrived as the last junior band was setting up. This band played admirably, and Mark detected early that the euphonium was the dominant instrument and possibly, therefore, a guest player who was a more experienced musician outside the age limits of Junior bandsmen. Also, Mark could sense there was a symbiotic connection between conductor and the band. They were well rehearsed, and while their sound was "thin," they were in tune and technically accurate in their responses to the scores. When it came time for the Hymn selection, the band played three verses of *Abide with Me* with the euphonium taking the solo for the second verse. This was a moment when Mark wished he could view the actual performance. The dulcet, full sound of the euphonium rose to fill the Town Hall and Mark had to swallow hard as the emotion embraced him. At the end of the third verse, the band played a reverent *Amen*. Mark was delighted with the overall performance and said to himself, "This is what it is all about. This is one C Grade Junior band on its way to B Grade!"

Suddenly becoming visible to the audience, Mark emerged from his cramped adjudicator's box and walked on stage for his brief comments on the Junior Bands' recitals. He praised the level of musicianship and thanked the parents, schools, communities and players for the privilege of listening to their music. He expressed his belief in music, and the "ability to play a musical instrument as a child" as being one of the useful components for achieving a healthy self-esteem as an adult. "And don't overlook the fact that the human voice is a musical instrument too; some say the greatest!" he added. Ever aware of the need to express succinct and pertinent comments, Mark proceeded to announce the winners according to place and category.

By the end of the first day of adjudicating, Mark was tired. It had been a day of heavy concentration. He drove home to Hahndorf and his weariness along with the light drizzle and fog in the Hills were such contrasts to the magic of the same journey the night before. Betty was still up when Mark arrived after 10 pm. She prepared a hot cup of Milo and a slice of German crumb cake. Mark was grateful and wanted no more. She could see that he was tired.

"What time do you need to be at the Town Hall tomorrow? she asked with empathy.

"Fortunately, I can arrive just before 9:00 am," said Mark, "and then we should finish by around 5 pm. Remember, Saturday night is the band concert for the public."

"You know that I won't be going to church on Sunday, Mum, don't you? I am going to be glad when these Easter Nationals are over. I must say again how badly I feel disrupting Easter for you all." Betty reached over and squeezed his arm and replied, "Think nothing of it. It has been wonderful to have you home with us. It makes Easter even more special."

Mark awoke before dawn and went for a walk around the farm. It felt good to know that this was Schubert property and had been in the family for four generations. He approached the pines but thought better of entering the childhood sanctity of damp, dew-soaked branches and pine needles. He moved on to the dairy and spoke with the two farm workers busy with milking. He left for the house as Gary was walking to the dairy.

"Everything Okay, Mark?" asked Gary, a little surprised to see that Mark had been up for some time.

"All is good," replied Mark, "just woke up early and needed to walk. Now, I need coffee and to get to work."

Mark had a quick cup of coffee and toast with his mother, then he made ready for his longest day of adjudicating. He was on his way to Adelaide at 7:00 am and in his cave ten minutes before the first A grade band was ready to begin the day's heavy roster of twenty-one competing bands. By 10:30 am, A grade was over. Mark had focused intently on the Test piece as the one common musical score within

182

each grade where bands could be directly compared one against the other. Especially in A and B grades, interpretation of the score was important, and often highly subjective. There were certain critical passages with the potential for numerous mishaps and these, again and again, reflected not only on players, but conductors too. Accordingly, it was the playing of these passages that often separated two perfectly matched bands. Another feature Mark watched for carefully was the solo parts that were tucked into the very fabric of the score. Was there good balance between soloist and accompaniment? Was the rhythm supportive? Overall, Mark was very pleased. He had listened to wonderful music and had little difficulty in awarding points that ranked the bands from winner to fifth place.

This was followed by seven B grade bands with lunch interrupting the flow, but by 3:00 pm this grade was completed. Next came C grade with its five bands and then a break of one hour. It was in the final two grades where Mark had issues with both the playing of the March and the Hymn. There was no question that an A grade band had to get the march *absolutely correct*. In the lower grades, rhythm, attention to dynamics and intonation were all necessary. Sloppy rhythmic playing was easy to detect. The Hymn section was frequently the most disappointing of the four contest areas. Music-wise, it was not so difficult, but many bands chose to play overly flamboyant hymn arrangements with multiple percussion flurries building to a voluminous conclusion. Mark, true to his religious inclinations, saw the hymn as a prayer where the band played a simple rendition of a unique hymn with good balance and intonation. Above all, Mark preferred a reverent ending, but admitted his bias and sought to remain impartial. Mark announced the rankings of the C grade bands and was appreciative of the thirty-minute break.

The evening slot fell to the four bands in D grade and the day's competition came to an exhausting end just after 9:00 pm. As he made his comments to the D grade bands, he strove to be encouraging and to thank both the bands and the audience for their patience as the long day concluded. It had been ten hours of concentration and thirteen hours on the job for this adjudicator.

Still not permitted to mix with the bandsmen until after the competition, Mark was glad of the excuse to leave early and drive home. He was tired, even a little stiff and cramped from sitting all day, but reflective. If he had discrete empathy for soloists, it was also extended to B grade brass bands. These were often well-established bands within communities or sponsored by industry or business. Similarly, many of the players were advancing in years, yet being part of a band was ingrained into their innermost selves. Belonging to a band gave them a sense of pride, meaning and, in unique Australian parlance, mateship. Intermingled among these older members were talented, eager younger aspirants who received nurture and succor to aim for the stars. Mark's one concern was that many of the mature players were content with preserving B grade status, yet he was realistic enough to know that their greatest contribution was still being engaged with banding. Not every player should be expected to retain that unbridled anticipation and excitement of their first success at a national band contest. Fortunately, no B grade band could maintain its classification unless all members were engaged. At the end of the day, they were to be admired; it was far easier to stay home and sip tea in front of the television.

Mark was less complimentary with C grade bands, but he recognized his views needed qualification. He saw C grade bands as either advancing or coasting. A C grade band, or even a D grade band, may be relatively new to banding, but when ambitious it was only a matter of time before it achieved B grade status. In such bands there was motivation and anticipation. Each player knew that to be acceptable as a musical unit was not good enough. With a good conductor these bands were Mark's favorites to work with as either a guest conductor or as a music coach. As Mark saw the matter, both C and D grade bands were always open to improving their position in the banding fraternity. On the other hand, many an Australian band did not seek to compete, and its purpose was to exist in its community and provide fellowship for its members and entertainment at fetes, church and civic occasions. Frankly, this was Mark's beginnings and as he neared the farm and the comfort of his bed, he was grateful for these bands too. He just knew that their longevity was not assured.

Saturday morning dawned fresh and new. There was a chill in the gulley as Gary and Mark called the cows for milking. Gary had several audible farming calls; one for cows, another for sheep and his third for chickens. Once again, Mark observed his younger brother's well-established proclivity for all things agricultural. Half-awake, Mark asked Gary if he ever grew tired of the routine of farm work.

"You mean rising at 5:00 am to milk cows on week days and then at 6:00 am on weekends? You mean checking on the chickens, the sheep, the lavender field, the vegetable garden twice a day, the pumps, not forgetting the lucerne patch, and to do all this every day of my life?" replied Gary in a tone Mark heard as defensive.

If Mark had not been fully awake, he was now, and he immediately said: "I didn't mean to ruffle your feathers, Gary. It was a genuine question; probably because our lives are so different. I guess I envy your routine."

"No, no, my problem. I've been thinking a lot about our conversations since you've been home. You say you are proud of my work on the farm and envious of the stability I have. From my side of the fence, I think I have always been a little jealous of you, your success and accomplishments. Don't get me wrong. I see you on TV or read an article in *Women's Weekly* about your views on music education and I say to everyone, 'there's my big brother!' But, in truth, I sometimes wish that I was known like you are and that people knew me as me, and not as Mark's brother."

"What? I didn't know you felt this way," said Mark, surprised.

"As I said, Mark, my problem, not yours! I didn't sleep much last night because Helen and I had words. She wanted us to take Mum to the Band Concert tonight and to ask you to have dinner with us in an Italian restaurant we like near the Central Market, and then we could all go and listen to the concert. But I told her "no" because Graeme Kaesler is coming to work on the pump at noon today. It would just push me too much," Gary blurted. He looked somewhat relieved to have gotten that off his chest.

"I get it. Again, I'm sorry," replied Mark quietly.

"Not your fault, Mark. It's me! You spoke of routine and that is what farming is all about. We have known this since we were kids. Truth is, I hate fighting with Helen and disappointing her. We rarely fight, and she just couldn't understand that I need to work with Graeme as he is doing me a favor in coming on Saturday. I must get the pump working as this dry spell is not good for the lavender or the lucerne. We need rain badly. When you asked about routine, it all clicked together, and I immediately felt sorry for myself. I must apologize to Helen when we finish milking and go in for breakfast. Once more, my problem. Always know that I am proud of you and glad that you are my brother; please let me be envious of you every so often!" said Gary, and this time he smiled and patted Mark on the back.

With that Gary suggested they get the milking done as quickly as possible since Mark needed to leave for the Town Hall just before 8:00 am. The Friesen herd was about 30 cows in the autumn season and two *milkers* could readily complete feeding and milking in one to one and one-half hours. Gary did not, in fact, take care of the milking during the week days because he had two full-time workers. One was married with a young family and lived in a farm cottage near the front entrance. The other was a single man in his early twenties. Gary usually appeared toward the end of the milking cycle around 6:30 am. On weekends, only one worker did the milking, with Gary providing the extra hand. It was a harmonious work arrangement and both men regarded Gary as a fair and generous boss. They witnessed, each day, Gary's dedication to his farming endeavors through innovative agricultural practices and current mechanization. Like his father, Gary was known for his fervent personality, but sometimes he was just a worry wart. All in all, however, Gary was a more natural farmer than Frank, and a true son of the soil.

Just after 7:00 am, Gary motioned to Mark that he had better go and prepare to leave for the Town Hall. Mark signaled that he agreed and, leaving behind the pulsating noise of the machinery, he returned to the house for his Weet-Bix and coffee. Just as he was ready to leave for Adelaide, Gary arrived.

"Have a good day, Mark, and again, I am sorry for being a knucklehead," said Gary.

"Think nothing of it. I am frequently a knucklehead several times a week," replied Mark as a means of ending the incident.

Noticing Helen and Betty looking at each other, Mark called out through the open car window, "I will see you around 10:00 pm." Looking through the rear-view mirror, he saw Gary move close to Helen and put his arm around her. Mark was glad, and for the sunshine and cloudless blue sky too.

It had been an eventful morning already, yet Mark's real purpose for this day lay ahead. The road through the Adelaide Hills was relatively free of cars on this early Saturday morning. He knew he had only a few more days left at home. His mind turned to Annapolis, then graduation, the packing and closure of his life in the United States and, most of all, to Christina. What was going to happen to their relationship? He had been so occupied with the euphoria of being home, with family, and dealing with his medical plans that, to be honest, he had rarely thought of Christina. Was this an indication that she didn't really have a firm place in his future? If this was true, how was he going to react when they saw each other in less than a week? Perhaps he was meant to be single. If ever he was to marry again, he wanted a relationship like Gary and Helen; one where trust and friendship were as evident as love and affection.

As the Toll House at Glen Osmond came into view, Mark quickly switched gears in his thinking, knowing that he was now only fifteen minutes from the Town Hall. He focused on his adjudicating role of evaluating and critiquing the best bands in this year's Easter National championships. Mark recognized that he was not, in his opinion, a professional adjudicator. He also knew that state and national brass band competition in Australia and New Zealand were not at the level of professionalism he found in his American experience. In many respects, Mark was glad for this. He was often skeptical—even amused—at the elongated degrees to which American musical adjudicators conspired to demonstrate their exaggerated credentials of *professionalism*. It was Mark's hypothesis that adjudication was more than a skill; it was an art form that required a balance between emotion and technical precision. Moreover, were not these also the necessary ingredients for a champion musician, conductor or even an entire band? Whatever the case, he felt comfortable in his role for the day. His one lament was that he was not given enough time to offer comments and recommendations to the bands.

He parked the car and with brief case in hand walked into the Town Hall. This time he was ushered to a side room far removed from the main hall and was tasked with adjudicating the lower brass open solo championships. Mark was appreciative to be told that a second adjudicator would be evaluating the cornets, flugelhorns and tenor horns. Otherwise, the contest would continue until midnight. He immediately saw that the barrier between the contestants and himself was less like a cave as it had been in the main hall. This time he could be seen by the audience, but not the contestants.

He liked this so much better. Mark anticipated listening to some outstanding solo music from Australia and New Zealand's best bandsmen and women. Several players on the roster were open champions three and four times over. These were the best of the best.

Three Eb basses, or tubas, were up first. Then came three Bb basses, the largest instruments in a brass band. Frequently regarded as the foundation instruments of a band, each of these soloists defied the usual myth that basses were only ever about the *oompah* sound. When it was played as a solo instrument, Mark looked for flawless technique exhibiting the low and high registers achievable by these big tubas. He was not disappointed. One Eb player rose above the others with his playful intonation, giving his solo a personality lacking in the other recitals. All six players demonstrated technical command of their basses and played with tonal quality and expression.

Regrettably, there was only one bass trombone in the contest this year. As an increasingly popular instrument internationally, Mark hoped there would be a similar heightened interest in Australia in the future. Instrument makers were now producing newer versions with greater capabilities and the bass trombone was emerging as an exceedingly versatile instrument. While this single soloist played well, he did not lift his performance to new heights. Mark felt let down, quietly noting to himself that he should promote the bass trombone as an instrument of choice within junior bands.

He was brought a cup of tea and biscuits as the tenor trombones made ready to perform. There were three soloists in this section; all were champions and had mastered their music. They played with accuracy and good tonal quality. One player, however, stood alone, with better interpretive skills and a superior grasp of the ebb and flow of a competition score.

Two baritone soloists were next. The repertoire for baritone and euphonium was virtually the same, and Mark knew this solo selection intimately through his own playing experience. He was pleased with each player's interpretative skills but noted that both needed guidance in phrasing where each played slurred notes above the *staccato* notations, and also missed a trill on the first movement. Even so, these were soloists of long standing and their performances were those of proven champions.

Finally, three euphonium soloists came before a euphonium-playing adjudicator. Again, Mark knew the music thoroughly, a beautiful and challenging work, perfect for a solo contest, as it permitted the soloist to demonstrate the range of the euphonium through different tempos and challenging technical segments. By the very nature of how contests function, there was one section in the score which called for the euphonium to rise in song through its tone and texture of sound. Only one player achieved this quality of expression, while the other players were less vocal and more purely instrumental, albeit with technical accuracy. Mark had found his champion of champions in this year's Open Solo section. He was delighted, but with one qualification having nothing to do with the performance just ended. It had to do with the music itself. All soloists used piano accompaniment. Mark had played this same piece of music with a full brass band accompaniment, and he missed the fullness of sound a band gave to the grandeur of listening pleasure. He was a purist through and through, and now relieved that his long-awaited adjudication assignment was over, or so he thought.

The President of the National Band Council of Australia came on stage and spoke in appreciation of Mark's "fine professional adjudication for this year's Easter Nationals." He called Mark to announce the winners of the Open Soloist Lower Brass categories and the Champion of Champions. Mark concluded by congratulating all soloists and all bands, their families and supporters for the dedication to Australian banding. He told the listening band members and the audience that he was returning to the United States for a few months and then would commence the next phase of his career in September in Melbourne. Finally, he invited all present to be at the next Easter Nationals event.

"I will be there too, and you can all come and talk to me because I will not be an adjudicator!" stated Mark with a smile on his face.

He received a loud and long applause. He shook the upper brass adjudicator's hand and walked back to retrieve his brief case. Out of the corner of his eye, he could see the president and two other band officials approaching him.

"We have a problem and are wondering if we might impose on your good nature and ask a big favor? One of the adjudicators for the grand march is not able to participate. Could you help us out between 1:30 and 3:00 pm and act as the third adjudicator?"

What could Mark say? He knew what he wanted to say, but the Council had paid his full air ticket from Maryland to Adelaide, largely because he had no accommodation expenses by staying with family on the farm. He was tired and eager to be alone. However, he agreed to assist and would meet them on the corner of Flinders Street and Gawler Place at 1:15 pm. This gave him over an hour. He excused himself and headed for Balfour's on Rundle Street, near Coles. He was going to enjoy a pie and chips for lunch with a green frog and coffee. Best of all, he intended to enjoy it alone!

Come 3:00 pm, the Grand March was over, Mark was glad that he had contributed. He was outside on a superb afternoon in the autumn sunshine. He was active in mind and body and the concentration factor was minimal when compared to his music adjudication role. Besides, marching bands always engendered a level of excitement that attracted crowds. With twenty-one bands participating in the march there was a level of activity King William Road rarely saw on a Saturday afternoon. The spectacle of the uniforms, the shine of the instruments, the rattle of the kettle drums and the steady resounding beat of the bass drums added an element of glamor to the stately bank buildings, insurance companies, government offices and retail shops for a ninety-minute segment of time. As Mark analyzed the entire scene on this Saturday afternoon, it just came down to it—the Adelaide Central Business District was having fun.

By 4:00 pm all the evaluation forms had been submitted and the rankings of the marching bands had been finalized, with announcements to be made at the Band Concert that evening. Now, at long last, Mark was free with no further obligations.

He was looking forward to a walk around the University of Adelaide, but as he was turning to walk down Gawler Place, he heard his name called. Surprised, he turned to find his entire family, Gary with Helen and the children, and Betty and his sisters with their children as well.

"Well, I never! What brings you all here?" Mark asked with genuine curiosity.

"I decided Kaesler's can fix the pump without me," explained Gary with a rush. "After you left this morning, Helen, Mum and I decided that this should be a family night before you head back to Annapolis next week. We want to have an early dinner and then come to the band concert with you."

"I'm delighted," responded Mark. "I was about to take off on my own and kill time for several hours. So, what shall we do before dinner? Do the kids want to do something or see something?

"Why don't we all go to the Hobby Shop? I bet that is where you were going anyway, right, Mark Schubert?" Betty asked with a twinkle in her eyes. She knew how all her children, especially Mark and Gary, asked to visit their favorite specialty toy shop each time they came to the city.

"Ah, Mum, you remembered!" said Gary. "Let's go there first and then we can slowly walk to the restaurant at the Central Market. By then the girls' husbands will be close to joining us."

What followed next was family time where Mark paused often and absorbed all the evidence of an extended family at play. His nieces and nephews were interacting with each other as siblings or cousins, his brother and sisters (and their husbands) caring for the children and each other, and Betty, now the matriarch, watching too, and fully aware of Mark's contemplative mood.

"I will never have what I am watching now," Mark said to her quietly.

"Perhaps not exactly like this, Mark, but there are many types of family settings. Maybe Christina is the one you are looking for, my dear," Betty replied as she linked his arm in hers.

"You are a sweetheart. You know where I am, don't you?" replied Mark. "We'll see Mum. I will see her in less than a week," added Mark, breathing deeply.

After a very good Italian dinner, the family entered the street to find night coming on quickly. The youngest children were tired, Mark's sisters' families decided they would skip the concert and take the kids home to bed. Mark understood the attraction of an early night.

The concert was excellent, and Mark was besieged by bandsmen he knew and those who wanted to meet him. His adjudicator's hat was off, and he appreciated the time to socialize with fellow musicians. After the concert, Gary and Helen left for home immediately, while Betty stayed with Mark. Before long, Mark recognized that there was no end in sight of people who wanted to talk to him. He ensured Betty was close by his side and then he began a deliberate five-minute effort to break away and head for the Adelaide Hills.

On Sunday morning no one under the Schubert roof went to church. When Gary and Mark returned from milking in the cold drizzle of an overcast day, they all had a lazy breakfast. When the St.

Michaels' bells tolled, Mark felt a rush of guilt knowing that he was keeping his family from Easter services. All were quiet and pensive knowing Mark was departing in less than a day, when Gary said he was going to light the first fire of the season in the family room. Soon, he had a crackling fire shedding light and warmth. Mark inhaled the unmistakable aroma of the burning eucalyptus logs. The family mood rebounded, and he spoke warmly of the wonderful time he had savored at home over the last eleven days. Besides, he reminded everyone, in just over two months he would be home again, this time to remain on Australian soil.

"That's right," said Gary, "And one more thing: Helen and I decided last night that I am going to come over for your graduation from Johns Hopkins. And, if this will work for you, Mark, and you do leave Maryland a few days later, then I want to treat us to a visit to the mountains in Colorado and the Grand Canyon on the way home. This will be at the behest of the Schubert Farm!"

"Are you serious?" asked Mark.

"Why not, and if we can find a way to ride that Durango and Silverton narrow gauge steam train in Colorado, we will do that too," responded Gary, thoroughly enjoying his burst of spontaneity.

"Well, I'm game to tackle all this, if you are? Everything except hand luggage will be shipped to Melbourne anyway," replied Mark.

"Okay, well, that's settled! I'm going to break my dull farming routine for once," said Gary with an impish look in his eye that only Mark fully understood.

Helen smiled broadly, while Betty tried to keep up with the conversation, but it was clear that she, too, was pleased.

"Ah, I like my two sons being adventurous together," Betty said as she went to check on the Sunday roast dinner.

The full Schubert family arrived for lunch. It was still bleak outside but the gaiety inside the home spoke of the extended family at its best. Too wet for the Easter egg hunt, the children were happy to receive their Easter baskets in the warmth of the living room. By late afternoon it was the immediate family alone again and they all went to their respected bed rooms for an afternoon nap. Mark and Gary had to leave at 4:00 am on Monday in readiness for Mark's 6:00 am flight to Sydney.

That evening Mark tried once again to contact Christina by phone. She did not answer. He knew that she had moved to a larger apartment with her sister and she did have the details of his arrival at Dulles. He was almost glad she did not answer as he was not sure what he would say. Every aspect of how Mark and his family saw his future was now tied to Australia, and none of this included Christina. Be that as it may, if Christina and Mark were able to find harmony in their relationship and truly fall in love, it still left the Australia problem. He knew she would not leave the United States, and he could not blame her for that. Nonetheless, after this visit home, with the next phase of his Navy career looking so appealing, Mark knew he could not turn his back on Australia. Perhaps in the early days of their relationship he might have been able, but no longer. He was a true-blue Australian. Now in his bed, with rain falling gently on the roof, Mark had to be honest: he could not see himself with Christina. Yet, to be certain, he had to go back to Annapolis to confirm this one way or the other.

Before 4:00 am the next morning Mark and Gary were ready to drive to the airport. Betty and Helen were in their dressing gowns sipping coffee, while Mark and Gary each downed a quick glass of water, knowing that they would enjoy coffee better at the airport. The parting, while emotional, was not arduous as all knew that in two months Mark would be back again on *terra firma*. Gary prayed, with the four of them holding hands. As Mark hugged his mother tightly, he thanked her for being with him through all the medical tests and discussions.

"We will get through your surgery too," said Betty, "Remember, I love you always. Have a wonderful graduation and we will see all those photos of your adventures with Gary as you go out West."

It was still dark as the car drove down the path to Balhannah Road, through sleeping Hahndorf, the Hills and on to the Adelaide West Beach Airport. Mark checked in and received his boarding passes all the way to Virginia. Gary came back with two coffees and a couple of donuts.

"Gary, I've been thinking about our trip out West. What if I kept the Buick and we drove it across the country? We could say that we made the full journey east to west and it would give us extra flexibility. I have a friend at California Lutheran University in Thousand Oaks in Los Angeles. He could sell the car for us. Overall, it will add a few more days, but I have time now to tidy up my personal details over the next month and we could leave the day after Commencement," said Mark.

"Sounds good to me," replied Gary, "So I would arrive a few days before graduation and we will leave the next day. I like that. But, Mark, all this leaves out Christina; you're not expecting a good outcome here, are you?"

"No, I'm not," muttered Mark as he finished his coffee.

The brothers shook hands and Mark turned and walked onto the tarmac to board his aircraft as the sun was poking its head over the Adelaide Hills beyond the city skyline.

The journey back to Maryland began. Mark reached into his hand luggage under the seat in front of him and took out his Walkman. The music on the cassette tape was that of the Mormon Tabernacle Choir singing traditional hymns. Listening through head phones to these hymns of his youth, Mark sat back deeply into his seat, suddenly feeling like a restless gypsy with no place to call home. The jet roared down the runway, climbed over the Gulf of St. Vincent and then banked east into the sunshine of a new day.

CHAPTER ELEVEN

BREAK UP — THEN GRADUATION

"Remember that sometimes not getting what you want
Is a wonderful stroke of luck."
—The Dalai Lama

Four hours later, Mark was high over the Pacific heading towards Los Angeles. No longer did flights need to refuel in Fiji and Honolulu. The direct flight was a long thirteen hours, but it was done in one hop. Half way through the flight, Mark realized he was not ruminating about his past life as he always did on long flights. Instead, he was relaxed and listening to music, history tapes and generally enjoying being in the now, and not the past. This is a first, he thought to himself.

When he landed at Los Angeles, he called Christina, but there was still no answer. Mark felt a little miffed, but if she was not at Dulles International Airport, he would take a taxi to Annapolis. It would be expensive, but it would get him to his apartment before 10:00 pm. Upon landing at Dulles, there was no Christina to be found. There was little point in calling again. Mark waited an hour and then took a taxi to his Eastport apartment. He was a little irked. Nonetheless, the positive side to this might be that Christina was having second thoughts too. The roads were relatively free of traffic at this hour and the driver made exceptional time through D.C., onto US-50, into Annapolis and then across the Spa Creek Bridge to his street. Strange, thought Mark as the taxi pulled up to his apartment, there seemed to be a light on inside.

He paid the taxi and walked to his door, put his luggage down and took out his key to open the door. Once inside, he set his luggage to the left in his lounge nook. He could hear noise and it sounded like people. He walked quietly through the living room; the sounds were more audible. He could distinguish voices and the sounds of movement coming from his bedroom.

"Who's there?" he called out and held his breath.

There was immediate silence. Mark moved closer and pushed the bedroom door open.

"Mark! What are you doing here?" gasped Christina.

He could see her frantically reaching for the sheets as another person squirmed beneath her.

"What the hell is going on?" exclaimed Mark swallowing hard.

"I didn't think you were arriving until tomorrow!" cried Christina. Mark flipped the light on. Christina rolled off her companion and clutched the sheets up to her neck, but not before Mark saw that both were naked.

He shook his head in disbelief. The shock of it all had momentarily dulled his senses. Then he grasped the full situation.

"I called you, Christina, several times!" His voice was trembling. "I'm going outside. I'll give you and your cavorting friend fifteen minutes and when I come back you had better be gone."

He spun on his heels and strode to the front door. He slammed it shut behind him and walked slowly toward the Chart House Restaurant on Second Street. How could Christina do such a thing? Was there no self-respect? Did she so despise their relationship that she could insult it by bringing another man into Mark's bedroom? Why? Mark and Christina had not even slept together. What sort of person was she?

All this and more, was seething through his mind, yet he felt a cold clarity coming over him. "That's done it," he said to himself. "There's no future for us." In a few moments he heard a car engine start and turned in time to see its headlights flick on. As they passed him, the engine roaring, Mark could see them staring straight ahead.

He went back to his apartment, his heart still racing. The door to the bedroom stood open. He could see the bed clothes pulled onto the floor and the pillows strewn across the bed. He left it all as he found it, closed the door, and stumbled into the other bedroom. Without bothering to change he threw himself on the bed and was asleep in minutes. Before falling off, he vowed never to sleep again in the other bed.

Jetlag woke Mark before dawn. He got up and walked into Annapolis to his usual breakfast restaurant and slowly ate his morning meal with several coffees. He wanted to be alone with his thoughts, but several acquaintances acknowledged him or came and shook hands, since he frequented this *deli* often. Mark needed a plan to deal with Christina on top of his overarching intention to conclude all his personal business in Maryland. He did need to speak with her and to end their relationship amicably. Already he had fulfilled all obligations to the Naval Academy, and he had alerted his landlord to his departure near the end of May. This left final payments to Johns Hopkins and the closing of his Maryland bank account. He had opened a new bank account in Adelaide two weeks ago and had a credit card to care for expenses after his graduation and the adventure out West. He was keeping the car for this trip.

He walked back to his apartment feeling sanguine that his remaining personal and business specifics were easily manageable in the next two months. Equally, he hoped his next conversation with Christina would go well too. While he did not understand why she had done what occurred last night, he knew that she always wanted more than he could give. Back in his apartment, he stripped his bed and put all the sheets in the trash. He would use this room as storage until his goods were picked up for shipping back to Australia.

That evening Christina called Mark and said: "Mark, I am so sorry. I had no right to use your apartment. My sister was at my place and I didn't know what else to do."

Mark was tempted to reply with several caustic comments that Christina had walked right into, but he decided against it. Instead he asked: "Can I take you to dinner tomorrow night, or can we meet over coffee? Whatever is best for you."

"Yes, I can do that. Aren't you going to yell at me? I was wrong, and I am so sorry," she whimpered.

"No, Christina, there is no need for yelling at each other. We need to talk and deal with it," replied Mark.

Mutually, they selected a restaurant away from Main Street and agreed to meet at 6:00 pm.

"Mark, I didn't realize you were coming home on Monday night. I thought it was tonight," she explained.

"It's Okay, Christina. Let's meet tomorrow evening and talk," said Mark calmly, knowing that Christina was sure to read his tone as being dispassionate and coldhearted.

"I will. I am so sorry," Christina exclaimed one more time.

Mark put the phone down and sat quietly for a while. He spoke out loud, "Don't get yourself upset. It's over!" Regardless, he could not help muttering, "So if I came into Dulles on Tuesday night and she used my bed on Monday night, then that would be fine—and we would carry on because I was not in the know. I don't think so!"

It was almost dark, and although Mark was tired, his adrenalin was flowing because of Christina's phone call. He put on his sneakers and went for a walk around the streets of Eastport. An hour later he returned to his apartment, had a shower and went to bed in his second bedroom.

The next evening Mark and Christina met at the restaurant. He was determined to act as nonchalant as possible and he let her kiss him before she sat at the table. It was a little awkward at first, but ordering their food helped the communication to flow.

Christina began by saying again: "Mark, I am so sorry. But look, here is the flight schedule you gave me, and you did say you were arriving at Dulles on Tuesday, April 2 at 7:00 pm. See, here it is!"

"Christina, I made a mistake. So, that makes it alright for you to be in my bed with another man the night before you thought I was coming home?" asked Mark incredulously.

"I know. It was wrong of me, but it is your fault I was with another man," Christina protested.

"My fault, please tell me how?" Mark asked.

Christina looked at him and shook her head slowly, sensing the nonsense of it all. Nonetheless, she began: "I wanted to date you from the first night I served you at the restaurant. We had so much fun for the first few weeks. I began to think this was the man for me. Then, you dropped the bombshell that you were returning to Australia, admittedly, only for two weeks."

She continued: "That crushed me, but I got beyond that and hoped that we would make love before you left. But, you wouldn't, it was against your religion. Mark, that damn religion of yours, it's got in the way of us. I even went to church with you, but I just don't know why you let it dominate your life."

"So, that's how you see it all?" asked Mark.

"Yes, I wanted you, all of you, before you left for Australia. Then, with you gone I felt abandoned and one night I met this guy who was pushy and wanted me," Christina said defiantly.

Mark looked at her and sighed. He placed his hands on the table and began to talk in a low voice, conscious that they were in a public place.

"Let's talk about this. I think if we are honest, we'll realize we are both lonely people open to finding a solid relationship with the right person. We have both been hurt previously and, at least for me, I am nervous of starting a new relationship. Neither one of us wants to fail again."

Mark paused, took a drink, looked around, and then continued: "If I am saying this the wrong way, please tell me. At first, I did feel good about us. I wanted to be with you, go for a walk and a movie, and just feel close together. But I think here is the difference between us. I do have this religion thing, as you say. It is important to me and it's a large part of who I am. I was raised in a practicing Lutheran family where we still believe in a personal God. Most people in Hahndorf are the same. When I was a child, I just accepted that all people everywhere believed in God."

"Now, I know what I have just described is not necessarily cool today. I may even sound outdated, old fashioned and even weird. But for me it is real. I don't force this on others and certainly not on you," said Mark aware that he must not lecture.

"I don't think you are trying to force your religion on me," Christina replied in a conciliatory voice. "I don't understand your need of God, but if that is what you need, then I am fine with it. Why can't we still date and see where our relationship takes us."

Mark nodded and then responded: "Yes, that is one approach, but it will not work for me. Christina, I am too intense a person not to have my girlfriend, maybe eventually my wife, in harmony with all aspects of my life. My faith is not a coat I can put on and take off at whim. It is who I am, and I want to talk about it, share it and use it in all that I do in life until the end. I feel more strongly about this than I did five years ago."

Christina sighed and shook her head. Her tone was bitter: "So, you are saying that unless I become a Lutheran, then our relationship is over!"

"Christina," implored Mark, "Nobody is going to force you to become a Lutheran or any other denomination. I am saying far more than that. I have just come back from my family and I am returning to Australia permanently in less than two months. While in Australia, I was praying about us. Then, I come back to my apartment and find you there. Everything is telling me that we have no future together. I think we should say 'good-bye' tonight. You need to complete your graduate degree and find a future for yourself here in your country. My future is in Australia. I just don't see it any other way."

Christina stared angrily at Mark. Her eyes blazed, and she snapped, her voice rising: "I could hate you for what you have just said. What I did in your apartment meant nothing to me! You should be mature enough to realize that!"

Mark shifted uncomfortably in his chair. They were in a restaurant and he could see that Christina was on the brink of full fury.

"No, Christina, it is much more than that. I don't think we are well suited together. Our worldviews are too far apart. I think we should separate, and both look elsewhere for happiness," Mark replied, firmly. He knew that his words were probably not the best for the moment.

Suddenly, Christina stood up, looked down at Mark and said, "I do hate you. You and your damn worldview—whatever the hell that means. I wish I had never met you."

She picked up her purse and stormed out of the restaurant, knowing that people were looking on and discussing in hushed tones their version of what had just occurred.

Mark put his hand up to his forehead. He looked down. He knew he was being watched and could not hide. He motioned for his meal check, paid his bill using his new credit card and walked out of the restaurant.

Sleep was difficult for the next few nights. Life seemed such a juxtaposition. At least Christina and he had faced each other and, as fractious as their dinner was, they were now free to go their separate ways. On Saturday morning, Mark was on the verge of a pity party by blaming himself for another calamitous relationship when Schulzy called.

"I know you are back from Australia, Mark. Why haven't you called me?" he asked.

"Ah, John, I am sorry. I have been a little pre-occupied, but I do need to see you. When are you available for some serious pastoral counselling?" Mark asked.

Mark's tone piqued John's interest: "I'll be here in the office all morning," he said. "Come whenever you want."

"I'll be there in fifteen minutes," responded Mark.

As he put down the phone he paused and thought about what he would say to John, his pastor and best friend in Maryland. Then, he stood up and said, "I'm going to see Schulzy. I'm not going to let this burden me any longer."

"Man, that didn't take you long," said John as he came from behind his desk to shake Mark's hand. "It's good to have you back in Annapolis. Let me get us some coffee and we can take our time and talk."

By the time John and Mark had finished their coffee, Mark had concluded the conversation about his trip home, the family, the farm, Hahndorf and the Easter Nationals. John took Mark's cup and, with his own, walked it to the kitchenette. When he returned, he said, "Now, my big question: how's Christina?"

Mark looked at his pastor, pressed his lips together while shaking his head slowly and replied: "My friend goes straight to the point!"

The next fifteen minutes were spent with Mark relating his torrid welcome-home encounter with Christina and continued until their parting at the restaurant two evenings ago. John listened and every so often he nodded in dismay or raised his hands in alarm. Mark leaned forward in his chair, looked at John eye to eye and said with a resigned shake of his head: "John, I just have to accept that I'm not particularly good in forming successful relationships with women. In fact, I'm probably more to blame than Christina for our sorry outcome."

John cut him off abruptly. "No, Mark, don't say that! You may recall that I was pushing you to look in the first place. Shirley and I saw you as a suave, out-going professional man who was so good interacting with people, and we asked ourselves, 'Why isn't this guy married, or at least dating?'"

Biting his bottom lip as he pondered, Mark agreed. "Yes," he said, "You did give me the initial nudge."

Continuing, John added, "But, you know, the few times Shirley and I saw the two of you together, the more we wondered how long it would last. Mark, she lacked substance in the things that matter to you and she certainly showed no interest in church, or things spiritual."

"Thank you for saying that," replied Mark, "I needed to hear that from you. We were not 'equally yoked,' that was for sure. I was beginning to beat myself up on yet another failure."

John jumped in quickly, "You have to stop saying you have failed. As I know your story, you courted and married Roslyn; that marriage was doomed before it started. Then, I think, Christina was the next girl in your life, and for several months only. This is hardly a record of failure in the love and romance department!"

Putting both hands up in defeat, Mark gave in: "You're right. I've just got to get beyond this and be more deliberate in the future."

"Schub—changing the subject—what about your medical appointments in Adelaide? Is there a clear plan to deal with your prostate cancer?"

"Yes, there is," replied Mark. "Actually, my trip home clarified more than the 'when' and 'where' of my surgery. And, breaking up with Christina has helped even more. For a while, I was thinking Christina and I might have made it. If so, I was prepared to think of calling America home. But, not now. Spending those few days with family on the farm and mixing with the Aussie banding world again, I know I must return home, and permanently."

"My surgery is booked for early June and I should be ready to start my new Navy job in Melbourne in early September. It's all coming together, if only over the last two days. I'm praying about it and beginning to feel good about my future."

"Well, I'm so pleased for you, Mark," said John. "You have been through more ordeals than most over the last couple of years. It's time for you to experience some sunshine in your life. I still can't believe you have cancer so young in life, but we can be grateful that it is not going to be life threatening and you can aspire to many more years of living. Of course, this is always by God's grace."

"I agree," replied Mark, "But, it is life changing. I'm still coming to terms with it all."

It was now after mid-day and both men had other duties looming. John had Sunday's sermon to complete and Mark was going to attend the first practice session of the St. Paul's concert band with the new conductor. Before they separated, John prayed for God's guidance, wisdom and protection to be given in abundance to Mark in the weeks and months ahead. There was a special bond which had been formed by both men over the last five years. As they embraced, for the first time each recognized that their remaining time together was short, yet their friendship would last forever.

For Mark it had been an intense morning and he returned to his apartment feeling weary. As a matter of fact, it had been an exhausting week; first the international flight, then the Christina saga and separation, and finally, a comprehensive conversation with his pastor. He had four hours before band rehearsal. He was alone. He went into the second bedroom, stretched out on the bed and went to sleep.

At 5:00 pm, Mark was jolted awake by the phone. He blinked, opened his mouth several times to shake off sleep and moistened his lips as he picked up the phone.

"Mark, are you alright? It's Gary. We have been trying to call you for your birthday on Thursday and to check that all is well with you," said Gary in a loud voice.

"Oh, dear me, Gary, I'm sorry. I should have called on Tuesday and told you that I arrived safely. I've been dealing with a lot of things. Christina and I are no longer an item. The end was rather dramatic. I am okay. This morning I spoke with John Schulz about it all. It gave me perspective and I will be fine. We can talk about it on our road trip. I won't say anymore now. But, with so much happening I forgot about my birthday until you mentioned it just now." The words poured out of him and Mark instantly regretted saying that he had forgotten his own birthday.

It was too late. Gary picked up on it immediately and exclaimed, "Mark, you forgot your own birthday! Has it been that bad?"

"Yeah, and then some, but it's over now and this morning my talk with Schulzy has made me determined to move on and not stress out on it all. Just got to let it go! Another sad lesson of life," Mark replied and fell silent, determined to say no more over the phone.

"Well, that's good. Can I tell Mum that it is over with Christina and that you are feeling relief?" asked Gary.

"Yes, please, that'll be good. Tell her that she can counsel me all she likes when I am convalescing under her care in June. Gary, I must go now as the St. Paul's concert band rehearsal begins in fifteen minutes. The good news is that my replacement conductor is being introduced tonight. Thank you for calling! We're going to have such a good trip in a few weeks from now," said Mark. He reached for a clean shirt.

The next six weeks went by quickly and Mark deliberately kept his pace of life at a low level of daily assignments and necessary accomplishments. He scheduled himself for an hourly euphonium practice session each morning except Sundays at St. Paul's. It was his luxury gift to himself; rarely had he had such a consistent, unencumbered schedule for his own music practice. He was mindful that he was soon permanently leaving another portion of God's acre that he had come to cherish for its natural beauty, rich history and vital significance in today's world. He walked as often as he could from Eastport to old town Annapolis and on to the Naval Academy, to his pondering bench gazing out at the Severn River and beyond to the Chesapeake Bay. Yet, there were other places he would miss too. He had become so familiar with Johns Hopkins University and its focus on cutting-edge research in so many fields of knowledge. He had come to love Baltimore, and especially the Mall in the nation's capital. There were so many historical sites that were so well preserved for posterity. He resonated with the national pride that was evident in so much of the Richmond-Washington-Baltimore corridor. He would miss it all, but never would he forget the memories he had locked away over the last five years.

By way of a poor comparison, he would often think of his home town of Hahndorf. It, too, had history, buildings and a way of life worthy of preservation. Alas, what a tragedy that tourism and greedy vendors had raped so much of his home town. It could make him angry. Yet, he had to admit that the tourists did not come in their busloads to see the *old* Hahndorf at work as Mark had known it in his childhood. They came to see the historic buildings and rustic farm implements, to learn of the German culture and to taste its food, its beer and frolic to its music. Indeed, isn't that what Mark enjoyed doing as he visited the numerous points of interest within the Greater Washington panorama? He finally had to agree it was all relative. As he digested all this, he determined to be kinder and more tolerant to the *new* Hahndorf when he returned in a few weeks.

One afternoon he found a card in the mailbox from Christina. He opened the envelope with mild trepidation but found she had written kind words wishing him future success and happiness as he returned to Australia. She also wrote that she did not want to think of an unfathomable bridge between them. Mark was touched emotionally. He felt good that she had taken the initiative that he dared not take himself. He went inside and picked up the phone and called Christina.

"Christina, it is Mark. I have just read your very kind card and I thank you for sending it. I want to wish you every success as well. I … I wonder if you would be interested in having all my china, cutlery, glassware and pots and pans for you and your sister as you continue to set up your new apartment. I was going to give them to St. Paul's next week."

Mark was acting spontaneously with his offer, but Christina was delighted.

"I'm glad you can use them. Why don't you come around next Wednesday; any time after 5:00 pm," said Mark as the conversation ended.

Gary arrived three days before Commencement. By this time, Mark's apartment was almost an empty shell. His books, papers and personal effects had been picked-up by the removing company and were anticipated to arrive at the Port of Melbourne toward the end of July. Christina had come by and gathered her kitchenware. What remained was basic furniture to house Mark and Gary until the morning after Commencement. Then, Schulzy and St. Paul's would collect the kitchen, living room, bedroom furniture and Mark's desk, chair and bookcases and distribute these into the community as they saw fit. Mark was left with two suit cases of clothes and personal items and his euphonium to take on their Western adventure, and then across the Pacific and home to the farm at Hahndorf. Mark told Gary that they were both about to understand what it is to "live out of suitcases for two weeks."

Two days before Commencement, Mark had his car serviced for the last time. He added new tires for the long journey and to provide incentive for its resale value as he dropped it off at Californian Lutheran University. With nothing else pressing, this was a day when Mark and Gary walked for hours not because they had to, but because they chose to. It was Mark's way of having Gary experience Annapolis as he had come to know and love it—on foot. Over the five years Eastport and Annapolis had been his home, he estimated that he had walked hundreds of miles over the same streets keeping himself physically fit and his mind focused on what was important in his life. Now, for the last time, his brother was part of his experience. Walking up to the Maryland State House was vastly different to the typical drive-around by most tourists. Gary, who had seen it before by car, along with Helen and Betty, was impressed to understand that it was the oldest U.S. state capitol in continuous legislative use, and for a brief period served as the nation's capital. Even walking past a salt water taffy store on Main Street was different because they lingered and watched a batch of taffy being poured out on a large slab of marble and then shaped into its recognizable form. Best of all, Mark gave Gary a thorough walk through the extensive grounds of the Naval Academy from the old Naval Cemetery to the new Alumni Hall to the Chapel to the center of campus and, finally, to Mark's pondering bench at the end of the sports field. Here they sat, rested and talked about many things and nothing of consequence. Both wished that their father could have seen Annapolis.

Weeks before, Mark had asked Gary if he would speak to the St. Paul's Seniors Club about life in Australia as a farmer. The final day before Commencement was occupied with this meeting and was followed by the final recital of the St. Paul's Concert Band, with Mark conducting. This was open to all parishioners and members of the community as well. Gary was anxious all morning about his presentation, and he kept saying to Mark: "I'm only a farmer and not accustomed to public speaking like you."

Mark showed little empathy, replying: "Nonsense, Gary. You are the *best* farmer and a great conversationalist. All you do is talk to these seniors about your life work, and as a Lutheran farmer in a historically Lutheran community you have a tremendous hook to capture their interest. You'll be a success."

That afternoon some fifty seniors gathered for their monthly meeting. Pastor Schulz gave a brief devotional and then introduced Gary as Mark's younger brother and mentioned their Western adventure after Mark's graduation and their return to Australia two weeks later.

Gary's slides of the farm, of Hahndorf and its churches and historic buildings, of cows, sheep, chickens, lavender fields, tractors and his family, including several of a much younger Mark, brought the church hall alive for almost an hour. He engaged his audience. His slides were colorful and attractive, and they complemented Gary's farm-life dialog. It was a complete success, with many asking how their Seniors Club could arrange a future visit to Australia with Hahndorf as the prime attraction. Mark and John sat back and beamed at how well-received Gary was by the older parishioners of St. Paul's. Perhaps the ultimate accolade came from a sheepish widow who asked if there were any older, single men in Hahndorf as handsome and charming as the Schubert brothers. The audience burst into laughter as the lady sat down absolutely enjoying her moment on the stage. Gary looked at Mark, back at the lady, and said: "Madam, if you come to Hahndorf, I will find a suitable man for you to bring back to Annapolis!"

That response brought forth gales of merriment and infectious guffawing as these elders resorted to their childhood past. Rising to restore some sense of equilibrium, Pastor Schulz used hand motions to quieten his senior flock who paid little attention to him, such was the pleasure of the afternoon. Pastor Schulz good-naturedly spoke over the laughter: "Ladies and gentlemen, or is it girls and boys, I don't know when I have appreciated and had more fun at a Seniors Club meeting. Your response has been delightful, and I suspect there is no one in this room at this moment who is feeling any aches and pains. Scripture tells us that laughter is good medicine and I think Gary Schubert has brought all of us the remedy of what may ail any of us this afternoon. Gary, thank you for your presentation, your photographs and for showing us a taste of farm life in Hahndorf today."

A few hours later, as the concert began the sanctuary was nearly filled to capacity with over four hundred and fifty people in the pews, including some thirty Naval Academy musicians in full uniform. Some had assisted Mark in the formation of the youth band at St. Paul's. All Naval Academy musicians knew of his focus on the development of community youth music. In the past four years, the youth concert band had grown to a stable forty members with feeder groups around Annapolis at the elementary, or primary school levels.

With some of his naval musicians playing in the concert band, it was a performance that St. Paul's would remember for a long time. The excitement among the younger band members was palpable and they gave of their best. Mark performed two solos during the concert, with his first the *Le Carnaval de Venice,* or the Carnival of Venice, with piano accompaniment. He knew this music by heart and the church acoustics with a full audience allowed his tone and dexterity to shine at his final performance. His last solo was Ennio Morricone's *Gabriel's Oboe,* the main theme from the film, *The Mission.* He liked playing this piece and was fully aware of the emotion it had engendered previously and again, this evening, as he concluded his five-year sojourn at the Naval Academy and his doctoral studies at Johns Hopkins University. It seemed an appropriate time to let sentiment loose.

No sooner had Mark ended his last high pause note, the audience burst into applause and rose to its feet. The Navy contingent toward the rear of the church came forward and surrounded their colleague in full support and appreciation.

Pastor Schulz approached the microphone and asked the audience to be seated. He began his final public farewell to Mark: "A musician from a foreign land came among us five years ago. He was one of us, a Lutheran directly descended from the first German settlers to Australia in 1839. They called themselves *Old Lutherans* and were escaping religious persecution from a region of Prussia. They landed in Adelaide, the capital of South Australia, the only Australian state that was founded without convicts, or indentured labor. They came to worship and live in freedom. Mark Schubert comes from a farming family and this afternoon the Seniors Club was fortunate to hear a presentation on farming life in present day Hahndorf from his brother, Gary."

"Mark and Gary, if I may, you are good, sincere, decent men who have modelled a believable Christian life with consistency and humility, and with a love of and for others. We will miss you, your ministry, your music and your fellowship."

"Mark, God bless you as you graduate from Johns Hopkins University tomorrow, as you both trek across the U.S. and then as you head home to Australia. You may call Australia home, but remember we will always keep a place in our hearts for you, and you are always welcome in Annapolis."

That night Mark and Gary went for one last walk across the Spa Creek Bridge to the Annapolis City Dock and back to the apartment. They both sensed the ending of Mark's American experience and were glad that they were brothers sharing these final days together. They went to their rest that night needing sleep.

Commencement morning had both men awake and down at Mark's breakfast restaurant long before the working day was under way. It was a sunny day with dotted clouds in the sky and the promise of an early taste of summer. Mark's graduation party included Gary, John and Shirley Schulz and their two children. They drove to Baltimore and arrived characteristically early. Gary was visibly excited to witness his brother's graduation from a prestigious American university. He was wielding his camera in all directions capturing buildings and people in academic regalia. As surreptitiously as possible he took as many photos of Mark bedecked in his lemon and black doctoral gown with velvet tam and its gold bullion tassel. Mark was certainly pleased to be graduating as it signified the culmination of his long-held ambition. He did feel conspicuous and somewhat uncomfortable in his elaborate paraphernalia; this from a person accustomed to wearing uniforms. On top of all this, he was beginning to perspire under the weight of his gown.

While John and Shirley and their children went to their assigned seating, Gary urged Mark to show him *quickly* the George Peabody Library. "It will have to be quick!" said Mark. Inside the Library, Gary stood transfixed, looking up at six, maybe seven floors, of the "most beautiful and dignified library I have ever seen." Taking photos in rapid succession, Gary muttered in hushed tones about its architecture, its stunning black and white marble floors, its lighting and its sheer elegance.

"Have you read this, Mark? It was George Peabody's wish to create a library 'for the free use of all persons who desire to consult it,'" said Gary, reading the insignia.

"Gary, we have to go," said Mark, looking at his watch. "You are right, there is so much dignity on this campus. You know, it was only a few years ago that Johns Hopkins and Peabody Conservatory joined together. It has worked in my favor as I have been able to do research across disciplines. Had this not been the case, I might not be earning a PhD today, but a DMA with a much more restricted focus. I'll always be grateful for my education at this University."

The next two hours witnessed Mark graduating with his Doctor of Philosophy degree along with many other doctoral recipients in many disciplines. The outdoor Commencement area was awash with the colors of academic regalia from universities around the world, with the fresh green of new leaves on the trees, with spring flowers and the brilliance of red, white and purple azalea bushes. Even the audience was colorful, with spring dresses on the women and little girls, and the men bold enough to wear summer suits and sports coats. Gary's camera clicked its way through the grand music, the speeches, the conferral of diplomas, and continued until Mark returned to his party at the end of the recessional. With that, he looked at them all, exhaled and declared, "I have done it!"

John announced that St. Paul's was taking the party to lunch in recognition of the ministry Mark had contributed to the church members, especially in establishing the youth concert band. The chosen restaurant was Haussner's, a well-known Baltimore landmark of some seventy years. Mark had eaten there several times and knew it was not for the faint-of-heart. It served 'old-world' style food and housed a large collection of cluttered art displayed on the walls. Again, Gary was in his element and shuttered away with his camera. It was a sumptuous meal with little attention to calorie intake. His best compliment was uttered at the end of a generous serving of German chocolate cake: "Phew, that was so good! You Americans eat very well. Mark, this food is truly the best of *Deutscheland kuchen!* It is Hahndorf food and what we grew up on from childhood. But it is going to sit heavy and there will be no tea, oops, supper for me tonight!"

They all agreed, laughing along with Gary that supper was not high on anyone's list. As the day wore on, Mark changed the mood of the table by announcing that this was his time to thank John and Shirley Schulz.

"John, how do I thank you for all you mean to me, and have given to me over the last five years? You have been my American brother away from home. You have been my pastor and the one to whom I have turned to when in need—and that was more often than I like to admit."

"Shirley, you have allowed John and I to spend a lot of time together. I sometimes felt guilty that I was stealing him from you and the children. Thank you for wonderful meals, the comfort of your home and, really, your care and love to this foreigner."

With a few more words, Mark bowed and gave the Schulz's a gift card, adding, "This is for a new TV, so you can all watch a bigger picture of the Redskins trying for the Super Bowl."

Both cars drove back to Annapolis and Eastport, Gary chortling on for half of the one-hour trip until he suddenly went quiet. It was apparent that the heavy German fare and his jet lag had gotten the better of him and he was dozing. Mark smiled: he was so glad his little brother had come to his graduation. Gary was a generous brother too, Mark reflected; it was his idea for the Schulz's to have a new television set. When they reached the apartment, they both packed and set aside toiletries and clothes for the next day. Then they walked down to the marina next to the Chart House and sat and talked about their journey starting early on the morrow.

CHAPTER TWELVE

A ROAD TRIP TO REMEMBER

"In life, it's not where you go,
It's who you travel with."
—Charles Schulz

Early Friday morning, Mark and Gary had a last breakfast with John Schulz at Mark's favorite diner. At exactly 7:00 am, they said a final farewell to John, gave him the apartment keys and got into their packed Buick Regal two-door, and pointed it westwards.

Once out of Annapolis heading towards Baltimore, Mark spoke to Gary about two things they needed to keep in mind over the next twelve days: "First, this is a long drive. It is longer than driving east to west across Australia. And the second point, I am going to have to watch more than you, there are hundreds of detours I wish we could take to look at special places and historic sites along the way. We just have to be at LAX by 6:00 pm on Wednesday, June 5, or even a day earlier."

"I hear you," responded Gary. "We don't want to miss our flight home. But, Mark, in the meantime, let's enjoy each day to the full as it happens!" said Gary, smiling. Mark smiled too and thought that he ought to adopt some of Gary's spontaneity for himself.

When they reached I-695, the Baltimore Beltway, they encountered morning traffic and settled into the slower pace. Fortunately, they kept moving all the time until they exited onto I-70W, the interstate highway, which would take them most of the way across the country. At Frederick, the undulating landscape gave way to the Appalachians, and as they climbed over the first range and into Hagerstown, they saw an old town experiencing a burgeoning growth as a bedroom community of Greater Washington. They climbed again, into Pennsylvania with its fertile valleys and farmland.

"Have you ever wondered what people in these isolated houses and small farms do for a living?" asked Gary, breaking a long silence.

"Probably whatever they can do to survive, raise families and just live as best they can," replied Mark.

"Yes, just to live, but is that good enough?" asked Gary, obviously with more on his mind. "I mean, you have your music and I have the farm, but how can people just settle to live to survive?"

"Gary, we are the lucky ones. Most people in the U.S., Australia, all over the world, do not have much choice as to how they work and where. They don't have a lot of options and most times they find work as they can and live paycheck to paycheck."

"Yep, that's right, pay to pay! Not very exciting, is it?" He glanced out the window and shook his head slightly.

"You and I have the farm and the sweat and good judgment of our Schubert ancestors all the way back," said Mark. "Now, how many *greats?* Great-great-great grandfather who was allocated his first block under the Hufendorf plan and built from there. You are the one who has fiduciary care of the Schubert farm. So, no reckless schemes and foolhardy ventures, little brother. We are counting on you!" said Mark with a sidelong glance at his brother.

"Oh, and one more comment on this: it is the farm that has made my PhD and time in America possible. How many other brass colleagues back home would have liked the opportunity that has been mine?" he said.

"I get it, but how many also had the original dream and how many would have worked as hard as you?" asked Gary. "I'm not trying to minimize any of this, but I think you would have still done all this, farm or no farm. It would have just taken longer, and you would be driving a VW Beetle and not a Buick!"

"Perhaps," agreed Mark. "One thing I know, and that is education makes a difference to the choices we have in life and, thereby, the lives we eventually live. I have seen too much evidence of this over the last twenty years, the last five in Annapolis and other parts of America."

"I accept that," said Gary. "But, as I look at these valleys and hillside roads, it's these people I was thinking about. Back home, it is people in Ceduna or Burra or Millicent, where they are isolated from large towns and cities and their choices are few and far between. Some of these people don't have the options that you gave your students at Luther College in Melbourne or at St. Paul's in Annapolis."

Mark looked at his brother: "I'm glad to hear you talk like this. You have plenty to occupy you every day in running the farm and with all your leadership duties at church and in the community. Yet, you can still empathize with the disparate poor—there's a term for you! These people are virtually trapped by their circumstances at a socio-economic level that perpetuates paycheck to paycheck survival. I want to help kids from these families find options through music and education. The issue for the near future is to see how much I can accomplish while being full-time Navy."

"Mark, returning to my fiduciary responsibility, tell me honestly how you felt when I first proposed planting lavender. You were in Sydney and supported the idea. Is that how you really felt? Most in Hahndorf thought I was going to lose big time," Gary asked.

"I did support it immediately. You did your research, you did a cost analysis and went in to it with your eyes open. Those who were skeptical were only revealing how much they were locked into the old paradigm that Hahndorf was a dairy, sheep, potatoes, cropping district, and should stay that way. Lavender was so foreign to them, they thought it would fail. You know, I remember Dad saying to me when you decided to go to Roseworthy College that he hoped you could learn to be a good businessman-farmer who was not afraid to think outside the box. You have done that with your lavender project," replied Mark.

"Thank you for telling me that," said Gary. "You know, the lavender deal has been so successful I can't keep up with all the demands and potential orders, even from Victoria. After, five years, it has returned all the money I invested, including the additional sheds for drying and extracting the oil. I thought I would be dealing with the Hahndorf tourist trade only, but I have cosmetic companies, herbal-medicinal practitioners and florists wanting more of our fresh bunches, dried lavender, oils and perfumes. I am so pleased I did it. Helen and Mum have gotten involved too, as you know, and it gives them a real interest in the business. I have to thank God for blessing this project."

"Yes, every day is a day given to us by God," replied Mark, as they fell quiet again. They drove through Breezewood and into West Virginia, crossing the Ohio river at Wheeling. Still on I-70, they stopped to refuel, have lunch and a good stretch, just south of Pittsburgh. For Mark, it was good to know that they would both be contributing to the driving on this cross-country trek.

On the road again, Mark mentioned that he wished they had time to drive north to see Frank Lloyd Wright's *Fallingwater*, knowing Gary's interest in architecture. While the potential closeness interested them for this once in a lifetime visit, they knew that Colorado was their fixed goal and it was still 1,600 miles to their west. This was ample motivation to keep them on schedule. By mid-afternoon they had travelled through Zanesville on their way to Columbus, Ohio's largest city. They stopped for gas and a needed break from sitting. This was their longest day of travel and an ice cream was a pleasant reward for their endurance.

Ohio surprised Gary with its flat landscape and interminable succession of farms scattered as far as he could see on either side of the highway.

"Yes," said Mark, "This is the Midwest, the breadbasket of the nation. Ohio is a very important state for its productivity."

"It must be," exclaimed Gary. "Look in any direction, and the pattern is the same: farm house with sheds or barns and some trees, then crops and cultivated land. Each farm seems close to the other, so it must be fertile and productive land. It's all so neat and tidy, like a giant has a massive railway layout in his garage and he has placed homes, barns and trees at regular intervals, and we are driving through it all. I just love it!"

The endless, flat farmland continued for two hours until the tall buildings of the Indianapolis skyline appeared on the western horizon. As they by-passed Indiana's capital, various highway signs caught their attention and alerted them to the landmarks they had no time to visit; "Crossroads of America," Home of the Indianapolis 500," "The Benjamin Harrison Presidential site."

"I always thought it would be good to go to an Indy 500 race," said Mark. "It would be a memory-maker, for sure. I think it is still the largest one-day sporting event in the world."

"Yes, I agree. I loved Paul Newman in *Winning*," said Gary.

The landscape west of Indianapolis became mile upon mile of gently rolling terrain. An hour along and they came to their stopping point for the first day of travel. Located on the banks of the Wabash River, and the largest city in the Wabash Valley, Terra Haute provided Mark and Gary much-needed relief as they pulled into the parking lot of their hotel. After they checked in, they walked to a small diner, ate lightly and returned to their room for a shower and a review of their next day's journey. As the sun was setting, they went to their rest, neither wishing to watch TV from bed.

Next morning, they were on I-70W by 7:00 am with a goal to reach Ellsworth, Kansas, in about eleven hours. The miles covered would be less than the previous day, but they were on a carefully prepared road trip, and by sundown they planned to have covered over twelve hundred miles of their nearly three-thousand-mile journey from Annapolis to Los Angeles International Airport. Indeed, it would be more than this in total miles because they were stopping at chosen sights along the way.

They crossed the Mississippi River and by-passed St. Louis. A while later, they passed over the Missouri River twice, drove through Columbia and approached the outskirts of Kansas City, spanning the former stockyards and rail yard. They crossed yet another river, the Kansas River, entered Kansas and drove on to Lawrence, Topeka, and Abilene. Just after 7:30 pm they finally reached Ellsworth.

Gary was hungrier than he had thought as he dug into his meal in the restaurant. He nodded vigorously, his mouth full, as Mark lamented all the places they had had to pass by.

"We could have spent a full day in St. Louis, perhaps two in Kansas City; I would have liked to see their railroad station, the photos are beautiful. Then, we could have easily spent half a day each in Topeka and Abilene. Dwight Eisenhower came from Abilene. He is perhaps my favorite president after WWII, and I would have liked to see his presidential library and his boyhood home. Just so much to feast our eyes upon if only we had the time," said Mark breathlessly as he finished his peach cobbler.

"Well, we knew we had to be selective in the time we had and so what are these two farmers doing? We are checking out mountains, steam engines, the Grand Canyon and a big lake in the mountains above Los Angeles because you said that I must see it," said Gary, bent over Mark's itinerary of their journey.

"Don't forget Laguna Beach. You are going to wish Helen was with you when you see the Pacific Ocean from its western shores," said Mark.

On their third day, they were again on the road by 7:00 am. This time there was a certain anticipation they both were feeling as they knew that come late-afternoon they would be peering into the Rocky Mountains. This was geography and topography not found on the Australian mainland, although there was some semblance of jagged mountains in the western side of the island state of Tasmania. In the meantime, both were fascinated with the far-reaching prairie, its farmlands, and the rolling hills of Kansas.

Suddenly, Gary, who was driving, looked over at Mark and said, "You actually walked in on Christina and some fellow in your bed in your apartment?"

"Yes, I did. And, I am trying to eradicate that scene from my memory," sighed Mark. He was not entirely sure why his brother was bringing up this painful memory.

"I'm sorry, Mark," Gary said, with a pained expression. "I was concerned about you. I was thinking of Helen and the kids and how happy we are together. Then, I started to worry about you because I think you would like a good wife to love and to have children," Gary blurted in a rush.

"I understand," said Mark. "The reality is that I do envy you and wish that I could have experienced a successful marriage with Roslyn. No, not with Roslyn, but with a girl who could love me genuinely and let me love her the same in return. She cheated me in being able to love her; it still hurts. I wouldn't like to tell you the hundreds of hours I have spent trying to undo all that unhappiness in my mind. When I was at HMS *Cerberus* in those first few years in the Navy, I was virtually a musical hermit trying to find happiness in my craft. I pushed myself so hard. It didn't work. I knew it then and I know it even more now. My music brings me contentment, satisfaction and acclaim, but it hasn't given me the kind of happiness that you have."

"Mark, I feel your hurt and pain, but I still believe there is someone out there for you," said Gary. "I think it is good you are coming *home* so that you can find that special person in Australia."

"Yeah, I think you're right, but after Christina, I just don't think I am much in the intimacy relationship department," admitted Mark.

"Nonsense!" barked Gary. "You've had a bad run twice, but you really aren't looking as I hear you tell the story. For years you have been preoccupied with your music; you just haven't taken the time to stop and think through what you want and need in a soul mate. Schulzy told me that he felt badly because he nudged you into the Christina situation."

"The Christina situation, that's a good one. Yes, he did push, and then I went along with the flow," confessed Mark. "As I think about it—and this has just come to me—the same happened with Roslyn. I just went along with the flow. Both were aggressive, and like an idiot, I went along with their notions of romance and marriage."

"Well, if we're honest, we did grow up a little naïve," said Gary. "I think this can happen when you come from a good, harmonious family. We were oblivious to anger and to infighting and all the manipulation that goes on in most families. Added to this, we came from a farm and from Hahndorf,"—he paused dramatically—"essentially a peaceable hamlet on the edge of Adelaide at the cusp of the modern era."

"Goodness me, listen to *you*!" exclaimed Mark. "So, little brother, what's your point?" He found himself rather impressed by his brother's thoughts. "I'm going home to Australia, I'm facing prostate surgery in less than three weeks and, bingo, the next happenstance will have Miss Wonderful walk into my life, we fall in love and live happily ever after. All this, even though I may be permanently wounded in the romance department, if you get my drift!"

"Come on, Mark," implored Gary. "I'm trying to be helpful! Frankly, I think you keep matters too close to your chest. There are some things you need to talk about, maybe explore some different scenarios. Maybe I was lucky in finding Helen, and maybe you weren't. But you're not going to die with this prostate problem. Thank God you had your physical check-up when you did. You have years ahead of you and I hope and pray that you will find the girl of your dreams even yet!"

"I'm sorry," said Mark. "I know you want the best for me. I need to get a grip and trust that God will see me through all of this. Now that graduation is behind me, I think—I know—I'm getting apprehensive about my surgery."

"And that's natural," agreed Gary. "But we'll be there for you, God is with you too. We'll all get beyond this in just three weeks. You'll know how matters stand in the intimacy department. You'll be home as you heal and then you'll begin a new phase of life. There's a certain excitement about all that!"

"You're a good brother," said Mark. "Here's Oakley coming up. We've got to leave I-70 and take US-40W and then US-160W into Durango."

The brothers followed US-40W to the small town of Kit Carson in Colorado. They marveled that only some two hundred people lived in this town, a distinct contrast to the large and legendary status of its American frontiersman namesake. While not yet 11:30 am, Mark and Gary wanted to eat at the Kit Carson Restaurant, so they could brag about it when they returned home. The food, however, was only average and so they agreed to not mention the eating experience, just the privilege of being in Kit Carson.

It was Mark's turn at the wheel, and from hereon they saw mountains dominating their vista to the west. Their altitude was already over 4,000 feet and they knew this would increase dramatically in the next few hours. They came to La Junta, the intersection of the old Santa Fe Trail and a pioneer road to Pueblo, now a prosperous city largely through its steel mills in this highly mineralized region.

"You know we are approaching high desert country," said Mark. "It is hot in summer, but extremely cold at night all year round."

"Look at that beautiful clump of trees over there. Are they aspens?" Gary wondered. "If so, I would love to see this part of the country in the autumn."

"Yep, those are aspens and we'll see a lot more over the next two days. I think they are related to the Poplar family. They're delicate, at least I think so, and remind me of the dogwood, perhaps my favorite American small tree," replied Mark.

Onward they drove toward the southwestern section of Colorado, just north of the New Mexico border. Their objective was the Durango and Silverton narrow gauge railroad in the San Juan National Forest within the Rocky Mountains. They were both aware of approaching some of the most beautiful territory in the United States. Even in early summer, the high elevations held large snowfields which would remain into July. It was too early for the spectacular displays of alpine wildflowers, and it was not possible to linger until July. By late afternoon, the vast open spaces of the last three days gave way to towering mountains and steep valleys with the road winding through heavily wooded sections dotted with abandoned homes, barns and small enterprises now left to rot away.

The surrounding mountains blocked out the late afternoon sun and Mark and Gary were anxious to arrive in Durango before they needed to use their headlights. Their road speed had slowed, and they continued to climb in elevation. They both were feeling excitement at the anticipation of riding the Durango and Silverton steam locomotive as this notion had grown in their imaginations since they first mapped out their final route in Annapolis. They were true Australian boys of the 1950s who loved steam engines and played with Hornby train sets. More than this, they had a father who would, at times, chase steam locomotives along various rail tracks as steam was phasing out to be replaced by diesel. Here they were, approaching one of the most celebrated historic steam locomotive journeys in the world.

They made good time and came to Durango in the Animas River Valley just on 7:00 pm. They followed their map and came to The Strater Hotel. It was a relief to get out of the car and to stretch vigorously, having now completed three days of travelling over six hundred miles each day. Gary looked over at Mark and said: "I can't believe we are here. Look at those mountains and the river flowing through the town. This is heaven to me."

Mark smiled and replied: "Well, let's come down to earth, get our gear, check into the hotel, freshen up and go have our supper. I don't mind admitting it; I am ready for a solid meal and a slow cup of coffee."

After their meal, to aid their digestion, they walked down to the fast-flowing Animas River and then back to the hotel for a good sleep. There was a sense of fulfillment, knowing that they had arrived at their first destination. The next morning, they were awake with the first rays of sunshine. They walked out of the hotel into the brisk mountain air and determined it was going to be "a corker of a day," as only farmers can. Once they had the day's weather settled, they walked back into their century-old hotel with its period decor, including authentic creaks in the floor boards. They ate a hearty breakfast and were among the first to assemble for the first train to Silverton.

Both carried cameras and were intent on recording their train ride for family and friends back home. The morning was warming up by the time the steam locomotive was ready to depart. The tourists arrived in hordes, the whistle blew, the excess steam was discharged, and the conductor announced the departure of the Durango and Silverton train. The distance to the mining town of Silverton was forty-two miles. This was a good stretch, ample time for steam enthusiasts to thoroughly absorb the journey.

With his head and shoulders out of the open window, Gary called out to Mark who was also looking through the next window: "This is amazing. I just can't believe we are on this train journey. This morning before breakfast I was feeling a little guilty that I wasn't with the boys and helping with the milking. I am over that now!"

"Wouldn't Dad have enjoyed this?" asked Mark, with nostalgia and a thousand other thoughts rushing through his mind.

The steam locomotive chugged out of Durango as the outskirts of the town disclosed broken-down dwellings and scattered debris in the form of cars, trailers and discarded machinery. This untidy scene soon gave way to rural, open countryside and then woodlands, mountains on either side of the valley floor and the energetic Animas River flowing into the town left behind. As the train crossed a road, the engineers gave a long whistle and hung on as if they were seeking everyone's attention. The brothers looked at each other, aware that they were remembering the words of their father who described "hobby train engineers" as "mere children" when they get control of the train's whistle. Soon, the locomotive began to climb at over a two-percent grade. Steep cliff faces, thick forests in the distance and the river shrinking below captivated the enthusiastic tourists on board. The train crossed bridges made of steel trusses and timber frame and once at the high line the canyon floor was four hundred feet below. As the track followed the cliff face, the train slowed to ten miles per hour. It was all staged to provide perfect opportunities for the photographers to have a field day. Mark and Gary were having such a day.

"I just can't believe the rugged beauty at every angle I turn," cried out Gary as he contorted this way and that, seeking to capture photo after photo in rapid succession.

"I know," replied Mark, "But, I am going to stop taking so many photos and concentrate on visually storing these scenes in my mind. I doubt any camera can capture what our eyes are seeing today."

The journey to Silverton took over three hours. The Durango

and Silverton narrow gauge railroad had run continuously since 1881 and was one of the few places in America to see the uninterrupted use of steam locomotives. After World War II, as the freight business declined, tourism in Durango grew exponentially, making this one of the most popular attractions in the nation. As the train steamed into the Silverton depot, Mark and Gary saw their hotel close by. It was the century-old Grand Imperial Hotel. They had brought only basic needs for their one night's lodging. Tomorrow they would return to Durango for their last night in Colorado.

It was a half hour before noon, and they knew that they needed to watch the time. Gary wanted to have a quick bite to eat and for them to both head off on a five-mile hike to Ice Lake. He was completely captivated by brochures on the Ice Lake Basin of the Weminuche Wilderness, almost the size of Rhode Island, in the San Juan National Forest. He wanted to experience high mountain desert and see an alpine lake in its natural setting.

Silverton boasts numerous day hikes, but few can compare with the sheer scenic beauty of Ice Lake. Mark agreed to go along, but helped his brother curb his fervor by not hiking to all three lakes; one was acceptable, and maybe two. Time was against them and Mark knew he was not as physically fit as his little brother. Within the hour they were on the trail and after two miles had gained altitude by climbing 1,600 feet. They walked through forests and along meadows that were soon to be filled with wildflowers. When they reached the beautiful Lower Ice Lakes Basin, they were astounded at the sheer beauty and majesty of four mountain peaks, each rising to over 13,000 feet. They saw waterfalls dropping from hidden alpine lakes and gazed upon snowfields still abundantly covered with snow. When Ice Lake came into view they gazed on its turquoise-blue waters nestled in a cirque of sculpted ridges and peaks.

"Oh, Mark, this is more glorious and beautiful than I ever dared to imagine," whispered Gary, as they knelt on the grassy slope to take the best photos they could muster.

"You are certainly right there. I have never seen anything so pristine in its unspoiled natural beauty," responded Mark.

"I just need to sit and absorb the whole scene as best I can," said Gary.

"You sit there, and I will go down by that rocky outcrop and spend a few minutes with my mouth piece," explained Mark as he stood up and took out of his shoulder bag his euphonium mouthpiece.

"What, we are in the middle of some of the most beautiful scenery I have ever seen, and you have to blow your mouthpiece?" Gary questioned incredulously.

"I know it must seem bizarre, but it's been four days since I have played my *eupho,* and I just feel the need to keep my lip in good form," Mark said sheepishly. "Call it force of habit, I guess!"

"It's alright, Mark. I get it. Seriously, I understand," replied Gary. "But, if you had brought your euphonium, you could have played *The Hills Are Alive* from the Sound of Music. "

As Gary laughed at his own humor, Mark threw several stones in his direction.

After ten minutes, they ventured on towards the next lake and saw waterfalls cascading down rocky crevasses and water flowing across the grassy sloping landscape where there was a natural depression and into rivulets which carried the icy water into the lakes.

"I bet this must be a fabulous scene when the wildflowers are out in a few weeks," Gary enthused.

"Yes, indeed," responded Mark, "It is a vista you don't see in Australia. Perhaps in Tasmania. I would like to explore the south-west of Tassie sometime."

"Well, let's do it before we get much older. I am up for it whenever you are," volunteered Gary.

"Gary, it's just after 4:00 pm," said Mark. "If you're ready, let's head back to Silverton and check out the town. I'd like to ride that stage coach," he said.

They stood up, looked at each other and laughed, knowing that they had experienced an afternoon they would never forget. Gary thought to himself how much Helen would have enjoyed this. When they reached the town, Mark could feel a little tenderness in his muscles, but "it was not too bad overall," he thought. They rode the stagecoach, walked around some of the stores and then entered their Victorian hotel for their evening meal. The live entertainment for that evening was a lecture on discovering gold in the San Juan Mountains in 1860 and life on the goldfields. The speaker was an interesting resident who lived in Silverton in his retirement and was a wealth of information about the region, especially about surviving harsh winters in the mountains.

The next morning was day five of their trek across America. The train back to Durango did not depart until 2:30 pm and arrived at 6:00 pm. By noon Mark and Gary had exhausted what was available in Silverton and realized that they would not be able to see all that was in Durango, since they had to depart for the Grand Canyon early Wednesday morning. However, they had come to ride the railroad and to see the alpine lakes, and they were pleased to have done both. At a book shop in Durango Mark bought a book on the Anasazi heritage in Colorado and New Mexico. This opened a new perspective for them both as they recognized that an entire week or more could be devoted to delving into the cliff dwelling Anasazi culture in both states, especially near Taos and Santa Fe. Again, tourists must make choices.

Durango to the North Rim of the Grand Canyon was about eight solid hours of travel. In Silverton and Durango, fellow tourists cautioned against driving the full distance in one day. "You should stay overnight at Monument Valley." "You will miss so many scenic stops if you drive straight through." "No, not a good idea. You must see Mesa Verde National Park, Monument Valley and Antelope Canyon. Who knows when you will come back, if ever?"

"Good advice for sure," said Gary, "but we are on a schedule and we can't deviate any more than weather and road conditions dictate."

The next morning, as they stepped out of the hotel before breakfast, Gary took a long look at the morning sky and said, "There's bad weather ahead for us today, Mark."

"Yep, it sure looks like it. Let's get some breakfast and hit the road as soon as we can," replied Mark.

By 6:45 am, the brothers were on the road with a full tank of gasoline and some 375 miles to drive. They knew that most of the journey was a single lane highway and that frequently the flow of traffic was hindered by campervans traveling as slow as molasses. The road took them through the Navajo Nation and road maintenance was often an issue. Beyond doubt, they were traveling through beautiful, rugged and largely empty land. They were on the Colorado Plateau at elevations in the 5,000 feet to 7,000 feet range.

By late morning they reached Monument Valley and decided to take an hour to stretch and look around this famous and magnificent panorama. The foreboding cloud formation was not what they had hoped for; they wanted the clear blue skies like most postcards showed of Monument Valley. Despite the heavily overcast sky, there remained a dramatic landscape before them. They took more photos of each other than at other stops because the background was so spectacular.

Back in the car, they had another four hours of driving before they reached the North Rim of the Grand Canyon. They knew it would take longer with the rain coming. For over two hours, the dark clouds loomed ominously, yet there was little wind and no thunder or lightning. Mark was at the wheel, keeping the car moving towards the Grand Canyon. It was good that they had the road mostly to themselves.

After the turn off to Antelope Canyon, the droplets of rain began. Slowly at first, and then larger in size and sound, until a sudden downpour caused Mark to slow down to a crawl. After five minutes it ceased, and they were able to return to a cautious speed.

"Well, that was different," said Gary.

"Sure was, but we know there is more to come. Why isn't there any wind?" questioned Mark.

"We have about another ninety minutes before we reach the North Rim and it is only 4:00 pm, so we have plenty of daylight ahead of us should a real storm develop," reasoned Gary.

Neither spoke for some time as they drove on, staring at the growing intensity of the dark clouds that now surrounded them on all sides. They looked along the sides of the road and noticed how the downpour had already been absorbed into the porous red soil. Looking out at the flat, treeless high desert terrain, there was hardly any sign that heavy rain had fallen at all.

"You know, I have seen many spectacular thunderstorms around the Port Pirie region and over on the Eyre Peninsula. Some have been frightening, but on all occasions the wind has never been tornado-force as so often in the U.S. Midwest. I wonder why?" queried Gary.

"If you don't know, then I'm sure I don't," replied Mark. "All I know is that many colleagues at Hopkins and the Naval Academy who live, or have lived in the Midwest, admit to being fearful of living in that part of the country because of the frequency and sheer intensity of tornadoes."

"When I think about it, America is clearly one of the most beautiful countries on planet Earth, but also one that has more natural disasters than any other country. It has the wildfires in the Southwest, tornadoes in the Midwest, blizzards in the Upper Plains states and New England, and hurricanes in Florida and the Gulf States," reflected Gary.

"You're right, but it is also a heavily populated country where people are permitted to live in mountainous wildfire terrain or on the coastline where hurricanes strike first. Australian zoning is much more controlling," added Mark.

They were now climbing into the Kaibab National Forest, passing through lush alpine meadows and forests of fir and pine with very little sign of any development. When they came to the small town of Jacob Lake, they turned onto US-67S with the only paved road into the North Rim.

"Only another forty-five miles to go," announced Gary.

"I don't think we are going to make it," said Mark as a drizzle began.

The impending storm distracted them from peering beyond the pines to signs already of the Grand Canyon. It was not the way they had imagined their first views of this magnificent landscape. In fact, the entire area looked rather drab. Suddenly, there was a flash of lightning and they both awaited the thunder clap to follow. After twenty seconds it came, faint and weak in its arrival. Gary looked at Mark and said:

"We might make it to the Grand Canyon Lodge before the storm breaks. The thunder is way behind the lightning."

"It would be good if we can," agreed Mark.

More lightning lit up the sky and the wind began to blow as Mark pressed on, now behind other cars presumably making their way to accommodation at the North Rim as were they.

"I remember reading about the weather patterns at the Grand Canyon one afternoon when you went over to the Naval Academy for a meeting. It said that as spring transitions into summer, temperatures fluctuate, and strong northwestern winds occur as the jet stream from the Pacific coast begins to flow north. Apparently, there are numerous short-lived thunderstorms around the Grand Canyon over the summer months," said Gary.

"I sure hope we get some blue skies and sunshine over the next two days," replied Mark. "We have both wanted to see the Grand Canyon since we were kids playing Cowboys and Indians in the pines."

"Me too," said Gary. "The North Rim is less crowded and less sophisticated than the South Rim, but I am thinking that the South Rim may have been easier to get to."

"Perhaps, but there is the Grand Canyon Lodge ahead of us and we do have time to see the North Rim only," said Mark. "We'll make the best of it." He maneuvered the car into the parking lot around other tourists who were eager to be inside the lodge.

"Let's leave our luggage in the car and register first. I want to get some photos of the lightning over the North Rim," suggested Gary.

They both took their cameras and hurried inside as the drizzle turned to light rain. Once inside, there was a dazzling lightning flash and, immediately, a loud and dramatic roll of thunder. It caught all the people in the registration line by surprise and even the staff paused from their work and looked towards the large glass windows in the lounge.

"Mark, I have to go outside and take some photos," said Gary as he moved quickly toward the observation deck overlooking the wide expanse of the North Rim. The storm clouds brought an early dusk and blocked any sign of a westerly sunset. Mark followed Gary, who was already taking photos on the deck. Registration, luggage, their room and an evening meal would have to wait. Right now, there was a sense of excitement in arriving at another of their planned destinations, and the spontaneity of being able to act and react to the drama of nature around them.

Mark glanced at Gary as they tried to take photos with as much precision as a bewildering thunderstorm permitted. The flashes of lightning streaked across the sky and the thunder bellowed. It was nature on display, startling and awe-inspiring, and its manifestation was a fanfare of pomp and pageantry.

Mark could see that Gary was overwhelmed by it all. Trying to find the right words, Gary gestured helplessly and blurted out: "Don't we serve a magnificent God? Look at the beauty and power of his nature on show."

"What's wrong with you, fella? There's no God here. It's a thunderstorm. There's a perfectly logical explanation for it that doesn't need some archaic belief in a supernatural God," declared a heavy-set man standing near Gary. He lowered his camera and glowered at them both.

"I'm sorry?" said Gary, surprised. "I didn't mean to upset you." He glanced over at Mark anxiously.

"Ahh, you Christians are all the same," growled the stranger. He took a step toward Gary. "You're all naïve, you don't even know how the real-world works! You're stuck in an obsolete paradigm. There's no God. That's the natural world out there!" He waved an arm across the sky. "It's doing what it's always done—following its cycles forever. We have cycles too: we're born, we live, and we die. End of story."

"Well, if that's your viewpoint, then you're welcome to it. But it isn't mine and I ask that you respect mine," countered Gary. "We've taken our photos and now we need to register for the night."

"Sure, go on. You Christians are all the same. You run away because you have no argument," snarled the man.

"No, we're not all the same. But we know when we're talking to a brick wall, and frankly, we have better things to do," said Mark over his shoulder as he and Gary walked away.

"Man, where did *that* come from?" Gary asked. He shook his head impatiently. "All I did was utter a statement of wonderment."

"Let it go," said Mark. "You will never win with some people because all they can see is their own fuzzy point of view. We need to register, and then get our luggage—then we can head to the dining room."

As they were registering, the skies opened up. It was loud and forceful and stymied the idea of taking their luggage to their cabin before dinner. So, they ate and watched the thunderstorm unravel through the large panoramic glass windows of the Lodge. The flashes of lightning were so breathtaking and gigantic in their diorama that Mark and Gary ceased from eating and were transfixed, along with the other diners, by the breathtaking display. The claps of thunder were so loud and so close that many people clung to each other nervously, in need of reassurance that this grandstand play would soon be over. Once the rain lessened, the dining room emptied quickly, and the unlikely spectators of one of the greatest shows available anywhere in the world scattered to their cabins, humbled and quiet.

The next morning broke with all the freshness of a cleansing after the epic thunderstorm. There was a new smell of pine in the air and, after 6:00 am, this mingled quickly with the aroma of breakfast emanating from the Lodge dining room. Mark and Gary decided against a constitutional walk before breakfast as the ground was still moist and, in some places, just muddy. They would let the sun dry the trails for an hour or so before they commenced their explorations.

An hour later, with the ground much firmer underfoot, Mark and Gary determined to make as much use of the clear skies and sunshine as possible. The park rangers had cautioned everyone that the weather patterns for the next few days were unpredictable. Bright Angel Point was a short, but steep walk, and presented spectacular views into Roaring Springs and Bright Angel Canyons.

"Look at those views!" exclaimed Gary. "Wherever you look it's just sensational in every sense."

"I know," said Mark. "You get tired of using superlatives, but what can you do? It's impossible to gaze out onto such scenes and not say anything."

"You're right," said Gary. "I remember when I first peered into the Blue Mountains. It was a fabulous moment. And, you know, I remember at that time wondering just how more splendid the Grand Canyon must be. Here I am, and totally blown away."

The brothers leaned on the safety rail and took photos, allowing themselves to be swallowed up by the immensity of it all. They shared binoculars, and a half hour soon went by as they explored the geology of the rocks and cliffs and all the flora and fauna they could see in its magnified form. Walking away from the observation point, Gary said: "When I was at Roseworthy, I remember enjoying, yet being disturbed by, lectures on erosion, especially erosion caused by the stupidity of man. The teacher made a comment I have never forgotten. He said that the Grand Canyon was one of the spectacular examples of erosion anywhere in the world. Because it's nature at work, it's beautiful and majestic. When humans are the cause, erosion is ugly and destructive."

Returning to their cabin, they sat on the porch and rested a while. They decided that since the day was so stunning, they would drive to a few trails and viewpoints around the North Rim. If they did this today, they'd have no regrets should tomorrow be overcast or even raining. They drove back to the office and around to the Uncle Jim Trail. Here, they walked part way, but were interrupted several times by mule trains coming up the trail. They had to step off the trail, keep still and follow the wrangler's instructions as the mules and their uneasy riders passed by. They returned to their car and drove onto the Vista Encantada, Roosevelt Point, Walhalla Overlook and, finally, to Cape Royal. This was the most southerly viewpoint of the North Rim, with expansive views of the canyon east and west and a close-up look at the natural arch of Angel's Window.

"If only we had time and patience," said Mark, "I bet we could get some astonishing sunrise and sunset photos."

"So true," replied Gary. "Mark, it's after five now. We really haven't had lunch. Sunset is another three hours or more: do you want to stay for those sunset photos, or do we go back for dinner and an early night? With the sun and all today, I'm feeling weary."

"Me too," agreed Mark. "I'm feeling the toll this entire journey is taking on us as well. Let's go eat."

Half way through their meal, a man approached their table and asked if he could talk to them. It was the same person who had bristled at Gary's exclamation during the thunderstorm the night before.

"I don't want to take much of your time, but I need to apologize for my words and behavior last night," said the man.

"Thank you," said Gary. "It did bother me, actually, because I was only uttering what I felt, and I did not mean to offend you."

"I understand," said the man. "In fact, I was feeling the same, but I've tried to deny my feelings about God since the death of my little girl, four years ago. She had acute leukemia. My wife and I prayed so desperately for God to heal her and give us a miracle. It didn't happen: I've been at war with God ever since. Last night, for the first time since the death of Lucy, I was sensing the power of God once again. I tried to suppress it and then I heard what you said." He looked at Gary. "I lashed out in anger. I apologize."

"Are you here alone?" asked Mark. The man shook his head and motioned to his wife who was sitting near the large windows, watching them. "Why don't the two of you join us?" said Mark. He pulled out the chairs next to him at the table as the man's wife came over. Thus, began an extended dinner lasting over two hours.

Back in their cabin, both were somewhat somber as they got ready for bed.

"Mark, you were terrific tonight," said Gary. "You gave Ben and Rebecca a wonderful and caring testimony of having a personal God in our lives. I have never heard you speak like that before. I don't think I have heard a better explanation of how there is no logical answer for why God supposedly condones death and violence, unless we view it through the eyes of faith. This has bothered me too. And to say that *this is God's world, but not as He would have it be*, is a great saying. I'm going to write that down and use it."

"I've had a lot more practice than you," offered Mark. "I left Hahndorf as a century-old, well-respected, conservative Christian-based community and I stepped into secular Australia with little time or need for Christianity. I've had to ask questions about my own faith journey and fight battles that have probably never come to you." He paused: "For over twenty years I've been weighing my Lutheran faith against the supposedly smarter and more enlightened ideas and practices of a secular society. There are some aspects of my belief system where I am no longer as rigid as we were raised, but I'll defend the Gospel story in all its wonderment until the cows come home!"

"Interesting, isn't it," said Gary reflectively. "Probably half the people I know are either atheists, or agnostics, and many are lapsed Lutherans, but no one has ever given me grief about my religion."

"That's because they know what you believe and represent," said Mark. He sat on the edge of the bed and slipped off his shoes. "They accept it and don't challenge you. I also don't think it hurts that you are a decent man who is respected in your work and your contribution to the community—and I know that means certain activities in Adelaide as well."

He continued: "I have taught courses in *Jesus and the Gospels, Christian Apologetics* and preached and taken talks and workshops on many aspects of Christianity, even comparative religions—which is fascinating. It's a tough world out there for Christians and some of us don't present a pretty picture of what it means to be a follower of the Christ. I try and say as often as I can that the best example of the Gospel is a loving and a loveable Christian. The fact is that some of us aren't all that loveable!"

"Okay, so how is it best to present Christianity as the best way to live?" asked Gary. He slipped under the covers and raised up on one elbow.

"Two words," said Mark. "Live it! Live it every day, good and bad, live it so that people watching you can only say, *"What you are shouts so loudly in my ears I cannot hear what you say!"*

"And one more thing," he added. "Christianity doesn't claim to solve all the problems of life, but it does have an answer for them; it has a worldview that works and provides a place where we can find peace of mind. I am not suggesting this is easy, but it *is* a start. I think this is how you see it too," said Mark. "I'm sorry if I've gone on too long!"

"I agree with all that you say," replied Gary. "I just don't see Mr. and Mrs. Average wanting to delve into the inner workings of God and Christianity."

"That is because in this modern day and age, with prosperity and materialism all around us, who needs God?" responded Mark. "Billy Graham was astounded at all the empty churches in Britain when he was conducting his evangelistic campaigns in the 1950s, when these very same churches had been full during the terrible days of WWII."

"It's times of adversity which drives men and women to their knees. Who needs God when too many of us act as though we are our own 'god'—and always with a little 'g.'"

"We better go to sleep," said Mark. "If I say anymore, I'll need to collect an offering!" He turned out the light: "Good night, and we can be grateful that Ben and Rebecca left us tonight in a better frame of mind. I hope life is good for them going forward," said Mark.

It was Saturday morning, seven days into their westward adventure, as Mark and Gary pulled out of the North Rim. They had a comfortable seven to eight-hour drive ahead of them. Big Bear Lake was their next destination and another of the brothers' chosen essential landmarks on their way home to Australia.

"I'm so grateful to have seen at least the North Rim of the Grand Canyon," said Gary, as he drove back to Jacob Creek, then onto Marble Canyon.

"But," added Gary before Mark could comment, "I am beginning to miss Helen and the kids incredibly, and the farm and Hahndorf. I miss home!"

"It's true," replied Mark. "You can only take in so much before the call of home signals. Here I am coming home to a whole new chapter of my life. And, if I'm truthful it is a little intimidating to think of what is ahead. Especially when I think about my surgery in two weeks and all the changes that will bring."

"Mark, the first bonus in your new chapter will be an assurance of life," stated Gary firmly. He was intent that Mark should not delve deeper into his prostate issue in the middle of high desert country.

"Yes, I know," said Mark. He glanced away. "It's … it's just that it is starting to come to my mind every day now … and many times each day. I know that I'll be alright; I just wish I didn't have prostate cancer."

"And soon you won't," responded Gary. He was keeping the pressure on his brother, hoping for a change of subject.

"You're right," Mark said. Then he grinned, brightening: "Just think in six days you will be with Helen and the kids. We are now over half way through our adventure."

"I want you to know, Mark, just how much I appreciate you suggesting that we tackle this journey across America. It will always be something that you and I have shared as brothers. I will never forget the sights and places we have seen; and, I have the photos to prove it!" said Gary quietly.

From Marble Canyon, the Buick took US-89S through Cameron to Flagstaff, and then they were back on US-40W and driving along the perimeter of the Mojave National Preserve to Barstow. It was completely different terrain, and with an overcast sky and a new bank of threatening dark clouds, the miles of barren topography exhibited a moon-scape appearance. Mark was driving as they approached Barstow and Gary was napping. As the town came into view Mark was quietly relieved. The gas light was on and the gas tank was ominously low as the car pulled into the gas station. Gary jolted awake as the car stopped.

"Oh my, sorry Mark, I must have dozed off," said Gary.

"Yes, about one hour ago! You didn't miss much in the scenery department, I can assure you," responded Mark. "We're almost out of gasoline."

They were making good time and only had one hour before they would arrive at their destination. They pulled into McDonalds and consumed a fast-food lunch; something Gary was loath to do under ordinary circumstances. He lived by the adage that "if you eat good food, it would in turn be good for you." While Mark agreed, the long-time bachelor was guilty of many a fast-food meal.

Half an hour later, the clouds had given way to sunshine and they were approaching Big Bear Lake, situated in the rugged San Bernardino National Forest. The small city was touted as one of Southern California's premier four-season vacation destinations. It had a mild summer climate, scenic beauty and a wide range of recreational choices for complete vacation or weekend getaways. Mark and Gary were determined to relax for one full day as they were spent from the pressure of keeping up with their own schedule. The brochures boasted a mile-long chair lift taking them to panoramic views, especially of the lake below. The biggest attraction was renting a pontoon boat for several hours on the lake, trying their luck fishing for trout and bass. As they drove into Big Bear Lake it was abundantly clear that this was a town geared towards the casual city-dweller either relaxing at the lake or trekking into the mountains. It had an ease and agreeableness about it.

"I think I'm going to like Big Bear, Mark," said Gary, as they walked up to the reception desk. "In fact, as it's just after 4:00, can we ride on the chair lift today? I want to get a look at the lake and the town before we commit to fishing tomorrow."

"Sure, I think that's a great idea," agreed Mark. "We need some exercise and fresh air. Let's do it."

The chairlift was well-patronized, but the brothers lined up and were soon ascending with sublime views of the lake and town. The cable ride was a mile-long and took them to an altitude of over 8,000 feet. The panoramic spectacle surveyed mountain summits near and far and a series of ranges as far as the eye could see. Closer to Big Bear itself there were dozens of trails revealing mountain bikers zipping along much too fast. This, too, was the natural world, but one revealing greater domination by people and their human activities. It was a far cry from the North Rim.

"Makes the little chair lift on Granite Island look rather pathetic, doesn't it?" said Gary. "I guess I shouldn't be too critical. All in its context, and I happen to like the Victor Harbor region just the way it is. There is already too much development coming into Port Eliott and it's moving closer to Victor."

"Yep, but everything changes when you consider size of population and demands made by people on nature," said Mark. "You've got to keep things in proportion."

In the restaurant that evening, Gary announced that their expenses for this westward adventure were less than he had anticipated, and so he recommended that they splurge a little on the morrow and rent a pontoon boat instead of an aluminum dinghy and make it a day of relaxed fishing. With no travel on the agenda for the day, they emerged from breakfast mid-morning and within the hour were slowly making their way to various parts of the lake, casting for trout. The sun was hot, but not unbearably so, thanks to their shade cover. The water had a blue coolness about it. Off shore, it was quiet and relaxing enough that the ease of the hour induced a drowsiness. They decided to drop anchor, take advantage of the added features of their pontoon, and soon they were both asleep.

Sometime later, they were suddenly awakened by the roar of an outboard motor and the shouts and laughter of the young boaters as they swept past.

"What the ... look at those kids, they're having the time of their lives, including that old dude driving the boat," said Gary. "I've got to admit that sure looks like fun!" He clung to the gunwales as the wake passed under them, rocking the pontoon until they slapped the waves.

"That's one thing we never got to do as teenagers," reflected Mark. "South Australia doesn't have lakes like this. Even if our parents hadn't been so frugal, we only had the Murray River an hour away, but we thought that was dirty and not fun for water-skiing."

"Yeah, but we did go to the beach a lot," said Gary, "and I will always be glad of that. Even at the Adelaide beaches we didn't see a lot of boats, did we?"

"No, that's true," replied Mark, "Hey, quick, check your line, I think one of us has a bite."

There was a bite on both lines. Gary had caught a placid bass which had probably been there for some time, whereas Mark's line had a fighting trout on the end, and it was not going to give in without a struggle. For the next ten minutes, Mark toiled to bring his fish to the edge of the pontoon so Gary could slip the net underneath and haul it up. It was a fair-sized trout, about five or six pounds, and after necessary photos were taken to record the catch, Mark reluctantly released his prize trout back into the lake.

"Well, there goes our dinner," pined Gary as he watched the fish blend with the waters of the lake and then disappear.

"Ha ha, but we did catch him—and we have proof," laughed Mark.

The whole episode was a positive tonic for Mark. He had been contemplating his surgery and its after effects. Try as he may, he could not stop bizarre speculations creeping into his thoughts at the oddest of times. He wanted it all behind him and to be assured that he had a long life ahead of him. In fact, he had a deeper enigma he had told no one, not even Gary or his mother. It had surfaced, as it rarely did, during his siesta on the pontoon. His subconscious was questioning whether he would ever find true, romantic love. His practice was to quickly suppress such yearnings. It didn't matter if it didn't occur. He had his music. He had his career, and both spoke of successful and satisfying days ahead. This golden dream belonged back under the pines, to the days when he was an idyllic kid engrossed in perfect outcomes which he so relished in story books or Disney movies. Now a mature man, Mark had to recognize that his future was not his to control. What if there was no princess, or true love and romance in his future? His matured obligation was to accept this *fait accompli*.

When the sun was clearly in its western trajectory, Mark and Gary decided they had satisfied their need of a relaxing day. The fish were not biting, and the brothers were feeling their appetite pangs as they only brought fruit and water with them. They returned the pontoon to its moorings and walked to a restaurant they had noted in the morning as a likely place for their evening meal.

"You know, Mum and Helen and the kids would have loved being on the pontoon today," commented Gary. "In fact, it makes me want to check renting a houseboat on the Murray next summer. It could be a lot of fun for the family."

"I think there are many aspects of this trip where you are going to try and find an Australian equivalent; a houseboat on the Murray, fishing in Tasmania, train journeys here and there. You are going to be one busy boy in your spare time," chuckled Mark.

"Well, you only get one shot at watching your kids grow up and I want them to enjoy some of the things we have done over these last few days."

"I appreciate that. You are fortunate to have kids … and I am not feeling depressed because I do not!" said Mark hurriedly, before Gary could go to work on him.

"I wasn't going to react, Mark. Frankly, I wish more than anything that you had kids too. I sure am looking forward to seeing mine in five days now," said Gary as he re-calculated the remaining days before he was home. "Yep, five it is!"

They walked back to their hotel. Mark had alerted Gary to the fact that they should not leave Big Bear at their usual early hour as they needed to avoid Los Angeles morning drive traffic. It was less than two hours to Laguna Beach, and they would still get there before noon if they departed from Big Bear around 9:00 am.

"So, it is the beach tomorrow at the Pacific Ocean. Man, this is a tough life being a tourist; I'm going to find it hard to settle back into farm work after all this! Good night, Mark." exclaimed Gary.

The next morning was overcast and much cooler. Mark and Gary were so accustomed to early departures by now, that they were eager to begin their two-hour or so drive before 8:00 am.

"By the time we get down to Redlands it will be approaching 9:00 am anyway," Mark said. "I just recall getting stuck in traffic last time." He glanced at Gary and grinned. "Now, I'm not going to say much about this drive until after we arrive at Laguna Beach. Then, I want to know what you think. I remember my first impressions about a year ago."

Mark drove so Gary could take in all the sights and sounds. It was not long before they left behind the ponderosa pines and the high mountain country terrain. They began to descend toward the coastal plain that was Greater Los Angeles. The road hugged the cliff face on one side, while steep gullies dropped away on the other side. Mark kept the car in a lower gear so as not to ride his brakes, and after half an hour they had dropped over 4,000 feet and were driving into the outskirts of Redlands. They had left the clouds on the easterly side of the mountains and the sun was shining brightly.

"That was something, but I will say no more until we get to the beach," nodded Gary.

They continued south-west into Riverside, and then Corona and Irvine. In many respects, it was mundane suburbia they were passing through with small trees and dry, almost uninteresting topography. Gary looked at Mark and said, "Similar to parts of Adelaide in many ways." They both smiled as Mark pointed at Gary as if to say, "You catch on quickly!" After Irvine there was an end to recent housing developments and a much narrower road through a small canyon with older and less substantial buildings on either side of the road. Then, suddenly, they turned a corner and could see glimpses of the sparkling ocean ahead at the end of the street with normal housing again on either side of the road.

"Wow, where did all this come from? Is that the Pacific Ocean?" asked Gary, as bewildered as Mark hoped he would be.

"Exactly! This was my reaction as well. It was about a year ago when I was with some Navy musicians and we drove up to Big Bear Lake and then in the afternoon we came down to Laguna Beach. I know that I just wanted to see it all again one day," declared Mark putting it all in context. "Wait until you see the beach and more of the Pacific."

Mark turned left and drove about one mile along Highway 1 to give Gary a taste of what they were to find at Laguna Beach on their last day and a half in the United States. Admittedly, it was still lunch time, but there were many people walking both sides of the road. They were ambling, hurrying, eating food as they looked in windows, assembling in twos and threes, having conversations and blocking the flow of foot traffic. Laguna Beach was a busy commercial seaside community. As they threaded their way down the street, Gary gaped at sidewalk cafes, restaurants, art galleries, small boutique hotels, professional businesses, a dental clinic, and a myriad of stores selling surfboards to baby clothing.

Mark turned right up a side street and said, "Well, this is Laguna Beach, what do you think?"

"It's sure not like any beach town I have ever seen before. This is like one of the busiest streets in Unley or North Adelaide, but even more so. What do I think? I love it. There is energy here and yet it all seems orderly."

"Precisely. I feel the same way," said Mark. He was feeling gratified that Gary agreed with his impressions. "Now let's go back to the beach, and then on to our hotel. It's upscale, but you said we are doing alright with the budget!"

Mark pulled into a one-hour parking spot at the main Laguna Beach. They had ample time to breath in the salt air, walk on the beach and eat a sandwich at a quaint seaside cafe. Both were relaxed and feeling pleased with themselves that they could now say they had successfully navigated across the North American continent from East to West.

"We've come a long way in nine days," reflected Gary around his sandwich. "I think this will become one of the more memorable happenings in my lifetime. I'm not sure it is right and proper for a vacation to be at the top of the memory ladder. It seems a little selfish."

"If it makes you feel any better, you could say it was the time you came to your brother's graduation and then helped him with his relocation to Australia," teased Mark laughingly.

"Nah, it doesn't matter, I can live with it either way. It has been such a tremendous experience. I think it is also different because it was just you and me and not us with our parents, or me with Helen and the kids. It's just been two brothers fulfilling some dreams together," replied Gary.

"Yep, it's been a special time for me, too," said Mark. "I've truly felt unencumbered and on vacation. This has come at the end of a long goal to earn my PhD. That was five years of intense work and study at the Naval Academy and Hopkins—but it *was* rewarding," he added, after a moment.

"Come on," he said, "Let's get back to the car before the meter expires, and then go up to our hotel. See it up there? It's the Inn at Laguna Beach," Mark said, and pointed up to the right.

When Mark slid behind the wheel and turned over the engine, the Buick made a whirring sound. He turned the motor off and turned it on again. The brothers looked at each other. Gary said, "Well, better to have a problem here than at the North Rim." They lifted the hood and quickly saw that the fan belt had broken.

"It's a minor problem compared to what could have happened," said Mark.

Putting several more coins in the meter, they went back to the cafe and found a young man they had been talking to while eating. He indicated that there was a GM body shop only five minutes away and he offered to take them. Within thirty minutes, they had the new fan belt installed, and the problem solved. When the car started again, there was no menacing noise and as they peered down at the engine all appeared in order.

They drove up the hill to the Inn at Laguna Beach and were dazzled by its location. It was an oceanfront hotel, reminiscent of a secluded villa. They registered, went to their ocean-front room and shortly after were on the beach in their trunks. The next few late afternoon hours were spent swimming, dozing, tanning and merely pondering individual private thoughts.

For dinner that evening they walked to a recommended seafood restaurant. Mark had the Wild King Salmon and Gary the Grilled Swordfish. It was a splendid meal made even more so by watching the sun set over the Pacific. They had to remind themselves that they had an entire day at the beach tomorrow, and it was the following night when they headed south-west across the vast Pacific for home. Once they had fixed this fact in their heads, they chatted mostly about small stuff and Gary began to shift his talk to the farm and his schedule leading into spring, the Royal Adelaide Show and onto harvest and summer. Mark looked beyond his immediate surgery and spoke of being settled in Melbourne in his work and his new accommodation by Christmas. He said that he now could look forward to coming home for Christmas without an ocean in between. They skipped dessert, deciding instead to sit on the sand for a while and listen to the gentle caressing of the surf on the shore.

"Mark, what if there is no God?" Gary asked suddenly as he gazed up into the starry night.

"What! Where did *that* question come from?" asked Mark, surprised. "Is there something bothering you?" He turned to Gary with a concerned look on his face.

"I'm just asking as you have more experience with questions like this than I do," said Gary. "I was thinking of that 'fella back at the Grand Canyon during the thunderstorm. It was when … err … Ben … that was his name … attacked me. There was real hatred in his eyes and a dangerous look. I haven't seen that before."

"Alright, now I understand where you are coming from," said Mark. "Remember, his anger was more at himself than at you. You said out loud what he was thinking, yet he was denying it to you and himself until he came to apologize."

"Gary, we live in a post-modern world where it is more acceptable to be anti-God than for God. I think we'll see this increase, and it may possibly lead to legislative changes in government and the demise of traditional values. Both America and Australia are based on Judo-Christian principles. I'm no theologian, but I know I believe in the God of the Bible, of Luther and our Protestant tradition. This is important to me, but I recognize that not everyone does. We all have a choice here and I know where I stand and, I think, I know where you do too," said Mark. He was beginning to feel like a teacher.

"No, I know. Ben has me worried, that's all. I find myself looking at all the people I see at every stop, and I wonder how many of them are atheists," confessed Gary.

"The good news is that it's not a disease in choosing not to believe in God. You are not in danger because of their atheism or their indifference to spirituality or religion," counseled Mark. "Most of my colleagues and friends may or may not have a faith-based worldview—perhaps this term will be useful to you—but most of them know that I am a practicing Christian."

"I guess that was a stupid question," admitted Gary.

"No, no, don't feel like that," consoled Mark. "You're revealing yourself to be the product of our upbringing. We come from Hahndorf. Worship and the way we lived Lutheranism was very intentional. Most South Australians took religion seriously until after the Second World War. Even when we were kids, radio stations were careful what music they played on Good Friday and movie theaters were closed, and always closed on Sundays. There was a time when most kids went to Sunday School, but now you are dealing with the first generation of Australians who have never been to Sunday School or inside a church to worship God."

"Most of my friends still go to church, perhaps not a Lutheran church, but they are Anglican, Uniting or Catholics," said Gary.

"That's my point, Gary," continued Mark. "Even now your experience is different to most. Years ago, when I was studying Christian Education at Immanuel College, I read a quote I use often from Carl Jung, who was a student of Sigmund Freud. I memorized it. He said, *'Side by side with the decline of religious life, the neuroses grow noticeably more frequent.'* He was talking about life in early 20th Century Europe, and he was advocating the practice of a religious belief system, as much as a belief in God, as a means of helping with the problems of life. Look at the way technology is changing our lives, but are we calmer, more at ease and living less stressful lives? Wherever I look, the answer must be a resounding NO! For me, I choose to have faith in an interventionist God who watches over my 'comings and goings.'"

"Me too!" replied Gary. "Thanks for that!"

Mark added one more comment: "When we get home, I'll give you a reading list, little brother, and suggest that you get involved in some discussion groups to explore ways to confirm and share your faith. On that note, let's head back to the hotel for some shut eye."

The next morning, they ate their breakfast on the terrace that was decked in bougainvillea, wisteria and other fragrant summer blossoms. They were early enough to watch the beginning of another sunny day at Laguna Beach. The foreshore was placid like glass, even though there was an occasional ripple on the surface. The absence of wind made the calm waters possible. The beach below, and the coastline to the south, were dotted with early swimmers and sunbathers. The beachfront businesses, hotels and cheerful cottages were awakening to a new day. Altogether, it was a slow-moving colorful canvas locked in the moment and it seemed like it was for their eyes only.

"Our last day to do nothing specially," said Gary. "I say beach first, shops next, and beach again. What say you, Mark?"

"Well, great!" said Mark. "Sounds like you've got the day's agenda already worked out. I'd like to explore a few art galleries, too. Before we do this, I must call Chris Greville at Cal Lutheran and confirm the drop-off of the Buick," he said.

Forty minutes later they were on the beach where a breeze was encouraging small waves to break on shore, much to the delight of young surfers. The wholesome breakfast had induced a need to doze a little as the heat of the day mingled with the ocean breeze and, for some time, the brothers succumbed to a light slumber. They knew all too well that a thirteen-hour night flight was ahead of them, and with this came little sleep and a lot of discomfort.

"Gary, we'd better be careful that we don't burn in this sun," said Mark.

"I know, as wonderful as it is, I can feel some burning too," replied Gary. "It does feel good though, especially knowing that we are heading back into winter."

"What about those art galleries?" asked Mark. He slipped on shorts over his swimming trunks, added a shirt and hat, and then they both joined the throngs of people walking the Laguna streets.

As they dawdled along, they happened on several art galleries, one or two antique stores and several women's clothing stores. Gary bought several items of clothing for Helen and his daughter, while Mark followed suit and bought a colorful summer dress for Betty; she adored bright colors tastefully presented. They stopped for lunch at an Irish pub and enjoyed fish 'n chips, and they fell into conversation with an elderly couple who had lived their whole lives along the southern Californian coast. Once a week, they would go on a lunch date to a restaurant between Huntington and Laguna beaches. They were fascinated to learn about Mark and Gary's background and their road trip across America.

Later, back on the beach in the late afternoon, Gary chuckled, remembering their animated conversation with their new friends, Rex and Vivian. "Imagine California being short of females for over a century. Did you see the sparkle in Vivian's eyes when she said she made sure that she got her man?"

"That *was* cute, wasn't it? Amazing that it wasn't until 1950 that California reached a 'normal' male to female ratio of one to one. Australia was like this in its early days. But up until 1950 ... phew, that was very surprising," responded Mark.

"I am going to make a personal study of the American orange and citrus industry when I get home," said Gary suddenly. "I wish we had time to go to that citrus park in Riverside. A million orange trees in Orange County alone, and now, hardly any left." He shook his head. "I really enjoy learning about the agricultural developments in other countries. The Riverina region, back home, can be very proud of what they have accomplished in fifty years."

They finished up their day with a swim in the hotel pool. Like every location they had visited on their frenzied journey to this point, Laguna Beach was leaving them with good vibrations they could recall in the dreary months of July and August as Mark recuperated and Gary waited for spring to arrive.

The next morning, they were on Highway 1 by 7:00 am. They knew they were confronting morning drive traffic, but they had to drive across the metropolis to arrive at Thousand Oaks to the north.

Point to point it would normally take just over two hours, but this was Los Angeles, where it could just as easily take up to four hours. They drove up the coast to Newport Beach, then on to Huntington Beach, and finally to I-405, skirting Greater Los Angeles to arrive at the campus of Californian Lutheran University.

Chris Greville came out of his music building to meet Mark and Gary. Mark and Chris had been lower brass colleagues for just under ten years. They had met by attending church on a Sunday in the middle of a music conference. Shaking hands and embracing, Chris looked over his shoulder and said: "Hello Gary, I'm Chris. You boys have sure been on an adventure this last week or so. I would love to tackle a cross-country road trip one day. Got to wait until the kids are off our hands though, and it's just Judy and me," said Chris as he greeted Gary.

Chris looked over the Buick quickly and pronounced it to be in good shape. He thought it ought to sell within the month. Gary added another $500 to the amount Chris and Mark had agreed to a month ago.

"No, you don't have to do that, Gary. I am happy with the agreement as it stands," protested Chris. "I trade a few cars each year with the help of an auto mechanic friend. Actually, he's a member of the University Church. It keeps me in touch with the business my Dad was in when I was a kid."

"I insist, Chris. I have had a fabulous time with Mark on this trip across America. The Buick made it possible and you are key to helping Mark recoup a few dollars on his car. We are under budget in our expenses; I keep telling Mark this. Honestly, it is my pleasure to give you more—or should I say make it $500 less that you send to Mark," responded Gary, the farmer-businessman in his element.

"I won't argue. Thank you, Gary. It's a deal," said Chris with a broad smile. "Now, come up to my office for some talk, then we will have lunch in the campus café. I will take you on a brief tour and then, about 5:00 pm, we will head to LAX. You need to be there about 6:30 pm."

Over the next ninety minutes, Gary was the superfluous member of the trio, and he liked the fact. He had the immense satisfaction of listening to, and watching, his brother in action with a fellow musician and educator. Chris explained his role at Cal Lutheran as a music professor, chorale conductor, a part-time session player for recording studios and a community music promoter and educator. Like Mark, Chris' background was lower brass instruments in high school, college and community concert bands and orchestras. The bass trombone was his preferred instrument, but he played tenor trombone and some euphonium. Over the last decade, he had turned increasingly to choral conducting, at first because there was a vacancy, and now out of a passion for English choral music; the dulcet strains of John Rutter being his current obsession. Indeed, Chris described how his choral conducting had now become a fixture at the University Church; this bringing him both honor and burden. The chorale was now fully incorporated in the liturgical function of traditional worship services. Glancing over at Gary, Chris explained that much of his choral music was from the Baroque period, and the numerous Bach cantatas—these being originally composed by Johann Sebastian Bach—were intended for worship in a Lutheran church as his focus.

"Too much information," apologized Chris.

"No, to the contrary," said Gary. "I love it. Your passion and dedication; both are incredible. Never apologize, please talk as much as you like. Perhaps one day my daughter will come to California Lutheran University and study music under you. Now that would be wonderful!"

Chris looked at Mark, then back at Gary, and reached out to shake his hand.

"You humble me by your kind words," he responded with a smile. "It would be a pleasure to teach your daughter."

Over lunch, and then as they walked around campus, Chris and Mark engaged in more sharing of their work, their dreams and some of the frustrations hindering both. Gary sensed a genuine connection between both men and expressed his concern that 'too vast an ocean separated them from meaningful collegiality.' Both acknowledged that the distance made it difficult, while not yet impossible. There followed a brainstorming session of how they could collaborate on numerous projects and research. Not wanting to lose on their initial deliberations, they created a precis plan outlining the key possibilities over the next two years. They promised each other to flush out these projects in greater detail within the month.

During a lull in the conversation Mark shared with Chris the news of his forthcoming prostate surgery. Instantly shocked, Chris took Mark by the arm and said that he would pray daily about it. "Please let me know of your progress," he asked. "I want to know how your recovery turns out."

Too soon, it came time for Chris to take them to LAX. The drive to the airport provided Mark and Gary with a glimpse of Los Angeles in afternoon drive traffic. Chris avoided the congested freeways, yet there were ample views of bumper-to-bumper traffic in four lanes or more. They were glad to arrive at the Bradley building where Qantas departed for Australia.

So often, Mark had made this trip on his own and the hardest part was always the hours of waiting for the flight to depart. This time he had company and Gary could share his embarrassment as they watched Australian tourists arrive with all their Disney paraphernalia and their loud voices and obnoxious behavior. When it became too difficult to bear anymore, they walked the corridors for exercise. On their final traipse, both bought several boxes of *Sees* Candy for the family; *Nuts and Chews* for Betty.

Finally, at 10:30 pm, boarding was announced and just shy of an hour later, the loaded Boeing 747 lifted off the tarmac and climbed into the night sky headed south-westerly for Australia. Mark was going home, this time to stay.

CHAPTER THIRTEEN

NEW LIFE, NEW WORK

"Life isn't about finding yourself.
Life is about creating yourself."
—George Bernard Shaw

"So, this is what it's like when you walk off the plane and greet family," declared Gary as he walked across the tarmac to the waiting throng of family gathered at the Adelaide West Beach airport. Some fifty feet from the gate, Gary broke into a run, rushing to embrace Helen and his two children. Not far behind came Mark, a little resolute, yet swallowing hard as he felt his mother clutch him in her arms.

"Nice to have you home, Dr. Schubert," greeted Betty as she kissed him on the cheek and rubbed his scratchy face. The family, including Mark's two sisters and their families, crowded around Mark and Gary, all talking excitedly and seeking some recognition from the brothers. Once the luggage had been collected, and Mark checked the state of his euphonium, the various families went to their respective cars to return to the farm for a light luncheon. Gary announced that he was going to stay awake until evening as Mark had always done on his return from America. It was about "setting his body clock to good old South Australian time," he said wryly, now that he was an international traveler too.

It was an overcast day in Adelaide and the drive through the Adelaide Hills revealed a landscape heavy into winter. There was a chill in the air and a dampness as well. Coming into Hahndorf, the sentinel of trees on main street looked as forlorn as Mark could remember from his childhood days when he longed for leaves on those same trees and a change of season. As they entered the farm, Gary commented on the greenness of the pastures and the running water in the creek. "Do you have plenty of firewood?" Gary asked, turning to Helen and his mother.

"Plenty," said Helen. "The boys have looked after us very well and they filled the fire box yesterday knowing that you would check as soon as you arrived home."

"Well then, I must have more influence around here than I thought," responded Gary.

Mark and Gary showered and shaved and joined the gathered family for food, talk and gifts. It was a happy dining room with Mark and Gary home. At one point, Mark's eye's met Betty's as she quietly observed her family all together at home. Mark smiled, for he knew that his mother was feeling content, even if she had that familiar distant look in her eye indicating that she was thinking of her beloved Frank. Mark took her hand and said, "Now, no more than three Sees chocolates a day, young lady," as he squeezed her hand.

"Just thinking of your Dad and earlier times," she replied, smiling.

"I know, Mum, I could tell," replied Mark, patting her hand.

An hour later, Mark's two sisters and their families had departed. Evening was approaching, and Gary wanted to check on the farm before nightfall.

"Mark, do you want to come out with me?" asked Gary, putting on his heavy farm coat.

"Why, little brother, can't you do without me after being with me every day for three weeks?" laughed Mark.

"That's right; glued to the hip are we," responded Gary.

Out into the cold air went the two brothers, while Helen hugged Betty and whispered: "It's good to have them home."

As he knew he would, Mark awoke at 3:30 am and could not return to sleep. He put on his old dressing gown, donned his old slippers and edged his way to the kitchen without switching on any lights. It was raining. He reached for a flashlight and an umbrella and made his way gingerly to his father's study in the adjacent old house. He turned on the lamp at the side table and saw that the makings of a fire were already in the fireplace. Within minutes Mark had a congenial fire warming the chilled study.

He looked about the room, at his music stand, his first euphonium in its battered case, the familiar paintings and portraits of family, past and present on the walls. His eyes went to the abundance of books in the walnut-stained shelves. Almost unconsciously, he reached for one book, a small white covered paperback, entitled 'A Shepherd Remembers' by Leslie Weatherhead. Frank had encouraged Mark to read this after his first real disappointment in life, his first solo competition in Melbourne. Many years had transpired since that incident and on several subsequent occasions Mark had returned to read Weatherhead's beautiful devotional study on the Twenty-Third Psalm.

Mark turned to the last two chapters, his favorites, *Goodness and Mercy Shall Follow Me*, and *In the House of the Lord Forever*. He paused, walked down the corridor into the old kitchen, and opened the fridge, looking for some milk. There was none, and why should there be, he thought. There were cans of apple juice, so he poured some juice into a coffee mug and heated it in the microwave. Even if there weren't any spices for the Christmas drink he had come to enjoy in Annapolis, he'd make do. After all, it wasn't Christmas.

He returned to his father's desk to read the last two chapters. The nurturing words, the quietness of the early morning hour, the flickering of the warm fire, being in his family home, and sitting at the desk of his father—all this gave Mark assurance that all was well as he looked ahead to the biggest challenge of his life. He would face his prostate surgery next week, not so much with the exact words of Scripture in his thoughts, but more in harmony with the little girl, as told by Weatherhead, who misinterpreted the first verse of the Psalm as she recited it. 'The Lord is my shepherd, that's all I want,' she said. Mark smiled as he came to those words once more. "Yep," he said, "That's what I believe and that's all I need."

By 11:00 am that morning, Mark and Betty were in Dr. Lawson's waiting room. It was still raining as they walked from the car park and they were glad for the warmth of the waiting room. It was now six days until Mark's surgery. Ten minutes later, Dr. Lawson bustled into the room: "It's Dr. Schubert, I presume." They both smiled broadly and shook hands. Dr. Lawson asked Betty to wait while he arranged for Mark's blood to be drawn and then he said he would ask her to join them as they reviewed matters pertaining to Mark's surgery next Thursday.

Inside the confines of his office, Dr. Lawson said: "Once in a while, I find I connect with a patient on a personal level. It can be dangerous as I have always tried to adhere strictly to the ethics of the doctor-patient protocol. With you, Mark, I am drawn empathetically to a young man dealing with prostate cancer. More to the point, I see a man who could marry again in the next few years and who would want to start a family. That's why I reached out to you in my letter. I was glad that you liked my suggestion."

They talked more on the matter and Dr. Lawson agreed to make an appointment for Mark at the sperm bank the following Tuesday. Mark nodded his head quietly. "Thank you for being more than my doctor!"

After blood was drawn, Betty came into Dr. Lawson's office and it was arranged for Mark to return on Tuesday to review the results, plus sign papers and go over details for the arrival at the hospital. Mark was to be in the hospital for at least one and a half days, perhaps two, and then released in the care of his mother.

After all the medical and technical matters had been attended to, Dr. Lawson asked, "Now, tell me, on that marvelous adventure across America, is there one thing that stood out?"

Mark thought for a moment and then replied, "The road trip must be experienced to be believed, the scenery was inspiring and humbling, but the one factor that trumps all else was being there with my brother for the entire journey. I have done too much alone in my life."

Dr. Lawson looked at Betty and said, "Hmmm, that's quite a statement. 'No man is an island.' That's John Donne, I think. I'm going to think on your words."

It was still raining as Mark and his mother made their way back to Betty's car. She took him to a favorite restaurant of Frank's for lunch. They both ordered King George whiting and chips. When their plates of food arrived, Mark declared that he was 'in heaven' and that the fish 'n chips at Laguna Beach a few days ago was not a patch on his King George whiting now. They ate slowly and talked a lot about trivial things. Betty called it 'just catching up.' Towards the end of the meal, Betty said that one thing both impressed and bothered her in the doctor's office.

"Well, Mum, tell me?" questioned Mark.

"You gave a wonderful answer to Dr. Lawson's question about your trip across America. You said that having Gary with you was the best part. That was good for a mother to hear. Then you said that you have been alone too much, and that bothered me," responded Betty.

"If I am honest, Mum, it bothers me now more than ever, but I can't snap my fingers and expect the perfect partner to appear out of nowhere. Look, I am more worried about this surgery than I am letting on, but I need to go through with it. I worry what it may do to me. . . physically," he said, his voice trailing off.

"Oh dear, Mark, I had not thought of that," replied Betty.

Then Mark told his mother of what he had done in the early morning hours and related the reading of Weatherhead and the story, at the very end of the book, of the little girl who had not memorized correctly the first verse of Psalm 23. Then, as a declaration Mark took his mother's hand and said boldly: "'The Lord is my shepherd, that's all I want!' This is my new mantra, my new catchphrase. I am going to get through this surgery and recover to begin my new work in the Navy band in Melbourne in September. And, then I am going to be intentional about finding the girl of my dreams—slowly and deliberately. God willing, it is going to work out."

"Gary has sensed this is where I am, but I am going to say no more about it. I am going to get on with life and watch for something wonderful to happen. You know, for years I turned away from any possible relationship. Not now, but this is between you and me."

Betty nodded, smiling, then added, "But you need to know that my prayer every day is that 'the girl of your dreams' comes along soon."

"I am not going to argue with that. Heck, I am now 41, and I want it to happen while I can still chase this dream girl on the beach!"

That Sunday the family went to St. Michael's as was their custom. Mark was besieged by friends and church members who knew that he was home in Australia permanently and wanted to wish him well. He was asked to play his euphonium the following Sunday, but declined without saying why, recognizing that the reason would come out anyway within the week. Succumbing to prostate cancer so young was news enough in itself, and to add a mild celebrity status to this was just more fuel to the fire when it leaked, as it would very soon.

Two days later, Mark was back in Dr. Lawson's office, this time without Betty. He had persuaded her that he could not always have her with him. She reluctantly agreed. The results of the blood tests indicated that Mark's PSA was rising. This did not surprise the doctor, as it is often an aggressive cancer when found in a patient so young.

"It will be good to remove that prostate this week," remarked Dr. Lawson. "Once out and gone, it can do no more harm."

"Gone for good, I hope," replied Mark.

"Yes, but in my business, we avoid speaking with complete confidence about cancers," said Dr. Lawson. He looked closely at Mark. "We will get it all, but if something should come back, we will tackle that when it comes. Don't get alarmed by this. Believe that it will be gone and gone for good," he said with finality.

"I get it," said Mark.

The nurse came into the room as they reviewed the steps to follow on the morning of the surgery. Mark would be released on Friday afternoon, or at the latest, on Saturday. As Mark prepared to leave, he shook hands with Dr. Lawson and confessed: "For $20, I would not keep my next appointment."

"I understand, but in a few years, you will thank me!" replied Dr. Lawson.

An hour later Mark emerged from his appointment at the sperm bank, vowing never to repeat the experience. He chuckled to himself as he thought of the irony of the statement. "You donkey! That's more of a prophetic statement than you know."

He drove back to the farm in a reflective mood. Later that afternoon, he walked around the farm alone. Gary was attending a meeting in Mount Barker and so Mark could wander as it suited him. Eventually, he found himself drawn to the pines that had been his psychological refuge since he was a boy. He stood for a long time staring into the trees and their trunks. No longer was there the same protection that the branches afforded when the trees were younger and gave him the shroud of secrecy that had appealed originally to his young mind. The more he gazed, the more he realized that he could let go of this childish fetish he had clung to for too long. He was a mature man now and he no longer needed the pines. He was grateful for their presence in his earlier life, but he was home now and entering a new phase of his life and his career. 'The Lord is my shepherd, that's all I want,' he said to himself as he walked to the house. He felt emboldened.

On Thursday morning, with some apprehension on Mark's part, he ate no breakfast but drove himself to the private hospital in Adelaide arriving, as requested, before 7:00 am. Betty accompanied him, while Gary remained with his family, but would join Betty at the hospital before the surgery began.

The only paperwork to be completed was Mark's registration on the day of the surgery. When this was done, he was shown to a preparation room where he undressed and donned the ridiculous garment that he "never in his life ever wanted to wear." After this thought, he calmed himself down and reminded himself that he needed to endure the next few hours, the next few days and the next two months of recovery time. There was to be no more *"why did this happen to me?"* Rather, it was time to cling to medicine's solution to a needless death sentence and to clasp hold of new life with all the determination he could muster. "Are you ready for surgery, Mark?" he asked himself. "Do you believe all will be well?" "Yes," he answered truthfully to both questions. "'The Lord is my shepherd, that's all I want.'"

He wavered for a few seconds as he mounted the gurney and the nurse connected his arm to an IV and gave him an initial sedative. Then, he was wheeled into another room where his mother leaned over, kissed him on the forehead and said, "You are in God's hands."

Mark nodded without speaking, and within minutes he was being wheeled down a long corridor. He found himself thinking of movies he had seen where the patient is looking up at the ceiling as the gurney speeds down the hallway to the operating room. He tried to smile at his musings, but he felt very drowsy. With effort he opened his eyes to see Dr. Lawson peering down at him and smiling encouragingly.

"Good morning, Dr. Schubert," said the doctor, "'No man is an island,' right? My team and I are going to begin surgery now. We will …" Mark heard no more. His surgery was underway.

Before noon the operation was over, and Mark was wheeled into his private room, still under the anesthesia. The nurse ushered his mother and brother into the room and told them that he would be awake within minutes. When he finally stirred, they leaned over his bed: "Mark, it's me," murmured Betty. "Your surgery is over, and Gary and I are here with you. The doctor says that everything was successful." Mark stirred, struggling to understand.

In a few minutes, he was conscious of someone speaking to him. This time it was Dr. Lawson with a nurse at his side. He had been talking to Betty and Gary and then came over to his patient: "You have done very well, Mark. Your surgery was successful. You will gradually regain consciousness and your mother and brother will be at your bedside for the afternoon. I have asked that no other visitors come see you until tomorrow. In a few hours, the nurse will bring you some food and I want you to eat something, even if only a little. I will go now and see you in the morning."

Most of the afternoon saw Mark dozing off and on. Try as he might, he could not hold a consistent conversation with his mother or Gary. He knew they were at his bedside and that brought consolation. He felt no pain and if there was any sensation he was experiencing it was one of floating above the ground, perhaps in the clouds. As evening approached, the nurse brought some food and Betty tried to help Mark eat. He was not cooperative but did drink some juice and swallow some jelly. Gary suggested to Betty that they should leave and let Mark have a good sleep. They would be back around noon tomorrow and then perhaps they would be able to take Mark home in the late afternoon. Mark thanked them for coming, although he was not sure why they had come or why he was in the hospital.

As the nurse settled Mark down for the night, she reminded him to press the button on the railing of his bed should he experience any pain. When the pain came about an hour later, he pushed the button. Then he slept, and he dreamed. In the morning, he was fully awake and aware of his surroundings. He ate breakfast and spoke to his mother on the phone. She would be with him around noon. About mid-morning, a male nurse came in and told Mark that he was going to help Mark walk along the corridor.

"I really don't feel like walking or even getting out of bed," protested Mark.

"I understand, Mr. Schubert, but it's important that you get some exercise as soon as possible," he replied, kindly but firmly. "I'll help you all the way."

Recognizing he would lose any further argument, Mark struggled to sit up and roll out of bed and then, holding onto the IV stand with one hand and the arm of the nurse with the other, he began a slow, clumsy walk along the corridor. Within minutes he was feeling better and greatly pleased with himself. "Perhaps recovery is going to be faster than I was told," he thought. This optimistic notion encouraged him to walk faster, until the nurse turned him around and they headed back to his room.

"We mustn't do too much too soon," he said as he helped Mark back into bed. "You did very well. Now you should rest."

In fact, Mark was glad to rest. He pushed his pain button to alleviate a dull ache he was encountering after his walk. He slept for some time and was awakened by the nurse checking on his vital signs. This was followed by lunch and then the arrival of Betty. She brought flowers and said, "I know you are probably being released this evening, but you can enjoy these for a few hours." Gary was at a meeting and would arrive later in the afternoon. He would help Mark into the car and then take him home if this was still with the doctor's approval. Betty was encouraged to see Mark awake, alert and so alive. They settled into a long conversation and when there was a pause, Mark said, "Mum, I want to tell you, only you, something that I experienced last night. I know it was largely to do with my medication and I really ask that you keep it to yourself."

"What is it, Mark?" queried Betty. "If you ask me not to tell, you can trust that I won't."

"I feel a little embarrassed even telling you," he confessed. "Last night I dreamed possibly the best dream of my life. I was asleep here in this bed and I woke up sensing that someone had an arm around me. I asked, 'Who's there?' A soft feminine voiced whispered, 'It's me and I've come to watch over you. Go to sleep and know that you are loved.'"

"Mum, I know it was still the medication in me," Mark continued intensely, "but it was such a real dream and the best I've ever had. The reality of the closeness of this gentle person was amazing. It was a sense of warmth and affection I have never known in real life."

"How lovely for you, Mark," said Betty. She smoothed his cheek. "You need to believe that somewhere out there such a person is waiting for you."

"Now let me tell you something I don't want the world to know," she continued. "There are times when I miss your father so much, I wonder how I can carry on without him in my life. It is a good thing that I am living with Gary and Helen and the children. Sometimes I dream of days gone by when your Dad and I were together, other times I can almost feel him holding my hand when walking on the farm or along a jetty at the various beaches he loved so much."

"I guess it is all good," responded Mark.

"Yes, it is, and remember, at all times, there is a loving God above wanting us to experience life in all its abundance," said Betty. "For me, I am content with my memories, but for you there is still much more to come. Don't let it slip through your hands."

The conversation ended as Dr. Lawson walked in, looked at Mark's bedside chart and then said: "Everything looks good, Mark. I am going to release you today and you can go home this evening. You are very young to have undergone this surgery. It was a precise operation and we got the prostate out with no problems. I am going to release you early this evening in the care of your mother. Just know that your catheter may begin to irritate you within the week. When this occurs, call me and I will have you come in and I will remove it. Also, the staples can cause trouble as well. Try not to move quickly in your lower abdomen. Sometimes one or more may come unattached and it makes healing longer and scarring more noticeable. You can go home when you are ready."

It was dark and raining as Gary pulled out of the hospital onto a busy road with cars and buses streaming by, getting thousands of working people home for the evening. Mark was in the front passenger seat, sedated and reasonably comfortable. He looked at all the vehicles and saw in their lights a kaleidoscope of confused color jumping around through the falling rain. Gary was now on Glen Osmond Road passing many semi-trailers in his eagerness to reach the Toll House and leave the city behind as they climbed into the Adelaide Hills. Mark prattled on loosely about how he was glad that the surgery was over and that he had his mother and brother to look after him. Betty leaned over and placed her hand on his shoulder, quietly suggesting that he close his eyes and rest.

"Great idea, Mum," agreed Mark. "Am I rambling? I feel groggy."

"It is the medication the nurse gave you before you left the hospital," replied Betty.

When he hobbled into the kitchen after arriving home, Helen had prepared split pea soup and toasted cheese sandwiches for the evening meal. This was a favorite winter meal for Mark and Gary when they were children. Mark insisted on sitting at the table while he ate. Gary's two children clung to their father's legs as they asked after Uncle Mark. They had not seen him incapacitated before and their concern was real. After his meal, Mark was more than ready for bed. He went to the spare bedroom, and his mother ensured that he was comfortable. A few minutes later, he was asleep. His recovery cycle had commenced.

Awake at 4:30 am, Mark lay still as he sorted in his mind all that had occurred in the last three days. He sat up, sipped some water and then fell back on his pillow. He ached in his torso and found that if he lay on his back, the pain was less. By 7:00 am he could see that the rain had stopped, and sunshine was greeting him as the day began. He stared at the ceiling and the corners of the room and matched shapes and angles as he did as a child to relieve the boredom of being confined to bed. He was pleased when Betty knocked on his door and asked if he wanted his breakfast in bed. He wanted to sit at the table, but needed assistance getting himself there.

"Well, I know this recovery effort is going to be a real drag. I wanted to get up earlier this morning but found I just didn't know how to go about it. I have to get beyond this handicap stage," protested Mark.

"My dear, patience has never been your strong suit. This is your first morning home after surgery. It is going to take a few weeks. You know this, and you need to pace yourself," counselled Betty.

"Frankly, Mark, it is all the more reason why we must concentrate on the exercise schedule Dr. Lawson gave you," she added.

Mark knew there was no magical formula here, and to follow doctor's orders was the quickest way to recovery. His mother was right, as she had been consistently throughout his life. He determined to tackle each day as a single unit and to map his progress accordingly. Within four days he understood why Dr. Lawson warned that the catheter could become irritating. This was an understatement. Try as he may, Mark could not stop the discomfort that was edging on mild agony. No matter if he was standing, sitting, in bed on his back or on his side, the sheer irritability seemed to increase with every hour. Dr. Lawson's instructions were to call him when this occurred.

That same afternoon, Mark and his mother drove to Dr. Lawson's rooms. He greeted them with an unexpected statement: "This is a good sign, Mark. You are healing ahead of schedule and the catheter must come out."

Dr. Lawson took him into another room, removed the catheter and Mark returned to his mother.

"Oh, my goodness, it is instant relief," he declared.

"It is unique to each patient," Dr. Lawson remarked. "The largest factor here is that Mark is very young—my youngest patient ever. It's a good sign that he is recovering so quickly. It looks as though the staples will be ready for removal in about another week." He turned to Mark, "We should make an appointment for you in eight days from today."

The drive into the Hills gave Mark time to sit back and let Betty navigate the twists and turns of the eighteen-mile journey. He was quiet and somewhat chastened by the recognition that he had had no control over the irritation he had felt from the catheter.

"There was nothing I could do to stop the level of irritation," Mark mused out loud. "It wasn't pain in the real sense, but it was getting worse and would not go away. I couldn't stop it." He looked over at his mother.

"Perhaps you are beginning to feel your vulnerability. It happens to us all at some stage or other in life," she responded, her eyes on the road. "You're entering an age when you will find you have less control over health and other matters."

"Your father and I talked about this quite a bit after his heart attack," she continued quietly. "He couldn't believe it was happening to him. Then, when we diagnosed it all, we came to realize that stress was the culprit. While he lived a life of calm on the outside, he was full of stress and conflict on the inside." She paused, her eyes filling with tears. "He really should have been permitted to study for the ministry. It was his father who said he had to take over the farm. Your father acquiesced, but he always carried some regret and disappointment inside," she added.

"Mum, I didn't know it was that bad," responded Mark. "I always knew that he had a love of books and music and the arts, but I thought he took over the farm from Grandpa understanding this was the best thing to do. You mean he lived with deep regrets?" asked Mark.

"Yes, Grandpa was very vocal that your Dad was *not* to go to Immanuel College and study for the ministry. The war didn't help and neither did the thought of losing the Schubert farm after three generations. It wasn't all bad and we were happy together on the farm for a long time, but I knew those moments of doubt and regret when your father would retreat to his study. It was his escape from farm life when it became drudgery in his thinking. Your father was a good, mechanical farmer whereas Gary is a natural and passionate farmer. You are more like my Frank," concluded Betty.

"I didn't realize. Thank you for telling me this, Mum. Stress is a killer. There is no question about it. I am going to try and live a more balanced life as I start my new role in Melbourne," said Mark.

"Glad to hear it," replied Betty as they drove into Hahndorf, onto Balhannah Road and to the farm.

As the weeks went by, Mark continued to heal and recover ahead of schedule. His mind was shifting toward his new work with the Royal Australian Navy Band. Phone calls and letters were increasingly part of every week day as he approached the month of September. Towards the end of July, the media learned of Mark's return to Australia and, more significantly for them, his prostate surgery. The news releases were brief and almost incidental at first. However, as the media realized they were not getting easy access to Mark, they became more intrusive. Death by prostate cancer was on the rise in Australia and to learn that even a minor celebrity had succumbed to this male curse was of special interest. Mark was known for his personal competitive success in Australian brass band circles, for his music education and his attractive persona as a discussant on television. The biggest news of all was his age; forty-one years and a prostate cancer survivor. This was the ugly side of media. Mark became fodder for hungry journalists working for popular weekly journals. They wanted pictures, they wanted comments, and soon the phone was ringing many times a day. Mark asked the Public Relations office at the Melbourne Naval Yard for assistance, and together they agreed on a strategy to satisfy media interest in Mark and to provide a smoother segue into his new work in music education with the Navy after September. Mark did one interview with a leading weekly journal and another with the *Adelaide Advertizer*. After this, the phone stopped ringing and Mark continued to prepare for his new work.

It was six weeks before he could play his euphonium. Breathing was the issue, and it still hurt his diaphragm if he blew for more than ten minutes. He needed a gap of about an hour in between each attempt. As frustrating as this was, Mark accepted the restraints and focused on effortlessly playing hymns, chiefly to keep him calm since he was chafing to play more challenging music. A week later he went to band rehearsal with the Hahndorf Town Band. Most of the members had seen him at church or on the streets shopping, but even so they applauded him when he entered. During the break they insisted that he tell them about his time in America and what he planned to do in Melbourne. Mark was pleased for the opportunity to give his first talk in Australia, impromptu though it be, to band members, some of whom had known him from the days when he was a lowly third cornet player. He spoke in soft tones at first, expressing his gratitude for Hahndorf, its people, its Old Lutheran traditions ("which mean more to me today than ever before"), its rural location and the town and farm connection which permitted someone like Mark to feel equally at home in either place. He spoke of his appreciation for family, including the town as an extended family (something he had not always valued as a youth). He addressed the younger players and asked them rhetorically if they had dreams about their future. He challenged them to think big and to do so with confidence, always knowing that Hahndorf 'has your back.' It had worked that way for him, he declared with vigor, and clenched his fist as he said that thinking of home helped him through his 'hardest moments.' Finally, he spoke of his next chapter and how he would only be 'one day's drive away from home.' He hoped to encourage the wider expansion of community music throughout Australia and to enlarge the numbers of young people experiencing practical music opportunities.

He ended with a question: "I believe that the ability to play or sing music adds to the quality of a person's life. Would you agree?"

There was not one member of the band who disagreed.

"Well, then," said Mark, "Encourage others to learn to play music!"

He drove home after the rehearsal and shared the details of his first playout since leaving Annapolis, with Betty, Gary and Helen over hot

Milo, with a toasty fire burning in the family room. He felt ready to resume normal activities.

In the last week of August, Mark met with Dr. Lawson for a pivotal appointment. He was seeking medical clearance to return to full-time employment with the Navy band in Melbourne in the second week of September. Even Mark was a little tentative about going back to a full work week in his first month. Was it overly ambitious? What would the doctor say? He had always been truthful with Dr. Lawson; dare he hide his own concern if asked?

"We are at that moment, Mark!" Dr. Lawson greeted Mark with the blunt reason for their meeting. "You have come a long way since your surgery. After checking all your charts, your wound, and listening to you say that you want to begin work on September 9, here is my recommendation."

"First, I suspect you recognize that you are still regaining strength and I think you know that working too hard in the first month will not be good for your continued healing."

"So, I'm clearing you to return to work on September 9, but I am going to state in the Navy medical report that you should be restricted to no more than eight-hour days in the first month. I wish this could be restricted to six hours. Also, you must be careful in playing your instrument too vigorously. We want the scarring to be minimal and, remember, it will always look worse to you than anybody else."

"Other than this, my friend, I wish you good health, happiness and may that princess walk into your life sometime soon!"

"My mother has been talking to you, hasn't she?" questioned Mark with a sly grin.

Betty was in the waiting room as Mark emerged with Dr. Lawson. They agreed to schedule an appointment for mid-December, they shared a few pleasantries, and then Mark and Betty stepped out into the brisk winter air. Mark drove home, and both were full of talk about the relief to have this cancer business behind them. They looked at each other and Betty pointed upwards as if to say, 'God willing.'

That evening the Schubert family kitchen was an especially happy place. They gave thanks to God for his care and keeping of Mark throughout his prostate cancer ordeal. Once again, Helen had excelled with another favorite meal of the brothers. This time it was rainbow trout (boned and 'butterflied'), from their own pond, with string beans and mashed potatoes.

After eating, Mark and Gary shared with Betty and Helen the flight details and agenda for their trip to Melbourne to get Mark settled temporarily and ready for work on the second week of September. Mark had been assigned to the Defence Force School of Music at the Simpson Barracks until the New Year. He would occupy one of the available furnished flats offered to him. When the dishes were done, and in conjunction with their flight to Melbourne on Thursday, Gary announced that he had a surprise for Mark. They pulled on coats and boots and walked in the cold and dark over to the main shed where the tractors were kept. Everyone but Mark knew what was coming. Gary strode over to the main power box and put on the lights. Where the main tractor usually stood was a tarpaulin draped over a car-shaped object. Gary told Mark that this was something he could accept or reject, and if so, then Gary would stake a claim for it. With that he whisked the tarpaulin off Mark's old Monaro GTS, sporting a new coat of paint and new wheels. It looked like a restored car.

"I didn't sell it, Mark, after you left for America. I have a strong impression that this will become a much sought-after car in the next twenty years or so. It is not completely restored, but almost. If you don't want it, I'll keep it. I believe it is going to fetch a lot of money in a few years," said Gary.

"Gary, you-old-devil, I can't believe you didn't sell it! It looks beautiful. Of course, I want it. I just have to forget that it also belonged to someone else too!" said Mark, putting it all out there.

"Yes, I thought of that. If that's a problem, you can take the utility and trade it whenever you want on the car of your choice," said Gary. "Otherwise, just bring back the Monaro when you are ready. Whatever car you buy, it will always be a business car from the farm. You know that!"

"Thank you, Gary," said Mark with considerable emotion. This little brother of his had matured into quite the businessman, with a generous spirit.

"Thank Dad and Mum. They passed a farm to us that has provided the Schubert family with financial security and a love for the land," stated Gary as he hugged Betty.

Before dawn on Thursday, Mark and Gary drove to the airport and flew to Tullamarine airport in Melbourne. The Defence Force School of Music (DFSM) had requested that Mark attend a planning session prior to commencing his duties as director of public relations for the Royal Australian Navy Band and associate musical director of the Royal Australian Navy Band in Melbourne. Gary accompanied Mark, as he and Betty wanted to ensure Mark had family support should he become fatigued at any point. Ever the businessman, Gary arranged to meet with a lavender producer in Wandin North and could, thereby, claim the trip for business purposes.

Gary dropped Mark at the DFSM Simpson Barracks in Watsonia and proceeded onto the Yarra Valley. Mark was welcomed by old and new faces as Navy and Defence Force leadership had changed in the five years he was overseas. Navy Strategic Command from Canberra had sent its Warrant Officer to participate in the meeting. Mark was greeted warmly by the Royal Australian Navy Director of Music from Sydney and he sat next to his immediate supervisor, the Musical Director of the Royal Australian Navy band in Melbourne. Surrounded by twelve military uniforms, Mark felt somewhat conspicuous dressed in a business suit. As the DFSM leadership team had called the meeting, the Commanding Officer chaired proceedings and estimated a projected conclusion at 2:00 pm, followed by a late luncheon.

The agenda began with a review of the state of current Australian military music, including the challenges of expanding offerings of musical genres, increased funding needs and revitalized public support. DFSM announced that it was using Microsoft *PowerPoint* as its presentation program for the first time. Admitting that there was a certain nervousness by their technicians, the co-chairs expressed their delight that, successful or not, it was clear the days of overhead transparencies were almost over.

PowerPoint worked flawlessly and there were expressions of interest in seeing this new program distributed to all music units under DFSM. Mark's mentor, the Royal Australian Navy Director of Music from Sydney, spoke next. He reviewed the dark days following the Vietnam War when public support for "all things" military was at a low ebb. Only in the last year or so, had he detected, along with others in the military, a renewed interest emerging nationally in Anzac Day attendance and a sense of national pride. Laughter ensued when he suggested that he hoped this was not merely a fleeting upswing after the popularity of the movie, *Crocodile Dundee*. Rather, he said, many were hopeful that public support of Australia's military would continue to improve, and exponentially so, as they moved into the 1990s. Next, he promoted the need for military music as an obvious public relations tool for the Australian Defence Force, to understand what the public expects from military music and how DFSM can transition to exceed public expectations in the musical domain. Speaking specifically of the Royal Australian Navy music contributions, he said: "Gone are the days when the Navy only had two offerings: a parade band and a brass or concert band. Sydney and Melbourne now have Big Bands and, to some extent, jazz groups—but here we often draw upon Army and Air Force to assist. We need to be thinking of a rock group and to develop, more intentionally, small groups like brass and wind quintets. It is my challenge to RAN musicians to dare to be innovative in ways and means to win greater support from the Australian public. I pledge my support to the DFSM as it plans and executes new policies and procedures, and then implements new musical offerings for all branches of the total Defence Force."

There was full agreement by all gathered around the table as the RAN Director of Music sat down. It was time for the Commanding Officer of DFSM to provide a summary of all that had occurred in the meeting and to recommend a series of actions to be explored, researched and acted upon immediately. It was at this point that Mark was officially introduced to the group and his new role explained: "Lieutenant Mark Schubert will be joining us at the DFSM at Simpson Barracks in less than two weeks. As a newly minted PhD, Dr. Schubert will be carrying a dual title as Associate Musical Director of the RAN Melbourne Band and, a new title for you today, Mark, as Director of Musical Innovation and Community Outreach at DFSM. His first title is understood by all. His second title is the best we could find for the moment. It may change as we are asking him to shape and mold DFSM strategies as we jointly seek to engage better relations with the Australian public."

"Mark—and I am speaking at a personal level now—has achieved a fine record of successfully interacting with local communities as a Navy musician. We're asking him to show us how it can be done throughout all branches of the Defence Force nation-wide."

"Between September to December holidays, many of us around this table will be working hard to create a new vision, mission and programs for Defence Force music to, one, enhance the professional careers of the hundreds of current musicians serving in our musical groups and, two, to engender greater support from the Australian public."

"I want to end with a comment which may seem out of context, but here we are looking to create new directions for military music. Unless I am missing something, I find it interesting to note that there never seems to be any question about the high degree of support for our Pipe Bands. Why is that? Perhaps we will find some answers through our research."

Mark was asked to make a few comments. Nodding his head to those gathered about the table he began: "It is good to be home in Australia, and permanently now. I am humbled by the confidence you have in me and grateful to know that the challenge before us is to be shared by many military musicians and administrators who already sense where Defence Force music must go if it is to remain relevant, buoyant and popular. Your comment, Commander, of public support for Pipe Bands is noted and will be included in our research."

"Between September and December, several of us at DFSM will tour all branches of Defence Force music facilities and utilize various data-gathering techniques in an honest attempt to assemble and understand the opinions and ideas on changes to the current status quo. It is very appropriate that we should seek input internally and ask our own military musicians what they see as a new direction for Defence Force music."

"You all know that I have just completed my doctorate at Johns Hopkins University on the benefits of local communities investing in musical opportunities for their youthful populations. I founded a youth band at my Lutheran church only a mile away from the Naval Academy in Annapolis. This band would not have developed as it did without the help of my fellow Navy musicians. I am passionate about professional musicians working within local communities to foster programs in youth music."

"Given the restraints of budget, I believe the DFSM can produce a new vision and mission for a new thrust in Defence Force music. This will attract the best musicians into our three branches and provide innovative strategies to connect in meaningful ways with the Australian public."

"My final comment is this: All that we do must be done in the quest of excellence. There is no substitute. In a few years, it is possible that the best musical performance and recordings in all of Australia will be those of Defence Force musicians. Dare to imagine with me military music which is not only excellent, but also entertaining. We're going to make it happen."

"I thank you for the opportunity given to me."

The last comment before the group broke for lunch came from Canberra's Navy Strategic Command Warrant Officer: "Today, I sense a determination to make Navy music better, and the same with Army and Air Force music too. We all know and appreciate that music is such an important part of our lives."

"Welcome home, Lieutenant Schubert. To you and all at DFSM, help the Defence Force make excellent and entertaining music."

This was Mark's introduction to his new work. Driving to the airport in the early evening, Mark was telling Gary all about the day. He had seen his appointed flat and said that he found himself longing for his Eastport apartment, but he could make do until the end of this year. It would permit him to settle into Melbourne once again and he could think of finding accommodation outside of DFSM for the new year.

"One other matter, I know I must be careful as to what I say and to whom I say it, but I think I am going to feel a month or two of culture shock. Let me say this and then give me feedback. I miss the U.S. I miss the architecture of the Naval Academy. I miss the size of Navy music in America and readiness to bring about change quickly. I miss American professionalism. I had a wonderful meeting today, and I am going to be given more help than I thought, but it is still going to be tough and always restricted by budget. It is simply the restrictions that come from a country with around 20 million people to one with almost 300 million. It is not Australia's fault in any shape or form. It just hit me in the meeting today."

"I understand completely, Mark," said Gary. He admitted that he, too, had taken a few days to orientate back into Australian ways. He had also decided to keep it to himself, but he continued, nevertheless.

"I felt it too, and I was only in America for three weeks with you. I have got it back in perspective again now. Overall, I see Australia as a less complicated country than the U.S., and one that is kinder to the average Joe. It may lack the spectacular and the sensational, but that is always in the mind of the beholder and most of us don't live at those levels for long anyway. I'm not sure how to describe what I felt, but I know I'm glad Australia is home."

"Me too!" echoed Mark. "I do know that it is important for me to organize at least three notable music events between now and Christmas. I need to video these and present them as examples of military music making a favorable impact on the Australian public. There won't be much time for any more innovation, as the rest of my time will be consumed with gathering data input on the future direction of

Defence Force music. There will be three of us leading this project. I think my territory will be Victoria, Tasmania and South Australia."

"What type of events, Mark?" asked Gary as they were approaching Tullamarine Airport.

"Well, I have been thinking on this for about a month, knowing in broad terms what my first three months would entail. I would like to put together a Navy rock presentation with five male singers performing forty minutes of the Four Seasons. You know, Frankie Valli. I can imagine this happening at Federation Square after work in Melbourne. In fact, we have already asked the City Council if we can do this on the second Thursday in December from 5:30 to 6:30 pm. They are working hard to approve this on short notice. I saw this done in D.C. and it was a tremendous success. If it goes ahead, I've got to pull out all stops to make it happen."

Gary interjected: "If you can make this happen, then I will bring Mum, Helen and the kids on a shopping spree so we can see this with you. It sounds exciting!"

"Yes, and scary, 'cos the stakes are high here for me," noted Mark. "For it to bomb is not an option. I think the next two events I would arrange with the Kewsick Army Band in Adelaide. The first would be to video a successful march in the Christmas Parade and the second would be a stage band performing Christmas music in the Adelaide Mall in the middle of December."

"And, again, what's the purpose of these events?" asked Gary, as they pulled into the rental car bay at the airport.

"The point is to demonstrate to DFSM, and Defence Force leadership in general, that here are three recent success stories of how Defence Force music is impacting, in a positive way, the Australian public. The full details of the review won't become available until the following year," responded Mark. "I just think it's important to make a positive splash as the research and review gets under way."

Three hours later they were entering the farm after Mark's first day of work since his surgery. As it was still not late, the family gathered around the kitchen table and listened with keen interest to the exploits of the trip to Melbourne. Mark and Gary ate their split pea soup and toasted cheese sandwiches as they told of their meetings, their driving in Melbourne's busy streets and of their flight home. Perhaps because he was sensing that in a few days, he would be leaving home again, Mark took note of the inestimable value of belonging to such a family. He was truly blessed.

CHAPTER FOURTEEN

BACK TO WORK

"Confront the difficult while it is still easy;
Accomplish the great task by a series of small acts."
—Tao Te Ching

A week later, Mark had packed the Monaro with a few personal things and as much clothing, towels and bedding as he needed for the next three months and drove out the farm gate just after sunrise. His new chapter was under way, and as he drove to the freeway heading to Murray Bridge and onto Melbourne, his first sensation was to know that he was alone again. Gary had been his constant companion for so long and then his mother, for the last three months. He was not a loner by choice, despite his protestations in days gone by that he liked to be alone. Gary had been such a vigorous conversational road trip partner, the journey to Melbourne seemed unbalanced without someone sitting in the passenger's seat.

There was no question, Gary's work on the Monaro had brought it to a high degree of restoration. Mark liked the new additions of a modern wood compound steering wheel, air conditioning and a new radio and CD player. The car drove well and responded quickly to a touch on the accelerator. Mark had to remind himself that this was a muscle car of the '70s and that Australian speed limits were less generous than in America, and heavily enforced.

All the same, he arrived at the Simpson Barracks as the work day ended and within the hour, he had all his belongings inside his new flat. He had three days to acclimatize once again to the Eastern suburbs. He was less than an hour from Luther College; probably where he would go to church on Sundays. As the daylight faded, he needed a substantial meal. He had had more to drink than he had eaten while traveling. He had seen an Indian restaurant about ten minutes from the Barracks and decided it was time to indulge in a cuisine that he enjoyed once in a while. The lamb curry was satisfying and that night he slept solidly knowing his new work was about to begin.

The next three months were a flurry of activity as Mark wore several hats as a Navy musician, his preferred term for himself when people asked him what he did for a living. He was a euphonium player first and foremost, but he was now doubling more frequently on bass trombone. As such he was a member of the RAN Melbourne band, and this required him to drive to *HMS Cerberus* regularly to participate in as many of the band's appointments as possible. He also reconnected with the Navy public relations office and his colleagues in both the Melbourne and Sydney offices. Finally, he had his permanent office at DFSM at the Simpson Barracks and it was here that most of the survey data gathering project was designed and implemented. Overall it pleased Mark that he did not have to bother with the design or statistical aspects of the survey; he was a team member and the 'face' of the survey as he visited Defence Force music locations in the three states allocated to him. He was out of the office for ten days gathering data input and was very much conscious that the clock was ticking. He had to make his *Frankie Valli* Federation Square concert a success.

Through the concerted efforts of Defence Force administration and Navy lobbying, the Melbourne City Council approved the RAN band occupying the Federation Square space for a one-hour slot on Thursday, December 12 from 5:30 to 6:30 pm with one hour on either side for set up and take down. Achieving this was quite the coup, and Mark was relieved when approval appeared in writing.

He had already been in contact with many colleagues and friends seeking five likely Navy men who could sing and entertain, a combination not easily found among Navy personnel. The RAN Melbourne band had already scored the six Four Seasons songs and brought together an ensemble of fifteen musicians. They had scrutinized Federation Square and plotted out all the logistics to seat about 200 people, allowing for a constant pedestrian traffic of thousands who would look in, but walk on by over the hour of the concert.

Once the right combination of vocals was in place, it took weeks of rehearsal to make these amateur sailors confident and engaging enough to perform before a live audience. Serious coaching was necessary, and someone suggested that they should contact Normie Rowe, the '60s teen-idol who served in the Vietnam War, and was now an entertainer mostly in Sydney. He was flattered to be asked to assist and he gave creative energy and long hours willingly in the preparation of these five fledgling performers. By the end of November, the program was ready. Mark remained tense, as he knew this had to be an outstanding success. He was looking for a "WOW" factor, not only from the audience, but from the Defence Force administration, the City Council and himself, always his own harshest critic.

With all that was on Mark's daily agenda, he found it impossible to restrict his work to an actual eight hours a day. Nevertheless, he knew his physical limitations and that he must not push himself too hard. He had little time to socialize and to meet new people. For now, this was to his health's advantage. He worked, he fulfilled his music obligations, he ate, and he came back to his flat to rest and to sleep. His only consistent non-work activity was his frequent visits to the music studios across from his flat to practice. Once or twice, he recalled his hermit days at HMS *Cerberus,* and he recoiled at the thought of letting himself slip back into that frame of mind. Back then, he was endeavoring to squash sentiment, whereas today he was open to being surprised by ecstasy. He knew his physical health and well-being were dependent on his pledge to Dr. Lawson to be circumspect in his daily schedule.

Gary was true to his word and drove the family to Melbourne for a two-day shopping spree, with the express purpose of coinciding with the Navy band concert. They arrived on the Wednesday night and took Mark out to dinner near their motel. On Thursday, they rode the suburban train into Flinders Street station and shopped until late in the afternoon. Burdened with shopping bags, they met Mark at Federation Square at 4:30 pm. He was in his white dress uniform and so were the arriving Navy musicians. The stage was all set and the sound checks were being finalized. Mark showed his family to front row seats and next to some fifteen seats reserved for Navy and City Council guests. Mark said the Navy administrators may show signs of anxiety as they were invested in a successful outcome of this 'music performance experiment.' Mark said he would explain more later.

By 5:20 pm, the Navy officials had arrived, including two female officers in their dress uniforms. They were followed by the City Council members, taking their seats as directed. Television cameras were in position and the two Navy videographers were well placed to capture the sense of excitement and audience response. All the chairs were occupied, and people were sitting and standing in every space possible. The anticipation was palpable.

Mark walked onto the platform right at 5:30 pm. He gave a Navy welcome to the audience and introduced the RAN Melbourne ensemble and their *Tribute to the Four Seasons*. The band began with its introduction and on stage walked five male sailors in their dress whites. The concert was underway. Immediately, the atmosphere at Federation Square was alive, pulsating with the beat of the '60s, and *Sherry*. There was no evidence that these five crooning sailors had not done this performance a hundred times before. They had been coached well. They were energized, natural and having a grand time as their hands, legs and smiles evoked raucous responses from the crowd. Normie Rowe stood next to Mark, both emanating pleasure (and relief) on their faces. The six songs flowed into each other with impressive and dramatic segues by drums and piano leading into *Big Boys Don't Cry*, followed by *Walk Like a Man*, the half-way point in the program.

As Mark and the other Navy observers reporting on crowd reactions looked about, they saw that nobody was leaving their seats. Indeed, the homebound workers were not walking past either, but were clustering in their hundreds until one could not see through the milling crowd in any direction. Everyone was caught up in the concert ambiance.

Rag Doll was next and was the one that aroused the most response from the audience. One of the singing sailors came down from the platform and approached the audience, moving towards the Navy officials. At the critical point in the song, the sailor targeted one of the female officers as his rag doll, and the two of them played out the song. The crowd lapped it up, and Mark could see the looks of pathos on people's faces as they mouthed the words of the song. The singer reached for the officer's hand and twirled her under his arm, then, as he sang, he clasped her hand in his as they moved together. At the end of the song he bowed respectfully to the officer as she sat down. The audience was in raptures.

This was followed by *Let's Hang on to What We've Got* and, the finale, *Oh, What a Night,* the song where the five sailors interacted so well with each other. The happiness factor at Federation Square was unmistakable as the audience stood, clapped and cheered.

Mark came back on stage, thanked the audience for coming, and wished them a Merry Christmas and a Happy New Year. The RAN Melbourne ensemble played three Christmas songs as the crowds dispersed. The concert was over; it had been an outstanding success.

The two Army and Navy band events in Adelaide were more routine. They presented none of the logistical nightmares that Mark and his team confronted in producing the Jersey Boys Tribute at Federation Square. The success in Adelaide resulted more from the quality of the video-taping than anything else. The weather was favorable at both the Christmas Parade and the Rundle Mall Christmas playout, and the South Australian Army and Navy musicians were resplendent in their uniforms. On both occasions the crowds were positive and enthusiastic. What made these two events successful in the eyes of DFSM was the audience enthrallment. Mark had given one directive to the videographers to 'capture audience pleasure and participation.' Once the footage was edited and delivered to DFSM, it was obvious that both Adelaide concerts were crowd-pleasing performances. The delight with military music by the audience was seen in the footage of children talking to the musicians and having their photographs taken holding instruments—all effective moments depicting strong audience support.

Before Mark left Keswick Barracks, he gave a packet of music to his colleagues, many of whom were Army and Navy reserve musicians, one of them even from the Kensington and Norwood band when Mark was still a student at the University of Adelaide. While he could not promise, he had requested a lower brass workshop at Keswick Barracks in February and if this was approved, he hoped they could promote a Saturday night concert.

Several of them looked at the music, and smiled, "If you can make this happen, Mark, we are with you all the way. This is exciting music for a brass band."

"Thanks!" he replied. "We need to change the face of military bands. We're great at marching and playing traditional music, but can we entertain at the same level, or even better, as a rock group? I think we can because we will do it in uniform!"

Six days before Christmas an initial debriefing meeting occurred at DFSM with many of the original group who met with Mark when he was initially introduced at Simpson Barracks in late August. They were there to informally review the activity of the last three months, to gauge opinions, and to come up with new suggestions for the New Year. Everyone recognized the nature of what they were aiming to accomplish: providing commendations and recommendations about the future direction of military music within the Australian Defence Force.

The Commander of DFSM placed only two items on the agenda: an initial review on the data gathering exercise from all military musicians throughout Australia and personal feedback on the Jersey Boys Tribute at Federation Square. The reports on the data gathering were verbal and given by Mark, his two colleagues and several at DFSM presently collating the data. Still early days, but the data gathered suggested there were three main themes emerging from military musicians: one, they appreciated the opportunity to contribute input; two, they were looking for greater professionalism and career-path opportunities as military musicians; and, finally, they were urging the Defence Force to modernize its understandings and delivery of military music.

As these were introductory findings only, there was not much discussion. The Commander noted the organizational need for increased professionalism and career security. He announced that this was to be his major emphasis in the time remaining for his term at DFSM; "Our career musicians have every right to be able to grow and develop as professionals just as if they belonged to the best musical bodies anywhere in Australia."

"Alright, now to the *Jersey Boys Tribute*. I can sense your keenness to begin the discussion on this event, perhaps a seminal event in DFSM music. Mark, we all realize that this germinated from your ideas and experience in the U.S. Do you wish to lead us into our discussion?" asked the Commander.

"No sir. I would like to listen to frank comments from others around this table," replied Mark.

"I understand. Then who will be first?" asked the chair, as he raised his arms to all in the meeting.

There followed a spirited discussion for almost an hour, extolling the extraordinary accomplishments of the Federation Square happening. The consensus was one of profound appreciation for the sheer tenacity in conceiving, shaping, rehearsing and implementing the event. Several spoke of the amazement expressed by some in the audience that the Navy band could, or would, produce such a musical presentation. It was as if audience members were surprised about the "modern music" and such "professionalism" emanating from military music. Three DFSM members spoke to the "bravery and boldness" shown by Mark and his team in making such a quantum leap from regular military music to this "extravaganza" approach. They recognized that this must be a harbinger of similar events ahead for all Defence Force music. The Commander expressed his approbation for the animated and open discussion and continued: "We all sat, or stood, less than two weeks ago in Melbourne as the work day ended, knowing that something seismic was occurring for the future of military music at public events. I want to add a few thoughts about the unadulterated excitement I sensed, the captivated involvement of the audience ... err ... what else ... the raptness, the happiness. We all felt it. And, when Able Seaman Petersen took the hand of Lieutenant

Fields, I thought the audience was going to come unglued completely. She was so gracious and feminine in working with Petersen. It was
excellent entertainment."

"And, one more comment. Less than four months ago, Mark, we
sat around this same table and heard you say something that I have not
forgotten. We all know it, but on that day, I heard it with a new sense
of urgency. You said that as we contemplate change to military music,
we must always insist on *pursuing a quest for excellence*. I saw excellence
in action at Federation Square. Your turn now to say a few words," said
the Commander.

"Sir, I am grateful for the kind words, but it took a team to make
December 12 happen, including a support team who *set up* and then
broke down with a minimum amount of fuss," began Mark.

"There is one area no one has spoken of, and yet I know we all
know it was the ingredient that made the difference. This is the human voice, the most perfect instrument known to man. And, when
combined with the rehearsed routine, we saw the audience response."

"The Commander and I have spoken about this several times and I
have talked to Navy colleagues in Sydney and Melbourne. I know there
are issues here, not to mention a funding nightmare, but, some way, we
must strive little by little, to develop small singing groups as a part of
military music. Admittedly, it will not happen overnight," said Mark,
knowing that he had said enough, and that he must not come across as
too reckless in his dreams.

"We hear you, Mark, and it is a viable topic for judicious promotion in the years to come. In the meantime, we need to be content with
baby steps as we bring about change to military music," responded the
Commander as he brought the meeting to a close.

"For now, I want to wish you all a safe and happy holiday season.
Mark, you leave tomorrow morning. How many others are going interstate? May you all travel safely."

"One last comment: As we return in the New Year, we will continue completing the data gathering survey. I am told by the end of
January the editors will have completed the video on the three events.

We will use this as an integral part of our overall presentation to the Defence Force committee in the autumn. Happy holidays to you all."

As dawn broke the next morning, the Monaro pulled out of Simpson Barracks and Mark was on his way to the farm; no planes, no oceans to cross, no airport stops along the way, no Sees candy for his mother. He was driving home via the Western Highway and planned to arrive by mid-afternoon. He cleared the western suburbs before the intensity of morning traffic and was heading towards Ballarat with the heat of the early summer making its mark on the landscape. The air conditioning was working well and kept the interior of the car pleasant. Mark did not use the Monaro every day. He walked to work and to shops and a supermarket for his daily and weekly needs. His longest drive was to HMS *Cerberus* for rehearsals and meetings. He did this at most once a week, and as it was an hour's drive, at least it gave the car a solid work out. He enjoyed driving a classic muscle car, and he agreed with Gary in that in another twenty-five years or more the car would be a collector's item. Even so, he mused that in the next year he would return it to his brother and buy a new, less conspicuous car. For now, he was almost at Bordertown, where he would stop for fuel and lunch, even if he could no longer buy an Amscol Berry Bar as he did back in his Luther College days.

After crossing the River Murray at Murray Bridge, Mark always felt a certain excitement as the easterly section of the Adelaide Hills approached. He had made good time and so he decided to turn off the freeway and travel the old road through Nairne, onto Littlehampton and follow the railway line to Balhannah, where he would take the back road to the farm. Mark sounded the horn as he entered the driveway and his family spilled out from various doors, buildings, and even the clothesline as he pulled into a parking place.

"I'm home," he cried out as his mother rushed to his open arms. It was mid-afternoon, and time for afternoon tea. Everyone crowded into the kitchen, including the children, now home for the holidays, and they peppered Mark with questions. The next hour went by blissfully. The family was together again for three weeks. It was Christmas and a time to celebrate the birth of Christ and the harvest season. Gary had completed all his haymaking except one paddock that he said he was saving for Mark and himself after Christmas Day. As they went outside, there was the essential visit to the vegetable garden where Helen, Betty and Gary all provided their individual commentary as to the state of this year's garden. Mark could see for himself that it was flourishing and had expanded in size from when he was a boy. Betty admitted that it had become her obsession for the remaining years she had left to garden. Gary had built her some raised garden boxes that enabled her to stand and tend to her strawberries and radishes. Seeing the radishes drew a laugh from Mark as he remembered how a cadre of pioneer women from the original founding families of Hahndorf, walked in the middle of the night once a week to take garden produce to the indolent and malnourished people of Adelaide on market day. Radishes were the first vegetables to market; they only needed six weeks to mature. Betty loved her radishes.

The St. Michael's church calendar was busy for the Christmas season. On Sunday evening there was a *Carols by Candlelight* program at Memorial Gardens jointly sponsored by the Anglican church, St. Paul's Lutheran and Mark's church. For once in a long time, Mark appreciated being part of the audience. It was a meaningful occasion as families relaxed in the comfort and fellowship of their community. It was a cool evening and blankets were necessary after the sun had disappeared. The children's songs were quaint, and in a couple of cases they were performed poorly, but it was among friends and families. This was the formative level of young minds and future talent, Mark thought to himself. Who knew what sparks of creative artistry could have been ignited at this humble annual gathering? He was proud of his town for resisting the temptation to quell such traditions and leave it to television to denigrate the simplicity of the Christmas story with its crass and gaudy commercialization. He looked up into the starry night and sighed deeply. It was two days before Christmas Eve, and he was home.

There was one last appointment before the holidays began in full for Mark. The next morning, Betty and Mark drove to Adelaide for his doctor's appointment. Dr. Lawson was pleased with Mark's progress and said, "It is wonderful to see you looking so healthy and alive." He took blood and said that the test results would not be ready until the New Year. Mark made his appointment for the day after New Year's; he was returning to Melbourne the next day. After the doctor's visit, Betty and Mark went to Rundle Mall where Betty helped Mark buy some gifts for his nieces and nephews and for Helen and his sisters. She wanted to buy some nuts and chocolates from Ditter's Nuts in Gawler Place and Haighs at the Beehive Corner, and as they walked down the Rundle Mall towards King William Road a pan flute group played amplified music as the shoppers dropped their coins or walked on by.

Betty nudged Mark and said, "Small potatoes! Not like my son and the *Jersey Boys Tribute* at Federation Square."

Mark laughed and hugged his mother. "Oh Mum, just a little biased, am I right?"

They spent more on chocolate and other delights, like licorice, at Haigh's than they intended, but it was Christmas time. Haigh's Chocolates had become a confectionary tradition with most South Australians. It was high-end chocolate, though each customer believed it was more than chocolate being purchased. Even before entering the store, the tastefully decorated windows lured the chocolate aficionado inside. The shop attendants were astonishingly polite and extremely patient with customers, young and old, who changed their minds many times before the final purchase. Customers walked out of Haigh's feeling proud of the exquisitely packaged bag now in their hands.

"Isn't this the best chocolate store in the world? I remember coming into this shop each Christmas, every Easter and, I think, Dad or you came here to buy one birthday present for each of us as a chocolate treat. I hope Haigh's lives on forever," extolled Mark as much to himself as to his mother who was now into the middle of her purchase.

As they walked out onto the Mall, Mark looked at his watch and suggested lunch as he had promised Gary that he would help with the milking that evening. Betty nodded that she was 'peckish' herself.

With that Mark informed her that it was time for another 'South Australian culinary delight.' They were going to Balfour's for lunch. Just past Coles, the Balfour's windows were not as flawlessly cared for as Haigh's, but cakes, frog cakes and savory pies and pasties were on display. Mark and Betty had to wait for a few minutes while one of the booths cleared. They were soon eating their pasty with sauce, a frog cake for dessert and a cup of tea with the tea pot on their table. Betty was amused at her son and his devotion to revisiting childhood practices from days when the family came to the city.

"What is it in all of us that we need to revisit pleasantries from earlier days," asked Betty.

"I hope it never changes, Mum. Think of how fortunate we are to be able to live in Australia where we have freedom, prosperity and gradual change. Imagine what it must be for those who do not have what we can sometimes take for granted," replied Mark.

"I stopped at Bordertown the other afternoon to refuel and buy a sandwich," continued Mark. "I really wanted an Amscol Berry Bar. This is what I did when I was at Luther College. As soon as I had crossed the state border, I bought fuel and an ice cream because it was Amscol. It's no longer around and I miss it. But that is nothing compared to losing all your belongings in a bush fire or living in some war-torn land where your cities are destroyed."

"Ahh, I'm sorry, Mum. I do go on. I think there for a moment I thought I was talking to Gary. We talked our heads off on our cross-country adventure. It was a fabulous time with memories that will last a lifetime. In fact, that is the answer to your question. We need to revisit the past, especially the good times, to remind ourselves that we have history and to make the present relevant. Remembering the difficult and sad times, helps us be careful not to repeat them today. Does this make any sense?" asked Mark, recognizing that waxing philosophical with his Mother in Balfour's pastry shop was probably not a conversation guaranteed to keep going.

"Yeah, I guess," she responded. "It helps. I like hearing my children remembering days from your childhood. I think back to my younger days before you. As children, we would only come to Adelaide a few times a year, and then it was usually to catch the train at Bridgewater. For us, that was our adventure, going to the city for the day. After the War and your Dad and I were dating, and even after we were married, we would drive to Adelaide or to Glenelg. Whenever we went to the pictures, your Dad would always buy me Haigh's chocolate covered almonds from the tray boys during interval. We had such fun together, and now he is gone … all so suddenly," said Betty, tearing up and reaching for her handkerchief.

"Oh, Mum, I'm so sorry!" exclaimed Mark. He touched her shoulder. "This is all my fault. I should have been more careful where my words were taking us. You and Dad were so wonderful together," he added.

"You remind me of your father so much, Mark," replied Betty, smiling up at him. "Gary talks a lot about that trip you did together. It was important for him. He has stayed by the farm and not been adventurous like you. I must admit that I like having you home again. Melbourne feels next door and I can handle that; Sydney not so much."

"Well, I am relishing being home," responded Mark. "Now let's tackle our green frogs, enjoy another cuppa' and then we go home. Sound good?"

"Sounds good to me, my darling," said Betty with her impish smile.

Back on the farm, Mark went to call the cows. There were over thirty to milk and it was the first day of the two-week break for the two farm hands. Mark wanted to help Gary as much as he could on this visit home since he had been incapacitated in the three months of last winter after his surgery. Now, in the summer season, he had regained his strength and he embraced the opportunity to work hard physically for a week or two. At the Simpson Barracks he was using the gym regularly, but this was nothing compared to farm work. Gary suggested that they cut, rake and bail the hay after Boxing Day, if the weather held. It would take them two days and they needed to be certain of stable weather. This suited Mark as he finished hosing out the dairy after milking. They walked the cows back to their paddock and stood for a moment, looking at Gary's pride and joy, his lavender fields, vivid with color in the late afternoon sun.

The next evening was Christmas Eve and the bells tolled and called the faithful to church. Mark had agreed to lead the congregation in a communal song service before the homily. There was to be no service on Christmas Day and church members had made an extra effort to attend the vespers program. The church was filled to capacity and the small organ strained as Mark turned up the volume and intensity of his unlikely choir with each carol. The emotional conclusion was unexpected by the congregation. Mark chose a non-Christmas hymn, often a funeral hymn, to end the song service. He asked the women to sing the first verse softly, the men, the second and softly, and together, softly on the third verse. He conducted the last verse as a prayer and had the voices blending as seamlessly as congregational singing could ever be. At the end, Mark said with assurance: "In life, in death, O Lord, abide with me."

The service ended as dusk greeted night. The church yard was lit in a most attractive manner for the season and the church members enjoyed mingling outside on this warm Christmas Eve wishing each other well for Christmas Day. Many came to Mark to thank him for the spiritual nature of the song service. As the Schubert cars left the church in the valley and climbed to the higher elevation of the farm, the family witnessed the last rays of light fading from sight over Mount Lofty.

Christmas morning, after milking, was a time for presents, a light breakfast and then preparation for Christmas dinner, the meal most looked forward to all year. The giving and receiving of presents centered on the children, although it was not always easy to see who qualified as *children*. In truth, it was a family occasion, and with Mark's two sisters and their families, the lounge room was stretched to seat fourteen persons. The Schubert family had a method to the distribution of presents. It was given over to the six grandchildren. The eldest selected a gift, read the name tag and handed the gift to the recipient. All waited for the gift to be opened and then the next child selected a present and handed it on. It was an approach that enabled the adults to remain in their chairs and the children to gleefully hand out the presents. The downside was the time involved as the family grew in numbers and, always, towards the end of the process, the women grew anxious about the meal preparation.

The turkey was already in the oven and its enticing aromas were beginning to waft through the house. Helen came into the kitchen and gave directions to her eager helpers. She began preparing the roast vegetables, potatoes, parsnips, carrots, small whole onions and pumpkin. The sisters topped and tailed the string beans and shelled the peas. Betty busied herself with her boiled fruit pudding, which she had made three weeks earlier and had let hang in the cool room. Now it was time to heat Betty's proud dessert, all encased in cloth. For those family members who did not like pudding, there was a trifle or just plain ice cream. The ever-popular *nibbles*, Haigh's chocolates and Ditter's nuts, were ready to be placed in their bowls after the table was set and just before the meal. Betty's best china, silverware and crystal were stacked and ready for use. Knowing how tempting it was to wait for food, Betty had placed one bowl of chocolates and one of nuts in the lounge room with instructions for the men to watch that the children didn't eat too many. Mark and Gary were assigned two salad bowls, but they were keeping out of the kitchen for the time being. They remained in the lounge and, at times, on the porch as the children came and went with their new toys.

It was a happy time, and a full three years since all the family had been together. When all the food had been cooked and placed on the two tables (a smaller one for the grandchildren), there was that moment when the awareness of Christmas stopped them all, and they looked at Betty. Mark sensed that tears were about to flow. Abruptly, he interjected and asked everyone to hold hands. He asked Gary if he would pronounce the blessing on the food this Christmas Day. Mark squeezed Betty's hand as he sat down; she looked at him and whispered, *Thank you.*

The men did the dishes on Christmas and Easter Sunday in the Schubert household. Apparently, Frank had started the custom. The ladies were given a few minutes to themselves and eventually made it outside to the wicker chairs on the long porch where they had a superb westerly view looking over the front paddock, the roadway, the next farm and all the way to Mount Lofty. To the right was the smaller of the ponds and the afternoon sun cast a golden haze on the rural scene. The men joined them soon after with a tray of cool drinks. They took the next hour to relax as a family on one of the few days of the year when they could do so.

When Mark and Gary began the milking, their sisters and families left for their respective homes. Helen and Betty walked with Mark and Gary to the dairy, with the children dashing alongside, and stayed with them as they milked the Friesen herd. When they were nearly finished, Helen asked Gary if they could go to Brighton Beach for Boxing Day. Mark chimed in to say he would enjoy that too, and so the next day became beach day.

"Tell me, Mark, do you really like driving this Monaro, or are you doing it to keep Gary happy?" questioned Betty as the two of them followed Gary and Helen on the drive through the Adelaide Hills to Brighton Beach.

"No, I like it, but it is heavy on petrol," replied Mark. "I'm actually thinking that I may drive it for one more year and then bring it back to Gary and get a new car. I do agree with him in that it will be a collector's item in the years ahead. I need to talk to him as he is the money manager of the family business."

"I love this section of Brighton Beach!" Betty interrupted. "I remember when most of these houses were being built. Your Dad never liked Glenelg because it was so crowded. We drove along these roads until we found a ramp close to some changing sheds and we decided to chance it. You children would not hear of us going anywhere else after that," reminisced Betty as Mark pulled up close to the ramp, just behind Gary.

Mark and Gary took the beach tent onto the sand and the ladies and children carried the picnic hamper, the towels, blankets and the beach balls and buckets. It was a milder day than they usually liked for the beach, and there was a fair breeze blowing as well. Helen and Betty knew that they must watch the children as colds could follow. When the tent was up it was time for a swim; then lunch and the mandatory hour after eating before swimming was permitted again. Mark and Gary played with the children, built sand castles and flew a kite.

By 3:30 pm Gary said, "I don't know that it is going to get any hotter. I am worried that we may get chilled if we stay much longer. Mark and I have the milking to do, and since the weather pattern is only going to get hotter over the next few days, I think we will tackle the hay tomorrow," suggested Gary to the family.

"You're right," agreed Mark. "None of us needs to catch a cold."

Within minutes they had packed up for the drive home, promising the children that they would have fish 'n chips on the weekend. When the milking was finished Mark returned to the house, feeling a little chilled. He ate his soup and toasted sandwiches and went to bed with Betty's proven medication: hot lemon and honey with a large handkerchief dabbed in Watkins Camphor ointment tied around his neck. As he snuggled down, Mark kept the covers close. He was determined to help Gary the next day with the haymaking.

The next morning, Mark was better, but not entirely himself. Gary said "Look, I don't really need you for the first hour. I'll cut the grass and then after it dries, you can rake it into rows. And if you could rake it again just before sunset, that would help."

"No, I'm staying with you," insisted Mark.

"That's it," announced Betty, "We're having a curry for tea. I am going to put extra curry in yours, young man, and that will fix that pesky cold before it gets any worse."

Together the two men went to the tractor shed and hitched the sickle mower to the tractor. Gary preferred using the much gentler mower when cutting grass for bailing. He used the slasher all the time, but never when cutting grass for hay. It was the old-fashioned way and it took longer, but the grass was not mulched as it would be with the slasher. Besides, it was easier to rake, and Gary felt that it made for better hay for the livestock. They attached the rake to the second tractor and drove both to the two-acre paddock sheltered by trees on two sides. Gary went to work immediately and within an hour had the grass cut. They left the sun to dry the grass for another hour and went back to the house for a cool drink. Then Mark raked the grass and the paddock looked clean and cared for at the end of his task. They would leave it for another hour and rake it one more time in the afternoon. Tomorrow, Mark would rake it after the morning sun had dried the moisture on the flattened grass and after lunch Gary would bale the hay. Gary anticipated about seventy bales, which they would load onto the trailer as Helen drove the tractor. By the time they stopped for evening milking on the second day, there were seventy-odd bales of fresh hay in the shed, and no rain had spoiled the animals' dry feed for the winter. Mark returned to the kitchen that evening with no sign of a cold, feeling invigorated after his hard labor. Betty's hot curry was the final act in terminating his sniffles.

CHAPTER FIFTEEN

A DREAM COME TRUE

"You, Beloved, who are all the gardens
I have ever gazed at, longing."
—Rainer Maria Rilke

The new day dawned fresh and sunny and the church bells called Hahndorf's Lutherans to church. As it was the last Sunday of the year, Gary and Helen ensured that their two children had two sacks of coins to take to the Thanksgiving Table below the pulpit at offering time. The first sack was cracked egg money that the family had collected from sales to neighbors and friends since October. The children gathered the eggs each day after coming home from school and they separated the cracked eggs. The second sack, always the larger of the two, was from the full sales of eggs Gary was now supplying to three of the town's restaurants. Other restaurants and bakeries were increasingly anxious to buy his 'local farm fresh eggs' and Gary was feeling the pressure to supply these or lose an opportunity forever. He had resisted the expansion of his poultry enterprise, although not entirely closed the door to it. Two thousand laying hens could easily become three thousand without much extra work or worry. Gary determined that he would talk with Mark about this before the New Year. It was a project that could be done, of this he was certain.

Church members participated in the quarterly thanksgiving offering and as the children would come forth with their own offerings, adult members who had no children would hold up paper money which the children would collect as they walked down the aisle. There was always some guarantee of amusement as eager toddlers wandered about trying to collect money several times, often taking it back to their parents. A church that involves its children is a growing church and this was the present state of St. Michael's.

After the service, Mark was asked if he could play his euphonium on Tuesday afternoon, the last day of the year. The solo euphonium player was away on Yorke Peninsula for holidays. Mark had retained his band uniform and kept it in his old bedroom closet. The Hahndorf Town Band was playing in a quadrangle of stores off the main street. The band was to play for about an hour in two intervals. This would entice potential customers to veer off the main street and to venture into the courtyard of stores and boost sales. The band earned good financial support from the vendors and over the course of a year, it brought in considerable funds to offset the costs of the Band's operations.

At the lunch table, Mark announced that he had complicated the beach outing scheduled for Tuesday.

"I am going to need to bow out of the beach outing and play with the band. Les Braendler is on holidays on York Peninsula. The band knew this ahead of time, but just didn't look for a replacement. I think I have got to do it," explained Mark.

"It's fine," Gary answered. "We will still go as we are meeting up with the sisters. This way our kids still get to eat their fish 'n chips. Mum, you will still come, won't you?" he added.

"Yes, I will go. I have some things for the girls, and I want to eat fish 'n chips with my grandchildren," replied Betty, hugging her grandson.

"But, Mark, I do want us to go Glenelg before you return to Melbourne. They still have the track 'n field tournament and you will see some of the changes which I don't think are for the best. We could do this on Thursday. You leave on Friday, remember." added Gary.

On the Tuesday, Mark was quietly pleased to have the day to himself. It was nothing more than his bachelor ways and the importance of having quiet time for himself occasionally. In the late morning the family drove down the farm lane. The band was playing between 2:00 and 3:00 pm; this gave Mark ample time to do nothing much at all, or something useful. He chose the latter and polished his black dress shoes first and his euphonium next. This was his second euphonium and it had travelled with him around the world in the Australian and the United States Navies. He noted to himself that he ought to explore the costs of a new euphonium soon. With time still on his hands, he took one of his two Christmas books out onto the porch and sat in one of the wicker chairs. Gary, his ever-resourceful brother, had managed to track down a second-hand book Mark had listed on his gift list, *The Righteousness of God* by Gordon Rupp. It was published in the 1950s and was a respectable study on Martin Luther, his writings and his struggles as he shaped a new religion, the Lutheran Church. Mark still enjoyed history even though he had little time to read it of late.

After fixing himself a light snack, it was time to change into his uniform and drive to the main street. Finding a convenient parking place was not always easy in peak tourist season.

As he drove out of the farm, he mused aloud to himself and his car: "Well, in a few days it will be just you and me heading back to Melbourne. I'm going to miss the family. Mate, you've just got to find new friends outside of military musicians in the New Year," he said, enjoying the rumble of the V-8 revving through the gears on the country road.

Rumbling down English Street and onto the main street, Mark parked in front of a boyhood friend's home, just down from Kaesler's Engineering. He walked to the quadrangle, arriving together with other bandsmen and women. Everyone pitched in and assembled the music stands, placed the banners on the stands, distributed the music folders and gathered the instrument cases to one side. Then came the fifteen minutes or so before playing began when the band sat in their chairs and watched the milling crowd watching them or watched as people shopped and moved around the quad. It was the time when the conductor gave last minute instructions and band members chatted amongst themselves.

Mark's attention was drawn to a little blonde boy sitting on the music stand box and gazing attentively at the band. He was probably about six years old and he had an intensity about him that seemed familiar to Mark. All throughout the recital, the little fellow was fixated on the band's performance. The last piece of music, *Waltzing Matilda*, always brought out the nostalgia in the audience. For Australians, this was the *lump in the throat* finale which had the toughest of men fighting back the emotions. The performance ended with the hymn, *Abide with Me*, which drew a warm and prolonged applause from the audience.

During the "break down," when all the music stands, chairs, banners and music folders were placed in their crates and loaded onto the trailer along with the instruments, the little boy, who had moved to a new location, looked on from the railing of one of the retail shops. Mark glanced in the boy's direction as by-standers came up to compliment him on the band's performance and engage in small talk. The next time he looked, he saw a woman by the boy's side.

When he could finally get away, Mark went over to them and said, "Your son has just taken everything in for the last hour."

The woman, whom Mark could see was cute, replied, "Luke wants to be a band boy! But he's not my son; I am his aunt!"

Something about that last comment registered immediately as Mark paused awkwardly for a few moments. He was struggling to remember why.

"You don't remember me, do you, Mark Schubert?" the woman asked in the awkward silence.

Mark looked at her closely. There was a hint of challenge in her voice.

"Do we know each other?" he asked.

She nodded with an impish grin. She was enjoying the advantage she had over this flustered man.

"You know, there *is* something familiar about those eyes. Hmmm … I'm not sure. There is something I remember. No, I don't know. Just a minute … that smile, that look. No way … Wait! You're young Claire Wagner, aren't you?" Mark stuttered.

Although he had not seen her for over twenty years, her name suddenly flashed into his mind and he realized that he had thought of her on the oddest of occasions. As a precocious teenager, she had left an indelible imprint on Mark in his last year of high school, and thereafter in a subtle way.

"Yes, it's me. I was too young for you, remember?" Claire replied.

"Well, you're certainly not anymore!" Mark said, and his face reddened slightly. She embraced him, and they laughed over meeting up again.

"Say, Mister, how do you know my Aunty?" piped up the little boy beside them. They'd almost forgotten him.

"Well, Luke, I knew your Aunty a long time ago back at high school," Mark said. He glanced at Claire, smiling.

"You know, I need to put my instrument in the car. It's just a minute away on the main street. Are you interested in having a coffee? I sure could do with one and a sandwich after all that playing," asked Mark of Claire. "We can get Luke a milkshake, or whatever he wants."

"Luke's parents are having a late lunch at The Hahndorf Inn. I didn't want a heavy meal, so I offered to take him to hear the band. Now, I am glad I did," replied Claire. "Do you want me to take Luke back to his parents, or should we have coffee with them?"

"Well, I don't mind either way," Mark said. "I have the rest of the day free. My family is at the beach. It would be fun to sit and talk and catch up on life. Are you interested?" Suddenly, he just wanted to be alone with Claire.

"Alright, I'd like to talk too," Claire said. She hesitated, trying to decide.

Mark came to the rescue: "Let's go to the Inn and see if Luke's parents will care for Luke, and you and I can go over there to that coffee shop."

He pointed across the road. "It used to be a *lolly shop* when I was a kid."

They walked to the restaurant and found Luke's parents still eating their meal. Claire introduced Mark to her sister, Julie, and her husband, Grant Giles. Julie, Claire's younger sister, perked up at the mention of Mark Schubert by name.

"You mean that you are Mark Schubert," she stammered.

"Yes, I am if that is alright with you?" replied Mark, not quite sure whether he was in trouble or in the clear.

"No, no, It's alright, Mark. I used to talk a little about you years ago," replied Claire, looking a little bashful.

"A little is an understatement," said Julie. "Well, I never expected to meet you after all these years. I mean, I've seen you on television and read about you in magazines, but never thought I would meet you in person."

Grant chimed in to save the day for Mark.

"Hello Mark, I'm pleased to meet you. I'm trying to figure this out. You and Claire are going for coffee, right? We're going to be another twenty minutes or so. We can wait if we need to, otherwise, we'll be heading home to Mount Barker. Claire is staying with us until she returns to Melbourne at the end of this week. Do you have a car? Do you want to bring her home after you've talked?"

Mark didn't hear much after the mention that Claire lived in Melbourne. He knew they were looking at him and expecting an answer.

"Well, whatever suits Claire is fine with me," he said. He wasn't sure what he had just committed himself to doing.

"Great, leave Luke with us," replied Grant cheerfully. "He can have some of my chips. He's listened to the band and is now good to go. Pleasure meeting you, Mark."

He waved a hand: "Why don't you both go for coffee now and talk your heads off."

"Thanks very much. Really nice meeting you both as well," said Mark, as he picked up his euphonium.

"Mister Mark is that heavy?" chirped Luke. "It sure makes a pretty sound."

"Yes, it does, Luke. Keep your dream alive of becoming a band boy. When I come back in a few months, I'll see if we can go listen to some more bands," offered Mark. He looked at Grant questioningly.

"Anytime is fine with Julie and me. Now, you two, get out of here," teased Grant as Claire and Mark turned to leave.

Outside, Mark took Claire by the arm and asked excitedly: "You live in Melbourne? You have a family?"

"Yes, and no. I live in Melbourne, in fact, in Box Hill, one of the eastern suburbs. No, I have no family. I am divorced." replied Claire.

Then, she looked at him and asked: "Your family is at the beach. Who is your family?"

Mark smiled and nodded.

"No immediate family. I divorced fifteen years ago. No kids. My family is my mother and brother and his family who live on the old farm less than two miles from here."

"So, it's just you and me?" questioned Claire.

"Yep, it's just you and me," he replied, smiling. He touched her lightly on the arm. "Come on, let's put my euphonium in the car and then get something to eat."

They walked across the road to the restaurant and Mark ordered coffee and sandwiches. They took a seat outside under a tree, oblivious of the tourists crowding past. It was a warm, perfect afternoon and they were transfixed with each other.

"I should have changed out of my uniform," said Mark, "but I thought I would be going straight back to the farm." said Mark. He was feeling a bit conspicuous. "At least I can take the coat off."

"No, don't say that," protested Claire. "I like you in uniform. It gives you an air of importance."

"And that's a good thing, right?" asked Mark as he placed his coat on the spare chair.

Their coffee and sandwiches arrived. Mark waited until they were alone and then he said: "There is so much I want to say and ask. I'm not sure where to begin. What I do know, is that I'm very glad we're here together."

Before Claire could respond, a car pulled close to the curb and the window rolled down. Julie leaned out and said, smiling, "Just checking on you two. Is everything good? We'll expect you home before midnight!"

They chuckled. "Everything *is* good," said Claire happily. The car pulled away and they turned to their coffee and sandwiches.

"You know," said Mark, pushing back his plate, "I look back and wish that I had not been so absorbed in my music at such an early age. It was kind of unnatural, but when you get to a certain level, you feel as though you must keep the momentum going. So, I kept climbing upwards. I had the support of my family and my music teacher, Mr. Paech, bless him, who was obsessed with my success."

He paused and glanced away. He was aware that Claire was leaning forward, completely absorbed in what he was saying. He continued, recounting his divorce, his moves across continents, his tours of duty, the education he had pursued, and his love of family. At last he paused, looking at his watch, realizing almost an hour had passed since he began his story. He looked at Claire; she smiled and drew a deep breath.

"That's some life, Mark. From the late '60s until now, almost twenty-five years. You've packed a lot of living into those years. You've had some big highs and some lows. I suspect those lows have been quite hard on you. Yet, here you are, Dr. and Lieutenant Mark Schubert. I'm glad you shared your story. I know it's not easy to talk about your own life," Claire said.

"Perhaps, but I didn't seem to have any trouble telling you!" countered Mark. "You made it easy. But it's your turn now. Would you like some more coffee?" He gestured to the waiter and sat back expectantly.

"My life is nowhere as impressive and as action-packed as yours," began Claire, "But it is my life over the same twenty-five years."

Claire told of developing an interest in accounting through the bookkeeping courses she took at Mount Barker High School. When she finished high school, her family did not have the money for full-time university, and she had to admit that she was not ready for a life of study anyway. She found work at *The Advertiser,* the state's main daily newspaper, as a junior accountant. Daily, she commuted from Mount Barker to Adelaide on the Mount Barker bus. Once in the city she had a short walk from Victoria Square to *The Advertiser* building which was down from the Post Office on King William Road. It was all routine, comfortable and convenient.

In her second year, Claire took a certificate course in accounting at the new Adelaide City Technical and Further Education College (TAFE). She enjoyed her work and her study in accounting: each reinforced the other. After two years of part-time study, she completed a Certificate in Accountancy and intended to continue with a third year of study to earn a Diploma of Accountancy.

By this time, she remarked, she was also dating John Baldwin, a Sydney television sales manager, working for Channel Seven in North Adelaide. He was ambitious and saw himself as a rising business executive. He lived a fast and selfish life with himself at the center.

"Sounds familiar," interjected Mark. "Claire, you don't have to talk about it if it is too painful," he said gently.

"Oh yes, I do," she said, and looked down. "It *is* painful, but I haven't really talked to anyone about it. I've kept it bottled up inside, and at times I feel as though I am going to explode. My family wouldn't understand. They lived in the Hills. Here, life lacks the drama those of us have experienced who have ventured outside the safety net," exclaimed Claire, tears welling up in her bright blue eyes.

"I understand," said Mark reassuringly.

He reached for his handkerchief and gave it to her. She smiled weakly as she dabbed her eyes and took a deep breath. He took one of her hands, noticing how small and delicate it was, and said: "You don't have to continue, we can talk another day."

"No, I want to continue," she said. "I think my original problem was that I was infatuated with you when I was thirteen years old. You were eighteen, and why would you give me a second look? I think I idealized you as my perfect man. I began dating John when you were becoming known by us locals as a success in the music world and then when I saw you on television, I think it prodded me to connect with John who was looking to reach the big time. I got caught up in his nonsense of parties and social life."

She shook her head and sighed. "There were so many people who were fake in almost everything they did. I was cute and vulnerable, and I went along with it," Claire explained.

"I dropped my TAFE diploma program and we became engaged

after a quick weekend in Sydney to meet his family. They were not like him at all, although his father was a hen-pecked husband who did not have a chance with his dominant wife. I guess that means that his mother was aggressive. I didn't care for her, but I only saw them a few times. After we got engaged, John got a promotion to television program production and went to London for six months. He wanted me to go with him, but I had the good sense to refuse and I stayed in Adelaide on the pretense that I had to organize my wedding. I busied myself with wedding preparations and worked with my mother to reduce the costs for my parents. Am I going on with too much?" she asked, suddenly conscious of the time.

"Am I boring you?"

"It's your story, Claire," said Mark, "and I want to hear as much of it as you care to tell." He smiled. "All I have to do is get you home by midnight."

"You're kind. Well, now I am almost twenty-three and we get married in September. We live in a flat in North Adelaide for three months and then he gets his big promotion in Melbourne. We move in March and he spends a lot of time in Sydney. I apply for accounting work at *The Age* newspaper and find that I am spending more time alone in a strange city without many friends, and certainly no close friends. Then I fall pregnant and this annoys John. 'Why did I let this happen' was his favorite saying for weeks. Then one night he hits me after coming home drunk. From that moment on I live in fear of having the baby. The anger and violence continued in the evenings, not a lot, but there was some. I lost the baby and he announced that we're moving to Sydney. I refuse to go, and so he leaves me. After no contact from him for a year, I file for divorce, and at the ripe old age of twenty-seven—and after four years of a poor marriage—we're divorced, and I am alone. I keep my work at *The Age* and get promoted several times. I then take myself back to part-time university study. Two years ago, I graduated from the University of Melbourne with a Bachelor of Arts degree in Accounting, and this coming May I will be awarded my Certified Public Accountant title and then become a Chartered Accountant after that. This means that in June I am going to have my nervous breakdown. I tell everyone I've earned it, and no one is going to deprive me of it!" exclaimed Claire, with a relieved laugh.

"Some story. Thank you for trusting me," responded Mark. "Look, Claire, it is just before six o'clock and I have only now remembered that I should be helping my brother with the milking. Would you like to come home with me and meet my family? I understand if you don't want to do this. Either way, I should at least call him and tell him why I am not home. I ... I just forgot all about the milking ... which comes around night and morning every day of the year."

"No, no, I will come with you, if you think it is alright. Let's go quickly," said Claire.

"Terrific! Thank you," replied Mark. He left a tip as they stood up from the table and walked across the road to the car. In a few minutes they were driving into the farm lane and up to the house.

Gary's car was in the garage and Mark could see that the cows were in the dairy already. He knocked on the front door and called out, "Mum, Helen, are you in the house?" They both came to the door, wondering why Mark would call out rather than just walk in. When they saw Claire, they stopped and looked as Betty wiped her hands on her apron.

"Mum, Helen, I want you to meet an old high school friend. This is Claire," said Mark as his mother and Helen came forward and each shook her hand warmly.

Neither one showed any recognition of Claire's name, but seemed pleased that Mark had met up with an old friend.

"Could Claire stay for tea, Mum?" asked Mark. "I'll take her back to Mount Barker afterwards." He turned to Claire, "I just need to change quickly and get out to the dairy to help Gary with the milking. Do you want to come along?" He wasn't sure how his mother and sister-in-law would react to this unknown woman showing up for tea. They walked over to the dairy as Gary looked up and saw them approaching.

"Ah, now it makes sense; you got a much better offer than milking cows, I see!" said Gary with a smile. He put out his hand to Claire. "I'm Gary, the little brother that does all the work on this farm."

"This is Claire, my old friend from high school days," replied Mark, as casually as possible.

At the mention of Claire's name, Gary immediately looked at Mark.

"You mean Claire *who was too young* from high school days?" questioned Gary, with a grin.

"Yes, she was at the band playout today," explained Mark, as nonchalantly as possible.

"I am very pleased to meet you, Claire. I know for a fact that you have never left Mark's thoughts over all these years," said Gary. He glanced at Mark, fully realizing that he may have said too much.

"Interesting," said Claire, casting a sly look at Mark. "You must tell me more, Gary."

"I don't know much more. I just know that you were too young for Mark, yet he never forgot you," added Gary. "Come on Mark, let's get this milking out of the way and then we can go back to the house and relax."

Rarely had the milking taken less time than it did on this Tuesday evening. The three of them walked back to the house and Mark and Gary disappeared for a shower and change of clothes, leaving Claire with Betty and Helen. The food was prepared. They had decided to eat outside on the porch so that Claire could enjoy the view as the sun slipped lower on the horizon. Betty spoke quietly to Claire as they carried plates, food and drink onto the porch table.

"Claire, forgive me, but are you the same girl from high school who was six years younger than Mark?" asked Betty.

"Yes, I am," said Claire. She was beginning to enjoy the reception from Mark's family.

"I am so glad that the two of you have met up again," replied Betty, with a warm smile and a hug.

Mark and Gary emerged with hair still wet but looking clean and fresh. Mark looked at the three women and sensed that all was well, but he knew he needed to say more—he just wasn't sure how much more.

"Claire and I met at the band playout today and then we went for coffee and time just got away. I looked at my watch and panicked as I thought of Gary doing the milking on his own. I agreed to take Claire home to her sister's in Mount Barker after we had talked and caught up on life. Then I asked Claire if she would come home and meet you, so I could help with the milking," Mark said in a rush.

"Mark, it's Okay," Gary chimed in. "Claire, I have a good brother and I'm grateful for his help. We only know a little about you from all those years ago, but welcome to our home! We hope you'll enjoy our food and company. Now, Mark, just relax!" He put a hand on Mark's shoulder. "No more explanations are necessary."

Mark shrugged and looked at Claire and they both smiled. "I didn't handle that very well, did I?" he whispered as they sat down to eat. Later, as they finished up with watermelon, Gary talked fondly of their beach outing. He pointed to his two children, sunburned and nodding off after an active day. "If you'll excuse us," Gary said to Claire and Mark, "Helen and I need to get these kids to bed."

"By all means, Gary," said Claire. She smiled at Gary and Helen. "It was so good to meet you and your children."

"Well, I'm sure we'll see more of you!" said Helen, stealing a glance at Mark as she shepherded the children out the door.

The rays of sun were almost gone from the Mount Lofty Ranges when Betty asked Claire if she worked in Mount Barker or Adelaide. When Claire told her Melbourne, Betty audibly choked a little on her iced lemonade. Mark looked at her and waved his index finger at her, and then all three broke into laughter.

"What have we missed?" asked Gary, coming back into the room. He looked at his mother, then Claire and finally, Mark.

"Mum has just learned that Claire lives in Melbourne," said Mark.

"Well, that's convenient, isn't it? I was wondering what I was going to do to make sure that you two kept seeing each other. Now, I can cross that off my list," teased Gary.

"Please, Gary, let Mark and Claire work this out," urged Helen.

"It's quite alright, Helen," Claire said. "Melbourne is going to be a much nicer city now that I know Mark will be there too. Our talk this afternoon has told both of us that we need a good friend. I'm looking forward to getting to know Mark better."

"On that note, I think I should take Claire back to Mount Barker," said Mark, rising. "One question, though." He turned to Claire. "When and how are you going back to Melbourne? I'm leaving early this Friday. Do you want to come along?"

"Sounds like a great idea to me!" said Betty, before Claire could answer.

"Thank you all, so much," said Claire, getting to her feet. "The meal was lovely, and you have made me feel very welcome."

The darkness was complete as they walked to the car. They had less than ten miles to drive to Mount Barker. Claire guided Mark through the various streets until they came to Julie and Grant's house. As they pulled alongside, the neighbor's dog rushed to the fence and began barking frantically. They looked at each other as the barking continued.

"I don't think that dog is going to stop," sighed Mark. "Let me take you to the front door and we will say goodnight. It's been a whirlwind afternoon and evening, but I am so glad we met up again! I was going to say so much before you went inside, but that barking is too much. Claire, thank you for coming home and meeting my family. They adore you; I can tell," said Mark.

"Whirlwind is right. I can hardly believe all that has happened in six or seven hours. You have a wonderful family. They're honest and upfront. I like that," Claire replied.

She leaned against him as Mark kissed her on the cheek.

"Have a good rest," he said earnestly. "Think about coming with me back to Melbourne. We have two days before we need to leave on Friday morning. Maybe we can do something together tomorrow or Thursday. I better go, or I am going to need to shoot that dog!" He turned and walked to his car, pausing while she went inside. He watched the door close and smiled to himself. Claire was home with an hour and a half to spare before midnight.

The next morning, as Mark and Gary were milking, Gary extolled the virtues of Claire at length and admonished Mark not to let her slip away. They were aware that there was only one morning left for them to share the milking routine together before Mark returned to Melbourne. They had developed a new brotherly bond since their American cross-country trip, and they had come to delight in their easy banter and small talk.

"Let her slip away! What's with you, Gary? I met up with the dear girl less than twenty-four hours ago! At this moment, there is nothing for me to *lose*," proclaimed Mark.

"Well, I know she's a quality girl, and I think you should go all out to win her," replied Gary.

"Win her for what?" shot back Mark.

"Okay, I will stop, but she sure did impress Helen and me," said Gary. He looked his brother in the eye. "Mark, she's beautiful and that beauty is inward as well. You can tell that. Not like that what's-her-name in your apartment at Eastport," said Gary.

"Let Eastport go, will you?" demanded Mark, as he turned the hose in Gary's direction.

"Okay, okay! No more! I promise I won't bring it up again," laughed Gary as he dodged the spray from the hose.

Once the cows were back in their new paddock for the week, and Mark and Gary had hoisted the milk cans on the trailer and taken them down to the loading station at the front gate, they went inside the house to wash up. Mark knew there would be more about Claire while he ate his Weet-Bix. He also knew that his family had seen in Claire what he had seen—that this was a person who fit right in with the family in just one evening. She had poise, a pleasing disposition and a gentle manner, yet possessed a mischievous side as well. There was an awful lot to like about Claire, and Mark had sensed, within their first hour at the restaurant, that she was affecting him like no other girl had done before. Right away, he knew he wanted to see her again. He realized with chagrin that they had talked last night about meeting up again, but he had not gotten her telephone number. "Typical of me," he thought, shaking his head ruefully.

"Mark dear, we all liked Claire very much. Are you going to see her today?" asked Betty.

"Well, I think today is better than tomorrow as I want that to be with just us. I didn't get her phone number, but it will be in the phone book," replied Mark.

"Will she travel with you to Melbourne on Friday?" questioned Betty.

"Mum, I don't know yet. I invited her again last night to travel with me. Frankly, so much was happening yesterday, I didn't want to push too hard."

"Well, if this will help, I would still like you to see Glenelg before you go," said Gary. "Today is the better day. You could pick Claire up and we could meet you at the Merry-go-Round."

"I like that," responded Mark, and then added, "Let me call at 9:00 am and see. Perhaps her sister and family may want to come too."

When Mark called, Claire jumped at the invitation for Glenelg. When Mark asked if Julie and her family would like to come as well, Claire hesitated, and when he added, as an incentive, that the Schubert family would buy the fish and chips, she said that Grant's family already had a picnic planned at Victor Harbor and his brother was returning to Mount Gambier on Friday. "Thanks for the offer," whispered Claire over the phone, "Grant's family can be pretty boisterous!" Two hours later, Mark was opening the car door for Claire, while the dog from the previous night snarled through the fence in a frenzy.

"I would have a war with that dog if I was around him too often," said Mark, starting the engine. They could still hear the dog's manic growls.

"He's very protective and settles down once he knows who is at either house," replied Claire.

"Well, Claire, how are you this morning?" asked Mark, changing the subject.

"If I say I'm still in a state of shock, will you understand?" she replied teasingly.

"Oh yes, it is less than twenty-four hours and my family wants you to come live with them, or me, or all of us together on a tropical island," laughed Mark.

"Well, I'm glad. I liked them very much. They were so natural and open to me," said Claire.

"I have a wonderful family, I know it. I wish you could have met my father, but he has been gone now for almost ten years," said Mark. He leaned over the wheel looking at the road ahead. "He was the moral exemplar of the family and my Mum always was, and still is, the life of the family. Dad raised us to always tell the truth, to deal honestly with people and to look for ways to make life better for others." He paused and glanced over at her. "He was a sad man in some ways. He didn't want to farm; he would have preferred to be a minister or a teacher of philosophy, or religion and history. But even so, he was a great father and we had a happy childhood. I'm probably more like Dad in many ways," Mark added, reflectively.

"You are your mother too," said Claire, "About that I have no question."

"Goodness, how did we get onto this?" asked Mark, surprised.

"I like talking about you and your family," replied Claire.

"Well, what about you coming with me to Melbourne on Friday?"

"I'd like to, but let's think about it," said Claire. "Are we doing the right thing? Is it too much too soon?" She hesitated. "I mean, I was going to fly back, but I bought a ticket that can be changed without penalty, so I could make the change as late as tomorrow."

"I don't want you doing this if you have some hesitation," said Mark. "Can you tell me what's not right about it?" he asked, befuddled.

"I guess there is no easy way to say this," Claire said, turning to him. "Meeting up with you yesterday was like a dream come true. Perhaps a dream I have held onto for too many years and one that I had all but let go. If there is any future for us, then I don't want to spoil it from happening. I am not sure *what* I'm feeling," she finished.

"Claire, I feel it too," responded Mark ardently. "I've been lonely for a long time. I've been afraid of relationships since Roslyn, the wicked witch of Horsham. See, I handle it by making fun of it, but I mustn't do that again. I busied myself with my music so much that I've given up on the idea of ever finding someone special again. I try to conduct myself with decorum and dignity every day, like my father taught me. People think I'm fine, but I'm hiding an emptiness inside of me. Then, yesterday, you walked into my life. Honestly, I just wanted to hug you and never let you go."

She was silent, and when he glanced over at her he could see that she was tearing up. He passed her a handkerchief and squeezed her hand as he drove. This was more than just attraction between two people. It was bewildering and happening too quickly, but maybe this was how things are when people were older.

Claire sighed and then said: "I'll drive with you to Melbourne on condition that I buy whatever food we decide to eat. I'm an independent girl of means and I will contribute to our road trip together."

"Sounds like a deal," said Mark. He reached out a hand and they shook on it.

"Thank you, Mark, for taking us seriously. I need a genuine friend before I need a lover."

She paused, and looked at him curiously, "Is that too much?"

"Not at all. It sounds honest. And, I agree, except that I may need you to remind me of when a friend crosses the threshold and becomes a lover!" said Mark, grinning.

"If I can figure that out, I'll let you know, Mark Schubert!" said Claire.

At Glen Osmond, Mark turned left onto Cross Road and after fifteen minutes turned onto Anzac Highway and, finally, to Colley Reserve at Glenelg. So much had changed, but they eventually made it to the carousel and met up with Betty, Helen, Gary and the children. Gary was playing with the children, throwing a frisbee, and after Claire was settled with Betty and Helen, Mark joined in the game. On one of the last weekdays before a new year of work, there were many families on the lawns. The fortunate ones were those who incorporated their annual leave with the Christmas holidays.

Helen called the frisbee players for lunch and Mark came willingly to the blanket next to Claire. He and Gary were puffing and starting to perspire, trying to keep up with the children. The picnic lunch was delicious, with Claire commenting on the culinary skills of both Betty and Helen. Before they finished up, Mark announced, to everyone's satisfaction, that Claire was going to travel to Melbourne with him. The children were impatient for a walk along the jetty. But before that came ice cream—a treat for everyone from Uncle Mark. As the children ran on ahead, the adults took their time, breathing in the salt air and remarking at the nearly-empty buckets of the jetty fishermen. Looking back at the foreshore, Mosely Square and the newly constructed Stamford Hotel, Mark agreed with Gary that the hotel added a handsome balance to the Town Hall and the view down Jetty Road. Claire and Helen and Betty played spot-the-fish with the children as they all peered into the water below the jetty and watched for fish swimming in between the pylons. Gazing into the water and letting his mind drift easily, Mark asked Claire if she liked to fish. "I've only tried it a few times," she said, "and I always felt sorry for the fish!" Back on land, they made their way to the carousel, but found themselves unimpressed with its condition and surroundings. However, it was still the Merry-go-Round of Glenelg and the Royal Adelaide Show, so Mark bought tickets for everyone and they all rode the horses of their choice.

The lazy, easy afternoon was coming to an end. It was time for Mark and Gary to get back to the farm for milking. Gary's farm hands would be back to work on Friday and that would give Gary some relief. Until then, essential work was calling. After milking, Mark and Claire drove back to Mount Barker.

"Mark, I know you are a church-goer, but are you religious?" asked Claire as they passed Windmill Hill.

He looked at her curiously. "It's a fair question. I am the son of my father. If I hadn't pursued music and education, I think I would have been a teacher, a professor, to use the American term, of Church History, especially Early Modern Europe—the Renaissance and Reformation period. Yes, I do take religion—and spirituality—very seriously. Hey, I am a descendent of the Old Lutherans who founded

Hahndorf," explained Mark. "Does this answer your question?" He looked out the window for a moment. "You see, I think 'spiritual' is more important than being 'religious'."

Claire nodded. "Spiritual is what I meant. I am a lapsed Anglican with Lutheran on my father's side. My family didn't take it seriously and then my ex-husband thought only weak men followed religion. He scoffed at prayer and church attendance. I want to understand it more."

"I don't mean to sound harsh here, Claire," mused Mark, "but over time I don't think we could remain together if you weren't interested in religion and spirituality. It is too much a part of me to let it go, and you would only become frustrated with me if we were at odds over practicing a daily walk with God. My beliefs guide me in the way I live my life. Many people do not agree with me, and that is Okay. What I don't need is for them to mock or taunt me over it. All my Navy colleagues know I am a practicing Lutheran," said Mark.

"That's another thing I'm grateful for since we have reconnected again," replied Claire with a smile as they pulled up at her sister's home.

The dog saw the car approach and commenced barking. "Maybe he has an aversion to muscle cars from the '70s," Mark growled. "Say, would leaving at 7:00 Friday morning be too early?" he asked Claire as they walked to the door. "That way, I could help you buy some milk and groceries before I go on to the barracks." She began to answer just as Grant swung the door open. "Won't you stay for a cup of coffee?" he offered Mark. Mark hesitated for a moment and then yielded, saying that he must not stay longer than half an hour. "I've got a lot to do before I leave for Melbourne," he said. "I need to spend some time with my mother, and I haven't practiced my euphonium in a serious way for over a week," he confessed.

"I notice a difference when I don't practice about an hour a day for at least five days of the week," explained Mark.

"Don't you ever find it boring going over the same scales and pieces of music you have repeated for years?" questioned Julie.

"Not really, Julie, no. Practicing relaxes me and puts me in a meditative state of mind. Probably sounds weird to a lot of people. For me, I need it to function properly," explained Mark.

"The way you describe it, I think we all need to learn an instrument," chuckled Grant. "Perhaps we should join the band when Luke becomes a member. By the way, Mark, when *should* Luke join a band?" he asked.

"There are three points to your question, Grant. Luke could be learning elementary music now. Next point, there is a difference in learning to play an instrument and joining a band. I think he could begin learning to play a cornet, my recommendation, at about nine years and join a band around eleven or twelve." He looked carefully at Julie and Grant. "It is very much an individual choice and depends on the child, parents and method. The Suzuki method works very well, but it starts with children younger than Luke. It is also rather demanding."

"Well, wonderful coffee, Julie. I really must go. I will see you all early on Friday morning," said Mark as he stood up and made his way to the door.

"I'll walk you out," said Claire. As they made their way to the car, the dog next door did not bark. "Maybe he's accepted that I'm not an alien and I belong here," said Mark, and speculated further it might have something to do with the fact that he was allowed in the house and this meant he was no longer a threat. "Makes sense," Claire agreed with a laugh.

"Listen Mark, I am going to begin praying for us tonight," she said, taking both of his hands in hers. She looked up at him and smiled. "Thank you for being you."

"I like how you put that, Claire. I think God is interested in you and me as individuals first, and as a couple next. When we're committed to God there won't be much that can come between us!"

He gave her a hug and kissed her on the cheek, and as he slid into the Monaro, he pointed at her through the window. "I haven't told you this, before, but you are a very beautiful woman, you know!" As Claire's mouth dropped open in surprise, he hit the pedal and drove off, accelerating a little more than usual. It had been another one of those good days.

Mark's last full day on the farm began early with the Friesian cows. Three weeks of milking had been good for him as he was able to experience again the early morning reflections he remembered so well from his younger years when it was just him, the cows, the pulsating of the milking machines and God. This morning, he prayed for God's guidance and blessing over Claire and himself. There was a freshness about early mornings, and, for Mark, it was possible to feel more serenity and tranquility than at any other time throughout the day. As he walked the cows to their paddock, he paused as he closed the gate and listened to the hush and stillness of the new day. He wanted to remember this moment.

The one matter Mark had to attend to on this day was a brief appointment with Dr. Lawson to review the results of his blood tests. Betty accompanied Mark. The doctor pronounced the tests routine and added that Mark needed to see him twice a year for five years, and then once a year until the tenth year. "Otherwise," he said cheerfully, "you can look forward to a long and productive life ahead!" "Does that sound good?" he asked, as both mother and son breathed a sigh of relief.

The remainder of the day passed quickly and at its conclusion, Gary, Helen, Betty and Mark sat on the porch and watched the sun set. There was not a lot of conversation as each was deep in personal thoughts of family, the farm, a new year and Mark in Melbourne, only a day's journey away. On this evening, however, a new thought entered their streams of consciousness; it was of Claire. In less than three days, she had become a real presence in their lives. The family liked her and saw her as the most positive indication that Mark's bachelor status may be coming to an end. In the meantime, the car was packed and ready to depart at 6:30 am.

The morning was overcast and cooler, as Mark stepped onto the porch, with Betty by his side and Gary and Helen behind them. He had only eaten a banana, along with his usual two glasses of water.

"We'll stop for breakfast at Tailem Bend," he said, as the family urged sandwiches and coffee on him. It was just easier that way, he reasoned, and what if Claire had decided to bring some food herself. At that, Betty and Helen relaxed. Mark gave his mother a hug and they bowed their heads as Gary lead out in prayer. They would see Mark, and hopefully Claire too, come April. As Mark drove away from the farm and on his way to meet Claire, he could see in the rear-view mirror his family waving from the front porch until he rounded the bend and they were gone from sight.

CHAPTER SIXTEEN

COMING TOGETHER

"I will find you. In the farthest corner, I will find you."
—Mary E. Pearce, The Kiss of Deception

The dog came to the fence as soon as Mark pulled alongside the Giles' home. As Mark walked to the front gate, the dog looked strangely at him, but did not bark. Mark made several complimentary comments to the dog, and it began wagging its tail. *A friend at last,* thought Mark as he knocked on the door. Luke came to the door in his pajamas and asked Mark to come into the kitchen where Julie and Claire were busy making a hot breakfast. Claire looked up and smiled. "We're assuming you didn't eat!"

"No," said Mark, "I wasn't sure what you would be doing, so I told Mum that I would wait until I picked you up. I was thinking that we could stop at Tailem Bend or somewhere not too far along the way."

"See, Julie, I told you that he would want to know what I was doing," said Claire smugly. "So, we figure if we eat breakfast here, then we can drive further and stop for petrol and food, perhaps, at Bordertown."

"Sounds good," replied Mark. "Please sit!" said Claire, as she placed a glass of orange juice in front of him, followed by scrambled eggs and fried potatoes and mushrooms.

The family ate with Mark and Claire, and Luke asked when Mark was going to take him to see some more bands.

"Well, Luke, that depends when I come back to Adelaide or you come to Melbourne. I will take you as soon as I can. That's a promise," said Mark as Luke beamed with satisfaction.

Grant followed up with a question of his own. "Mark, we have someone who has offered to teach Luke to play the piano. Is this a good plan before learning to play the cornet?" he asked.

"It's the best plan," Mark responded quickly. "The piano is a foundational instrument; I wished I'd learned to play it! I've done all the music theory and I can play several instruments, but I can only manage a poor song or two on the piano. If Luke begins with piano, you should link it with AMEB music lessons as well and give him theory too. By the way," he turned to Julie, "this is good coffee."

"Mark, we should go soon," said Claire.

"Right," said Mark, as he stood up. "Thanks for the good breakfast, Julie and Claire. It's been great meeting you all. Okay, we'll be off then." Within a few minutes they were in the car, and as they turned on to the street, Mark looked at Claire. "Thank you for coming with me," he said. She smiled: "How could I turn you down when you're offering door to door service?"

With that they fell into idle conversation and little by little they discovered more about each other. The road was relatively empty, and Mark told of some of the adventures Gary and he experienced as they crossed the United States from east to west.

"We missed so many sights and places. Gary has an interest in architecture and wanted badly to see Frank Lloyd Wright's home, *Falling Water,* in western Pennsylvania, but we just didn't have the time. I had to keep us fixed on our schedule. Besides, we knew we wanted to see the Rockies and Grand Canyon more than anything else," said Mark.

"I would love to travel and see so many places, but I've never had the right person to go with me. I just can't imagine travelling overseas alone. Even now, I'd be afraid," replied Claire.

Mark acknowledged Claire's hesitancy and said, "I think most people would agree with you; especially if it's travelling alone. Today, more and more people are needing to travel for work. I have done work assignments overseas alone and in small groups. As I think about it, I haven't gone overseas for pleasure or a holiday either; it's always been work-related. Like you, I haven't been with the right person. Perhaps this is going to change for both of us."

Time passed quickly. The mundane landscape of the Mallee region provided no reason for them to comment on geography or human endeavors outside the moving car. They decided not to stop at Bordertown. They would push on to Nhill and buy petrol as well as food; their breakfast was sitting well.

"What's in accounting that you like so much?" questioned Mark, breaking the silence of a minute.

"I'm not really sure why I liked it. I think it had to do with the fact that I understood it from the first. I wasn't confident in my schooling. What I didn't understand in the classroom remained a mystery. I never studied with other friends or talked to my parents about school work. Accounting, or Bookkeeping as it was in high school, was logical and sequential. I liked its structure and orderliness." Pausing for a second or two, Claire continued, "With English and history, they never came to an end; there was always more to read and more to learn. I never felt I knew enough to talk about them in class or to write on them with conviction."

Mark looked at Claire before he spoke. He hesitated, and Claire asked, "What's wrong?"

"I didn't like hearing that you didn't talk with your parents about schooling. Then, I didn't want you to think I was criticizing them if I told you that," explained Mark.

"It's alright. I now know that they didn't understand how kids needed their parents' involvement in growing up. Dad and Mum both left school at fourteen and found work as soon as they could. They never knew what it was to improve themselves. Mum always had good jobs in retail, but Dad hated his work and died unfulfilled."

"I'm sorry, Claire," Mark empathized.

"I guess I found myself feeling compassion for my Dad when my marriage didn't work out. I felt sorry for myself as I know Dad did because he was only a laborer. He would say, 'What have I got to offer any body?' I refused to wallow in self-pity. I remember having many talks to myself and realizing that I had a good job at *The Age* doing what I enjoyed. Accounting helped me turn my life around and gave me a sense of accomplishment I didn't have before. I need to get off this," said Claire.

"No, no, you don't," said Mark, "I want us to be able to tell each other anything and to be a support for one another. There's nothing you can't tell me."

"I am beginning to believe this, and it feels good," replied Claire as she squeezed Mark's hand. "Before meeting you a few days ago, I had a plan to leave *The Age* as soon as I earned my professional qualifications and work for a smaller accounting firm, perhaps in interior decorating, design or even an art gallery. I have worked for so long in large organizations and now I want something smaller and personable."

"Well, you should go for this. With us meeting up again doesn't mean you have to give up on your career plans," added Mark as endorsement of Claire's work preferences. "In fact, I admire what you have accomplished."

"Thank you, that means a lot," Claire remarked. "Remember when you were telling me your story at the restaurant after the band playout? One statement made me immediately see that we had things in common. You said that you turned inward and busied yourself with your music and your work when your marriage didn't work. Remember? Well, I liked that because it is what I did too. Yet, so many of my friends wanted me to 'let go' and join them in dancing, partying, drinking and just living in the now for a time until I felt better about myself. I just couldn't do it. I know you understand."

"Oh, yeah, the typical hedonistic response to recovering from personal hurt and pain. 'Eat, drink and be merry, for tomorrow you die,'" said Mark, feeling a certain indignation coming to the surface. "I went to the other extreme in almost turning monastic in my early Navy days, but I am beholden to good ole common sense and the nurturing of a devout father who always said that 'bright lights and fast living' never satisfy; all they do is dull your senses and leave you worse off in the end."

Claire looked at Mark and brought the discussion to an end by saying: "I like that we think alike."

At Nhill, they stopped for almost an hour. While Mark refueled, Claire bought lunch, and after they ate, they stretched and walked a little as well. Then it was on to Horsham, Ballarat and Melbourne.

"You mean Horsham where *the wicked witch* came from?" teased Claire as Mark pulled out onto the highway again.

"That would be the place," replied Mark, with a grin.

"You mentioned how you dated a girl in Annapolis for a while before you graduated. Do you mind talking about it?" asked Claire.

"No, I'll tell you, but I'm not proud of the memory. We weren't a good fit and I should have known it much sooner, but I felt pressure to try and find a relationship and meet the expectations of my friends, like my pastor and his wife," began Mark. He wasn't sure how Claire would handle the details.

When Mark had told the full story, including Gary's outburst on the trek westwards, Claire smiled. "You're right," she said. "Clearly not a good fit." She looked out the window, and when she didn't say anything more, Mark asked her why.

"Because I am not sure what more to say. I think of John and me. Not a good fit from the beginning, but I went along with the flow. I didn't tell you, but when he left Melbourne and I didn't hear from him for a year, he had found another girl and they lived together. Had I not begun divorce proceedings, I am not sure what he would have done. He was just a creep of a man; not very brave and not much character," she said, shaking her head.

"I understand. Isn't it fascinating that we go to school for a dozen years, and then on to university for a few more, to prepare for a productive life as an adult, yet what kind of preparation do we get for marriage and raising children, probably the two most important things we do in life?" He looked ahead at the road and thought for a moment before continuing. "Even though I came from a decent home, and I had an active church life, it wasn't enough for me. I was away from family when I was dating Roslyn and I was as naïve as could be. I thought that a couple who prayed together would stay together, but that fell apart when one of us decided that she did not want to pray. It was downhill from there and we just drifted apart."

"Sad, but I had pretty much the same experience," Claire responded. "Julie dated a monster before Grant. This guy had multiple affairs and told Julie that he was just doing what comes naturally for a man. He bragged about his conquests and showed no remorse for his behavior. Fortunately, Julie met Grant at an Echunga dance, and he punched out the brute one night. That freed Julie of him. Grant's a wonderful guy, but he has no ambition. He was content to drive a Jacobs milk tanker for the rest of his working life. When Jacobs sold out a few years ago, Grant panicked until he got another truck driving job. Nothing wrong with that. He's a good father and husband and they're happy. But I just couldn't live in Mount Barker for my entire life," said Claire.

"Look at me," said Mark. "I've lived all over, and now I want nothing more than to live in the Adelaide Hills, if not Hahndorf," he said. "Truthfully, I will always call Hahndorf home and I hope the farm is in the family for generations to come, but I've outgrown that lifestyle. What I knew as a boy will never be again." He looked at her searchingly. "The Lutheran school master will never drive his single milking cow up the main street while riding a bicycle and holding a bamboo cane to prod the animal. Those days have gone forever. So, what do I want? I'm still putting together the master plan. Nevertheless, I *do* know that I want to live in Australia, probably Melbourne, or Adelaide or the Adelaide Hills. I want to stay with the Navy for about another five years or so, and I want to continue to work in music education to help build professional music in Australia through community music programs." elaborated Mark.

"And that's it?" asked Claire, a little disappointed.

"Oh no, Claire! That's just the professional side of the master plan. Are you ready for this?" He took a deep breath and the words gushed out. "I want you by my side and to never leave it. I want us to be deliriously happy together and to live productive lives for the greater good. I want us to cherish our relationship, knowing what it took to come together after all these years. I want God to smile upon us and to give us the abundant life He has promised. There you have it. No small master plan, right?" said Mark.

"I think it is wonderful! We owe it to ourselves to make it happen," replied Claire.

The journey continued through Ballarat, Bacchus Marsh and into Melbourne. It was heavy traffic on a Friday afternoon and Mark turned off towards Footscray into Parkville and on to Doncaster and then slowly into Box Hill. They went to the supermarket where Claire bought groceries as did Mark, and then they drove to her flat. They took her suit case and the groceries into the flat and Claire opened the windows to air out the mustiness from the summer heat.

They stood in the kitchen and looked at each other. Here it was Friday evening in Melbourne. They had only made contact on Tuesday afternoon. Both were feeling bemused by all that had transpired in no more than four days. Years earlier it had only been a teenage crush, but the spark had been lit. Mark had never forgotten that charming, innocent thirteen-year-old face. He took her face in his hands, looked deep in her eyes and kissed her gently. There was no need for either of them to speak. They walked together to the front door.

"Shall I come to pick you up for dinner tomorrow at 5 pm?" asked Mark. "There's a place in Melbourne I used to go to often when I was at HMS *Cerberus*. I think you'll like it!"

"Of course," said Claire. She looked up at him, her face shining, and kissed him lightly on the cheek as he turned to go.

Mark drove to the Simpson Barracks, unpacked the car and took his groceries, euphonium and Christmas gifts into his flat. He sat and ate some fruit, gazing out the kitchen window as he thought, then took a shower and stretched out comfortably on his bed. He felt overwrought, yet entranced, by all that had happened in the last few days. *God moves in mysterious ways*, he mused, and he was grateful for that fact. He suddenly realized how tired he was and crawled under the covers early, knowing full well how early he would be awake the next morning.

It was dawn as Mark walked over to the practice studios with both his euphonium and the Navy bass trombone. He went to the most soundproof room he could find and began a grueling practice session. He told himself he needed to guard against becoming lax on his daily rehearsals, and he knew that with Claire in his life, it would require discipline. But he could do his playing in the early morning hours; he'd done it before and he could do it again, he knew. After his practice, he walked to the café where he often bought coffee and a pastry or two. Later, in the afternoon, he gave the Monaro a good cleaning and a polish. As he surveyed his work an hour later, he was pleased. 'Must keep the old girl looking good for Claire,' he said to himself.

Right on time, he knocked on Claire's front door. She stepped out into the afternoon sunshine in the prettiest summer dress Mark had ever seen. He took her by the hand and twirled her around, admiring her shoes, dress and hair. It felt good to be happy again. Claire looked at Mark in his grey dress trousers, blue striped shirt and navy jacket. "My handsome beau," she said laughing, and twirled him around. Suitably embarrassed, Mark ushered her to her seat in the spotless car and they drove into Melbourne. "This restaurant," said Mark as they arrived, "is classy, but not the Windsor!" They savored the food and their conversation, lingering over dessert and coffee until three hours had passed. When they emerged on the street, it was twilight and the street lights gave a soft glow to the evening. "Would you like to do some window-shopping?" asked Mark. "That was always my father's favorite kind of shopping: 'You can look, but you can't buy!'" Hand in hand they strolled down to Bourke Street, and then extended it for another three blocks, reluctant to return to the car park. As they drove back to Claire's flat, she remarked:

"Thank you, Mark. That was so much fun. I know so much more about you after our window-shopping," she declared.

"Me too," replied Mark. "I now know that you don't like bright red clothes and are more of a pastel person, and you are not really keen on earth tones—unless in the right setting."

"Okay, Okay, that's enough," said Claire, "but you have got it correct about me. However, I can be persuaded. I'm not a rigid person."

When they arrived at Claire's flat, Mark walked her to the door. "Do you want to come in?" she asked. "Best friends first," he said. She reached up and kissed him. "I like that," she murmured.

Both had chores to do on Sunday in preparation for their first day back at work, so Mark said he would call Claire Sunday evening. As he drove back to his flat, he could not remember when he had savored the companionship of another person as much. He had not wanted the evening to come to an end.

The full contingent of military personnel was not due back at Simpson Barracks until the beginning of February. Mark, still accruing his full holiday allotment, returned with the civilian staff and many other military persons as well. At the initial meeting on Monday morning, the commander asked each of his team to give a verbal report on their holiday ruminations about the survey and the video. He reminded them that they were planning for the middle of March, when DFSM would make a forty-minute presentation on the future of military music to the leadership of the Defence Force in Canberra, along with several political leaders.

No one had altered their thinking on the direction of the March Defence Force presentation should take, and all believed that the survey, once tabulated and analyzed, would provide a consistent sense of the areas where military music needed to adapt and change. All agreed that the brief segments of the video shared prior to the Christmas break had been a foretaste of the powerful message the final and complete version would carry about the positive affect military music could have on the Australian public.

After the meeting, Mark met with his Navy Musical Director, who confirmed that he would be conducting several performances in Brisbane and Sydney in the next three months as part of the department's public relations campaign. He would also be conducting a lower brass workshop in Adelaide in late February for three days. Mark returned to his office and called Keswick Barracks, spoke to his counterpart and alerted him that the workshop was on, and to expect some official announcement within days. He also asked how they were liking the music scores he had left them in November. The response was what he needed to hear: they could not wait to perform the music in public. Mark said that he had a weird routine in mind for the Morricone piece and they may reject it. *Bring it on* was the enthusiastic response and the conversation ended with Mark laughing as he pondered his suggested routine.

Other than these interstate assignments, Mark was fully occupied at Simpson Barracks and HMS *Cerberus*. Travel never bothered Mark in his work. It was never onerous or something to dread. To the contrary, he appreciated the break in routine, the chance to meet new people and see the progress in military and community musical groups. However, his perspective had changed since Claire had entered his life. Now, he felt the tug of being away from her, even for a few days, and he did not like it. He realized that he was suddenly in a new place in this relationship business. Claire was rapidly filling the void he had experienced for so long. He liked being only a short drive away from her, whether it be her work place or her flat.

In the next few weeks, Mark called Claire each night after work and they spent as much time together as possible on the weekends. On Sundays, they attended Luther College Church, unless they were out of town. The weeks went by, and the first week of February found Mark and his team presenting the complete survey report and the video to the full DFSM committee. Both were received with full approval and a brief outline was sent on to each branch of the military and to the respective military music administrators. Full details would be forthcoming after the presentation in Canberra. By mid-February, the commander at DFSM was engaged full-time in polishing the report to be made in mid-March to the Defence Force leadership.

Late February was fast approaching, and Mark was scheduled to fly into Adelaide for the lower brass workshop with a performance on the Saturday night. All South Australian brass and concert bands were invited, from high schools to community to the rarified professional musicians in Adelaide. There had not been enough time to advertise and promote the concert as was needed, but Mark as the conductor and concert master was a draw. Word was beginning to seep out that Mark was an agent of change for future military music. The Federation Square performance had made its impression. What would he do at this Adelaide concert?

Mark asked Claire if she would like to come with him to Adelaide. They thought about it for a day or so; was it worth it when Mark would be working all day and into the evening? Claire decided to go and obtained time off from work. Mark booked the tickets and they departed Tullamarine Airport on an early Wednesday morning flight, arriving in Adelaide in time for Mark to make his first meeting at 10:00 am at Keswick Barracks on Anzac Highway, not far from the airport. With the children in school, Gary and Helen, and Betty, drove two cars to the airport. Mark took one and drove immediately to his appointment. Gary, Helen and Betty took Claire to Mount Barker where she had lunch with her sister. Later, Claire decided to stay at the farm and not disrupt the schedule of Julie and Grant. Mark had invited them to bring Luke to the Saturday night band concert.

Mark arrived back at the farm before 8:30 pm. He was tired, but excited to see his family and, even more so, Claire *with* his family. He had not eaten and only wanted fruit and a cup of Milo. They talked until 10:30 pm and Gary suggested that three people in the room should go to bed. This left Claire and Mark on their own in the lounge room. They sat quietly on the sofa and talked about the day.

"I hope you are glad that you came with me," Mark asked.

"Of course, I am, but I did wish I could be with you several times throughout the afternoon. I wanted to see what you do in these workshops," replied Claire.

"Well, you can come if you want. I do think the entire day would be too much but think about coming with me on Friday. I won't be leaving the farm until after 9:00 am. I have a workshop until noon, specialty items from 1:00 to 3:00 pm and full band rehearsal from 3:00 to 6:00 pm. You could come into the Barracks with me and I will park the car. We can then go to the rehearsal building and I will show you around and you can go off, if you want, and come back at 1:00 pm and stay through until the end of rehearsal. Afterwards, we could go to Glenelg and relax in a restaurant," suggested Mark. "This will give you an understanding of what it takes to prepare for a concert."

"Wonderful, I would like that very much," said Claire as she reached up and kissed Mark.

"Now, young lady, we had better get to bed. I see they have put you in my old room and I am in the old house next to Dad's study. Good night, beautiful girl," said Mark as he kissed Claire again.

The next morning, Mark was playing his euphonium with his mute as Gary was returning from checking on the milking. Mark ate a quick breakfast and walked onto the porch with Claire and said good bye. He allowed one hour to arrive at Keswick Barracks. It was not Melbourne traffic and he should only take about forty minutes on the new roads, but he would not leave anything to chance. He was the workshop leader and he must arrive on time, or earlier.

He had a lot to accomplish this day. He had asked his Melbourne Navy percussionist to come Thursday afternoon for the first rehearsal of the Saturday concert. He needed a seasoned drum kit professional who could keep driving the beat of the modern arrangements. The Adelaide Army and Navy percussionists were welcome at the rehearsals, but for the concert Mark needed the professional. At the rehearsal on Thursday evening, he stood before thirty-five musicians and he complimented them for looking "a fine and handsome assembly of musicians. Let's make some excellent music together!"

They rehearsed the main full band pieces of music; *The Floral Dance, Grandfather's Clock* (with its perky part for three trombones), *Under the Boardwalk, The Lincolnshire Poacher, Colonel Bogey* march, *Y.M.C.A., Tom Marches On* and the final hymn, *Abide with Me.*

"I always finish with a hymn as a piece of music to calm the soul and to have the audience leave the comfort of the concert hall and go out into the night air with a sense of goodness about life," explained Mark. "This is a beautiful arrangement and we will work on it more tomorrow. It needs to flow seamlessly. Think of an organ playing and not a piano."

"We will spend time on *Under the Boardwalk* tomorrow afternoon as well. Mr. Bass, don't feel awkward about sitting down after the introduction. If anyone wants to hold that instrument all the way through the piece, then they are welcome to do so," said Mark as the band smiled with him. "That was beautiful flugelhorn playing, by the way."

"The two spoof pieces we are leaving until rehearsal at 1:00 pm tomorrow. I am so impressed with how the *Moment for Morricone* routine has come together; there has been true dedication in making this happen by these keen musicians who will entertain you as well. You will like it, I promise. I'm part of the William Tell Overture quartet and you will see this tomorrow also."

"Full band, please arrive by 3:00 pm and we can leave by 6:00 pm. Thank you everyone. Appreciate your commitment and great music. Travel safely as you return to your homes," concluded Mark as the band broke up and left for the evening.

Earlier in the day, he had spent a lot of time formatting the *Moment for Morricone* piece into a comedy routine. The group had been committing the music to memory since November and had not received the entertainment routine video from Mark until late January, when it was confirmed that the concert would proceed. This was to be the entertainment highlight of the entire concert. The three trumpets, three trombones (one as a bass trombone) and Bb bass had agreed to say nothing to others about the parody on the western movie music of Ennio Morricone, one of Mark's preferred modern composers, who was also the composer of Gabriel's Oboe from *The Mission*. Mark had first seen their rehearsal yesterday and he was delighted with how they had perfected their act from the video. Today, it was even better, and Mark exclaimed with enthusiasm, "I want to take you guys on tour with me all over Australia!" The seven musicians reacted like little kids and said, "We are going to keep you to that!" They laughed with relief that Mark liked their satirical performance, and he laughed because they were so good.

As he arrived at the farm and climbed out of the car, he was excited, knowing he would be with Claire in a moment. Is this what they call true love, he asked himself? It had better not be infatuation, he thought. He was too old for that nonsense. He wanted this feeling to last forever. He was beginning to feel complete as a person. As he walked inside the house, he restrained himself to hugging Claire and kissing her on the forehead.

Betty said, "We know you haven't eaten much all day. We have a salad and some fruit for you. Now come and sit down and tell us all about your day. Never mind the time!"

Claire sat next to Mark and he talked as he ate. They could all tell that he was energized, they just didn't know that the reason was two-fold: he was close to Claire and he was pleased with the rehearsal of all the items in the concert. He related what had happened throughout the day without giving away the two special musical entertainment routines; he spoke of these as surprises which he hoped would thrill the audience at the concert. Mark then asked what had occurred on the farm throughout the day. They all interpreted this as meaning, *Claire, what did you do today?* Again, Gary saved the evening and suggested that bed was mandatory now, except for Mark and Claire.

When they were alone, Mark put his arm around Claire and said: "I feel like an impetuous teenager who wants to remove everybody and just leave you and me."

"Me too, but we have got to go through some of this first, I guess," Claire reminded Mark.

"Alright, I will settle down. Are you still coming with me tomorrow morning?" asked Mark.

"You had better believe it! I have my clothes all laid out and am booked to have a shower at 7:00 am. Is that going to interfere with your shower?" asked Claire.

"No, I will have mine in the old house. I just must tell you about one of the items that will be darn good entertainment. I have asked all seven players to keep it quiet so that it will be a surprise for the entire audience on Saturday night. But let me break my request to them, and tell you," Mark said, beginning to feel tired.

He told Claire about his basic notion that in reshaping military music for the twenty-first century there was no magical formula. It was mostly about excellent music and entertainment value. He believed that a brass band or a concert band could compete with the best of rock bands and even orchestras by applying these two aspects. He said that the only component all music groups needed as their one essential was the human voice, and an animated body with that human voice. When combined with any musical group, the human voice and body can create in a live performance, an allurement, an enthrallment and a magnetism that no recording studio or movie production can produce with all the wizardry, all the illusion, all the hocus-pocus of technology and one hundred years of smart production. He admitted that these were bold claims and he might be proven wrong. However, he was in the business of transitioning military music in Australia in ways that the United States military had already done. Then he explained the *Moment for Morricone.*

Claire was beginning to see his zest for life and his passion for excellence, and she was pleased for him. She prayed he would maintain a balance in his work and learn to relax more and let go of stress, the silent killer.

It rained over-night and the skies were overcast as Mark and Claire came from separate directions into the kitchen for breakfast. Mark was stunned as he looked at Claire's pant suit; she wore a powder blue jacket and black pants and shoes. She looked adorable and Mark told her so, as Betty looked on admiringly. They ate casually, without the rush that Mark had felt the previous morning. Betty left the room and returned placing a string of pearls next to Claire's coffee cup.

"You can wear these today, if you like. I think they will finish off your outfit perfectly," said Betty.

"Oh, Betty, they are perfect! I would be honored to wear them. Would you mind putting them on for me?" replied Claire as Mark came to help as well.

Gary lead in a short devotional and prayer, and then Mark and Claire were out the door. Helen and Gary had several chores ahead of them for the day and would remain on the farm. Betty volunteered at St. Michael's and had agreed to several hours during the middle of the day. This was an opportunity to mix with her peer group, many of whom she had known since childhood. As Mark drove through the Hills, Claire expressed gratitude about how she had been enfolded into the family so quickly. Mark agreed, although he said that it had occurred because *it just feels right to everyone.* He remembered the icy reception his family had given Roslyn. No, he said, he took that back: she brought tension into the Schubert home right from the start. In fact, his family was long suffering and very tolerant of Roslyn's nonsense. Mark said that it was the exact opposite now, and had Claire noticed how Gary's children were now calling her *Aunty Claire?* She had, she said, and she had even helped Gary's son with his homework last evening.

As they came to the Eagle on the Hill hotel, Claire said, "It's a wonderful drive into Adelaide, isn't it? I never tire of it and I've never found it boring."

"I agree," nodded Mark. "When we were kids, we would close our eyes at Glen Osmond and know exactly where we were by the twists and turns as Dad drove towards Hahndorf. Gary and I made a game of it and Mum and Dad would listen to us describe the landmarks along the way home to the farm," said Mark.

They were approaching the Toll House, when Claire asked Mark about the day ahead. She didn't want to distract Mark, but she also did not want him to leave her alone either. "By the way," she wondered, "what are the musicians going to think of me being there?"

"First of all, they are all going to think that I have the most beautiful girl in the world," Mark said with a grin. "I am not going to leave you at any time. We are going to be fully occupied with rehearsing. I just want you to enjoy it all. I don't think you will be bored at any time, and the full band won't arrive until 3:00 pm. We will be focusing on the specialty acts, beginning at 1:00 pm. I hope you laugh a little at the staged antics. I will show you the bathrooms, and I think that is all you will need," explained Mark.

Moving through Greenhill Road, they entered Anzac Highway and Mark turned into Keswick Barracks. They walked to the rehearsal building and Mark showed Claire the bathrooms. "If you want you can go wherever you like," he said, "Maybe you could go to Glenelg. Just remember to be back here at 1:00 pm." She stood on tiptoe and kissed him. "Shall I bring you back a sandwich?" she asked. "Yes, thanks!" said Mark. He was enjoying how thoughtful Claire was.

The last session of the workshop was underway by 10:00 am., most of it concentrated on trends and techniques Mark had experienced in his five years while based at the Naval Academy Band in Annapolis. This had given him a global perspective in that military musicians from many nations were continuously interacting with their U.S. military counterparts. Added to this was his own adaptation of what was suitable for Australia's Defence Force music, and by extension, community and K-12 music as well. Most of the discussion over the ninety-minute session took a question and answer format. Many of the musicians in attendance were reservists, rather than full-time military. They belonged to the various brass and concert bands of the South Australian Band Association. That was their first loyalty, and many were concerned about the future of community bands because they were finding it increasingly difficult to recruit and retain a steady source of additional players. To this point, Mark added the concern that many of these players never aspired to excel beyond the level of mediocrity, and mediocrity was really going backwards. It certainly was not advancing.

After an hour, the direction of the conversation came down to one question: What can be done to ensure that South Australia has a dynamic and vibrant brass and concert band milieu? Or, as Mark rephrased the question: How do you build success and maintain it?

Mark wished he had time and a classroom setting whereby he could lead his fifteen lower brass players through a deductive reasoning session where they could answer the questions themselves. He had, however, thirty minutes and chose to make four salient points. First, nothing occurs in a vacuum. If brass and concert bands are to flourish in South Australia, champions, leaders, coaches are necessary to nurture these bands across the state. Second, there must be structure to whatever nurturing program emerges as a means of growing and developing new and better brass and concert bands. The South Australian Band Association is one example of structure, as is State Education department music education curriculum for K-12 and, even the Navy and Army bands in the state provide structure as a reference point.

Before Mark could embark on his third point, Claire walked into the room, hesitated and then sat down. All eyes turned to this attractive and well-dressed woman as she took her place. Mark glanced over at her and waved. "She's with me," he said, and smiled. "I'll introduce you shortly. Let me finish up quickly."

He continued with his third point by noting: "All fifteen musicians present here, today, have a mental checklist of the gradations of existing brass and concert bands across the State. You already know, with experiential accuracy, the best and poorest bands in the State. The South Australian Band Association's classification of A, B, C and D grade bands provide documented evidence on an annual basis of excellence, good, mediocre and struggling bands. Then, at the national level, it is the National Band Council of Australia which determines Australia's best bands. As an aside, Salvation Army bands do not compete in contests. We know this, but I must say that I have been astounded by the musical excellence and performance dignity of these bands in the UK and the U.S."

His fourth point called for effective channels of communication and the vigilant promotion of presence (meaning the advertising of marches, concerts and competitions) to continuously broadcast to the population of South Australia that these bands were in existence and offered wonderful opportunities for children, youth and others to learn and play music, or to encourage within the non-playing public a listening appreciation for this musical genre.

"There is so much more, but we will end here," he said, gathering up his materials. "Take a break for lunch and the *Moment for Morricone* players will rehearse starting at 1:00 pm. Before we break, we must not let go of those questions. Much of my work in the years to come, within the Navy and without, will be focused on growing and developing brass and concert bands in Australia. The word I used earlier is key; how to make bands *flourish!* Thank you," said Mark feeling as though he needed more time with his group.

As the group began to break up, Mark said quickly, "One more thing: If you want to meet someone special—come and meet Claire."

Naturally, they all came over, and Mark introduced Claire to the Lower Brass group, the backbone of a band. Claire, looking a little embarrassed and very demure, said 'Hello.' The boys, as Mark called them later, were eager to meet her, and many winked or gave Mark the thumbs up as he knew they would; in recognition of Claire's attractiveness and Mark's good fortune. Mark showed Claire to another seat close to the table with coffee and biscuits. She gave Mark his sandwich and he ate as 'the boys' came by to make coffee or take a biscuit. Her bashfulness continued, but Mark smiled and said, "I would want to look at you too, if I was them!" She blushed, and he asked her how her morning went. As he made them both cups of coffee, she told him where she had been, and as they sat sipping away, some of band members came over and made small talk.

The second rehearsal for the Saturday night concert began at 1:00 pm. The seven players of the *Moment for Morricone* piece emerged from a side room in their old trousers with braces, colored polo shirts and sneakers. They looked a disheveled lot, and Claire burst out laughing. Mark looked in her direction and said, "Don't they look charming?" The other musicians who were in the other two specialty items looked on, witnessing this act for the first time.

They were intrigued, and before the practice began, Mark told all in the room: "I need to say that these boys have worked hard on this performance. It is excellent music with good entertainment value all the way through. Ordinarily, I wouldn't wish to perform this type of item without more rehearsal, but these seven musicians have rallied and worked very hard, and yesterday I was absolutely thrilled at their performance."

Moment for Morricone was played with precision and exactness as the players walked about the stage and enacted their strange routine. It was a long performance lasting almost eight minutes. Mark was going to leave it until Saturday night to explain to the audience what was happening.

The *William Tell Overture Quartet* was next, and this included Mark on euphonium. This was a three-minute piece, but they all sat as

Mark did not want the Bb Bass holding his instrument all that time, the two Eb Basses were not as heavy on one's back.

Under the Boardwalk needed the full band, and until they arrived, Mark just wanted to go over the introduction with the Bb Bass and the flugelhorn.

This part of the rehearsal was over by 2:40 pm and provided a welcome break until the full band rehearsal began at 3:00 pm. On schedule, Mark stood before the band and said that they would rehearse according to the concert program, and would play full band pieces twice, paying attention to dynamics and volume. Again, Claire was a person of interest as she was the only outsider in the room other than the few technicians who had to transport the equipment to the Adelaide Town Hall after the rehearsal. Mark introduced her to the full body of musicians as his "guest." To make light of the moment, Mark, in return, introduced Claire to Abel Seaman Tony Hodge, the percussionist who lived in Melbourne at *HMS Cerberus* and said, "He's the only player I have to keep tabs on when we arrive back in Melbourne!"

The rehearsal went exceedingly well. Mark remarked that he was privileged to conduct such a disciplined and eager group of musicians.

"Conducting is easy and a pleasure when players are poised to give of their best. You have done that on both rehearsals. Thank you. I look forward to a terrific concert tomorrow evening. One comment about the concert. I have not been in the Town Hall for about eight years now. I am told that the acoustics have been improved and it has had a facelift. This concert, as you know, has been arranged hastily and we have our fingers crossed that the attendance will be worthy of the energy you have given to it. I am hoping for 300 plus. Again, your enthusiasm is inspiring. See you tomorrow at 6:15 pm, no later. Good evening to you all," said Mark as he closed his score folder and looked over at Claire.

After dealing with the usual small matters from various players, he walked across the room to Claire and as she stood, he kissed her on the cheek and said, "You are very patient and very lovely!"

"And you, Lieutenant Schubert, are a very fine conductor and an inspirer of musicians. They adore you," replied Claire.

"Adore me, hmm, I'm not sure it's that good, but they are enthusiastic. What I really like about them is that they want to make the best music possible. That's admirable!" said Mark. "Let's get out of here. Where do we go?"

"I have found a restaurant I want to show you right on the foreshore," announced Claire.

"Well, if you like it then we will eat there and just unwind for an hour or two," said Mark.

"I am unwound," said Claire, "you are the one who needs to relax."

They drove out of Keswick Barracks onto Anzac Highway and in fifteen minutes were parked and being ushered to a table looking out on the water. They were early enough and did not need a booking for a Friday evening. Claire confessed that she spent some time looking for other restaurants because she realized this was expensive. She could not find one she thought Mark would like as much, but she did worry about the cost. Mark took her hands and told her never to worry about things like this with him.

"I'm not rich by any means, but I have been on my own for a long time and I don't spend big on myself. I have a solid bank account and am fortunate in that I receive an annual stipend from the farm. Gary is a natural with business and farming and we have other investments too. We talk often about the finances of the farm, but I don't contribute much else." He looked at Claire closely. "Soon, I want to buy a home, and probably later this year I want to buy a new car. I'm hoping you will be part of both these decisions, Claire. I have waited a long time for you. We're going to enjoy life together and I pray that long life and health will be granted to us," said Mark.

That cleared the air. They both settled into a relaxed and pleasant dinner in the ambience of a fine restaurant. At one point, Claire asked Mark what he enjoyed doing most. He looked surprised. "Why do you ask?" he said. "Well, it's just that you seem to do so many things, that I wonder how you decide what you like best," she responded.

"Well, first," he said, and paused for a moment, "First, I'm a navy musician and a music educator who plays and conducts. That's on top.

Then, I'm also an administrator, a researcher, a teacher, a writer, and a communicator about music and education." He paused for breath. "It sounds complicated, but it's really not. Think of a post office, like the one at Hahndorf," he said animatedly. He made a square with his hands. "When I was a kid there was a whole wall of mailboxes and you needed a key to open yours to get your family's mail. Well, I've probably got a few more mailboxes than some people! I've got one for my euphonium, one for my conducting, another one for my bass trombone, a box for teaching, another for speaking appointments," as Claire shook her head, laughing. "And I've got a few more for other stuff," he finished triumphantly. "I don't know how you do it," she said. "I'll tell you which boxes I *don't* have," continued Mark. "I don't have one for television because I just don't watch it much. And I don't have one for drinking with the boys at the pub. Too many military musicians drink too much anyway," he said, trailing off.

"So, what about you?" he asked Claire. "What kind of boxes do *you* have?"

She laughed, saying, "I don't think I have as many as you do, but I may have more than I thought, if I use your classifying system." She paused and took a sip of water. "I have about six, I think, but I've got a new one since the holidays and it has your name on it!"

"Yes," said Mark, "You—or us—has become the largest box for me too. But it makes a strong statement about us and our priorities." He looked at Claire earnestly. "Spirituality is one of my larger boxes. I pray every day and I take time to read Scripture or works of theology and devotion. It just gives me strength and courage to face each day. And I believe it makes me a kinder person." Claire nodded as Mark continued, "Most of the world mocks much of what I have just said, but it works for me, and I know you have it too," he added.

Claire hesitated. "Maybe not as much as you think, but those books you have given me are wonderful and I like the idea that God's grace is a gift and all we have to do is accept it. None of us is ever alone when we have the Holy Spirit with us," she said.

"Spoken like a true believer, my dear," said Mark. "It is our

worldview, our way of life, and I think I live more productively because God is with me, you, us, all the time." He shifted in his chair and
leaned forward. "What I find so interesting is that many sophisticated
people spend a fortune on counselling or seminars or self-help gurus,
buying these best-sellers or attending seminars—all to try to find the
peace and calm that anyone can have from reading Scripture and belonging to a Christian congregation."

Mark brought himself up short, realizing how much he was talking. "I know I have strong views on these things," he said. He bowed
his head slightly and fingered his napkin. "I'm sorry if I'm talking too
much, but I just think so many people are throwing their lives away.
But as Christians we're all bought with a price and can walk through
life with God by our sides."

Claire squeezed his hand and replied, "I *love* listening to you talk!
You've got so much passion for what you do and what you believe."

"Ah, well, please stop me when I carry on too much. I guess we
need to head back to the farm soon," he said.

Claire went to sleep on Mark's shoulder as he drove through the
city and into the Hills to the farm. As he drove, Mark reflected on how
many times he had wanted to experience this same drive with the right
girl by his side.

After milking, Saturday morning was a lazy time for everyone. It
was the only day when Mark and Claire could mix with family for
most of the day. Claire was brimming over with superlatives on Mark's
conducting skills and masterful interaction with all the musicians at
the rehearsal yesterday, and Gary told Claire that if the concert that
evening was even half as good as the Federation Square event, then they
were all in a for a real treat.

Before lunch, blue sky and sunshine broke through the cloud cover
and made the light in the kitchen cheerful and warm. It made Helen
suggest that they should all go for a walk to the camp fire site and
breathe fresh air and get some exercise as well. That met with everyone's approval and Gary said that he was taking the trail bike, matches,
his mother and some sandwiches, instead of a full meal at home.

Claire looked at Mark questioningly. "The camp fire site?" "It'll be good," he said reassuringly, "you'll like it!" Hand in hand, they walked about a half mile, following the lanes along the fence lines as they climbed to the highest ground on the farm. At the top of the hill there was a heavy copse of trees and close to the edge of a steep slope there was a camp fire setting with heavy logs shaped and worn like bench seating. In the center was a stone fire pit. When the family wanted to have a barbecue or picnic, they would load up the tractor and trailer, or the utility vehicle, and drive to this favorite family spot, so much so that even birthday parties were celebrated here.

Soon, Gary arrived on the trail bike with Betty on the back. The walk was a little more than she felt she should do with the concert looming for the evening. Claire was enchanted; watching as Gary and Mark scurried around and built a fire with dry grass, sticks and fallen branches they broke down with their hands and feet. Helen and Betty brought some thermoses of hot coffee, cold juice and sandwiches from the saddle bags on the bike. Mark, Gary and the children made *damper* out of flour, water and salt, using their hands to wrap the dough on sticks and bake it over the coals. Then they added butter and jam to this very Australian campfire treat from eons ago. It was a pleasant few hours in the great outdoors.

Claire's mother arrived at the farm with Julie, Grant and little Luke around 5:00 pm. They were all looking forward to the concert and were delighted that Mark had given a special invitation to Luke. They had not met Mark's family before. Mark and Betty came to the door and invited them into the lounge room. Mark was wearing his black dress trousers and a white shirt. Grant introduced Claire's mother to Mark and Mark introduced them to his mother. They had just sat down when Claire came into the room. They all straightened up and looked at this honey-blonde with shoulder-length hair in a black velvet dress with a white lace collar, black shoes and a clutch purse. Mark said it first, "Claire, you look sensational!" She blushed as the others said how wonderful she looked too. Helen and Gary came into the room with their son and daughter in their Sunday-best clothes, and Helen and Betty and Claire served cool drinks, while Mark disappeared to complete dressing. When he reappeared, he was in full-dress uniform with cap in hand. They were ready for a concert and three cars were soon driving into Victoria Square and the Adelaide Town Hall.

When they arrived, Mark handed the tickets for his party of ten to the ushers and gave Gary the extra tickets for their two sisters and families. He excused himself, but before he left, he said to Claire, "I am going to be preoccupied somewhat from now on. In case, I forget to say this to you later, you look gorgeous, and I love you." He reached down and kissed her on the cheek and disappeared through the side door of the auditorium. Claire was sitting with Betty on one side and her mother on the other. She leaned over to Betty and whispered, "Mark just told me he loved me!" Betty squeezed her hand and whispered back, "I saw that the first afternoon he brought you to the farm! I'm so happy for both of you."

It was thirty minutes before the concert commenced, but there was enough pre-concert activity on the Town Hall stage to keep the whole family occupied and entertained. The drummer came out on stage and completed his set up. Sound technicians moved back and forth, and at one point, Mark came out for his voice check as conductor and Master of Ceremonies. Then at the fifteen-minute mark, the full band came on stage and the cacophonous sound of instruments tuning up began. At the five-minute mark, the drum major called the band to attention as the auditorium quickly fell to a hush. At the top of the hour, the President of the South Australian Band Association (SABA) came on stage and gave the official welcome to the joint concert by the Army and Navy Bands of South Australia and reservist players from other SABA bands. He introduced Lieutenant Mark Schubert by reviewing his Vita and then Mark came on stage in full uniform minus his cap. The audience of some five hundred strong burst into applause. Mark bowed, brought the band to attention and the concert began with *The Foral Dance*.

Following this first piece, Mark came to the microphone and said: "Tonight, you are going to hear music and see antics on stage that you may not expect from a traditional brass band. Brass bands are enlarging and expanding their repertoire and you can expect military and community bands to not only play excellent music but to entertain you as well. This next piece, called *Grandfather's Clock*, will show you how the tempo can change, and the entertainment can begin."

The audience applauded appreciatively, and Mark spoke again: "Many of us from the '60s recall a popular hit song called *Under the Board Walk* and we probably knew the words by heart too. Here is a brass band version with a Bb bass player and the haunting sound of the flugelhorn. You will see the Bb bass player sit down after a while. If you knew how heavy a bass is, you'd would want to sit too. Listen for the percussion and the neat finish at the end. By the way, you can snap your fingers and tap your feet. You're in the '60s now!"

By the end of this piece, the audience had loosened up and was clearly having a fun time. As they clapped, someone called out, "This is great! Keep it coming."

Mark turned to the microphone and said: "Thank you, Mother, I can always count on you to like our music." The audience laughed, and Mark continued: "Actually, my mother *is* here this evening. Why don't you stand, Mum, and let these good people see you?" Betty stood and waved at the people behind her as they clapped.

Mark waited for the audience to settle and then said: "The next item is called *The Lincolnshire Poacher*. The title may sound traditional, but I can tell you it is anything but! Enjoy the percussion introduction and the frolicking spirit of the euphonium and baritones which is continued with the cornets. This is just a fun piece of music."

Mark looked to the sidelines and saw that the next performers were ready; they needed as much of the front of the stage as possible. Mark returned to the microphone: "There are many parents here this evening who have children currently learning music. In fact, I am told that there are parents here whose children are on stage with me now. Can I see you stand if your son or daughter, or husband or wife, or close relative is on stage tonight?"

Everyone looked around and there were over one hundred people who had family on stage. Mark continued: "Music is a unifier; it brings people together. It calms the soul and it soothes the tough segments of life. It also provides the musician, whether it is voice, keyboard, woodwind, brass, percussion, acoustical instruments, or whatever, with an avocation for life. We can't always play football at 60 years of age, but we *can* sit down and play the piano or the trumpet. After this next entertaining piece called *Moment for Morricone*, we are going to have intermission. All the bandsmen and women on the stage will be on the floor in front of the stage. If you want to come and talk to them about learning to play music, then we want to talk to you. If you have a family member who might like to learn music, please come and talk to us as well. We have cards to give you explaining the next steps you can take after the concert."

"Now, I think you'll enjoy this next piece, *Moment for Morricone*. It is a parody, a spoof, a take-off of the music by Ennio Morricone who composed the music for the violent Spaghetti Westerns of Clint Eastwood. Morricone is a wonderful composer who also wrote the music to the movie *The Mission*. These seven musicians have worked hard to bring this to you tonight. They received their roles and music only recently and I am very impressed by their act. Ladies and gentlemen, *Moment for Morricone*."

The audience responded with cheers and applause at this act and musical presentation. Their prolonged clapping brought the players back to the stage twice before they stopped applauding. The President of the South Australian Band Association came to the microphone and announced a twenty-minute intermission. Mark was inundated, as were many of the band members, as the rush of people to the front of the stage was heartening, even if many were only coming to speak to people they knew.

The second half of the concert opened with the traditional march *Colonel Bogey*. Next, Mark talked about arranging music by a composer to suit the needs of a certain genre like a brass band. One such song was the rock n' roll hit of the '60s, *Y.M.C.A.* He told the audience to listen for the rumble of the basses and to enjoy the driving beat of the percussion.

Tom Marches On followed. At its conclusion, Mark asked the audience if they liked the lilting sound of the euphoniums and the baritones. He spoke of the admiration he had for all the musicians on the stage. They did not have many months to prepare for this concert and he was in awe of their dedication to performing excellent music.

He continued: "I cannot let them have all the fun in playing while I conduct. Therefore, in this next quartet, I will be playing euphonium and will be joined by three basses. We hope you like our version of Rossini's *William Tell Overture.*"

The basses came to the front of the stage and the players sat down. Mark stood next to them and led them into this fast-paced piece. At the end, the audience applauded wildly because they knew this music, and had a sense of its level of difficulty.

"We have two more items for you in our program this evening. The first is called *The Clog Dance.* It is another fun piece of music with huge audience appeal. Once again percussion drives the music, but at the end listen for the sweet sound of the flute to bring the dance to a close. Our final piece for you is the wonderful hymn, *Abide with Me.* You've been a great audience. Thank you for coming! And remember, you've been listening to the South Australian Army and Navy bands with reservist players from many local bands in your community. Travel home safely and good night."

As the applause finally died down, Mark and the band made one last bow and left the stage. The concert was over. Many in the audience remained in their chairs, slowly emerging from the state of elation they had been in for almost two hours. Mark had left them wanting more. He was relieved it was over because he had felt the pressure on all those who contributed to the concert. At first it was only to be a lower brass workshop, but then it had morphed into a concert at his urging. This had given the promoters little time to advertise, especially with Christmas and New Years in the midst and, finally, it was an enormous test on the loyalty of players in the band to rally and perform at this level of excellence. Mark felt indebted to his musicians and humbled by their dedicated effort. This evening would live in his memory forever, and not only because it was the first time he had told Claire that he loved her.

As soon as he could, Mark made his way to his family. Claire stood watching him with her hands clasped under her chin, her face alight with smiles as she nodded her approval. As he hugged her, she kissed him full on the lips.

"So, this is what you do for a living, huh, Lieutenant Schubert? It was unbelievable! It was the most exciting music I have ever heard," Claire exclaimed. "And, it was *your* music. By the way, I love you too!" said Claire, as she whispered in his ear.

Betty put an arm around Mark and told him that she was proud of him and she wished that "your Dad could have been here tonight." "I do too, Mum," said Mark, hugging her to him. Julie and Grant thanked Mark for the opportunity to hear the band, and Mark bent down on one knee and asked Luke what he thought of the concert. Luke stammered, trying to find enough words, and Mark helped by asking him which instrument he most wanted to play when he became a *band boy*. "Drums!" he cried, jumping with excitement. Mark looked up at Julie and Grant with a smile and said, "Let's see if this changes over time!"

It was another thirty minutes before Mark was free to leave the auditorium of the Town Hall. When they all walked out into the warm night air, it was good to feel fresh air.

"Are you exhausted, Mark?" asked Betty.

"Surprisingly, I'm not, Mum," replied Mark. "I am truly relieved to learn that over 500 people came tonight. And, I am humbled how the band rallied and worked so hard. Normally, a concert like this would be in the works for six months or so. We pulled this off in less than three weeks, with Christmas and New Years in the middle. I am very impressed and so grateful to them."

When they reached their cars, Julie and Grant said goodnight and thanked Mark again for the chance to attend the concert. Julie, Claire and their mother spoke for a few minutes, unsure when they would see each other again. Mark took a moment to talk to Luke, who was showing signs of weariness. As Grant and his family drove away, Mark said that he and Claire would follow Gary and the two cars headed back into the Hills, and to home. Claire snuggled next to him all the way home. They chatted easily, holding back some of their deeper thoughts. They had been dating for less than two months, but it seemed much longer. When they arrived at the farm, Gary and Helen were busy putting the children to bed, and Betty asked if Mark and Claire would like a hot Milo. They said no, and Betty kissed them both goodnight and went to her bedroom. Mark held Claire in his arms and told her that she was the best-looking girl in the Adelaide Town Hall that night.

"I seem to be saying 'I am grateful' a lot tonight. Well, I simply can't imagine being without you and it has only been two months. At least we get to fly back to Melbourne together tomorrow and are close to each other in our flats. But that's going to get hard too, isn't it?" he said with a sigh.

"Yes, it is," murmured Claire. "I think we'll need to talk about it all soon. I'm not saying when, I'll leave that up to you. Perhaps we'd better go to bed now. You look tired," said Claire.

They hugged and kissed and went to their respective bedrooms. Mark was weary more than tired, and he lay in bed pondering the concert, the workshop and his work since he had returned to his Navy position. It occurred to him that he must pace himself to ensure that he was not pushing too hard on some of his proposed changes. True, he had been assigned the role of a catalyst, and his work as a change agent was from the Navy Command and DFSM. Even so, he must not run ahead of his superiors. To do so could see him lose support from senior administration. He did not want this to happen as he was beginning to experience acceptance and respect from the Navy and DFSM for his professional prowess as a musician, administrator and innovator.

CHAPTER SEVENTEEN

THE REST OF THE STORY

*"For true love is inexhaustible; the more you give, the more you have.
And if you go to draw at the true fountainhead, the more water you draw,
The more abundant is its flow."*
—Antoine de Saint-Exupery

Early Sunday afternoon, Mark and Claire flew back to Melbourne. They did not talk much on the flight as Claire fell asleep on Mark's shoulder. When they arrived at her flat in Box Hill, Claire put her hand on his arm and said: "Before I get out of the car, Mark, I have to say something. I hardly slept last night as I was thinking about us and our future. I know we hardly know each other. You said it right the other day; it is less than two months since we made contact again. All I could think of last night was those last five words, 'since we made contact again.' If it wasn't that we have been thinking of each other for over twenty years after our flirtatious connection at high school, I could be braver and stronger. But, I'm not. I want to be with you permanently and I want that to start as soon as possible. Am I wrong in talking this way?" She looked at him anxiously.

"No, you're not wrong. I want it too," Mark responded. "I guess I am concerned about people and convention; what they're going to say if we were to get married, say, in the next three months. Some would say that we are rushing in and it won't last. Me, I want to think about it for a few days. I have a plan that is starting to take shape and I want to be sure before I tell you about it." He paused before going on. "I do want to ask you one thing now. You know my work is going to have me traveling. Rarely will it be overseas. It will be interstate travel and usually no more than three days, like this trip. Where possible, I want you to come with me. But how will you feel being alone at times, after we are together?" he asked.

Claire answered quickly. "I can tell you right now. I will be in our home, not in my flat and you in yours. It will be ours. I am not a clinging vine type. I will be fine and happy for you to travel as your work demands. I will spend time making our home as we want it to be, and I will have work of some sort to keep me busy. I just want to be together as soon as possible," replied Claire.

"I understand, and I would feel the same if you had to travel from time to time, and I remained in Melbourne," said Mark.

"Good, I know you think the same. I'll say good night now," responded Claire. She reached over and kissed him and then got out of the car.

"Hey, just a minute," called Mark getting out of the car too. "Let me get your suitcase and walk you to the door. One thing you need to know about me is that I am a big advocate for chivalry. I open doors for ladies and walk on the road side of the footpath."

Claire laughed and said, "I love my Prince Charming!"

"You had better," said Mark as Claire stepped into her flat, "It's your job from now on!"

Mark drove to Simpson Barracks and almost immediately went over to the studio to play his euphonium. It didn't come easy and he soon gave it up as a lost cause. He had too much else on his mind—two matters especially. He returned to his desk in his flat and made a start on his lower brass workshop report and, more particularly, the concert. The other matter was Claire. He refused to consider what most of his contemporaries would recommend, move in together, and then figure out the rest of the story. It wasn't that he was old fashioned as much as he refused to be like others and take what he considered the easy way out. He believed in courtship, then marriage and the bliss of being married to follow. Sure, he was from an *Old Lutheran* background and a traditionalist in many things, but that was not it. He lived by a set of principles, and these gave him values, and from those came behavior, actions and conduct. Since he was a teenager, he had vowed that he would never steal, abuse his body with drugs, nicotine and alcohol, or mistreat people. Once he had punched a drunken fellow sailor for beating up on a weaker man, but he had this code, and this had guided his life for the last twenty-odd years. In moments of introspection, he recognized the need for more flexibility, to be less rigid, but he didn't preach at others, and he only asked the same courtesy from them.

After this weekend, Mark knew two things were categorically clear: he loved Claire and she loved him, and they were both mature adults. As such, they had confessed to each other that they wanted to be together and this meant marriage. It was the word they had not used to this point. They needed to discuss it, pray about it and then act on it.

Mark picked up the telephone and called her. When she answered, he hesitated for a few seconds, then he said that he had been doing some serious thinking about their relationship. Claire jumped in when he paused and said kindly,

"Well, Mark, I hope you have been thinking positively about our relationship. You make it sound very formal."

"I guess that did sound detached. I didn't mean it to," he said apologetically. "The fact is I *have* been thinking seriously about us. I want you to just listen and then you can comment. We've had a wonderful weekend, and for the first time we've both said we love each other. We've used the actual word! Claire, if you are ready, I think we need to talk about getting married so that we can be together legally and in the eyes of God. We are not kids in our early 20s. Forget what some people may think; if we want this, then I think we need to decide to go ahead and plan to marry," he finished, still not confident that he'd said it the right way.

"I wasn't meaning to make fun of you acting properly," Claire said gently. "It's just that I've relaxed a little since I spoke those words when I got out of the car. I know that I need to lighten up and be patient because we're just weeks away from meeting again. We *do* need to talk, and I want to talk about marriage. Do you have a date in mind?" asked Claire.

Mark hesitated, "Well, this is something we need to decide together, but what if I said September?" He held his breath, waiting.

"September sounds perfect!" cried Claire. "Thank you, my darling. I love, love, love you. Now, we'd better get some sleep. I need to be at work early tomorrow to catch up after my days in Adelaide. Good night, my Prince Charming," said Claire as she put down the phone. She went to bed feeling more at ease than she had for several days. Mark smiled as the line clicked off. "Good night," he said softly.

The next few days saw March arrive, the first month of autumn and the month when Melbourne and much of Victoria had its most stable weather. Appropriately, the Moomba Festival was held in the second week of March. Its setting was the banks of the Yarra River and its most awaited event was the Moomba Parade on Labor Day. It was somewhat nostalgic for Mark to take Claire to the parade for he recalled the effort it took to have the Luther College band qualify as the only high school band in the state to be approved to participate in the parade. This time he was one of the million or more people who lined the streets to watch the parade.

They had agreed to enjoy being together as often as possible over the next couple of weeks without further discussion of marriage. They would save this until Mark's birthday in early April. Besides, Mark was absorbed with the DFSM presentation on the new directions for military music with the Australian Defence Force in Canberra in the middle of the month.

This was a vital meeting, although Mark only had to attend for the actual presentation. Several political leaders and Defence Force personnel spoke encouragingly to Mark and told him to be patient because the transition would be slower than he might want. Mark understood, but privately he suspected that public response would, in fact, speed up the call for change by politicians and military bureaucrats. The Commander of DFSM was in attendance for three days, and Mark was encouraged when he heard that the presentation was received with approval and that the videos made a strong impression on both the upper echelons of the Defence Force and the politicians.

By the end of April, DFSM had received its official mandate to modernize Australian military music, but there was no budget for vocal musical development, even though its value was recognized. DFSM was encouraged to promote this as a voluntary project, with another review in three years. This was acceptable to Mark who, as a realist, appreciated what DFSM had gained from the Canberra meetings. He told Claire that "you take what you get and press on!"

April 4, Mark's birthday, was on a Saturday in 1992. He was forty-two and feeling it as he told Claire when she called him early before he left for the studio to practice.

She talked softly to him over the phone and outlined the day's activities: "My love, I will come over at 8:00 am and we will play squash in the Barracks gym. I must continue to lose weight and besides, we both need to keep fit. Then, I am taking you to our favorite pastry shop where we'll have coffee and *one* pastry. Next, we shower and then go into the city where I want you to choose your gift from three which I have set aside. We will have lunch and walk along the Yarra—it's such a pretty day and then we'll come back to my place, chill for a few hours, and then I'm taking you to dinner in South Yarra."

Mark chuckled, surprised. "It sounds as though every hour is planned. I love it! I've never had a special birthday outside of my family. It sounds like it's going to be a lavish day with elegant company, splendid food and indulgent spoiling. I'm up for it, and I'm going to relish everything that happens today," responded Mark.

They went to the bakery in their sweat outfits and Claire ordered coffee and pastry. Before these arrived at their table she leaned forward and placed an envelope and a small gift in front of Mark. He kissed her and read the card first and then opened his gift. He threw back his head and laughed delightedly when he saw the Montblanc Royal Blue bottle of ink.

"You amaze me every day, Claire! Thank you so much. Can I assume my gift is this ink bottle?" he asked.

She smiled and shook her head. "This is the hardest thing for me, but I'm not going to say anymore. I want you to enjoy what I have planned for you," she replied.

"I understand. I can wait," said Mark.

As they left the pastry shop, Mark intended to follow Claire to her flat in Box Hill, thirty minutes away from the Barracks. When they got into her car, Claire said: "Mark, I suggest that we go back to the Barracks and you get your change of clothes for our trip into the city and lunch, and then a suit for our dinner tonight. Follow me to my flat and shower and dress at my place. It's silly to have you drive back and forth three times for the sake of convention." She added, teasingly, "I promise not to invade you while you are in the shower!"

"Never lose that wicked sense of humor," Mark said, kissing her. They drove the few blocks to the Barracks and Mark put his clothing and other necessary toiletries in his car. He followed Claire to Box Hill, and when they got to Claire's flat, a neighbor watched as Mark walked inside with his clothing.

Claire could see his discomfort and said: "Relax Mark, you're not doing anything wrong. She's a friend of sorts and knows we're dating. It's not going to ruin my reputation or yours."

Mark sighed contentedly. "You're so good for me," he said.

"You go ahead and have your shower," she said, smiling. "It's going to take me longer to get ready." When Mark was dressed, he sat at the kitchen table and hand-wrote two business letters he would later type up on the word processor. When Claire came into the kitchen, she stunned him yet again in a new pant suit: a cream short jacket and black pants with black patent shoes. Mark gasped and stood up. "Wow! Turn around so I can see you from all angles," he said, admiringly.

"I just hope that you're always as flattering to me as you are now," Claire said. "I just bought this yesterday and I am glad you like it. It's getting cooler and I'm going to be wearing a lot of these in the next few months."

Mark got himself a drink of water before they left the flat, and as they walked to his car the neighbor came out again. "Pleasant day, isn't it?" Mark called out to her as he held the door open for Claire. When he got in the car, Claire looked at him fondly as if to suggest, that's more like it! They drove to the city and after parking in the Southern

Cross parking garage, they walked to a specialty pen shop on Collins Street. As they leaned on the counter, Claire said, "I've picked out three different pens and you can choose the one you like the most."

Mark looked at each one, turning them over in his hands. "Claire darling, I like them all, but the one I like the most is also the most expensive. If I get it, let me help pay for it," he said, straightening. "This is a Montblanc *Meisterstuck* 149! It's got gold trim."

"You are the love of my life, Mark. I know we have been together only a few months, but it feels like years to me. There will never be anyone else but you. Besides, I am a working girl who makes good money, and I can afford this!" She tilted her chin. "Or don't you believe me?"

"Hmmm, never known anyone like you, Claire. Thank you so much. I promise I'll keep it forever and it will never leave my study. When I get a study, that is?" said Mark with a smile.

Ten minutes later they were walking towards a French Patisserie and Claire was busy explaining how it was different to the bakery where they had their pastry and coffee after their workout. She said that she liked the soups, several of the quiche, and there were about three salad choices that went well with various savory pies. Mark was enthralled by Claire's sheer delight in unfolding his birthday, moment by moment. She was alive, chirpy and such a warm human being that he couldn't help but adore her. Their lunch conversation was filled with the small talk of two people obviously smitten with each other, and the food was as good as Claire said it would be. When they emerged from the restaurant and looked at their watches, it was after 2:00 pm. Did they have time to walk along the Yarra? Claire said she had booked dinner for 6:30 pm and they had to drive back to Box Hill and change clothing and then return to the city again. Mark suggested that they not go back to Box Hill but sit in the car for a while and talk. He told Claire that she looked wonderful and was already suitably dressed for dinner, unless she had planned a dinner with the governor. He said that he was the one without a tie. Did he need one? What did she think?

They opted for a walk along the Yarra with all the fall leaves creating a romantic atmosphere. "You couldn't do better than this even in

Paris or Annapolis," added Mark. "Let's go back to the car and talk about our future," he said, squeezing Claire's hand.

"I am having the best birthday!" he remarked as they walked back. "By the way, I thought you may like to see my cards from the family: one from Mum, one from Gary and Helen, and two from my sisters. There's also one from Aunty Ruth—she never fails to send a card ever since I can remember, but I didn't bring that one since you haven't met her yet," said Mark. He handed the cards to Claire.

"Your family is something else. You mean they never fail to send cards for birthdays. What about Christmas?" asked Claire.

"That too," responded Mark.

"Before we talk, I want to look again at my Montblanc fountain pen. I've always wanted one. The Visconti and the Parker are wonderful pens, but the Montblanc *Meisterstuck* is the envy of all. I do have a Parker Duofold Centennial. I actually like anything to do with writing; fine stationery goes with fine pens," said Mark, aware that he was rambling, but Claire was still reading the cards.

"I see I will need to keep a birthday list and send cards religiously to family," responded Claire. "Actually, it will be good for me, us, to let family know that we are thinking of them. I like that custom a lot."

"Just love this fountain pen," said Mark as Claire was now with him again after reading the cards intently. As he looked at her, he began to untangle his thoughts: "Okay, darling girl, I've been thinking about our future. We've called it correctly; we're not kids, we're adults. I knew you were the girl I'd been searching for after the band playout over Christmas, and when I took you to the farm and I saw how my family responded to you, that was confirmed even more. You said you felt the same about me."

"So, I think we should consider getting married in mid-September, or certainly sometime in September. I'd like it to be St. Michael's in Hahndorf, but that is more your decision than mine. I want us to begin looking for a home over the winter months, perhaps in the Doncaster East area."

He paused and took a breath. "We have to think through your daily commute too. I would like to settle on a house no later than October. I am thinking that we will go home to the farm for Christmas and we can spend time with both families. I will work with Gary on leaving the Monaro with him and buying a new car for us. That's what I've been thinking."

He looked at her and added: "Incidentally, this is not a marriage proposal. That is for another occasion in the right setting."

"Well! You've covered a lot," said Claire. "I like what you're saying and I'm so glad that we're serious about spending the rest of our lives together." She looked down at her hands. "I like the house idea, too. It will mean we'll need to live in my flat for a month or two, right? And I'd love to be married in St. Michael's. Oh, and what about our honeymoon," she asked brightly.

"Thought about that too," said Mark, "but I figured you need to dream a little on this one. I have backed away from the big honeymoon and have a very pragmatic suggestion, but I would like to listen to your thoughts first," said Mark.

"No, please tell me your practical thoughts," asked Claire.

"Well, I thought of Hawaii, but then came back to a less expensive honeymoon in Adelaide. We could go to the Stamford at Glenelg for a week or so, and just take day trips. We could go to the Barossa, over to Yorke Peninsula, even two days on Kangaroo Island and to Victor Harbor. I scaled back my thinking because we are going to need to furnish a house and while we don't need everything at once, we are going to need a fair amount of basic furniture, and I want it to be quality furniture; nothing but the best for my girl! Then, I thought about going to Hawaii for our first anniversary, or somewhere else, maybe Hong Kong," explained Mark.

"Again, I like it all, Mark. Your thinking is practical, and it is how I want to live. I have one big question for you: what about children?" questioned Claire.

"Yeah, we haven't even mentioned that topic. It has entered my thinking a few times, but I wonder if I am not too old. And, how will you feel having a baby in your late thirties? Sorry if I am being blunt here," Mark blurted.

"Well, I have thought about it," replied Claire. "If possible, I would like to have one child. I think it will add so much more to our marriage. I agree that we are getting older and we would need to act on this sooner than later. Fortunately, for me I can work from home as an accountant and even part-time work will help us."

"I need to tell you something," Mark said anxiously. "My prostate surgery means that I can no longer father children. That's clear. But my surgeon wrote to me, out of the blue, after I returned to Annapolis before my graduation and the road trip. He knew I was young and may still marry and want children in the future. He suggested I freeze sperm at a sperm bank. Initially, I thought 'I can't do this,' but when I came back to Adelaide last June, I did freeze sperm before my surgery."

"My word," gasped Claire, "that was good of him."

"I agree now," replied Mark, "But at the time, I found it all off-putting."

"I know it's a lot to think about. It's all good and we can tackle all these factors one at a time," added Mark.

"It doesn't make you want to hold off, does it?" asked Claire.

"Not at all," asserted Mark. "But, to be honest, I have been so caught up in the romance of us, I did not think about children. I don't think there is a problem, but I need to confirm this from a good doctor; one that I like and can trust," explained Mark.

"Tell me about your prostate surgery. Where did it come from? Why so young? How did you cope with it all? I think you are going to be fine. It makes no difference to me, and won't alter my love for you," declared Claire.

"I know that, but it does make a difference to me. To suddenly think of being sexually active, and after prostate surgery, has brought me up short. I am alright, but I do need to seek medical confirmation. I have no clue where it all came from. There is really no cancer in the family. Dad died of a heart attack and not cancer," admitted Mark.

"Let's go for another short walk and then it will be time to go to South Yarra. I think we need some fresh air running through our heads," suggested Mark.

They got out of the car and walked hand in hand in the opposite direction from before, but still along the banks of the Yarra. They said little to each other for fifteen minutes but the emotion coming from their hands gave clear signals that they were bonded together forever.

Dinner was an exquisite meal in a trendy Italian restaurant in South Yarra. The restaurant ambiance was a unique combination of alluring charm and sublime efficiency. Their waiter symbolized both as he exhibited great proficiency with an affable manner. Mark's main course was *Salmon alla Griglia* and Claire ordered *Chicken Piccata Pasta*. Claire toasted Mark as her *Prince Charming* and Mark responded in kind by toasting Claire as *the girl he always hoped was out there!* It was an evening neither wanted to end and it gave them a momentary escape from the decision-making and weighty outcomes which lay ahead.

As Mark walked Claire to her door, he asked her if she would come with him the next day on another date, this time at his behest. She looked at him and replied with mild concern:

"Why, of course, Mark. Is anything wrong?"

"Nothing at all wrong. To the contrary, everything is so right. There is one more matter I need to ask you about. I want to take you to the Cuckoo for afternoon tea tomorrow. Can you be ready by 2:00 pm?" asked Mark.

"Oh, I love the Cuckoo! It has so much atmosphere. I've only been there twice. Yes, I will be ready at 2:00 pm," replied Claire.

Mark remembered his shaving gear and his clothing still in Claire's flat. They walked into her lounge room and Mark was about to pick up his gear when he put both arms around Claire instead and kissed her. Then he hugged her tightly and whispered, "I have had one of the best days of my life and it is all because of you. Thank you for arranging everything so carefully. Thank you for my fountain pen and for a delicious dinner. I love you forever."

With his gear in hand, he walked to his car and drove back to the Barracks. Inside his flat, he couldn't help but sit at his desk and look again fondly at his new fountain pen. He felt like a real collector now with five pens. Clearly, the Montblanc was head and shoulders above the others. His everyday fountain pen was a Waterman. Cheap next to the German pen, but it wrote well and felt comfortable in Mark's hand. Should he ever lose it, the world would still turn; it would be no catastrophic event. On the other hand, he would never forgive himself if he was to misplace Claire's fountain pen. He wiped it with the soft cloth one last time before returning it to its stylish case. He would fill it with ink tomorrow and write Claire a letter. It was time for sleep.

After his euphonium practice, he went for a jog around the Barracks. He had indulged yesterday, and here he was taking the two of them, the very next day, to one of the most sumptuous restaurants in the wider Melbourne area. He had his reasons though, and it had to do with the fact that the following week he was going to be in Brisbane for a conducting assignment. He was pleased that Claire did not quibble about going. He placed her gift, of sorts, to the right of his desk and then settled down to some editing of his doctoral thesis for a book format. He had a firm offer to publish his book in fifteen months, in time for the following year's Christmas trade. He had a good deal of work ahead of him, but he was under the guidance of a professional editor, something he was grateful for. Before showering, he filled his new fountain pen with ink and wrote Claire a hand-written letter.

When he arrived at Claire's flat, her neighbor was driving out of her carport. She waved at Mark and he smiled and waved back. Claire was waiting at the door and asked Mark to come in.

"Just checking," she said with a laugh. "I like coordination. I think we're a neat looking couple and I'd hate to be wearing sneakers when you're wearing dress shoes and a tie. You'll get used to me!" she said, with a twinkle in her eye.

"Yes, but I also know that you mean business," said Mark. "I promise never to wear a tie when you are wearing sneakers!" As they settled into Mark's car, he turned to her and said, "Claire, I know I haven't told you much about this outing, but I guarantee you will fully understand before you come back to your flat tonight. We ate a lot yesterday, so I thought afternoon tea would be better than a full meal. You'll enjoy what is ahead," he said as he backed out of the driveway.

When they reached the Cuckoo, it was part way through the afternoon tea schedule, and it took a few minutes to find parking. As they walked inside, they both looked at each other and smiled at the jovial and vibrant atmosphere. There was activity everywhere. Mark had not been inside since the days he was at Luther College. They were seated at a table for two near a window where they could look out on the trees and lawns below them.

An afternoon tea menu was given to each of them and Claire lost no time in saying: "I think your idea of having less food to tempt us has been shattered. Look at all the choices we have. Frankly, it looks terrific because I am more of a savory food person than sweets. I think you are too. Ah, Mark, I am so glad you brought me here. What a happy place this is!"

Even though they were given a menu, it was a buffet afternoon tea. Only the tea and coffee were brought to the table. Mark and Claire walked around the food stalls and then took their plates and served themselves. When they returned to their table, Mark laughingly said, "I don't normally like buffets. Too much food and I always take more than I need." Claire agreed, but nevertheless, they did enjoy the food. They laughed and sang along with the entertainment, and then got themselves coffee and dessert. As the dinner segment was about to begin, around 5:30 pm, they left and drove for only a minute when Mark turned off the main mountain road and onto a narrow two-lane asphalt track ascending upwards with tall trees on either side.

"I want to show you something," he said as they emerged onto a hilltop with a restaurant. Off to one side was a parking lot and viewing platforms.

"This is called SkyHigh and it's the highest point of the Dandenongs," he said as they parked. Through the windows the restaurant looked full, but the viewing platforms only had a few couples. Mark reached into the back seat and took out a travel blanket and wrapped it around Claire. The temperature was falling, and the sun had almost set on the horizon beyond the tall buildings of Melbourne far in the distance. Claire had not been here before, and she stood gazing at the panoramic view extending across Port Philip Bay and beyond. The city lights were not as close as those of Adelaide at Windy Point, but they could still be seen twinkling in their remoteness. Mark hugged her to him, and she snuggled against his chest as they enjoyed the marvelous vista before them.

After a few minutes Mark broke the easy silence between them and said: "Yesterday we talked about our future and we covered a lot of ground. Tonight, there is something else. Claire, I cannot believe how quickly I have fallen in love with you. You are the first person I think of in the morning and the last person I think of at night. I want to be with you for the rest of our lives."

"Claire, I am asking you to marry me."

Claire turned and looked up into his face.

"This is it, isn't it, Mark? Yes! Yes, of course, I will marry you." She straightened and took his hands. "I've loved you forever and I will marry you even if we have to live in a tent for the rest of our lives!"

Then they kissed slowly and lovingly, like they never had before. Claire clung to him and hid her face in his shoulder. He could feel her shaking and crying. "Heh," he said tenderly, but she would not look up and held him even tighter. Mark knew she had to do this, and he was thankful for how sensitive she was. Finally, she reached into his pocket for a handkerchief and dabbed at her eyes. "I'm sorry," she said, smiling through her tears. "It's just that . . ." her voice trailed off. "It's just that I'm so happy!" "I know," said Mark gently.

He kissed her again and then he reached into his other pocket and took out a small package and said: "Claire darling, here is a gift. Go ahead, open it and then I'll explain. It's not an engagement ring. That's coming later this week, when we choose it together."

"Mark, I don't understand," Claire said, confused.

"I know, I'm going too fast. Well, just open it and I'll explain," requested Mark.

"It's an engagement ring. Mark, it's beautiful!" She held it up to the fading light of the vanishing day.

"No, Claire, it is a small pink sapphire and diamond ring to give you tonight. I think it's pretty too, but I wanted you to have it, so you'd remember this evening," he said smiling.

"Later this week, perhaps Thursday evening, or Friday, or Saturday morning, we're going to a jeweler near the Town Hall, and you're going to choose your engagement ring. I didn't want to do this alone, but I know I want it to be a big, beautiful diamond that tells the whole world you are my betrothed." She was silent, looking up at him and smiling.

"You know that I am going to Brisbane the week after and so I wanted us to choose your ring this coming week," he added awkwardly.

"Mark, we're engaged! Can you believe it? Please put this ring on my engagement finger," Claire asked.

"Yes, we are engaged. I am going to remember this date as 4592; April 5, 1992," he finished.

They returned to the car and drove back to Claire's flat. Mark gave her the letter and told her it was written with his birthday fountain pen. At her door, they embraced for a long time. When Claire stepped back, she said: "I feel so happy. See, after all this time, I'm not too young for you anymore." She smiled up at him, so trusting.

Her words stung Mark a little, as he realized how much he must have hurt her, a young teenager, all those years ago.

"I'm so sorry I ever said those words, Claire," he said. He cupped her chin and looked down at her. "It was cruel and thoughtless of me."

"Not to worry!" she said, brightly. "I must stop saying it. It's just that I can't believe that we are engaged. I'm going to marry my first love. I'm so happy," exclaimed Claire.

"And I'm going to marry the girl who has taught me so quickly the meaning of real love. This 'fella from Hahndorf has finally found peace and happiness." He swallowed hard.

On Thursday evening, after work, they visited the jewelers. Mark nudged Claire to make it as soon as possible because he said he wanted to see the real engagement ring on her finger *yesterday!*

When they walked into the jewelers the lady who had assisted Mark before exclaimed, "Oh, she's even more beautiful than you described, Mark! Pleased to meet you, my dear. You have a man who loves you dearly and who knows what he likes. However, he has told me that it is your choice which finally counts, so let me show you a selection of engagement rings which I think will interest you."

Twenty minutes passed before they had narrowed the choice to five possible rings. Between them, they had decided that *their* ring must be elegant, dainty, peerless, flawless—and Mark added that he wanted the ring to sparkle and dazzle. Two rings were exquisite, but both were expensive.

Claire tried to resist, but Mark urged her: "Which one do you like the best? Forget the price. I want to buy you the ring you really want."

"Mark, I can't help it. I just worry about the money," protested Claire.

"Don't you worry about that," he exclaimed and took both her hands in his. "This is our engagement and I know the ring I want you to have. It is the most expensive. I am never going to get engaged again. And, I am not trying to be a big spender to impress you. Claire, I have waited my entire life for you, and I want a ring that is going to sparkle and, forgive me, tell the world that you are my girl."

Claire paused and looked intently into Mark's eyes. She shook her head gently and sighed: "This is the one I love the best, but still . . ." She stopped and looked away, smiling.

"Right, that's it," said Mark decisively. He motioned to the assistant. "We'll take this one, the hexagon diamond with the white gold setting."

"Go ahead and do all the packaging, but Claire would like to wear the ring now," he said as she reached up, grabbed him by the lapels and pulled him towards her for a quick kiss.

The ring *was* stunningly beautiful. Claire kept examining it, turning it this way and that in the light as they ate at the French restaurant nearby. "I think I may just wear it to bed every night," she said as they drove up to her flat.

Mark's family was euphoric with the news of the engagement. Immediately Claire, Betty and Helen went into wedding planning mode and bonded as a *dream team.* The telephone bills in both homes were deemed a necessary expense over the winter months as planning the wedding became the extra exigency in Claire's life. It kept her more than busy during the times Mark traveled interstate between June and August. However, it was not the actual wedding organization that absorbed the majority of Claire's free time. She and her dream team had all that under control in no time. For Claire, her time alone during these colder moths while Mark was not in Melbourne was her opportunity to dwell on the more personal, reflective and spiritual aspects of preparing for her marriage. She knew she was marrying a romantic, a wonderfully talented man who was intense yet sensitive, playful but serious, and devoted to his God, his family, and now to her. Claire spent her evenings alone reading some of the books she had borrowed from Mark's bookcase and listening to his music and his religious CDs. She was discovering new insights about her inner self. Altogether, these snippets of spare time only confirmed her love for, and commitment to, the man she was going to marry in the spring.

On most weekends, Mark and Claire spent time searching for a suitable home in Doncaster East. After two months of looking, they found a home only two years old belonging to an oil executive who was being relocated. It had all they desired. They began proceedings to purchase and to settle in early October. It was ideal timing and harmonized with the timeframe of their wedding, honeymoon and relocation plans.

Life has a way of compounding people and their work at the oddest of moments. Here were Mark and Claire entranced over the winter months with their engagement, and soon coming marriage. At the very same time, Mark's role in promoting the modernizing of military music was gathering momentum, and one of his Navy superiors told him to assume the guise of "a disruptive innovator; we need you to disrupt our way of doing music in the military!" This was official validation for what Mark had already incited.

It was apparent to all at DFSM that Mark was consolidating himself as the right person in the right place at the right time and rapidly becoming the face of military music innovation. It was not so much his genius alone, but that he was considered its impetus, or as one of his colleagues said at Mark's official retirement dinner years later, "Commander Schubert became the *spark plug* for military music change." The transition did not occur in a vacuum and it occupied almost two decades of Mark's remaining service in the Navy. For Mark, it was his career's work and, with Claire by his side, his quest was satisfying and consequential. Such were the work-related events in the winter before their wedding.

September came around more quickly than they had thought possible. On the last Monday of August, they drove to the farm at Hahndorf to savor four full days away from work before the wedding on Saturday afternoon. It was an untroubled four days, even though there was much to do, especially in the finishing touches. Mark helped Gary on the farm and was content to leave the wedding preparations to the women. He told Gary that he just wanted to be officially married to Claire. The night before the wedding, Mark and Claire went for a walk on the farm over towards the pine trees. Mark asked Claire how she was feeling.

"Calm and happy," she responded cheerfully. "You have such an amazing family. All of you have the uncanny ability to keep drama and stress out of most everything you do. When I look to my family and think back to my first wedding, which I don't want to do, and then Julie's, there was drama, tension, tempers flaring right up until the church service. I asked myself, how is it possible to avoid all this chaos? Having been part of your family now for almost nine months, I think I do know how. Your family has a level of love, respect, and trust toward each other that seems to take away the need for chaos."

"Hmmm, that's quite a vote of confidence in the Schubert clan. Thank you for that," replied Mark. "You know, I just don't recall there being much anger and turmoil in our family at all. I think a lot of praise is due to Dad here. I know he dealt with conflict between his father and himself. I think this made him determined to work hard to keep harmony in his own family. Mum and Dad were great listeners and we spent some of our best times talking over everything about life around the kitchen table. We also walked a lot and as kids were encouraged to talk about everything."

"We must do the same in our family," said Claire, putting her arm around Mark as they navigated a gate into another paddock.

"I agree," said Mark, rather distractedly.

"How are *you* feeling the eve before you give up your independence?" asked Claire.

"Oh, really intimidated by it all!" he replied, picking up on Claire's sarcasm.

He sighed. "Honestly, this is what I am feeling just now. I wish you and I could sneak back to the garage, quietly roll the car down the driveway and head off to the Stamford Hotel declaring us married. I'd like to skip all the formal stuff!"

"Mark Schubert, I can't believe you just said that. What about propriety, convention and following the rules?" taunted Claire, with mock surprise.

"Well, you *did* ask me what I was feeling," joked Mark.

"Here's a better answer perhaps: I feel weary from being alone for so long, I can hardly believe that this time tomorrow we will be husband and wife. Yet, I also find myself … what's the best word … bewildered, astonished, shocked that I have found you as the perfect fit for me in every way. 'Grateful' is another key word. I am grateful to God, to you for saying *hello* that day at the band playout. I am also feeling happy and carefree," said Mark as he took Claire's hand and they ran towards the next farm gate.

"Yes, I certainly understand weary and alone. I never thought I would find another person I could love; yet I loved you before you took me back to Julie's on that first night," said Claire, as they closed the gate behind them.

Night was fast approaching as they made their way back to the house. Inside, Gary, Helen and Betty could see their flushed faces from the cool of the evening and sensed their impatience for tomorrow to be over.

"I've been anticipating hearing the Monaro driving out of the farm and heading down to Glenelg to escape all the formalities of tomorrow," said Gary with a chuckle.

"Oh, Gary, don't say that. Who would want to skip out on Mark and Claire's wedding? We have waited for this wedding day for so long. I can't wait to see the floral arrangements and to watch this gorgeous couple taking their vows together. It is going to be the best of days," declared Betty.

Claire looked at Mark and they both laughed. "We'd already thought of that, Gary," said Mark. "I had to talk him out of it," Claire chimed in. Gary looked smug and said, "Do I know my brother or what!" "Who wants Milo?" he said, getting up. "I'm making." All hands shot up and the whole family, including the children, shared a hot drink and some plain Arrowroot biscuits before bed time.

The wedding day began for Mark with milking. After breakfast he was ushered out of the main house to the old house where he was to dress for the wedding and then leave without seeing Claire until she arrived at the altar. In the afternoon, Mark made sure that their honeymoon cases were in the car, and then he and Gary drove to the church in the Monaro, which had been cleaned, detailed, and waxed. When they reached St. Michael's Gary told Mark he had a surprise for him. They walked into the church and there stood the Annapolis St. Paul's Lutheran pastor and his wife, John and Shirley Schulz. It was Mark who shed tears this time as he hugged his dear friends and spiritual succors from his Naval Academy and doctoral study days in America.

"How did you pull this one off, and not say anything?" said Mark, shaking his head as he looked back and forth from Gary to Shirley and to John.

"The idea came to me that weekend you and Claire came over for the workshop and concert in the Adelaide Town Hall," explained Gary. "The next week, I received a very good check for the lavender sales, and I thought I would at least explore the possibility of bringing John and Shirley out for the wedding. Of course, at that time, you hadn't announced your engagement, so I was thinking of sometime in the future. But suddenly, the future came sooner than I expected, but we made it happen!"

The discussions and meetings Mark and Claire had had with the resident Lutheran pastor, mostly over the telephone, were divergences for the real officiating minister, although the St. Michael's pastor needed to play a role as Pastor Schulz was not legally registered in South Australia.

"Does Claire know about this?" asked Mark. Gary shook his head. "She'll find out as she leaves the house." Mark looked at his brother and said:

"Aren't you the devious one!"

Claire arrived five minutes late, as was suitably appropriate for a bride to her wedding. Grant, as her brother-in-law, acted in place of her father, and Julie was her maid of honor. Claire did not wish to wear a traditional bridal gown, but instead chose a cream suit and netted head piece with Mark complementing her in a black tuxedo. As Claire walked down the aisle, a trumpet trio from the Hahndorf Town Band played in harmony with the organ. She joined Mark arm in arm, looked at him, then at Pastor Schulz, and then at Gary, and shook her head several times. Then, they all laughed as Pastor Schulz told the wedding guests, in his American accent, of how the bride and groom had only now learned that he would be officiating for most of the ceremony. He told of the clandestine ruse with such good cheer, clearly labelling Gary as the chief conspirator, that the guests burst into applause and Gary turned to face them and took a bow.

The service was beautiful in its setting, in its words, in the music and in the church of Mark's family since its inception. As they uttered their vows to each other, to friends and family and before their God, Mark took a moment to look at the beautiful woman who was declaring her love for him. He felt humbled and inadequate by the sheer joy Claire had brought into his life. He was jolted back into the present when Pastor Schulz called for the wedding rings. He put his ring on

Claire's finger and she placed her ring on his. Then, they were pronounced husband and wife. As they kissed each other with the guests watching, Claire held Mark, and try as she might, she could not stop the tears. He whispered for her to take her time. It was made easier because the guests broke into applause as Pastor Schulz introduced them as Dr. and Mrs. Mark Schubert. This was enough time for Claire to regain her composure and they both stepped off the platform, kissed once again, and walked down the aisle of the church with well-wishers reaching out their hands as they passed.

The wedding reception was a jubilant occasion at the Hahndorf Old Mill and the mood was maintained by the lively waiters and waitresses dressed in traditional German folk costume. It was not a large wedding, but those in attendance were long standing family and friends and fully supportive of Mark and Claire. There was plenty of time for conversation and canapes. Mark and Claire spent a good while catching up with Pastor John and Shirley Schulz. Mark said that he was flabbergasted when he saw John standing in the church. Gary had brought the Schulzs out and was going to take them on day trips to various places during the next week. Then, the Schulzs would take a few days in Melbourne and Sydney before returning to Annapolis. Again, they all shook their heads at Gary's generosity and planning. Mark spoke with Gary and coordinated Wednesday as the day they would all go to Victor Harbor together.

It was as husband and wife that Mark and Claire drove away from the reception to the Stamford Hotel on the foreshore of Glenelg. When they walked into their hotel room, they looked at each other, hugged and Claire exclaimed, "We've done it!" They laughed, showered and got ready for bed. Standing in their pajamas, they prayed together for the first time as a married couple. Then Mark knelt by his suitcase and drew out a toy trumpet.

"Before you think your new husband has lost his mind, let me say that one of my father's favorite movies was *It Happened One Night* with Clark Gable and Claudette Colbert." He got to his feet and stood in front of Claire, his eyes dancing. "The movie plot has them falling in love on a bus trip from Miami to New York. She was a rich society girl and he was a struggling journalist. There are many obstacles and they end up in a rough motel where Gable puts up a blanket between them because they're sleeping in single beds in the same room. He called the blanket the Walls of Jericho because this was the 1930s and propriety must be maintained at all costs." Claire was giggling, but Mark went on. "Later, they do marry, and they return to the same scrappy motel. This time they are husband and wife. But before they get into bed together, Gable blows his toy trumpet like Joshua did and the Walls of Jericho come tumbling down." With that, Mark blew a blast on the trumpet and turned out the light.

"Come 'ere, Joshua!" purred Claire, and pulled him into bed.

EPILOGUE

S hould this be a story from Romantic literature, it might end with some reference about Mark and Claire living happily ever after. Or, if from the Western genre, about the couple riding off into the sunset. This story is neither of those. It is, nonetheless, fiction, although based on aspects of the lives of real people, baby boomers who, trying to find their place in a complex and complicated world, are now confronting retirement and early old age in Australia and the United States. Within that timeframe of seventy years, the two nations featured in the story have experienced unprecedented change in their societal structure. What was socially acceptable by way of customs, norms and attitudes in the 1950s had changed in the 1990s and, again, in 2019. Religious practice, especially Lutheranism in Hahndorf, was still vibrant in Mark's formative years, whereas it matters less today, unless you come from a family aligned to an effective congregation where the church is intent on serving the spiritual needs of its parishioners. St. Michael's (and St. Paul's) still serves families who value the inculcation of the Gospel message into fostering lives of practical Godliness. Some of these church communicants originate from the actual *Old Lutheran* families who founded Hahndorf in 1839.

Hahndorf remains recognizable from the 1950s, although it is no longer the original, quiet, merchandising German hamlet it had been for over a century (1839 to the 1950s). During this period, the town and its agricultural hinterland had been cloistered away from most of the intrusions of the modern era. Its German customs and Old Lutheran religion had shaped the Hahndorf community in its lifestyle, its industry, its agriculture, its food and its buildings. A record of this unique community was captured in art form (to a greater degree than any other community in all of Australia) by the artistry of Sir Hans Heysen (1877 to 1968).

By the early 1970s, those very characteristics which separated Hahndorf from other communities now became the essence of what attracted tourism to its main street. Gradually, and then with a rush, Hahndorf was invaded by business people from Adelaide (and interstate) buying up century-old homes along main street and turning them into commercial enterprises selling goods and wares faintly related to the German town's historic past. It was the parents of the Baby Boomers, along with the boomers themselves, who sold these homes; many needing costly repairs of plumbing, electrical and roofing to meet the standards of modern living. Even then, most were too small and ceilings too low to remain commodious. Places of business, like Smith's bakery on the corner of Balhannah Road and main street, no longer bake bread in the early morning hours, but sell all manner of items, none of which are related to bread, pastries and small goods. One building selling ice cream today once housed the town's bootmaker, a kindly man by the name of Hill. Perhaps the one unchanging aspect of Hahndorf life over much of this period has been the Hahndorf Town Band. Founded in the 1920s, it has been an immutable presence ever since. When the South Eastern Freeway was announced in the early 1970s, the old rotunda land on Pine Avenue was taken over by the Highways Department and a new practice facility was built largely by volunteer labor on Balhannah Road. Appropriately, in May 2018, the new rotunda in the Pioneer Memorial Gardens was named the L. W. E. Kramm Memorial Rotunda in honor of the founder and benefactor of the Hahndorf Town Band. Mr. Kramm was Gordon Kramm's father and his grandson, Greg, is trombonist and president of the band. Greg's mother, Kathy Francis [nee: Kramm], is its faithful secretary, and Gordon and Kathy are brother and sister.

The writer is one of these baby boomers and remains a close friend of the Francis/Kramm family. He was born in Adelaide, but his parents moved to a farm off Balhannah Road in 1948, and Hahndorf became home and nurturing community for the next 20 years. He is not of German heritage, not Lutheran and he did not play with the Hahndorf band, but with one in Adelaide. In 1968, he left Hahndorf and travelled interstate to a church-related college near Newcastle, New South Wales, where he played under his old Adelaide bandmaster in the community brass band in a small rural town with many similarities to his home town. Several years later, he became a high school teacher at a boarding school in the Melbourne eastern suburbs, and later its principal and business manager. During this time, he played in a church-related brass band based in Nunawading and expanded the fledgling school band from a junior brass band into a junior concert and marching band. It was the writer who obtained permission for this high school band to march in the Moomba Parade and ANZAC parades too. On several occasions he interacted with Luther College.

Later, he travelled to Maryland and completed his doctorate at the University of Maryland College Park. He visited the United States Naval Academy many times and endeavored to be on campus whenever the Naval Band, or segments of it, was performing. He returned to Australia as a higher education administrator in late 1989 and played again in a community brass band. A few years later, he was back in Maryland as academic administrator of a church-related liberal arts college and he enjoyed playing in the college concert band.

A divorce ensued, and he experienced first-hand the fragmentation of lives which occurs when a family breaks up. Curiously, departing from higher education while he sorted out his life, he worked in Annapolis for nearly two years with an office in Eastport looking back at Old Town Annapolis and the Naval Academy. Fortunately for the writer, he found love again, remarried, and has now lived in the U.S. for almost thirty years. After six years as an international higher education administrator at a university in south-west Michigan, he has recently retired and relocated to Charlotte, North Carolina where he has joined a lower brass group for older musicians. A few years ago, the writer's wife bought him a Besson BE 967 Sovereign Series Silver

Compensating Euphonium. It is his pride and joy. The writer still calls Hahndorf home and returns as often as money permits.

Even so, the story has not concluded.

The end of the story ...

Mark and Claire's honeymoon was an enraptured time, but it was over too soon. After ten days, they drove back to Melbourne and stayed in Claire's flat until settlement on their first home in Doncaster East in early October. Mark and Claire settled happily into married life and completed furnishing their home within a year. It became their castle. They both showed a flair for gardening and rearranging the landscaping to suit their tastes, and soon planted a small vegetable garden, with radishes as their first harvest.

Claire became pregnant with twins and gave birth to a boy—**Glenn Oliver**—and a girl—**Emma Rose**—in late November of the next year. The twins added to Mark and Claire's happiness. Both children were introduced to music early. They were tutored in the Suzuki method and piano became their first instrument. At least once a year, the family traveled to the farm and the children developed a love and appreciation for rural life, Hahndorf, the Adelaide Hills, and visits to Glenelg and Brighton beaches. Melbourne was home during their childhood and adolescent years. Schooling was at Luther College. Mark and Claire invested heavily in providing a loving and supportive home for their children. The evening meal around the family table became a valued time together with open and honest conversation.

Betty came to Melbourne as often as she could in the twins' early years to spend as much time as possible with her grandchildren. She lived to see them both earn their drivers' licenses. Betty remained a gracious, dignified and active woman until her last days. She died in her 88th year.

Glenn Oliver did not take to brass, but gravitated to his father's tenor saxophone and, after the piano, this became his second instrument. As Glenn Oliver entered his teen years, it became clear to Mark and Gary that there was another farmer emerging within the family. After completing high school, Glenn Oliver decided to work with

Gary on the farm. He studied agriculture at University of Adelaide and completed his AMusA diploma in piano in his first year of university. Jazz was his avocational preference and he doubled on piano and saxophone at some of the best clubs and restaurants in Adelaide.

Emma Rose excelled at piano and transitioned to organ in early high school. Never as intense as her father with music, she, even so, pursued her organ lessons with deliberation, especially classical organ. After high school, and as her parents relocated to the Adelaide Hills, she enrolled at the Elder Conservatorium of Music at the University of Adelaide. Similarly, she completed her AMusA at the same time as her brother. Before long, Emma Rose was sought after as an organist in Adelaide churches. Always her father's daughter, she ventured to the Peabody Music Conservatory at Johns Hopkins University and earned her Master of Music degree in organ literature and church music. It was her privilege to play on the 3,000 pipe Holtkamp organ in the conservatory's historic Griswold Hall.

Gary's and Helen's son became an accountant and, later, a very successful financial advisor in Adelaide. While he had no agricultural interest in the farm, he did become the Schubert farm financial advisor with Claire doing the accounting.

Gary's and Helen's daughter did study music at California Lutheran University. She took a double concentration in Musical Theatre and Performance. She joined two ensembles; the Cal Lutheran Choir and the Women's Chorale. Continuing graduate study in the U.S., she earned her Master of Music and Doctor of Musical Arts in Voice at the University of California Santa Barbara. She married a choral conductor and established her home in southern California.

Luke became a band boy and continued with his piano lessons as well. He played cornet for two years and then switched to percussion. There was little challenge for a percussionist in the Hahndorf Town Band. By good luck, he took drum kit lessons from a new resident of Mount Barker and became adept as a drummer in rock 'n roll groups by the time he was twenty. As he matured, he transitioned to jazz and, later, Luke and Glenn Oliver played jazz together in Adelaide clubs and restaurants.

Mark's career with the Royal Australian Navy continued for another 22 years. He was promoted to Commander and assumed leadership of the Defence Force Music School for his last ten years of service. He was a gregarious and methodical leader, and confidence in military music went from strength to strength during his term of administration. He did not retire from the Navy until the transition of traditional music to a broad offering of music was evident in all branches of the Defence Force. Vocal groups were gradually funded as a second instrument and the entertainment value of military music was appreciated among all sections of the Australian public. Mark continued to have a social media profile and authored four more books and numerous articles on the benefits of music for individuals and the wider community. He was a frequent spokesperson for community events and radio and television programs. Upon Mark's retirement from the RAN, Mark and Claire (and Emma Rose) decided to return to the Adelaide Hills, not only to be with Glenn Oliver, but also their wider families. As Mark often said, "The older I get, the more my heart turns toward home!"

Mark and Claire returned to Hahndorf for their retirement years. It was time to let go of the vicissitudes of the working life. Rather than building a home on the farm, they chose to build in a new sub-division off Balhannah Road and, fortuitously, their patio faced directly westwards towards Mount Lofty. They both helped on the farm, Mark more so. Mark played euphonium and bass trombone for the Hahndorf Town Band, although he declined requests to be conductor. However, he did agree to tutor the band to greater excellence. The band responded, worked hard and became a B grade band in three years. Surprisingly to many, Mark fostered an interest in English choral music in his last years in Melbourne. Once established in retirement at Hahndorf, and through Emma Rose's organ interests, he renewed his earlier contacts at St. Peter's Cathedral and became choral director for some seven years. The choir was much in demand for high church calendar festivals and government events.

Gary's health was becoming an issue and he suffered a heart attack in the first year Mark and Claire returned to Hahndorf. Gary offered his nephew, Glenn Oliver, the opportunity to take over the family farm, with both Gary and Mark there to support him in his first few years of farm management. After retiring, Gary and Helen relocated to the same subdivision as Mark and Claire, with their new home a mere two-minute walk away. In the years ahead, the two couples took leisurely trips to Tasmania, Queensland and New Zealand.

Glenn Oliver had a mind of his own and dreamed of changes he wanted to make on the farm. It was right and proper that he do so; Gary had done so with the lavender investment as his largest innovation. Glenn Oliver brought four major changes to the farm offerings in his first decade of stewardship. He closed the dairy after much angst; it was too labor intensive, and he was faced with either growing the dairy or closing it. Second, to keep cattle on the farm, he introduced Angus and Hereford beef cattle. He also planted twenty acres of radiata pine as a long-term investment. Glenn Oliver's last innovation came from noting the continued growth and development in Adelaide and the Hills. He planted another twenty acres with lawn turf and, over time, expanded this enterprise to include a delivery service. For over eighty years, his grandfather, and then his Uncle Gary, had planted walnut trees in carefully chosen locations all over the farm. Glenn Oliver continued this custom and, at last count, there were over forty walnut trees on the Schubert farm.

Glenn Oliver was an active lay member at St. Michael's Church and worked with the youth as his major contribution. He sponsored a mission trip to Papua New Guinea, and, on the second trip, he became friendly with a nurse from Adelaide who had joined the mission team as a mandated nurse practitioner. Beth Bowman was raised on York Peninsula at Ardrossan on a fourth-generation wheat and barley farm. A year later, Glenn Oliver married Beth and they honeymooned in Hawaii. Then, they met up with Mark and Claire in San Francisco and journeyed onto Washington, DC where they attended Emma Rose's graduation in Baltimore. Mark took enormous pleasure in showing his family around Annapolis, the Naval Academy, Johns Hopkins University and, best of all, staying for several days with John and Shirley Schulz, who had retired to the Eastern Shore on Chesapeake Bay.

Emma Rose met Allan McGowan at Peabody. He was a music teacher from Sydney who was studying euphonium at North Texas University. He was attending a summer workshop in brass banding when he was introduced to Emma Rose at an outdoor concert in Baltimore. Allan's father was a RAN bandsman and favorably influenced by Mark years earlier. Emma Rose and Allan began a long-distance relationship as friends. After graduation, she returned to Adelaide and began her career as organist at St. Peter's Cathedral and conservatory lecturer in organ and organ literature. After his graduation from North Texas University, Allan took a brass teaching position at Prince Alfred's College in Kent Town, Adelaide. Emma Rose and Allan married two years later.

It was through Emma Rose that Mark was asked to become choral director at St. Peter's Cathedral, and he injected a necessary energy, enthusiasm and vision into the cathedral's music program. Father and daughter made a winning duo, and church membership grew along with stewardship and a genuine interest in worship as the first focus of a church. Mark, with his love of John Rutter's compositions, established excellence in English choral music not seen before in Adelaide, long known in Australian folklore as the *city of churches*.

Growing older for Mark and Claire was a new phase of life neither could have predicted, even given the opportunity to do so. Its vexing aspect was the gradual recognition of aches and pains as normal features of daily life. Its joys were remaining in close contact with family and friends. They loved their immediate family and were grateful to God for His bountiful blessings. One of their greatest pleasures was to sit on their patio in the evening and sip lemonade in summer and a hot Milo in the autumn. They liked to reminisce as the day turned to twilight: Mark never tired of hearing Claire say that at first, he thought she was too young for him, and Claire never grew weary of hearing Mark declare that "you are the first person I think of in the morning and the last person I think of at night." They loved each other immeasurably.

Now ends the story of a boy from Hahndorf who had to come home to find everything he ever wanted in life!

AUTHOR'S NOTES

Chapter One: The Epiphany

1. Of the many sources helpful as background for this fictional story, one stands out in particular: Walter O. Forster (1953*). Zion on the Mississippi: The Settlement of the Saxon Lutherans in Missouri 1839-1841.* Concordia Publishing House, Saint Louis, Missouri.

   This book concerns the influence of Martin Stephan and his volatile brand of Protestantism over a sizable group of Saxons and their migration to the United States in 1838 to 1841. Forster describes the religious, social, political and economic factors in Germany of the early Nineteenth Century. Contrary to the basic desire for freedom motivating the East Prussian immigrants to Hahndorf, the *Stephanites* left Saxony for the United States not because of principle, but a person—Stephan himself. It is a fractious saga and only elevates the immigration goals of the East Prussians and their benefactor, Fife Angas.

2. As a boy, I was puzzled why Captain Hahn, a Danish sea captain, would bring the German families from Hamburg to South Australia. The ship, the Zebra, departed from Altona, the westernmost urban borough of the German city-state of Hamburg, on the right bank of the Elbe river. From 1640 to 1864 Altona was under the administration of the Danish monarchy and Denmark's only real harbor directly to the North Sea. (Wikipedia: Altona, Hamburg.)

Chapter Two: The Formative Years

1. As an anomaly in the British colonization of South Australia, the

German immigrants of Hahndorf gave deliberate attention to the education of their children and youth. As Old Lutherans, they were intent on preserving, and advancing the faith, language, cultural traditions, and economic skillsets of their Germanic fatherland. Education was paramount and understanding a history of the Hahndorf Academy (which became a Lutheran teacher's college and seminary after 1877) is recommended by the writer. It was closed in 1912 and almost demolished in the 1960s. Fortunately, today it is an art gallery and museum.

2. While Hahndorf of the 1950s and 1960s may not have been as protective of its children and youth as depicted by the writer, it remained a predominantly German town until the late 1960s. The discrimination by fellow Australians in WWI and WWII was felt profoundly by people of German heritage not only in Hahndorf, but in Lobethal, the Barossa Valley, and further afield.

3. To travel beyond a twenty-mile radius of Hahndorf was still regarded as adventurous in the 1950s. The writer recalls being considered a privileged student at the Hahndorf Public Primary School because he had been to Melbourne by car. Some teenagers on an adjacent farm had not been to Adelaide—only 18 miles away.

Chapter Three: Repositioning

1. There are some seventy towns within the geographical region of the Adelaide Hills. Sporting activities were alive and flourishing in the summer and winter months of this story's timeframe. Australian Rules Football was, and remains, the most popular sport.

    It was entirely natural that Mark would take up football after his debacle in the Easter National championships. Men at their workplace and at the local pub, high school teenagers and upper primary boys would talk of little else during football season.

    However, there was little provision for music (instrumental or vocal) opportunities for children or teenagers. Primary school offered some group choral experiences and the recorder was the only instrument of choice. High schools typically provided no music education in the 1950s and 1960s. Parents were forced to turn to private music teachers and, even though there were pockets of the Welsh *Eisteddfod* festival in Adelaide, it was not readily available or convenient to most families in the Adelaide Hills. The Tanunda *Liedertafel* German male choir dates back to 1850 (based on an entry in *The South Australian,* January 10, 1851), but this was for adult men. Most musical opportunities (group and individual) occurred under the auspices of the various Christian denominations in South Australia.

2. Paul Althus (1963). *The Theology of Martin Luther.* Fortress Press, Philadelphia, p. 19

Chapter Four: A Year on the Farm

While Kensington & Norwood Brass was founded in 1898, the Tanunda Town Band was established in 1857 (sometimes listed as 1860) and is the oldest continuing brass band in the Southern Hemisphere. Both brass bands have a celebrated history and are ranked consistently as A grade bands.

Chapter Seven: International Tour and Divorce

1. The 1960s and 1970s were years when television was changing Australian society. It kept families in their homes, and it provided a wide range of entertainment. This was also the era when large rock 'n roll concerts were held outside. (The writer as a youth educator attended the Sunbury Rock Festival north of Melbourne in 1973. It was Australia's equivalent to Woodstock. However, by 1975, these mega rock festivals failed financially and ceased.)

2. Sources for this chapter in writing about international music education came from internet searches and, more particularly, from the writer's notes and memories of colleagues in music education who made summer visits to certain concert halls around the world. The most vivid recollections spoke of the disappointment of the physical appearance of both Carnegie Hall and the Royal Albert Hall. In the late 1990s, the writer visited Carnegie Hall on numerous

occasions and was pleased to see it restored as one of America's prestigious concert halls.

Chapter Ten: The Easter Nationals

1. This chapter was the most contentious for the writer. He has seen the aggression and emotional tension in teenagers subjected to long bouts of solo and band competition stress.

    Now, in early retirement, he remains ambivalent about competition in the banding world. Along with many conductors and musicians, he promotes the enjoyment, passion and excellence to be found in bands not involved in the continuous cycle of state and national contests. Even so, he acknowledges the distinct outcomes of regular competition involvement; prestige and funding as the most desired benefits. Plus, contesting plays into the psyche of younger musicians in the pursuit of being the best or playing with an A-grade band.

2. Among the useful resource materials in writing about the Easter Nationals and the adjudicator's role and function were: various interviews with brass band adjudicators; Eric Andersen (2010). *How to Judge a Band/Solo Contest: One adjudicator's approach*; Howard David Taylor (2017). *Examining the Professional Practice of Brass Band Conducting*. An unpublished Master of Music thesis, Queensland Conservatorium, Griffith University.

3. One final comment. This fictional story has retained the contest category of Under-18-Years, recognizing this has been dropped as a state category in those states that once listed Under-15 and Under-18. (The writer, as drum major, won a marching contest in 1966 at a regional South Australia Brass Band Association event in the Under-18 category, one day before his eighteenth birthday.)

Chapter Eleven: Break Up—Then Graduation

Haussner's Restaurant opened in 1926 and became one of Baltimore's most famous landmarks over the next 73 years. The restaurant closed in 1999, and its collection of fine art was auctioned by

Sotheby's for $10 million. The Haussner's building was demolished in 2016 and in its place is a high-rise apartment building.

Chapter Twelve: A Road Trip to Remember

1. This chapter took the longest to write but was the most fun. Google Earth and the Internet were indispensable tools as the writer vicariously made the East-West journey across America. Wikipedia and various websites provided factual material and an abundance of information about travel, weather, geography, landmarks, nature, people, history and tourism.

   Altogether, the writer was able to do what his father would often do from his bed; explore a roadmap of different states of Australia and, with his enthralled children onboard, he would catapult away to Tasmania, the Snowy Mountains or to the Great Barrier Reef.

   Soon after the publication and launch of this book, the writer (and his wife) intends to take this same journey across the United States with essential pauses at the Durango-Silverton railroad, the Grand Canyon and a week's vacation at Laguna Beach.

2. Carl Gustav Yung (1933). *Modern Man in Search of a Soul*. Kegan Paul, Trench, Trubner and Company, London and New York, p. 236.

Chapter Thirteen: New Life

Most of the prostate surgery account is factual. This was the writer's fate at 50 years of age; the most difficult year of his life to date for many reasons. The sperm bank occurrence is fiction because the writer was seeking a full life for Mark and, at 41, true love was still on the horizon and this included the possibility of children.

Chapter Fourteen: Back to Work

1. The description of the role of the Australian Defence Force School of Music (DFSM) at Simpson Barracks in Watsonia was all researched using DFSM website information and a few discussions

with Navy musicians.

2. It is important to recall that the late 1970s was post-Vietnam, the 1980s was at time of high inflation and, in 1989, the Berlin Wall came down. By late 1991, the Soviet Union had dissolved and the Cold War era (1947-1991) came to an end. Australia's re-evaluation of its military resulted in smaller attendance at ANZAC services and lesser interest in Defence Force bands. Then, Australian patriotism suddenly surged upward. *The Man from Snowy River* (1982) film tugged at Australian emotions in the re-telling of the Banjo Paterson poem. Australia won the coveted *America's Cup* in 1983 and *Crocodile Dundee* (1986) took the world on a fanciful dance into a surreal concept of an Australian hero. These examples, and many more, highlight the upswing of Australian confidence in its self-image, its role and purpose in an emerging global world. Thirty years later, Australians attend ANZAC services in record numbers and Defence Force music competes with the best in Australia. DFSM has done a laudable job!

3. Normie Rowe's Management and Agents graciously agreed that I could use his name and person in the Federation Square sequence. (I agreed to provide Normie with a copy of this book upon publication.)

Chapter Fifteen: A Dream Come True

1. For those who have been through divorce, and then found real love again, you will recognize Mark's tentative nature for many chapters. *How do you trust again, and how to you let go and share your true self with someone new?* Mark ponders these questions and more and tests the patience of Gary on their road trip together. Yet, Claire walks into Mark's life at the right time and in the right way.

2. Gordon Rupp (1953). *The Righteousness of God.* Hodder & Stoughton, London

Chapter Sixteen: Coming Together

1. Even now, in early retirement, it is the hope of the writer that this

story may encourage local and community music wherever it is to be found. Surely doing what you love to do, and with others, are goals we all need to enrich our lives. The challenge is to put before pre-teens the opportunity to play music. It is never easy, and many will drop by the wayside. However, some will persist and learn the joy to sing with confidence, or to play the piano or some other musical instrument. Once a certain competency is achieved, the skill acquired will last a lifetime.

2. Community music, whether it be vocal or instrumental, is scarce in today's neighborhoods. To thrive, it needs support and always a champion. Four months ago (November 2018), the writer was 'home' for 13 days. He renewed acquaintance with Ray Sadler after fifty-one years. Ray is struggling as conductor of a community band about 30 minutes south-east of Hahndorf. *It's hard to compete with all the distractions of modern life.* Previously, he had contributed eleven years of service to Taiwan as a music teacher. Community music can add so much flavor to a community, but it is not straightforward. The writer recalls how much Ray inspired him all those years ago as he first heard the melodious sounds of Ray's euphonium.

Chapter Seventeen: The Rest of the Story

It Happened One Night (1934). Starred Clark Gable and Claudette Colbert. Directed by Frank Capra.

Epilogue

Perhaps the story should have ended with *lights out* in Glenelg's Stamford Hotel.

However, the writer is hopeful readers are left wanting more. *It's taken an entire book for Mark and Claire to come together, and the writer offers nothing beyond their wedding!*

Rather than writing another 300 pages for a reading audience accused statistically of reading less pages than ever before, the writer offers this bullet format providing more information about the lives of the main characters. The overall aim is to conclude with a satisfying ending.

A Statement of Appreciation:

In the later half of 2018, I asked Dr. Barry Casey, a friend and colleague, to provide editorial assistance and general encouragement as this story was nearing its conclusion after ten years in the making. We have known each other since the days we were newly-minted PhDs in the late 1980s in Maryland. Barry and I have similar interests in biblical studies, world religions, history, philosophy and literature. His career path has steered him in the professorial role as a consummate teacher and guide. I, on the other hand, have followed the administration track, and lectured on the side.

Barry came onboard and soothed my anxious soul so eager to finish up my story. Barry has read, reviewed, made suggestions and been my friend and guide for the last nine months. In my mind, my story will always be partially his!

Barry happens to be the best writer I currently know. You can read some of his work on his blog at www.*danteswoods.com*.

Forever grateful!

And Finally:

Thank you to all who read this book. Although fiction, it is an adult adventure and aims to deal with real-life situations. I realize that you have used your imagination as I originally used mine in crafting this story. It is my hope as you reflect on this narrative you will think about the rhythms of change encapsulating all of us, you will appreciate the immense gift given to us through the arts (in this case, especially music), you will, at least, ponder the loss in our lives when we jettison transcendence, and you will seek goodness and peace of mind as ingredients in living that abundant life.

You can write to me: lynraybartlett@gmail.com

Quia non est alius—Give peace, O Lord, in our days